WINGS OF THE STORM

www.**penguin**.co.uk

WINGS OF THE STORM

Giles Kristian

BANTAM PRESS

LONDON · NEW YORK · TORONTO · SYDNEY · AUCKLAND

TRANSWORLD PUBLISHERS
61–63 Uxbridge Road, London W5 5SA
www.penguin.co.uk

Transworld is part of the Penguin Random House group of companies
whose addresses can be found at global.penguinrandomhouse.com

Penguin
Random House
UK

First published in Great Britain in 2016 by Bantam Press
an imprint of Transworld Publishers

A CIP catalogue record for this book
is available from the British Library.

ISBNs 9780593074558 (cased)
9780593074565 (tpb)

Typeset in 11/14.5pt Meridien by Thomson Digital Pvt Ltd, Noida, Delhi.
Printed and bound by Clays Ltd, Bungay, Suffolk.

Penguin Random House is committed to a sustainable
future for our business, our readers and our planet. This book
is made from Forest Stewardship Council® certified paper.

1 3 5 7 9 10 8 6 4 2

For Simon Taylor, with heartfelt thanks for believing in my tales and for making this writing lark a pleasure when I suspect it ought to be somewhat harder work.

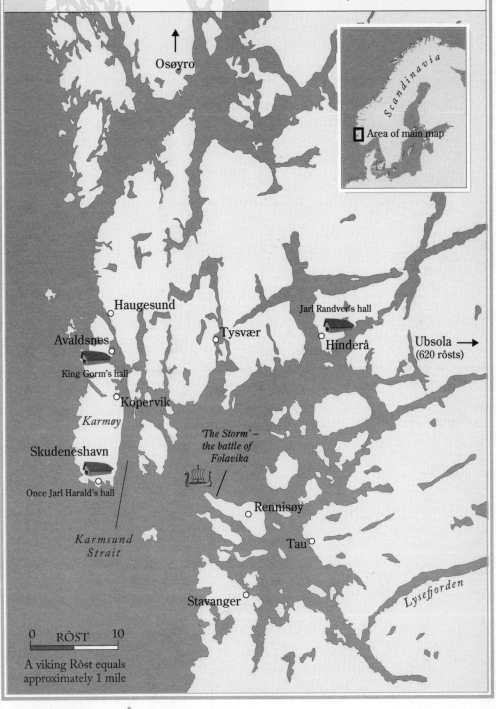

SIGURD HARALDARSON'S WORLD–
THE WEST OF NORWAY, AD 785

Osøyro

Scandinavia

Area of main map

Haugesund

Jarl Randver's hall

Avaldsnes

Tysvær

Hinderå

Ubsola
(620 rôsts)

King Gorm's hall

Kopervik

Karmøy

'The Storm' –
the battle of
Folavika

Skudeneshavn

Once Jarl Harald's hall

Rennisøy

Tau

*Karmsund
Strait*

Stavanger

Lysefjorden

0   RÔST   10

A viking Rôst equals
approximately 1 mile

When the wind god rides across the sky
With his host of hounds and the ghosts of men
And the spirits of these long dead fly
In the wild hunt over wood and fen
And in their wake the widows cry,
Beware old One-Eye and Sleipnir then
As spirits are from their bodies torn
By the gusting winds on the wings of the storm.

Sigurd Haraldarson's Saga

PROLOGUE

The boy had not been invited to cast his spear when at last the king's hounds' noses led them to the bull elk deep in the pine woods to the west of Gorm's hall.

'We can't take any chances, boy, not after last time,' Harald had muttered to him, though he had already spun the picture in his mind of his spear bringing the great beast down. Of the steel-tipped shaft flying from his hand like a spear of lightning from the sky, and of King Gorm slapping his back and laughing because amongst grown men, a king and a jarl no less, it was he who had laid that mighty elk down in the bracken.

But neither the king nor the boy's father had allowed him to cast the spear which he had gripped in his hand these past four days, since they had last seen the creature and tried to claim it for honour and the king's table. On that day his throw had won him King Gorm's praise and his father's pride, the spear having struck the bull elk in his right hind quarters, though there had not been the muscle in the throw to keep it there. His father's throw had been almost saga-worthy, but the beast had swerved and the jarl's spear only gouged a furrow in its neck, and then it was gone, roaring as it galloped off through the pines.

This time, though, there had been no chance of escape. Having stayed ahead of the pack the mighty elk had at last come to the end of its life's thread. Trapped between the hunting party of hounds and hearthmen, and a rocky prominence down whose grey, moss-festooned face the rain coursed, he had turned to face his pursuers.

'I hope when my day comes I will face death with the same courage, boy,' his father had said, stepping forward at the king's invitation to cast his great spear. But that had meant nothing to the boy. He was still sulking at being denied his moment of fame.

'Take him in his heart,' King Gorm said, gripping his own spear in readiness should Harald's not strike true, or if the elk bolted at the last moment. Behind them, the men had leashed their dogs, which barked and snarled at the beast, clamouring to get at it, though some would surely die before the elk did. For the bull's antlers were massive. They swept up, out and back from its great head, six tines and twelve points in all, spanning some five and a half feet and more than capable of tearing open a hound's belly. Or a man's.

Imagine what they could do to a boy.

'I am sorry I did not kill you last time we met, friend,' Harald told the elk, who lifted those magnificent antlers like a warrior showing his sword to the gods before his last fight. He gave a shrill, air-fogging call which sounded like that from a small horn blown by a big man, and the boy thought the beast would charge. His father thought so too from the way he suddenly put both hands round his spear's shaft and brought it in front of him, at the same time throwing a foot behind him and bracing. But the creature was already finished. He had nothing left, neither fury nor defiance. He just stood there. Waiting.

Harald did not make him wait long. The jarl took two steps and on the third launched the spear and it flew straight and true, plunging into the elk's chest with a sound which had the dogs frenzying and snapping their jaws. The bull skittered backwards a pace or two under the impact, gave a guttural grunt and then emptied its bladder, the stream of it steaming in the rain-chilled day as the king's hearthmen murmured and *hoomed* in appreciation of the jarl's throw.

For a long moment he stood there, that great beast, with Harald's spear shaft protruding from his chest, but every man in those woods knew that the blade had ripped open his heart.

'A fine animal,' King Gorm rumbled, and even the boy, with only seven summers on his back, got the sense that those words were the king trying – and failing – to sweeten an occasion which had soured.

The elk's forelegs gave way and he fell to his knees, his lifeblood filling his chest like water rising through a hole in a ship's hull. Then his hind legs gave way and he fell on to his side with a derisive snort and the dogs ceased their barking now because even they knew it was over.

The boy followed Harald and the king forward, his nose filling with the bull elk's musky scent, until he was standing over the once-proud animal, whose clouded eyes stared at nothing. The boy's own eyes saw well enough though. They were full of those impressive antlers. They stood before him like an ancient, storm-killed tree, its branches half covered in a mossy skin which would have peeled away completely by the end of summer, and a hirðman muttered that the beast had been rightly proud of those mighty weapons and that other bulls must have feared them.

'Your kill, Harald,' King Gorm acknowledged. 'The boy's too, hey?' he added, pointing his own spear at the prize. That was when the boy saw the wound which he had given the elk four days previously, the gouge between the animal's rump and the muscled flesh of its upper right hind leg. A raw gash. Writhing with maggots, as was the blood and pus-matted furrow which Harald's failed throw had ploughed in the flesh of the beast's neck.

'A bad way to go,' Harald growled into his beard, heavy-browed as he hauled his spear from the elk's chest, noting the dark heart meat clotted where blade met shaft.

The rain came properly then. It seethed through the pine boughs so that the king's hounds slunk into themselves and some of his men cursed because they had come a good way from their lord's hall and it would be a long time before they were dry and comfortable. But the boy barely noticed the rain. He was staring at the maggots in that wound and he knew without a doubt that the reason his elders had not allowed him to throw his spear was not because they feared the elk bolting and escaping, as it had the last time. It was because they did not want to taint him with the killing of this once-mighty but now suffering beast. In the end there had been no glory in it. The bull elk had been doomed. It had been rotting alive and would have fallen down dead in another day or so anyway, for all it had somehow managed to stay ahead of the king's hunting party until now.

Still, it was a rare beast and there were rituals to be observed, pissing rain or no. Harald drew his scramasax and knelt by the elk's head, growling at the boy to do the same. The boy knelt. The jarl plunged a hand into the wound which his spear had made and when he pulled it out it was steaming with the beast's hot blood. 'I claim this kill in honour of Ull, lord of the hunt,' he said and brought his hand up to his face and flicked his fingers, spattering his cheeks and beard with crimson spots. Then he did the same to the boy, who blinked at the splash of warm droplets and breathed in the strange but not unpleasant scent of the blood which had coursed through that magnificent animal.

Then Harald saw what held the boy's eye and grunted. 'Ale,' he called over his shoulder, and Olaf took a bulging skin from a pony's back and came forward, winking at the boy as he handed the skin to his jarl. Harald pulled out the stopper and poured the ale into the pus-slick wound which the boy's spear had made days before. With his hand he scooped out the maggots and then the boy caught a stench in the damp air as he swiped the rain from his forehead and saw that the back of his hand was smeared with the blood of the kill.

'There will come a day when you can throw a spear like your father, lad,' King Gorm said, scrubbing the boy's head with a big hand.

'Ha! Do not forget that Grimhild is the boy's mother,' Harald told the king, standing and rinsing the gore from his hand with more ale. 'With her blood inside him the boy will out-throw me by the time he is into his first beard.'

'I look forward to seeing that, my friend,' Gorm said, grinning at his men, who grinned back at him in spite of the rain. A grizzled old warrior named Gerik said that the boy had the look of a jarl about him even now and that Harald ought to watch out in case he came back to his hall one day to find the boy sitting in his high seat gripping Harald's own mead horn. This raised a peal of laughter and his father smiled at him, enjoying the attention his boy had earned.

Then the king gestured at two of his men to come forward with their butchering knives and set to work on the elk so that they could all get back to the dry warmth of their king's hall.

No one could say King Gorm was a bad host, or that he did not know how to throw a feast which had men crawling back to their beds after or sleeping in the floor rushes with the hounds and the mice. Nor did he neglect to honour the gods before men's beards ran with mead and ale and juices from the meat which was piled halfway to the rafters.

'The king means to impress your father,' Olaf said under his breath as the folk of Avaldsnes gathered outside the great hall on the hillside overlooking the Karmsund Strait, that narrow channel which might as well have flowed with molten silver, such were the riches King Gorm wrung out of the skippers and crews who passed through it on their way north. 'Wants us to see how generous he is to those who are pledged to him. He wants your father's oath, boy.'

'Will my father give it?' he asked.

Olaf cocked an eyebrow and lifted his horn, downing a great wash of mead, which was hardly an answer. So the boy looked at the other guests, many of whom wore the finest cloaks and brooches and dripped with silver and amber. At least half the men wore swords at their hips and boasted arm rings of twisted silver and finger rings, and several had even brought their own drinking horns, some of which were silver-mounted and all of which were decorated with etchings of wolves or eagles or serpentine beasts gripping their own tails.

Tunic sleeves and hems were embroidered with yellow, red or blue thread. Brightly coloured beads and beard rings and shiny Thór's hammers defied the grey day. Belt buckles, strap ends and sword hilts glinted like fish scales whenever the cloud parted and shafts of dusk sunlight hit the crowd gathered on that hill.

None of it, though, shone as brightly as Aesa, King Gorm's young wife. She giggled and flitted through the chattering throng the way a butterfly floats aimlessly through a summer field, and, young as he was, the boy knew the effect she had on the men.

'Don't look at her, boy, she's trouble that one,' Olaf murmured, bending down to his ear though his own eyes followed Aesa like gulls after the plough. 'Trouble like a split hull strake.'

A slap on the back released Olaf from Aesa's spell. 'Some bull hey!' Harald said, squeezing the boy's shoulder and nodding at the snorting beast which the thralls were pulling across the hill for all to see. Ruddy-cheeked and mead-full, Harald had been speaking with a handsome man named Randver who rumour had it would soon be wearing a jarl torc at his own neck. The boy had heard that the jarl over at Hinderå was withering from some gut ailment and would likely be dead come winter.

'I've just told the boy she's trouble,' Olaf said, because Harald's eyes were no longer on the bull. They were on Aesa too.

'Aye, listen to Olaf, boy. They're all trouble,' his father said, as Aesa giggled and shone like a brook in the sunlight.

'The king wants your oath, Harald,' Olaf said, turning to his lord. 'More than wanting. I am thinking he needs it. To ensure he gets others.'

Harald made a *hoom* in his throat because he knew as well as everyone on that hill that he was the king's honoured guest. And as such, Harald was the real reason why six of Gorm's thralls were hauling on those ropes and halters, wrestling with that horned fury which was the most impressive bull that the boy or his father had ever seen.

The bull fought the thralls because it knew it was to be sacrificed and was not altogether happy about it. It snorted and kicked and shook its horned head this way and that, eyes bulging, the hair standing bristle-stiff along its back.

'This should be good,' Olaf said as the thralls at last got control of the terrified bull and the king himself took the long-hafted axe which one of his hearthmen offered him. One of a matching pair, its blade was inlaid with silver and its twin was carried by another hirðman who, at the king's invitation, stepped forward and gave it to Randver of Hinderå.

Randver gripped the haft, tested the weapon's weight and grinned, dipping his head at Gorm in acknowledgement of the honour, for with that gesture the king had all but put a dying man's jarl torc round Randver's neck. That moment with the axes was not lost on anyone and the boy heard Olaf mumble that Jarl Engli's gut rot would never get the chance to kill him after all. Engli would find himself dead shortly after Randver had tied his boat to the jetty in Hinderå.

'This will be something to see, lad,' Harald said. 'Something to remember when your beard bristles are white and your knees creak.'

'Aye, but we should probably move back a step or two,' Olaf said, at which they and the other guests around them shuffled backwards as Randver came to stand in front of the snorting bull, his back to the boy as he gripped that beautiful axe, one hand at the end of the haft, the other clutching the heel just below that

GILES KRISTIAN

silver-chased head. Having removed his blue cloak and given it to his young queen, the king stood off to the side, his hair loose and well combed but for the braids hanging either side of his face. Even though for the last four days they had spent more time under pine boughs than under the king's rafters, roaming the woods in search of the wounded elk, Gorm's beard was neat and lustrous and to the boy he was the very image of a great king, a man closer to the gods than other men. In the boy's eyes only his father could match their host in stature and impressiveness, and yet he was certain that for all the king's silver and all his ships, his warriors and his golden mead which Olaf said was the best he had ever tasted, he could never throw a spear as far as his father. Nor row as far, nor wrestle an angry ram or soothe a nervous cow better than Harald. The boy knew all that without a sliver of doubt as he watched the king roll his great shoulders and nod at Randver to be ready with his axe, as the bull lowed and tugged against the ropes which the thralls clung to, pulling against each other to keep the beast as still as they could.

'Óðin! I slaughter this beast in your honour that it will give you strength, and that you will know that I, Gorm son of Grimar, am a worthy king. That I am a ring-giver who feeds his people with meat and mead in return for their loyalty.'

Gorm's hearthmen were chanting 'Óðin, Óðin, Óðin' in low voices and other folk took it up too, some looking to the cloud-swathed sky, others watching their king who they must have believed was as Óðin-loved as a man could be, judging by the feast they would soon be wolfing down at the benches in their lord's hall.

Then those silver-etched axe heads flew. Randver brought his up and over, twisting the haft as he swung so that the poll came down and not the blade, striking the bull between its bulging eyes with the unmistakable crack of a skull being staved in. A heartbeat later the king's blade bit and the crowd gasped at the enormous strength behind that axe which cleaved through the thick flesh, gristle and bone of the bull's neck, parting head from body before sheathing itself in the earth. Blood sprayed from the raw stump like red rain. It flew twelve feet or more, spattering Sigurd's shoes, pumping from the severed flesh in rhythmic gouts as the bull's legs gave way, just as the elk's had, and the great beast collapsed to the ground.

Randver turned to the crowd, his face blood-slathered and his teeth white amongst the gore of it, and men, women and children alike cheered.

But no cheer came from the boy.

Then King Gorm handed his axe to a retainer and came over to Harald, throwing an arm over his shoulder. 'And now we drink!' he said, and Harald grinned as the two of them, the king and the jarl, led the way back up the slope towards the open door of the great hall: the hall which loomed above the Karmsund Strait and because of that was more like a giant's sea chest, filled with hacksilver from every ship which sailed past. That hall was a hoard-chest upon which King Gorm sat, and around which other rich and powerful men gathered in the hope that its silver-lustre would shine on them too.

'You have some tales to take back to Skudeneshavn now, hey, boy,' Olaf said. He and the boy had both been seated at the king's own table, around which only his closest and longest-serving hirðmen sat. Harald himself was shoulder to shoulder with the king. 'Tell me why the king just beheaded his finest beast, lad,' Olaf said, holding out his horn to a serving girl who filled it from a jug which was so heavy she could barely lift it.

'He wants everyone to see how generous he is,' the boy answered. He knew he should be wide-eyed and open-mouthed at all the food on the table in front of him, the trenchers of boar, goat, horse, goose and hare. The loaves of hot bread and the boiled gulls' eggs, the piles of ripe red berries and plums and the cheeses and the bowls of skyr and honeycomb. But something about how that proud bull had died had soured his stomach.

'That's part of it,' Olaf said with a nod, drinking and dragging a hand across his moustaches. 'But why did he do it himself?' Olaf nodded at the kingsmen across the table from them. 'He could have had any one of these men cut the bull's throat and be done with it. Nice and neat.' A big man across the way caught Olaf's eye and the two warriors raised their drinking horns to each other and nodded before rinsing their insides with mead.

The boy shrugged. Olaf leant in close enough that the boy could smell the mead's honey's sweetness on his breath. 'The blood was part of it, of course,' Olaf said. 'The way it flew like that and soaked our shoes. That was for the gods. But it takes skill and great strength to take off a bull's head like that, even with such a sharp and pretty axe.' Olaf smiled. 'Had to get the swing just right too, or the beast might have dropped from Randver's dint on his thought box and the king would have buried that shiny blade in nothing but mud. Not the same kind of reputation to be earned cutting worms in half.' The boy could not help but grin at the idea of that while Olaf drank again. 'King Gorm wanted us all to see how he can handle an axe, for it takes more than silver, more than a feast or three to show men such as your father that you deserve their loyalty. Wants Harald to kiss his sword, he does. Wants everyone here to see it too, for he knows your father is a warrior.' He swept his drinking horn through the smoky air. 'Everyone in this hall knows it. So now and then the king needs to remind us all that *he* is a warrior too. Understand, lad?'

The boy nodded, thinking. 'Could you do it, Olaf? Take off the bull's head with one swing?'

Olaf considered that for a moment, dragging an arm across his glistening bristles. 'Even with the haft end, lad,' he said, grinning, 'and with only half a swing.' He laughed and the boy laughed too and then the king leant forward and called down the board to Olaf, asking him to share what had him and Harald's boy giggling like a pair of young bed thralls under the furs.

'At this end of the table we are talking about ship taxes and what to do about the island karls who are late bringing in the cows, pigs and grain which they owe me,' Gorm said, smiling. 'We will enjoy a funny tale if you have one.'

All eyes turned their way and the boy felt them like heat on his skin.

'Lord king,' Olaf said with a respectful nod, 'I was just telling the boy of the time his father and I were put on our arses more than once by a ram. Now, that bull of yours was a giant, no one can say otherwise. But that ram was another Grendel, hey Harald?'

'I still shudder to think of it,' Harald said, 'but *there* is a story with a good ending,' he added, raising his drinking horn at Olaf, though King Gorm did not seem to like being left out of that. Or else perhaps he knew full well that Olaf and the boy had not been talking about a ram and did not like being lied to. Either way he was a king and had enough wile in him to pick up the thread and spin it his way.

'It is a good lesson to teach the boy, Olaf,' he said, pointing a thick, silver-ringed finger. 'Harald's boy would do well to remember that size and strength alone are not always a warrior's greatest weapons.' The hall had fallen silent now, but for the flap and crackle of the hearth flames and the sound of one of the king's hounds gnawing a fleshy knuckle of bone beneath the table. 'Brawn will get a man only so far,' King Gorm said, then tapped his skull and the boy heard it from where he sat. 'The wits in his head are his greatest possession.' If the feast that was spread across that table had been for Harald's eyes, this now was for the jarl's ears and everyone knew it. 'I did not become king by raging round the place making enemies. A man must have patience if he hopes to rise.'

Everyone knew how Gorm had become king, how he had raided in the south and the east along the Svealand coast, filling his sea chests with plunder but sitting on most of it, biding his time until he had enough silver to persuade the jarls and warlords and the wealthy karls within a week's sailing of Karmøy to support his bid for Jarl Grubbi's high seat. And then once he had it, having put a spear in Grubbi's belly himself, how he had gone about narrowing the channel in the strait below with boats lashed securely to the rocks. No crew could hope to slip through without either paying Gorm for the privilege or making a fight of it which they would almost certainly lose.

He made himself king not long after that, and none of the jarls had disputed it. They might as well tell the rain it could not fall on their roofs.

'Patience is what separates the great hunter from the hungry one, lad,' Gorm said, 'as you yourself know, for did we give up on the great elk when he vanished into the woods four days ago?' The king's eyes bored into him until he could no longer hold on to his silence.

'No, lord king,' he said.

'No, we did not,' Gorm said. 'You cast your spear like a little god, like a young Thór, and you bled that mighty bull elk. Then you bided your time, never doubting the outcome, until in the end we caught up with him and your father finished the job.' With that he banged his mead horn against Harald's. 'Your boy knows how to bide his time, Jarl Harald,' Gorm said. 'But so do I. Which is why we have been friends for a long time now and I have never once asked you to swear an oath to me. Not once. I have never asked you to kiss my sword, even though other jarls have kissed it and so has every man at my table.

Harald nodded, acknowledging that this was true. He knew that his time at Avaldsnes drinking the king's mead had all been about this moment, and that while his friend had indeed bided his time, showing himself to be a patient and skilled hunter, that time had drawn to an end.

The boy tried to grasp all this, but it was too much to fit in a young boy's head, even with Olaf beside him steering him through it all. Besides which, he had a boy's drifting mind and was already thinking of other things, like the maggots in the elk's flesh. Like the way the soon-to-be-jarl Randver and the king had slaughtered the bull and how the blood had flown, painting the day with a crimson arc, like a gory, shimmering Bifröst linking the worlds of gods and men. His shoes were stained with it. It had been a day of blood, but now it was a night of feasting and drinking, of skald-song and friendship.

And later, when the oil lamps were starting to gutter and the hearthflames were low, and some men and women were falling asleep at their benches still clutching their horns, Jarl Harald gave the king his oath.

CHAPTER ONE

———

THE HILL FORT AT FORNSIGTUNA BELONGED TO ALRIK NOW, AND SIGURD was Alrik's man. At least, he had won the place for the Svear warlord, tricking his way through the gates to sow death amongst the defenders, who were sworn to Alrik's enemy, a Svear jarl named Guthrum. Sigurd and his half crew, along with some of Alrik's men, had come to the borg under Guthrum's own banner of the white axe, and Guthrum's men, seeing that banner and thinking their lord had returned, had opened the gates. Only, that banner was not Guthrum's own. Nor could the jarl have ever laid eyes on it, seeing as it had been nothing but a scrap of sail cloth and a boar spear before Sigurd had Solmund get to work with his needle and thread.

With Loki-cunning and war-craft and in a welter of blood, Sigurd and his wolves had won Alrik the borg. But Sigurd would not swear an oath to the warlord, and if Alrik was sour about that he did a good job of hiding it. Mostly.

'He's had enough out of us without needing our oaths on top of it,' Olaf had told Knut, Alrik's most trusted man, when Knut had suggested that Sigurd and his men could do worse than pledging their swords to the warlord and helping him defeat Jarl Guthrum himself, who was bound to turn up at the fort sooner or later.

Knut had looked from Olaf to Sigurd, wanting to hear the refusal from Sigurd's own mouth.

'We've made Alrik a rich man, Knut,' Sigurd said, which was understating it, as Knut well knew. Calling Alrik rich was like calling the sea damp, and Knut had nodded and raised a hand as if to say he would not press the matter further for now.

For the borg was full of silver and iron: sea chests crammed with hacksilver and stacks of iron already smelted and beaten into bars, enough to make the rivets for twenty ships, which was more iron than most people saw in their whole lives. And it had all been Guthrum's. The jarl had sat on this hoard while he built a war host large enough to take on King Erik, who was the real power in that part of Svealand, controlling the trading port of Birka and lands as far south as Götaland.

But Alrik, whilst he was not even a jarl, was an ambitious man and a hardened fighter, and he had grown powerful enough to challenge Guthrum, for all that he and his war host had then been stuck outside the borg as their beards grew long with the grass. Alrik had craved the place like a man who lusts after another man's woman, until Sigurd and his Sword-Norse had come and Sigurd had delivered the borg and its treasures to him. And so the warlord could make do without Sigurd's oath.

Not that Alrik was ungenerous. In the aftermath of the bloodletting he had given Sigurd a sea chest carved with ravens and eagles, and heavy it was too because it was stuffed with silver and iron: finger rings, sword and scabbard fittings, Thór's hammers, brooches, lengths of fine wire and solid ingots, iron bars, axe heads and even some gold, and in that one chest was a hoard as big as Sigurd's father Jarl Harald had ever owned. There would be more of the same, too, Alrik promised, if the Norsemen stayed and fought for him until Guthrum was carrion for the crows and his war host was scattered to the winds.

With such riches Sigurd could buy spearmen and maybe even ships. He could build his own war host and return to Norway to take on the oath-breaker King Gorm, and maybe he could have his revenge and so balance the scales which had been tipped against him and his kin since this whole thing began. That was the dream. And it was the gleam of all that plunder which blinded Sigurd and his crew to the presence of a man in Alrik's war band by the name of Kjartan Auðunarson, whom the skald Hagal Crow-Song – not that Crow-Song did much skalding these days – had recognized. Though it had taken him a while to pull that memory out of his thought box.

'He was Jarl Randver's man before he was Alrik's,' Crow-Song had said, turning all their thoughts back to that bloody fight in the fjord by Hinderå. Sigurd himself had killed Jarl Randver but now Hrani Randversson wore the torc and he wanted his revenge on Sigurd.

'What is to stop this Kjartan going home and making himself rich by telling Hrani Randversson where we are?' Olaf asked Sigurd when they had been thinking what to do about Kjartan.

'We kill him,' Svein had said with a shrug of his great shoulders, combing the fiery red beard of which he was so proud.

'He has to go,' Solmund agreed. The old skipper who had bound his wyrd to Sigurd's would rather hold a tiller than a sword, but even so he knew when someone needed killing.

'Of course he has to go,' Bram said. 'But the how of it. That's the question. We can't just go up to the man's bench and spear him when he's asleep.'

Sigurd and Olaf agreed it would take some thinking about, but then Alrik's men had brought that heavy sea chest in and all of them forgot about Kjartan Auðunarson.

Next morning, when they spread throughout the borg looking for the Hinderå man, there was no sign of him.

'What now then?' Olaf said when it was clear that Kjartan had gone, vanished 'like a fart in the breeze', as Bjarni put it.

'You are rich now, Sigurd,' Olaf went on. 'You've enough silver to put a proper crew together.'

'Not rich enough to take on the oath-breaker,' Solmund pointed out, which was true enough. Not that anyone liked hearing it.

'Seems to me we can stay here on this hill and earn more silver fighting for Alrik,' Bjarni said, lifting an eyebrow. 'There are worse places to live.'

'Even if Kjartan *has* slithered off back west to sell word of us to Hrani Randversson, it will be a long time before we have to concern ourselves about it,' Aslak said.

'True,' Olaf agreed, 'and weaving more reputation around here won't do us any harm.' For their war gear and the way they had won Alrik the borg had made the other men inside that ring of timber treat Sigurd's little crew warily and with the same respect as they did Alrik and Knut.

'Why get bogged down in a blood feud between two Svearmen when we have our own feud, which has a king in it?' Moldof put in, sweeping his one arm through the smoke-hung air. And this got some murmurs of agreement. They had avenged themselves on Jarl Randver by sending him to the sea bed and many of his men to the afterlife sooner than they had thought to go. But Randver had only been a sword wielded by King Gorm. Gorm was the poison which tainted the very air for Sigurd. A nithing king who had shared mead and the feast table with Sigurd's father Harald. Who had laughed and hunted with the jarl and called him friend, but had in the end betrayed him, first in the ship battle in the Karmsund Strait, by not coming to Harald's aid when Harald was fighting Jarl Randver's ships, and then in the woods near Avaldsnes, by greeting Harald with swords and spears instead of with the mead he had promised.

'Moldof has a point there,' Bram admitted. 'Much as I am enjoying killing these Svearmen, we could end up stuck here. Going down with Alrik like the ballast stones in a sinking ship. And the oath-breaker king will be free to keep being the rancid goat's turd that he is for many years yet.'

That was not a happy picture in anyone's mind and so Sigurd told them he would think about it over the next days and decide what he would do.

But three days later the choice was taken away from him because Jarl Guthrum came. He brought with him the rest of his war host and it made for an impressive sight, spilling out of the tree line to the west of the borg, men's spear blades, axe heads and shield bosses glinting in the pink dawn light. Some of them owned helmets, fewer had mail, but it was the size of Guthrum's army which had Alrik's men cursing, fingering the Thór's hammers hanging at their necks and looking to their war gear. They checked that blades were sharp and shields were strong. They piled more spears and rocks against the palisade up on the earthen ramparts. They carried more pails of rainwater up the bank, setting them down around the perimeter twenty paces apart, ready to be flung at any fires should Guthrum try to burn the fence stakes.

'Silver or no, I am beginning to think we should have joined Guthrum instead of Alrik,' Solmund said, as still more warriors came out of the trees. Alrik had ordered Sigurd to man the rampart above the gates as this was the most vulnerable part of the fort, where he wanted his best warriors.

'You won't be saying that when Guthrum strolls through those gates and gets a gut full of spear,' Olaf said as a horn sounded, formally announcing Guthrum's arrival.

Sigurd looked at the axe banner hanging on its long boar spear above the palisade, the wind stirring the cloth so that the white axe flickered, and in truth he did not think it would be as easy as Olaf said. The trick had worked once. Seeing that banner, which was the same as their jarl's, Guthrum's men in the borg had assumed their lord had come and they had opened the gates, inviting death into the borg. And now it was possible that Guthrum, having come at last, would see that banner and think that his men still held the fort. There was a chance, a hope at least, that Jarl Guthrum would walk into their trap and die easily.

But something told Sigurd that they would not be so lucky a second time.

Alrik had one of his men sound a horn in reply and those of his warriors not manning the ramparts thronged either side of the gates, shield and spear ready, waiting to spring their ambush.

It was worth trying, this ruse, but it was not without risk, as Bram pointed out. 'If enough of them get inside before we can shut the gates on the rest, their numbers will end up getting the better of us.'

'Not if we kill Guthrum,' Sigurd said. 'I have seen a hen run around after its head has been pulled off, but it does not know where it is going and soon falls down.' He shrugged. 'With Guthrum and his best men dead, the others will not know what to do.'

'I would like to see them all running around like your hen,' Bjarni said, grinning.

And perhaps they might have done, had Guthrum been fooled by that axe banner and walked into the borg to his death. But that did not happen and there was no steel-edged death for the jarl that day. He skirted the hill fort and came within an arrow-shot of the gate, close enough for Sigurd to see that he was a very big man, long-legged and broad in his brynja that reached almost to his knees. His silver jarl's torc glinted at his neck. His helmet had eye guards like Sigurd's own, so that they could not make out much of his face but for the big fair beard, and yet there was something about the man which told Sigurd that here was no fool. And sure enough Guthrum raised a hand and ordered his men to come no nearer to the borg. They waited, some two hundred Svearmen with their shields before them because they smelt the fox in the coop.

'Whoreson knows,' Olaf said.

'He does,' Sigurd agreed. 'But look how he controls his temper.'

Olaf nodded. 'Ice in his veins this one,' he said. 'He knows that if Alrik is cosy up in his borg it means the rest of his men are most likely dead. Also knows he'll lose more men trying to kick us out.' Olaf pulled at his beard. 'That's a hard thing to swallow.'

It was, and yet Jarl Guthrum simply stood staring up at the borg. No cursing. No red-hot fury. No threats.

'Here we go,' Svein said as Guthrum took a spear from the man beside him who was even bigger than he was, and strode up the hill towards the gates.

'Guthrum is coming,' Sigurd called down to Alrik.

'I see him,' Alrik replied. He was standing on a barrel peering through a crack between the gate timbers.

'He's close enough,' Valgerd said, an arrow nocked on her bow string, the stave bent and straining. The shieldmaiden was the only woman in that borg, but there was no one in Alrik's war band or in Sigurd's crew who was better with a bow. Few better with a blade either. 'Want me to put this between his teeth?' she asked.

'No,' Sigurd said. 'If Alrik wanted to he could take three or four men out and pull Guthrum in here before the rest of his men got halfway up the hill. Let us hear what this jarl has to say.'

But Jarl Guthrum did not say anything. He ran a few steps and hurled the spear high and it soared over the palisade and Sigurd looked up at it before it plunged into the borg behind Alrik. It was the kind of throw that skalds sing about. More importantly, it meant that Guthrum was claiming the borg and every man in it.

'It'll be war then,' Olaf said.

'Did you think he would offer Alrik a horn of good mead and discuss a truce?' Solmund asked.

'I would have been disappointed in the man if he had,' Olaf said.

Jarl Guthrum turned his back on his enemies and walked back down the hill to rejoin his men. Then, protected by a shieldwall of fifty warriors, the remainder of his army made camp on the ground where Alrik's men had camped previously.

*

It was a grey, rain-filled day the first time Jarl Guthrum sent his warriors against the borg. Fifty attacked the eastern section of the palisade, fifty the west, and one hundred came at the southern perimeter, the bulk of them massing before the gate. Only, it wasn't really an attack. They brought ladders and ropes but never intended to climb. Instead they came close enough that Alrik's men had no choice but to throw spears and drop rocks, most of which did little more than split a few shields or send Guthrum's men away with cuts and bruises.

'Don't waste your spears,' Olaf said to those on the rampart above the gate, he being the first man in the fort to guess what Guthrum was up to. 'He's testing us, that's all,' he told Sigurd, 'and will be pleased with himself when we end up with nothing left to throw but clever insults and buckets of piss.'

The second time Guthrum attacked, his men did the same thing, and again the borg men tried to kill some of them, though they did not try as hard as before and did not throw many spears or shoot many arrows. The third time was different because this time some of Guthrum's men threw their ladders against the palisade and began to climb, their shields held over their heads, while archers on the ground loosed shafts at those on the ramparts. All the while Guthrum kept an impressive-looking skjaldborg facing the gate as a deterrent to Alrik leading a sortie out of the place. Some of the climbers made it over the top and on to the ramparts and fought ferociously too, but these brave men were soon sent on their way to Valhöll.

The fourth time the jarl attacked, the defenders did not know what he intended. They hurled their spears and dropped their rocks, killing seven of Guthrum's warriors and wounding a dozen more, which had Alrik's men cheering as though they expected Guthrum to turn round and lead his beaten army back into the forest.

'Why doesn't he come for the gate?' Thorbiorn asked, seeming disappointed. A prince amongst the Danes, Thorbiorn was more used to bed slaves and mead-soaked nights in his father's hall than days manning ramparts and dropping rocks on other men's heads, but King Thorir hoped his son would learn sword-craft and the warrior's way as part of Sigurd's crew, and in truth Thorbiorn seemed to be enjoying this new life. 'Why doesn't he just come?' he asked again.

'Because he's not a fool like you, that's why, boy,' Olaf gnarred.

'He knows we're here,' Sigurd explained to Thorbiorn, watching the fighting at the other walls. 'And he knows we are killers.'

'Well it's not right,' Svein said, gripping his big axe but having nothing to hit with it. 'It's like watching other men eating and drinking when you are hungry yourself.'

'He'll attack the gate tomorrow, Red,' Bram said, hopefully. 'Aye, he'll come at us tomorrow, if the gods want to watch the blood flying.'

What no one expected was another attack that very night when Guthrum should have been dealing with his own dead and, as Olaf put it, scheming about his next move. They came just before the dawn, men with ropes and grappling hooks, and they came from the north.

The first Sigurd and his crew knew about it was the shouting, followed by a moaning of horns from those sentries manning the northern ramparts.

'That Guthrum is a cunning shit,' Olaf grumbled, sitting up in his nest of furs and scrubbing the sleep from his face while the others groaned and cursed around him.

'I was beginning to like the man but he's ruined it now,' Bram said, downing a cupful of ale which someone had left on a stool by the hearth. 'Waking me up when I am dreaming about a beautiful woman is not the way to get on my good side.'

'Whoever the woman was, she owes Guthrum for sparing her your stinking clutches, Bear,' Valgerd told him, shrugging into her brynja and sweeping her golden hair back to tie it. A simple enough thing for a woman to do, and yet the watching of it hurt Sigurd like a blade in his flesh. In some ways . . . in one way . . . Valgerd was closer to him than any of them. They had been lovers, if only for a night. But he had less command over her than any in his crew. Valgerd was no more his than had the cascading water of the falls where he had found the shieldmaiden living been hers. She and the völva of the sacred spring had shared a life and perhaps Valgerd had belonged to the völva, but the seeress had withered and died, for which Valgerd blamed the gods. No, Sigurd thought now, watching Valgerd prepare for battle. He could no more claim that she was his than he could claim ownership of the hearth smoke which rose to leak out through the thatch above them.

'Ready?' Olaf said, giving Sigurd a newly sharpened spear and a look which was sharper still. Sigurd nodded.

They did not rush, as the other men sharing the longhouse did, tumbling out of the place half asleep, their bladders still full of ale and their blades as much a danger to themselves as the enemy. But when Sigurd's crew were fully into their war gear, some of them having relieved themselves in the ditch outside, Sigurd led them through the borg towards the fighting.

Guthrum's men had not got far into the borg, but there must have been thirty still alive out of those who had made it over the palisade and more were still clambering over, spilling into the place while their companions fought Alrik's men, half in the moonlight, half in the shadow of the north wall. They had won a good part of the ramparts in that spot, allowing the next in line to get over the wall with relative ease. The borg men manning the rest of the perimeter could do nothing to prevent it, since to leave their own stations would invite the enemy to flood over the wall from all sides.

'Wait!' Sigurd said, stopping Black Floki and Bram who would have walked right into the fight without breaking stride. The rest halted at Sigurd's shoulder while he stood there, eyes sifting the chaos ahead.

Alrik himself was in the thick of it, bellowing encouragement to his men and hammering shields with his sword. There were no shieldwalls as such, just two opposing tides which mingled here and there. Small knots of warriors making their own steel-storms.

'We take back the wall and let Alrik deal with these,' Sigurd said, gesturing with his spear at those enemy fighters already inside the place, and Olaf nodded because it was what he would have done. They split into two groups, six going with Sigurd, six with Olaf, and skirted round the mass of fighting men, resisting the urge to join the slaughter. Then they clambered up the bank either side of the point where most of Guthrum's men were coming over the wall, Valgerd stopping halfway up to draw her bow and put an arrow into the thigh of a warrior straddling the stakes. Pinned to the wall, the man screeched like a vixen and Sigurd knew that Valgerd had meant the shot, knowing the man's plight would put fear in the bellies of those on the other side who had yet to climb.

'Shieldwall!' Sigurd yelled, and those with him moved with the fluid ease of long practice, drawing level and overlapping their shields to form a rampart to which each of them entrusted their lives.

'Now kill the goat turds!' Svein roared as a spear clattered off his shield and Floki bent to put his axe into the skull of a man who sat with his back against the palisade having somehow snapped his leg coming over it.

They drove into Guthrum's men, hacking and stabbing, as Olaf's skjaldborg swept towards them along the rampart, two killing waves swamping all before them, trampling the dead, while Valgerd loosed arrow after arrow, the dull thud of shaft striking flesh announcing men's doom.

Sigurd speared a warrior in the shoulder then slammed his shield boss into the man's face, dropping him. Hagal cleaved a head in two and Bram spilled a man's guts. Holding his long axe halfway along the haft, Svein hooked the crescent head round his opponent's neck and hauled him on to Asgot's sword, which was quite a thing to see. And then there were no more living men between Sigurd's skjaldborg and Olaf's.

'Come then!' Bram yelled up at two of Guthrum's men who were half over the wall, but when they saw what was waiting for them they scrambled back down and were gone.

'You wait here in case any of those turds change their minds and want to die,' Olaf told Sigurd, pointing his gore-slick spear at the palisade. 'We'll help Alrik with this lot.'

Sigurd nodded and Olaf took Moldof, Bjarni, Bjorn, Floki and Svein back down the mound to hit Guthrum's men in their rear. But those men, knowing that they could expect no more reinforcements to come over the wall, did not fight on for long. One by one they threw down their swords and axes, clamouring to be spared, and some of them died on their knees, hacked to death before Alrik threw the leash over his own men and put an end to the butchery.

Men stood panting for breath, spitting, coughing, grimacing with pain or grinning at friends who had also survived. Some were already looting the dead, while others growled insults at Guthrum's men, the dead and the living. A handful of survivors stood around boasting that they had known their wyrds would not be severed that day, which Solmund muttered was a bold thing to claim.

The wounded were helped back to the dwellings where those most skilled in treating injuries waited with bone needles and horsehair thread, strong ale and herbs to numb the pain, and red-hot irons to seal cut flesh.

Sigurd looked out into the night and saw the backs of Guthrum's men as they retreated across the moon-silvered meadow and melted into the forest. Then he ordered some of Alrik's men to resume a watch from that place so that he and his crew would not have to, and no one questioned the order or refused it, even as weary as they were.

'Guthrum would be a fool to try that again,' Alrik told Sigurd, which was as much acknowledgement of Sigurd's part in that fight as he would give. The warlord was blood-spattered. There were beads of it on his long moustaches, glistening by flame and moonlight or dark against the pale skin of his neck where his Thór's hammer sat. His hair was cropped to the scalp at the sides but long enough on top to be braided into a rope which was pulled back over his head and tied between his shoulder blades.

'I would not put anything past Guthrum,' Sigurd said, and Alrik answered that by striking a kneeling prisoner across the temple with his sword hilt, dropping him. Then he turned and barked at his men to get on with the binding of the fourteen prisoners who, unlike the earlier boasters, must have sensed that they had come to the end of their wyrds now. The Norns, those spinners of men's futures, were poised with their shears.

'This feud you two have between you is a thirsty bitch, Alrik,' Olaf told him, looking at the carnage around them. 'She drinks blood like we drink ale.'

Alrik could not argue with that, though he did not like hearing it as he crouched to pull the silver rings from a dead man's fingers.

'It is a shame Guthrum did not have the courage to lead his men over the wall,' he said, running his sword through a scrap of wool torn from a tunic. 'He would be a corpse now and a good number of his men would pledge themselves to me.' With that he called to one of his men who looked up just in time to catch the two silver rings which Alrik threw. 'They would join my army because I am a more generous lord than Guthrum,' Alrik said, locking eyes with Sigurd. 'As you have seen for yourself, Byrnjolf,' he added, using the name by which Sigurd went amongst these Svearmen.

'Silver is of little use to dead men,' Sigurd said, which was not quite insulting Alrik's leadership but not far off. It was not that Sigurd disliked the man particularly, just that Alrik did not seem gods-favoured in any way, and that was disconcerting. Besides which, the strain of this feud was carved in Alrik's face like runes on a standing stone, which did not fill anyone with confidence.

'Byrnjolf has the right of that,' Olaf said. 'More nights like this and you won't have a war host to speak of,' he said, which was true. Sixteen of Alrik's men would never fight for him again, because they were dead or halfway dead: which was slightly better than Guthrum's losses, but still. Guthrum could afford to lose more men because he had more to begin with.

'Earn your keep, Norsemen, and we shall all come out of this silver-rich,' Alrik said, turning his back on them to greet Knut, his second in command, who had come to report how things stood across the other side of the borg. It seemed this at the north wall had been the only real assault, though Guthrum had made another feint at the gates to lure some of Alrik's men away from the proper fight.

'Earn our keep? Is that what he said?' Svein growled, clutching a fistful of arrows which he had gathered and now gave to Valgerd like a bunch of spring flowers. The shieldmaiden smiled and thanked him and Svein spat on his axe head and rubbed it with a handful of hay to get the blood off. 'If not for us Guthrum would be drinking mead from Alrik's skull by now.'

'At least he's a fighter, unlike my last lord,' Bram said with a shrug, which got some nods from the others who were milling around wondering what to do now. They had heard the story from Bram's own mouth, of how he had insulted his lord, a jarl named Otrygg, in his own hall because Otrygg had become a soft-bellied, hearth-loving jarl who had forgotten how to raid and live like a man should. And how Brak, Jarl Otrygg's champion, had had no choice but to defend his lord's honour and die for it too. Because Bram, whom men called Bear, was as skilled as he was strong and would fight Thór himself for the fame of it.

'Even so, this is not fighting,' Bram added, curling a lip at the sight of the prisoners who were being herded together by Alrik's men. 'You can all stay and watch this, but I am going back to sleep to see if that beauty in my dream is waiting for me.' He walked off, his shield slung across his back and his helmet under his arm.

'Wait for me,' Hagal called after. 'I do not want to watch these men get their throats cut.' Neither did any of the others, it seemed, and so they made their way back to the longhouse, leaving Alrik to do what he would with the prisoners. Not that anyone expected him to spare a single one.

The truth was that this attack had nearly succeeded, and almost certainly would have, had Sigurd's crew not retaken the rampart and turned the tide against Guthrum.

'Not that Alrik will admit it,' Olaf said as he and Sigurd wriggled out of their brynjur and laid them over a sea chest by their beds.

'Wager he expects this to buy him more dead enemies yet,' Sigurd said, touching the chest, which was carved with ravens and eagles, and leaning his shield against it. He drew his scramasax to check the blade. Wouldn't hurt to take a whetstone to it. His blood still thrummed with the battle thrill so it wasn't as if sleep would come to him any time soon.

'Aye, I think you're right with that,' Olaf admitted, yawning and taking the ale mug which Svein passed him. Nearby, Bram was already snoring, the sound of it like a rockfall.

Right he might be, but Sigurd suspected there was another reason for Alrik's having bitten his tongue rather than admit that Sigurd and his half crew of Norse had stopped Jarl Guthrum becoming king of that hill in Fornsigtuna. Alrik was beginning to feel the worm of jealousy squirming in his gut. As much as the warlord needed Sigurd's crew, he was a proud man, and whilst his own men were dying, it must have been a hard thing to recognize that here was a young warrior whose reputation was beginning to shine like a moon-washed blade.

Or a flame-licked blade, Sigurd thought, as by the flickering light of the hearth he ran the whetstone along the knife's edge.

Still, Alrik had more important things to worry about than reputation, either his own or Sigurd's. With Guthrum for an enemy they all did.

It was a golden day on Fugløy. A breeze rattled the birch leaves so that the rocks and long grass were dappled with dancing light. Bees threaded the air, going from flower to flower, the hum of them almost drowning out the distant clack of wooden swords as a group of Freyja Maidens practised in the clearing. The sky was endless and blue but for a few wisps of white, like a god's waking breath still lingering on the cool dawn air. The gulls soared and floated high above the island, at the edge of sight, seeming more inclined to revel in the day than dive for fish or scavenge snails and worms or leftovers from the midden.

But the sea was the richest treasure in the hoard of that day. It shone like a dented old helmet after a good polishing and was almost too bright to look at. A sleeping sea this morning, after the wind-tossed rollers of the previous day. Good for rowing, fishing, or taking a skiff to the shallow places to snatch up crabs or tempt them with meat on the end of a string. Good for washing in too, Runa thought now, squinting against the silver glare of it.

'I'm going to bathe,' she said. 'After that I must get back to milk the goats. A wash wouldn't hurt you, you know,' she told Ingel, raising an eyebrow at the man who lay back on his elbows in the grass beside her. The young smith was soot-stained and sweat-grimed, and yet from the way he grinned at Runa now anyone would think he was proud of his own stink. Not that Runa had minded it as she had straddled him in their nest of dewy grass, the two of them having sneaked away while the other women were beginning their daily tasks and Ingel's father Ibor was bringing the forge up to heat with the bellows.

But that was then. Now there was work to be done and, with the thrill of their coupling fading in Runa, receding like the tide, she was aware of the dirt on him, matted in his long hair and beard and ingrained in his skin so that the creases at the edges of his smiling eyes were as white as milk on the rare occasions he wore his serious face. Which he did now, though it took every effort by the looks.

'I'll bathe for you, Runa Haraldsdóttir,' he said, 'even though I do not see much point, for I will be covered in soot and grease again before midday.' He raised a callused finger. 'But only if we do it together. I swim like an anvil and will need to hang on to you so that I do not drown.' Now the smile came to his lips and Runa struck his thigh with the back of her hand and tutted at his nonsense, for she had seen him swim like an otter more than once, the last time being when he and his father were off shore with the nets. She had watched Ingel jump over the side to cool down after rowing halfway round Fugløy and hauling in a bilge-load of mackerel.

'You are a hopeless liar, blacksmith,' she said now, pursing her own lips on a smile she did not want to give him. She almost resented Ingel for his arrogance. For his knowing that he could have her, even looking like a black elf from one of the stories Runa's father Jarl Harald used to tell her when he wanted to frighten her.

No, when I wanted him to frighten me, she thought, remembering. 'Come then,' she said, climbing to her feet and looking back towards the tree line to make sure none of the other women had come looking for her, however unlikely that was. With the High Mother Skuld Snorradóttir off seeking guidance from the gods, there was a slackness to island life, the Freyja Maidens working with only half the usual purpose and endeavour. Skuld's absence was not the only reason for this. It was more than the mice playing while the cat was out of the way. Runa knew that the Prophetess's words about the future of their fellowship, her questioning of their way of life in uncertain times, had been like the serpent Nídhögg gnawing at the roots of the World Tree, so that the Freyja Maidens of Fugløy truly believed their way of life might come tumbling down.

And yet a good many of them were more than a little excited by the prospect of leaving the island and returning to the world. The idea of that had turned their heads and their thoughts from the everyday patterns which they had lived by up to now.

Runa's friend Drífa had been born on Fugløy and knew nothing else, no other life, but that only made her more eager to leave and she for one desperately hoped that the High Mother would return with the pronouncement that the Maidens were to leave this place and venture forth.

'It is hard to worry about next winter's hay when we may be living in King Thorir's hall by then,' Drífa had said when their friend Vebiorg announced that they should be cutting and drying what little grass grew on Fugløy while this good weather lasted.

'What makes you think the king will have us under his roof and share his meat with us?' Vebiorg had asked. 'He is happy to send us his smoked mutton, his weak ale and his blacksmiths, because he thinks it will buy him a place in Freyja the Giver's hall when he keels over, but he does not want a hall full of blade-wearing women.'

Drífa had frowned at her, but knowing nothing of the world beyond Fugløy's shores she could not put up an argument.

Still, with Skuld away there was more sword, spear and shield work going on than mundane tasks such as spinning shorn wool into thread or searching for gulls' eggs or scything grass to feed the animals next winter.

'Wait for me!' Ingel called after Runa, finally dragging himself to his feet now that Runa was up to her ankles in a rock pool a crab's scuttle from the lapping tide.

She shivered at the water's touch and looked out across the sea which shone like the silver of a jarl torc. Later in the day the air would be warm enough to bathe and not shiver half to death after, but she was up to her knees now and would not let Ingel see that she was cold. He already knew too much about her. Knew her body as well as a man could, which was itself such a shock to Runa; she wondered what her brother Sigurd would make of it were he to find out.

At least her thoughts and feelings were still her own. Ingel could not have that part of her. Not yet. Perhaps when they were married.

'It's cold,' he said, coming to stand beside her, bending to bring handfuls of water up and on to his skin to prepare his body for the plunge. Runa laughed and took his hand, leading him deeper, her feet gripping the weed-slick rocks as Ingel cursed the chill water and huffed and puffed.

Was she really thinking of marrying him? They had never brought it up, but neither had Ingel been with any of the other Freyja Maidens since he had lain with her. That must mean something. Certainly he did not seem to mind the scar which some nithing raider's arrow had carved in her face from just below her left eye to her ear. A disfigurement which Runa had been ashamed of but which Skuld the High Mother had told her to be proud of. 'Such battle runes speak for us, Runa,' Skuld had said. 'They tell our tales as well as any skald.'

Runa felt the sea breeze on the scar now, as gently as Ingel's lips had brushed against it earlier. A shiver ran through her and she tried not to think of what her brother would say if he could see her now, arse-naked and hand in hand with a filthy blacksmith who was cursing as the cold water shrivelled the snake between his legs.

You should not have left me behind, Sigurd, she thought, setting her jaw as the water shocked the skin between her hips and waist. Wondering where her brother was now and resenting him for abandoning her. Wishing he could see how good she had become with sword and spear, as much as she dreaded him knowing about Ingel.

'There,' the smith said, 'see there.' He was pointing with his free hand to the north beyond the pine-covered sliver of the island which jutted out into the sea. 'You see it? There! An arrow-shot off shore.'

'Too small for *Storm-Elk*,' Runa said, having been struck with the sudden fear that it was King Thorir's ship come to take Ingel and his father back to Skíringssalr. The blacksmiths were the only men permitted to set foot on the island, tasked with repairing the Freyja Maidens' weapons and forging what needed forging. But even they must return to Thorir's hall when the king sent for them.

No. Runa could see now that the boat being rowed towards the bay beyond that knife blade of land was just a færing. She sharpened her eyes upon it, which was no easy thing because of the glittering glare coming off the sea. Two pairs of oars, no more.

'Sibbe and Guthrun?' Ingel suggested, for those two had gone off fishing before sunrise. But Runa shook her head.

'They will be on the west side,' she said. She had lived on Fugløy long enough by now to know that if you wanted to make your arm ache from pulling in mackerel and, now and then, something bigger like a codfish, you took the boat out to a place which the women called Flea Rock because the water there was as thick with fish as fleas on a dog.

'News from the king then,' Ingel said, his gaze lingering a moment on the distant craft before he turned to make his way back to dry land and his clothes and shoes which lay piled in the grass.

But Runa was already splashing through the rock pools then throwing her own tunic over her wet skin and thrusting her legs into her breeks. Because perhaps whoever was in that færing had word of Sigurd. What if he were dead? What if King Gorm or Jarl Hrani had caught up with him? No. She would not believe that. He had left her on this island because he would not make her endure the outcast's life he had chosen for himself after King Gorm betrayed their father and Jarl Randver had brought slaughter to their village. But he would not leave her alone in this world, would not make the journey to the afterlife without her.

Runa thought all this as she ran across the rocks and long grass, scattering butterflies and bees before her and looking up to the bluff where one of the other women was on watch. That woman was standing on the rock at the edge of the bluff to get a better look at the boat and its crew, and Runa saw that it was her friend Vebiorg. She waved at Runa now to acknowledge that she had seen the craft, then turned and was gone, back to warn the others that they should expect visitors.

So Runa ran, leaping a fallen tree and ducking a spider's web which shimmered between two hazels. Then through the birch and thickets and up to the higher ground that would take her over the ridge and down into the bay where those in the rowboat meant to come ashore.

And Ingel, despite not yet owning the brawn that his father had earned from a lifetime in the forge, could not keep up with her.

Runa watched as the man pulled the little boat up the beach, the small stones crunching beneath its hull as he dragged it beyond the high-tide line with the woman still in it. Her brown hair had spilled from a white linen head-dress and her teeth worried her bottom lip as she sat on the bench, clinging on to the sides as the little færing jerked and bucked to a stop.

And then Runa realized why the woman had not leapt out of the boat into the shallows and either helped the man pull the boat up or else at least lightened the load for him. She was enormous with child and grimacing as she stood in the thwarts, holding out her hand so that the man could help her out of the boat, which almost tipped with her weight as she hoisted a leg over and set a foot on the strand. Runa was reminded of a whale she had once seen on the east coast of Karmøy. The beast had washed up on the shore and her father had sent a score of men and women to butcher it on the beach and bring the meat and fat and even strips of its skin back to Eik-hjálmr. She stifled a grin and felt mean for thinking of it now.

21

'You cannot come ashore here,' she told the man, still breathing heavily after the run. 'It is forbidden.'

The man raised a hand to her to show he had heard, but did not say anything as he helped the woman walk across the loose stones up the beach towards her.

'You must get back into your boat and row away from here. You cannot stay,' she said, and again the man raised a hand but kept walking towards her and Runa felt a stab of irritation. Was he deaf? Or just arrogant?

'She looks ready to drop it on the beach,' Ingel said, coming to stand beside Runa, breathing hard, eyes wide at the sight of the man half pulling, half pushing the woman up the slope.

'She can't,' Runa said. 'They should not even be here.'

Ingel shrugged. 'Then you'd better put her back in the boat and hope the seep water in the bilge isn't deep, for she will drop the bairn in there,' he said and Runa frowned because he had a point.

'Who are you?' she asked the couple, thinking that if the man raised his hand again she would draw her scramasax and cut it off, expectant wife or no.

'My wife is fit to burst,' the man said, letting go the woman's hand to come closer to Runa. She could smell the boat tar and sweat on him. 'She began the pains,' he said, 'the ones that come again and again like waves on the shore.' He frowned. 'But something is wrong. Or else the child is being stubborn, for it will not come.' Fair-haired, his face pitted with little scars, he was a man in his middle years and not rich by the looks of his clothes and his lack of a sword or any war gear to speak of, though he might have left his belongings in the færing. He had no beard to speak of, either, but for a few mossy patches and the dark bristles on his neck.

'I know little of such things,' Runa said, thinking that she should perhaps start to learn more given what she got up to with Ingel.

'My name is Varin and this is my wife Gudny,' the man said, looking from Runa to Ingel, arming sweat from his forehead and pressing hands into the small of his back. 'We have come far. Rowed through the night to get here.'

'Why here?' Ingel asked before Runa had the chance to.

'You can see that she is in pain,' Varin said, thumbing back towards his wife who stood there looking about as uncomfortable as a person could who was not suffering from either the runs or painful arse berries or serious over-eating. 'My wife needs help or the child will die inside her and kill Gudny with it.'

'But why come here? Surely there are women near your steading who can help her,' Runa said.

'I have heard about the old woman who lives here. The witch,' he said in a softer voice. He touched the little iron Mjöllnir which hung at his throat and knew from Runa's expression that she needed more explanation than that. 'My brother is a shipwright. He worked on *Storm-Elk*, King Thorir's ship, and he is a friend of her skipper, a man named Harthbren.' He raised that hand of his again but this time it was lifted like a shield against Runa's next question. 'This Harthbren did not tell my brother where this island was . . . before you have King Thorir flay the skin from his flesh. But Biarbi was able to stitch the where of it together from what he learnt by talking to the man.' He forced a smile. 'My brother knows this sea better than he knows his own wife.'

He turned and beckoned to his woman to come closer. Her face was tear-stained and miserable-looking as she waddled forward, hands cradling her huge belly. There was blood near the hem of her kyrtill, Runa saw, which did not bode well for either her or the life inside her. Runa knew that much.

She looked at Ingel who shrugged as if to say he was just a blacksmith and who came and went was no business of his. She looked back at Varin and decided there was no point in telling him that men were not allowed on the island, not with Ingel standing there still flushed from their coupling in the grass.

'They will likely send you away,' she warned instead, this to Gudny, who was giving her such pathetic eyes that it was uncomfortable to look at her. 'Certainly they will not allow *you* to be here,' she said, turning back to Varin.

He set his face, the little muscles tensing beneath the pockmarked skin. 'I will not leave my wife,' he said. 'The bairn needs to come out of her. We need the old woman to weave her seiðr. She can help us. I know it. She will save Gudny and the child too, if the gods will it.' Gudny groaned then and swayed as if she might fall, and it was Ingel who stepped forward to steady her, earning the woman's mumbled thanks and a scowl from Varin, who took hold of his wife again though he did not refuse Ingel's help.

'Will you take us to her, girl?' Varin asked. 'Or will you stand there and watch my wife and bairn die?'

There was an edge of threat in the man's voice now, an air of violence about him, though it was not worth making a thing out of it, Runa thought, confident that she could handle him if she needed to; wondering why she had even thought about how she would take him down, this desperate and frightened man.

And so she nodded, turned her back on the sea and the couple who had come across it, and walked over the rocks towards the long grass and the birch and scrub beyond which lay the grazing meadows and, beyond them, the settlement where the Freyja Maidens lived their lives undisturbed.

'Come then,' she called over her shoulder.

Guthrum came three more times over the next six days. The last of those attacks brought terror to the borg, for as Sigurd knew only too well, few things frightened men more than fire in the night: ship-burning, hall-burning, man-burning fire.

Guthrum had bided his time, letting one rainless day follow another until the palisade, as well as the fuel he had gathered, was as dry as they were likely to get. Then, in the gloom of night, his men ran forward with arms full of sticks and dried moss tinder which they piled against the wall in four places, setting light to it. Alrik's men doused two of the four fires before they caught properly, but the other two, being fanned by a breeze coming out of the south-east, licked the stakes and then bit deep. It did not help that Guthrum, seeing the flames beginning to do their work, arranged all his archers before those two fires, so that they kept up a steady rain of arrows which, if they did not kill many, nevertheless kept Alrik's men's heads down when they should have been busy flinging water.

'What are we going to do about this, then?' Moldof asked Sigurd and Olaf, waving the stump of his right arm – all that was left of it since Sigurd's father had cut it off in a fight which the skalds sang of. A more grievous wound still because it had lost Moldof his position as King Gorm's champion and prow man, and this the warrior could not abide. Thinking he could reclaim his honour by killing his king's enemy Sigurd Haraldarson, Moldof had journeyed north alone, intent on finding Sigurd in his lair up in Osøyro. But in the event it was Sigurd who had offered Moldof a chance to rekindle his fame. Fame and the sword-song, or a bad death, cut into a stump and rolled into the fjord: that was the choice Sigurd had given him that white, frozen day on the fjord's edge. Moldof had chosen the first option and now the former champion fought for Sigurd, though Sigurd and the other Skudeneshavn men still felt the strange prickle of that like nettles on the skin, Moldof having been their enemy not so long ago.

Men were coughing now, choking on the smoke which billowed over the palisade into the borg, enveloping the huge mass of Moldof who scowled at it as if that would turn it back. And it might, given how ugly Moldof was.

Flame-glow showed like copper against the night sky.

'Now would be a good time to take your snake out of your breeks, hang it over the side and piss out that fire,' Svein told Bjarni, who was not above boasting about the size of the thing given any opportunity.

'I won't risk burning it. Not for the sake of this lot,' Bjarni said, gesturing at thirty of Alrik's men who stood with them on the ramparts, peering round their shields at Guthrum's war host massing on the slope.

It was one thing to make light of it all, Hagal said, but no one would be laughing when those burning stakes gave way and Guthrum's men poured into the place.

Alrik's men were bringing pails of water from all across the borg and tipping them over the wall, while their comrades shielded them from arrows and spears, and when a cheer went up fifty paces further along the rampart, Sigurd knew that the fire there had been put out. But the one eating the palisade where he stood was growing, tongues of flames now and then stretching above the pointed stakes to singe men's beards.

'Well, Byrnjolf?' Alrik said. 'What do we do?' The warlord was looking at the enemy rather than at Sigurd, and the question had leaked from the corner of his mouth like pus from a wound.

Sigurd had been asking himself the same question and had not liked the answer. But he shared it with Alrik anyway. 'A few of us slip over the wall and loot Guthrum's camp,' he said. Arrows streaked over their heads and thudded into men's shields around them. 'We burn his tents if we get the chance and we make a lot of noise about it.' He nodded towards the horde on the hillside, fully revealed in its war-glory now by the glow of the fire. He fancied he could make out Guthrum himself standing in the heart of that body of warriors, taller than those around him. 'If they think we are into their sea chests and slashing their ale skins they will hare back to the camp.' He shrugged. 'It may give your men a chance to deal with this fire at least.'

Alrik scowled, considering the idea. 'Anyone who makes it as far as those trees without being carved up will be tempted to keep going and not look back.'

'You think I would run?' Sigurd asked.

'You have sworn no oath to me,' Alrik said.

Here it was again. 'And neither will I,' Sigurd said. 'But tell me, Alrik, is my oath worth more to you than this borg?'

26

To his right Olaf cursed as an arrow *tonk*ed off his shield boss. He picked out the archer who had just tried to kill him and bellowed at him, calling the man a nithing son of a flea-ridden bitch. Then he turned back to Alrik.

'You won't have to worry about anyone leaving you here in the shit, Alrik,' he said. 'No one is going out there. Not us, not your oath-sworn.'

'What do you have in mind, Uncle?' Sigurd asked.

'We'll let the arse-leaves come to us instead. Only thing is, we need to lose this part of the wall to save the rest of it. If the fire spreads we're dead men.'

Sigurd knew what Olaf was thinking then.

Alrik knew too. 'But if there is just a small hole we will be able to plug it,' he said.

Olaf nodded, then called to Svein and Bram to bring their axes. Alrik ordered some others to help and they set to work, going at those flaming stakes like woodsmen while others went off into the borg to find the timbers they would need as replacements.

The first of the stakes fell with a shower of embers and the rest soon followed, and were kicked away down the slope from the palisade by Alrik's men, their shields raised against the heat as much as the arrows. Then Alrik himself stepped into the breach and his skjaldborg built itself around him. He was lucky in one way because the burning timbers lying on the bank checked Guthrum's advance. Yet he was unlucky in that those burning fence posts lit up his shieldwall so that Guthrum's archers could hardly miss.

'He can smell blood now,' Bram said. He meant Guthrum, who was pacing up and down in front of his men, yelling at them, inciting them to the coming slaughter, rousing them with promises of plunder and arm rings and fame. Men were flooding in from the surrounding darkness, swelling his numbers because they knew that this breach was their best chance of retaking the borg.

'All we have to do is hold!' Alrik called. 'We will kill them. We will bleed them and they will lose heart. Jarl Guthrum

will show himself for the pale-livered, pus-filled prick he is.'
His men cheered this, thumping swords and axes against their
shields, showing their defiance. One of them loosed an arrow
at Guthrum which hit him square on the helmet between the
eye guards. But Guthrum did not flinch. He pointed his sword
at Alrik, roared something to Óðin Hrafnaguð, Ravengod, then
led his army forward. They came up the slope as though they
never doubted that they would win, as though they would
punch through that gap in the fort's palisade like a rivet through
a ship's strake.

But Alrik had not become a warlord by being an easy man
to kill. Nor was he afraid to lead from the sharp end, and he
held like a rock, striking men down, hammering them with his
sword, splitting skulls and lopping limbs. Knut was there too and
he was a deadly fighter, cunning and quick, his spear striking
like a snake and laying men low.

'They're doing well,' Svein admitted grudgingly.

'Aye, they need to,' Solmund said. For now they stood back
from the fighting because Alrik already had two lines of men
filling the breach and there was no room for more.

'Hold your crew in reserve,' Alrik had told Sigurd. 'My men
will fight harder knowing that you are at our backs. But if we
break, you must hold the breach.'

'You won't break,' Sigurd had said, and so far he was right.
And now those men they had sent off to find timbers were
returning with their heavy loads, so that whilst Alrik and
Guthrum's skjaldborgar clashed, their blades biting, Olaf took
charge of the new defences. He had Sigurd's crew digging holes
and setting the new posts in them, but not so that they made
a new palisade, for being rushed it would be weak. Instead
they set the timbers at a slant and supported them so that they
pointed towards the breach. Old roof timbers, posts from the
animal pens, even split planks from long tables were set in place,
clustered thick as sea urchin spines, and then Olaf had them
take axes and sharpen the ends of the timbers. And as they dug

and hacked and sweated, they kept one eye on the battle in the breach, hoping that Alrik's shieldwall stood firm. Because if not, his men would be driven back on to those spikes and the enemy would surge in.

The sword-song rang out into the night, accompanied by the shrieks of the wounded and the gruff shouts of encouragement from men who knew only too well that they each depended on the other, that the shieldwall was only as strong as its weakest man. And it was a hard fight between those two warlords that night, with men falling on both sides, their bodies hauled back so that others could step up and take their place.

Still, try as he might, Guthrum could not break Alrik's shieldwall and force his way into the borg. And in the end, exhausted and bone-weary, Guthrum's men pulled back from the carnage in the breach, and Alrik's men up on the ramparts could not even sting them with arrows as they retreated down the hill, for they had long run out of shafts.

The mangled and the dismembered lay there like a grim burial mound, a testament to the savagery of that fight and to the stubbornness of both sides. But Alrik still held the hill, for all that he had paid a heavy price for it.

'I don't think we can take another night like that,' Svein said to Sigurd. Dawn was breaking and he had come with Sigurd to look at the hole in the palisade and see what Alrik was doing about it. 'I am thinking we should take our silver and iron and leave while we still can.' Svein had braided his thick red beard into one rope, which he pulled now as they watched three dogs licking the blood-smeared grass of the slope where the corpses had lain. Now Sigurd realized why Svein had got out of his bed to come with him while the rest were still half asleep in the longhouse. This was not the sort of thing his friend would say in front of anyone else. 'You know I would stay here and fight beside you until Ragnarök, Sigurd,' he said, tugging at that red rope, 'but how will that help us avenge our kin? This is a good fight but it is not our fight.'

They stood beside the sharp teeth of the makeshift defence, looking out across the rock-strewn meadow which was thick now with yellow flowers that showed even in the weak light, reminding Sigurd of home and Runa.

Now and then the breeze brought the low hum of men's voices from Guthrum's camp, but there was no sign that the jarl was going to attack the breach again. Which was why Knut was making the best of it and had his men digging out the last stumps of the ruined timbers, like rotting teeth from raw gums, so that they could be replaced properly.

'You think Guthrum would let us walk out of here and back to *Reinen*?' Sigurd asked.

'I think he would be glad to see us go,' Svein said, then held his tongue while two of Knut's men walked past hefting a long timber between them. 'Guthrum has lost too many warriors already,' Svein went on when the men were out of earshot. 'He wants this borg and the iron in it. He won't sacrifice more of his men fighting us if he doesn't have to. Not if we show him our backs.'

'It wouldn't be much of a fight. Not out there in the open,' Sigurd said, which was true enough. Even armed like Týr, Lord of Battle, they were just fourteen, whilst Guthrum still commanded as many as one hundred and fifty warriors. Even so, he suspected Svein was right and that Guthrum would just be glad to see Sigurd's crew fly the coop, leaving Alrik in the mire of it.

'We will never kill the oath-breaker if we die here,' Svein said, his mention of King Gorm like the stab of a cold blade in Sigurd's guts. There was no argument Sigurd could make against that and so he said nothing, which allowed a silence to spread between them like a bloodstain.

It had taken a lot for Svein to suggest that they turn their backs on Alrik and leave his men to Guthrum's army. And yet Svein was right, this was not their fight.

'Alrik will think we are cowards,' Sigurd said after a while.

'Alrik will not be alive for long after we leave so what does it matter what he thinks?'

But Óðin will know, Sigurd thought, *and I have not come this far, having got old One-Eye's attention, just to prove unworthy of it now.*

Sigurd looked along the rampart and saw Alrik doing his rounds, walking the perimeter and talking to the clusters of men manning the palisade. Down in the borg his other warriors were spilling out of their dwellings now, stretching aching muscles and preparing for whatever the day might bring. They were good men. Loyal men.

'We just have to beat Guthrum,' Sigurd said. Svein raised one thick red eyebrow but Sigurd pressed on. 'We beat Guthrum and we leave here as rich men.'

Svein nodded, which was his way of saying that whatever Sigurd decided, that was fine by him.

Sigurd nodded too. All he had to do was come up with a way of killing Jarl Guthrum and he would earn silver, fame and the Spear-God's respect. He was still wondering how this might be done when Svein tramped back down the bank into the borg to find something to eat.

It was not until four days later that the answer came to him. And it was Guthrum himself who came up with it, laying it before Sigurd like a gift.

'The horse prick is trying to put the worm of fear in our bellies, breathing down our necks like this,' Knut said. After three days of rain it had dawned bright and golden. The breeze itself was warm and what little cloud there was drifted through the blue sky like unspun wool.

Alrik, Knut, Sigurd and Olaf had gathered on the ramparts above the gates because the sentries there had called down into the borg that Guthrum was coming.

But the jarl was not attacking. Rather he was moving his whole camp up the hill towards the borg so that it was more than a spear-throw but less than an arrow-shot from the walls. Not that he need fear Alrik's archers taking long-range shots, because they were saving what few arrows they had scavenged or made for Guthrum's next attack.

'He thinks that if he puts his war host in full view, my men will lose heart at the sight,' Alrik said.

Olaf nodded in agreement. 'He wants this thing over with,' he said, 'and is coming at us like a hand round a throat. And his own men are going to want to finish it sooner rather than later for they will be fed up with living on a hillside and rolling out of their beds.'

It took most of the day, but by the time the sun fell behind the mountains in the west the enemy had set up their tents again and were sitting round fires, or rather lying because of the slope, drinking and talking, laughing and singing, and all of them ready in their war gear, shields and spears within reach. It was a sight which had Alrik's one hundred and ten fit men gripping sword pommels, spear shafts, axe hafts and Thór's hammer amulets with sweaty palms. But of all of it, one thing had Alrik spitting curses and telling anyone who would listen that he was going to pull Guthrum's head out of his arse, stick it on a pole and leave it for the birds. That was the sight of the jarl's own tent sitting nearer the borg than any of the others, as if Guthrum were announcing to gods and men that he was a man without fear of death. That he could snore the night away almost within spitting distance of his enemies and have no concern that he might wake with a blade in his belly.

Guthrum's tent was of red sail cloth and the upper ends of its cross-timber supports were carved to resemble snarling wolves; the whole thing now being where it was made for a decent insult. It was Jarl Guthrum saying that Alrik was too afraid to come out and fight him amongst the spring flowers, man against man, skjaldborg against skjaldborg.

And it was a sight which had Sigurd's heart pounding against the anvil of his breastbone. When *he* looked at Guthrum's red tent he saw opportunity, a chance to win this fight for Alrik and cut out the despair which was spreading through the borg like rot in damp wood.

'What is on your mind then?' Olaf asked him. They were sharing bread and some cheese and a skin of ale that was only a little sour. 'When you are quiet like this it usually means you are waist-deep in some scheming.'

'Not this time, Uncle,' Sigurd said.

But that was a lie.

CHAPTER TWO

THEY CALLED HER WISE MOTHER — THOUGH RUNA HAD NEVER HEARD of her having children of her own and so she supposed the Freyja Maidens of Fugløy, most of whom would never bear fruit themselves, were the old woman's family. She was a seiðr-kona too. A prophetess. A witch whom Runa had met in the depths of winter up in Jarl Burner's old hall in Osøyro, which in itself had enough of the strange about it to stand her neck hairs up when she thought of it. Knee-deep in snow out hunting a wolfpack, Sigurd, Olaf and Svein had found the witch – or perhaps she had found them – her galdr song holding the wolves at bay, stopping them from ripping out her throat until Sigurd and the others could put their spears to use.

The witch had come to warn Sigurd that there were men hunting him, warriors on their way to kill him and so end Jarl Harald's line. She had lived with them in that hall, her presence sensed more than felt, like a dark shadow in the corner, and she had told Sigurd other things which he had kept to himself. Meeting the old woman again, here on this island, and learning that the Freyja Maidens sought her wisdom and prophecy had stunned Runa like a blow from Drífa's leather-bound spear. So had the witch's words about Runa herself.

'The time of kings and jarls is ending,' the old woman had said. 'There will come a day when one king will rule everything beneath the sky as far in every direction as a raven can fly. And he will not support the Freyja Maidens. He will bend his knee to the White God. All across the north, few kings and one god. That is what I have seen.' But then she had gone on to say that in spite of this changing tide, there were still those in whose lives Óðin, Thór, Loki and Freyja liked to meddle. 'One such woman is amongst us here this night,' she had announced, the Freyja Maidens spellbound by her every word. 'Runa Haraldsdóttir and her brother are threads in the hem of the kyrtill of all this which I have spoken of.'

Runa had not known what to make of that, but the women of Fugløy had looked at her differently since that night. Not that the Wise Mother had done much far-seeing since then, she thought now, coming through the trees into the clearing, the man and his waddling wife on her heels. She had known where to find the witch, for the old woman did not range far these days. Not on her own two legs, anyway. In her mind, though, who could say?

'I'd better get back to work,' Ingel said, letting go of the woman and leaving her in her husband's care.

'Aye, run back to your hammer and your fire, my brave Völund,' Runa told him, half grinning as the smith frowned and made his escape, for she knew he was afraid of the seiðr-kona, as were most men, and would do whatever he could to avoid her.

There she was, just where Runa knew she would be, outside the longhouse in the shade of the eaves. It was where the old woman spent the long days, sitting on a stool, bent as a bow, hunched over, her grey hair itself like a tapestry hiding her face as she pushed the bone needle through the cloth over and over again, times beyond counting. Runa had yet to get a proper look at her work. Truth be told, her own dislike of being in the prophetess's presence was stronger than her curiosity where the old woman's needlework was concerned, though she had caught a glimpse of a horse's head, the brown threads of its mane flying. A hunting scene perhaps. Mounted warriors chasing a deer or a boar?

'What have we here?' the old woman said without looking up, head tilted, her face all pucker and frown, so that she could easily have been talking about the needlework on her lap.

It was a wonder she could embroider at all, given her old fingers and eyes and the slight trembling which seemed to fill her now and then, though not today, Runa noted.

'Well?' the old woman said, looking up with watery, unsurprised eyes, measuring the situation like hacksilver in the scales.

'She is called Gudny,' Runa said, jutting her chin at the woman, 'and she should have had the bairn by now but it is stuck inside her.' As soon as the words were out Runa realized that the old woman was not talking about Gudny. The prophetess lifted a claw-like hand, the bone needle in it pointing at Varin.

'Not her, young Runa. *Him*. What is he doing here on Kuntøy?'

Runa felt the heat in her cheeks at that name and avoided the eyes of several other women who had gathered at Vebiorg's warning, but the witch waved away her embarrassment with that needle. 'I know what King Thorir's men call this place, girl. Ha! I was not always a dried up old crab apple.'

Varin squirmed under her gaze as well he might.

'You know that men are forbidden to set foot on our island, Runa,' the witch said. 'Other than that young stallion you have taken to riding in the mornings. And his father, who still makes a straight iron bar whenever it is called for, so I hear.'

'Wise Mother, this man is unarmed. I saw no threat.' Runa gestured at the young woman. 'His wife will die if someone does not help her.' *The bairn may be dead already*, she thought but did not say.

Varin was brave enough to take another step towards the witch, though he pulled his wife forward with him. 'You can work some seiðr, Wise Mother,' he said, laying a hand upon the young woman's barrel belly. She was sobbing now, moaning with discomfort and still trying to lift the burden in the sling of her entwined hands. 'You can help her, Wise Mother. Give her some brew for the pain. Weave some spell to make the bairn come.' He glanced at Runa now and then as though hoping that she might speak on their behalf. But Runa did not think that anything she said would weigh in the couple's favour. She had done what they asked and brought them to the Wise Mother and whatever happened now was out of her hands.

Varin looked round at the dozen or so women who had abandoned their work to come and see what was happening and to ensure that these visitors posed no threat. Most were armed with spears or bows and they eyed Varin with suspicion, some of them asking each other how he had been allowed to come ashore and who was to blame for it.

Varin's fists balled at his sides and sweat glistened in the scar pits of his cheeks. 'You can help us,' he told the Wise Mother again. 'You can save my wife. I know of no one else with the seiðr. You must get the bairn out of her.'

'So you say,' the witch told him, and looked down, pushing the needle and thread through the cloth on her lap. 'I could coax the bairn out, hey. Perhaps with a song. Or maybe the promise of some warm milk and honey will do it. Out it pops like a bung from a flask. Like a fox cub from its den.'

Gudny groaned again and one of the Freyja Maidens said that if the woman burst like a boil where she stood, she would not want to be the one who had to clear up the mess.

'What say you, young Runa?' The Wise Mother looked up at Runa though her fingers were still busy with their work.

'We should help her. If we can,' Runa said, nodding at Gudny, who, in between grimace and groan, was trying to hum to the bairn in her belly now.

The Wise Mother was staring at Runa, her head on one side. Runa could smell her catskin clothes from where she stood. 'You know what Skuld would do?' the old woman asked.

Runa did not know what the Freyja Maidens' leader would do, but Skuld was off practising utiseta at the Freyja tree. She was under the cloak, as the women put it, seeking guidance from the gods in light of the warnings which the old prophetess had brought back with her from her travels, news which had bent her as a sackful of grain would. The gods, perhaps Freyja Giver herself, would tell Skuld if she should lead the women from Fugløy's rocky shore; if the warrior women should abandon their secluded way of life and make a place for themselves out in the world, a world which was changing, so the witch said.

'Skuld would throw him back into the sea like a codling not worth splitting open,' the old woman answered for Runa. 'As for his cow,' she added, 'Skuld would put her back in the boat they came in and let her spill that calf in the thwarts.'

Varin looked horrified. 'A woman would never—'

'Hold your tongue!' the Wise Mother spat at him, pointing her needle at Varin who must have feared she was going to put some curse on him. He held his tongue. The witch swung her gaze back to Runa. 'But if *you* think we should help these strangers, these nobodies who have violated our island, tainted this day like dog piss in the milk pail . . .' she shrugged, 'then we must do what we can. Though some spell is not what is needed here. Runa, fetch your young stallion's tongs,' she said, snapping her fingers and thumb together, 'the smallest pair he has for holding moulds of hot metal and such.' She gave Varin and Gudny a gummy grin. 'Or pulling bits from the fire,' she said. 'No, no, 'tis not seiðr that's needed but a steady hand.' She made several more stitches then folded the tapestry and stood, putting the cloth on the stool. 'Get her inside, then,' she told Varin. 'And you, girl, what are you waiting for?' she asked Runa, and so Runa ran off to the forge.

None of the sentries on the ramparts noticed the three of them slip over the palisade one hundred paces from the gates, where the brow of the hill partly shielded them from Guthrum's camp.

Even so, they crouched for a while at the base of the wall just to make sure, Sigurd's chest tight but his bowels loose as water.

He had chosen Floki because the ex-slave would not question his plan and because Floki could kill as easily and quietly as drawing breath. And he had brought Valgerd because she could be stealthy as a hawk and her skill with the bow might come in useful.

The only other person in on it was Moldof, who would stay behind and who, being no great talker, was unlikely to let Sigurd's plan slip out of his mouth even by accident. King Gorm's former champion would wait with a rope on the ramparts, ready to haul the three of them back into the borg when the thing was done.

Neither Floki nor Valgerd, though, had been impressed with that choice of Sigurd's.

'We have given a one-armed man the job of pulling us back over the wall with Guthrum's war host on our heels,' the shieldmaiden had said when Sigurd told the three of them of his plan.

Moldof had said nothing to that but it was a good point and Sigurd felt his face flush.

'If Guthrum's men are after us we won't need much pulling,' he said, glancing at the one-armed warrior. In the event they were discovered they would climb that rope like mice up a barley stem, he assured them. 'Remember, we are the only ones in this. The others must not know.' Floki and Valgerd shot each other wary glances then, for no one could say those two were friends.

'You won't tell Olaf?' Valgerd said.

Sigurd shook his head. 'He would say it was a mad scheme and try to stop me. Some of the others would want to come, but think of Svein and Bram sneaking around in the night.'

'They would wake Guthrum's whole camp,' Black Floki said.

In truth the three of them seemed pleased to have been chosen and when it was time, Sigurd had found them waiting for him in the shadow of the grain store, full of the same thrill that had his own blood simmering in his veins.

Now, outside the timber wall, he nodded that they should move. Valgerd pulled her hood forward so that her face was in shadow. Keeping low, they left the relative safety of the borg, moving down the slope to skirt round the tents and fires and warriors of Guthrum's war host.

It would have felt less risky to stick close to the borg, but then one of Alrik's sentries on the ramparts was bound to see them and, thinking they were Guthrum's men, raise the alarm or rain spears and arrows down on them. So they had to first move away from the borg before walking brazenly into the enemy camp, and it was as well that the night was black as Hel's arsehole, as Bram had put it when he had set off to buy more ale from one of Alrik's men.

Sigurd glanced up at the night sky, which was hazed by Guthrum's men's fires. The sliver of a waning moon that had been visible earlier was now hiding behind silver cloud, so that Sigurd wondered if Óðin was helping him. This was, after all, just the sort of undertaking that the Allfather relished, for it was said that Óðin sometimes came down from Asgard to walk amongst men, disguised as an old wanderer in a wide-brimmed hat.

Floki hissed and they stopped, eyes sifting the darkness for what the young man had seen. Valgerd was pulling an arrow from the quiver at her waist when Sigurd saw what had alerted Floki. One of Guthrum's men was pissing against a rock not a spear-throw away. He was swaying like a man adrift on the ale-sea and mumbling to himself. Then he hawked and spat, tucked himself back in his breeks and turned, walking away having never looked up in their direction. Which was lucky, for being seen approaching the camp from that side of the hill would have aroused suspicion even in a drunk.

Then they were moving again, more or less following the man in amongst the tents and fires, the sounds of a camp at night washing over them, and now Sigurd straightened and threw back his shoulders because he wanted to look like one of Guthrum's men, full of swagger and ale. Those of Guthrum's men that were awake, anyway. Most were snoring in their tents and the sentries who could be seen did not expect trouble. Why should they? Alrik had shown time and again that he would not leave the borg. Even Guthrum's ploy of moving his whole camp up the hill had not drawn Alrik out – for Sigurd was sure that was why the jarl had done it, not simply as a boast or to rub Alrik's nose in it.

And so Sigurd was going to Guthrum.

Yet, even now there was a part of him that would rather be behind those wooden stakes that loomed above them at the top of that steep bank, instead of walking through the heart of the enemy camp.

'Óðin be with me,' he whispered as somewhere a dog snarled and barked and a man growled at it to be quiet.

Tents to either side of them, they trudged back up the hill to where they knew they would find Guthrum's red tent a few feet closer to the borg than any other, and Sigurd's hand went to the bone grip of his scramasax. He would use that shorter blade to kill Guthrum. Far easier in the dark confines of a tent than a sword like Troll-Tickler.

If he found Guthrum asleep it would be easier still, though he would wake the jarl up just before he cut his throat, even if it risked the man crying out. A jarl deserved to know who was killing him. Perhaps he and Sigurd would laugh about it together in Valhöll when they met again.

The three of them stopped again now because they were almost on top of the jarl's tent and Sigurd knew that after the next steps there would be no going back until the thing was done.

Off to their left, twenty paces away, seven or eight men lay sprawled round a fire. They were talking in low voices and one of them looked over and raised a hand in greeting, perhaps thinking that Sigurd was someone else. Sigurd pretended he had not seen it, instead looking at his companions to make sure they were ready for what they were about to do. They were standing beyond the reach of the fire's glow and so he could not see their eyes well, but both nodded which was good enough, and with that they strode on up the hill towards Jarl Guthrum's tent.

They expected guards, because they had seen them from the borg ramparts earlier, though it had been too dark to tell how many there were. As it turned out there were just two, sitting on stools in front of Guthrum's tent. They had a tafl board set up between them on another stool and were playing by the light of an oil lamp, which reached only far enough to illuminate the board itself and the men's faces.

Kill the guards. Kill Guthrum. Run up the hill to the borg where Moldof will be waiting. Simple as that.

Now the three of them split, Sigurd walking down one side of the jarl's tent, Floki and Valgerd going down the other, drawing their scramasaxes as they went. Then Sigurd came round the end and the two guards looked up at him, their hands falling to their sword grips.

'Who is winning?' Sigurd asked, but neither man could answer because each had a hand clamped over his mouth and a length of steel slicing through his throat. Sigurd did not wait to see it done, instead pushing inside the tent. Where Guthrum was waiting.

And the jarl was not alone.

There were ten warriors crammed into that fug-filled tent, though Sigurd only saw eight at first. They looked as surprised to see him as he was to see them, and they jumped up from their stools, mailed and helmed, swords and axes already in their hands, as a sword struck Sigurd across his back. His brynja stopped the blade biting, yet it still felt like a hammer blow and drove him forward into the press of warriors. Then he was down and they were slamming their shields and sword hilts at him, battering him to the ground when he tried to rise, and he wrapped his arms round his head while the blows rained down, his nose full of the stink of the old animal skins beneath him.

A trap, then. Even through the pain and confusion of this beating, he was struck by that even more savage blow, that this had all been a trap and he had walked right into it.

'Throw down your blades or he dies,' a man threatened in a voice that demanded respect. The knot of warriors stepped away from Sigurd, who gasped for breath and tried to turn his head to look up at his enemies. But the point of the sword pressing against the back of his neck, forcing his face back to the ground, made it all but impossible to move. 'Where are the rest?' the man standing over him asked. The clatter of arms, along with the cool night air, filled the tent, announcing the arrival of more warriors. 'Well?'

Sigurd knew without doubt that it was Guthrum speaking, that it was Guthrum's sword at his neck now.

'All quiet, lord,' a newcomer replied. 'This seems to be all there is.'

Sigurd managed to squirm round far enough to see Floki and Valgerd standing in the tent's entrance empty-handed, their faces poorly lit by the lamp hanging from the ridge pole, which was swaying and sputtering having been knocked in the commotion. One of Guthrum's men, perhaps the one who had struck Sigurd from behind, lay dead at Black Floki's feet, but the others had greeted Floki and Valgerd with levelled blades. Still more of Guthrum's spear men stood behind them outside in the shadows.

'Again I find myself disappointed in Alrik,' Guthrum said. 'I really thought the temptation would be too much for him. That he would attack.'

'Aye, and we've been stuffed in here all night like cats in a sack,' a black-bearded warrior growled. He was the massive warrior Sigurd had seen from the walls, Guthrum's champion if Sigurd was to guess. 'Hardly worth it for these three,' he said, then he and another warrior bent and relieved Sigurd of his scramasax, his sword and even his eating knife. Then Guthrum squatted beside him, keeping his sword point pressed into the hollow of Sigurd's neck just beneath the skull.

'At the very least he could have come himself if he intended to kill me in my own tent as I slept,' the jarl said. He pushed the blade and Sigurd grimaced against the pain. A little more pressure and the sword would break the skin. More than that and it would slice into his brain. 'Instead he sends two lads with barely a beard between them,' Guthrum said. 'And . . . a woman.' That last was said with something resembling awe.

He ordered his men to stay alert and do a sweep of the camp in case any more of Alrik's men were skulking in the darkness. Then the sword point twisted a little and Sigurd felt the skin break and blood trickle round to his throat from where it dripped rhythmically on to the animal skins. 'Who are you?'

Sigurd said nothing. A big hand clutched his hair and hauled his head back.

'I asked you a question.'

Sigurd could see Guthrum properly for the first time and what he saw in that face was a dangerous combination of cruelty and cunning. If only he could have killed the man before the others had a chance to stop him. Now he would die for nothing. Floki and Valgerd too.

'Byrnjolf, lord,' Sigurd said. Even as far from the lands of the Norse as they were, it would not be a clever thing to tell this man who he truly was. If it even mattered now.

'Why did Alrik send you, Byrnjolf?' Guthrum asked.

Seeing there was no attack coming from the borg, some of his hirðmen slipped out of the tent, cursing when they saw Black Floki and Valgerd's handiwork outside.

'He did not send me. He does not know we are here,' Sigurd said.

Guthrum's eyes narrowed. 'I've seen you. Seen your face above the wall. Did you really think I would fall for that trick with the banner? The axe on it did not even look like the one on my own.'

Sigurd shrugged. 'Your men in the borg fell for it,' he said, unable to resist. Guthrum's face twisted at that. It must have been a hard thing knowing that half of his army had been slaughtered when Alrik took the borg. And yet from the look in the man's eyes Sigurd knew that he was at least relieved to know now how it had happened, how his men had lost the place.

'You are young to be tired of life, Byrnjolf,' Guthrum said, letting go of Sigurd's hair and standing. He gestured at his men who came and hauled Sigurd to his feet, one of them coming behind him to lock his arms round Sigurd's neck. 'Did you really think you could kill me and hop back over the wall to claim your reward and boast about what you had done?'

'I thought killing you would be the easy part, Jarl Guthrum,' Sigurd managed through the choking neck grip. 'I was having doubts about the wall. The man waiting with the rope has only one arm.'

Guthrum did not know what to make of this and Sigurd wondered why he was still alive.

'We thought that killing you would end this war,' Valgerd told the jarl. Guthrum stared at her. He was not alone. Half the men in that tent were staring at her. Had been before she even opened her mouth.

'Who are you?' Guthrum asked her.

'Does it matter?' Valgerd said.

'It might,' Guthrum said. Then he turned to his men, who were still waiting to see if there was killing to be done. 'Bind them,' he said, and one of them went to find rope.

'What will you do with them?' the huge warrior with the pitch-black beard asked his lord. He was the one who had complained about having to wait all night in that stinking tent in case Alrik attacked.

'I don't know yet.' Guthrum frowned. 'The gods will tell me in their own time.'

'And if they don't, I'll cut their throats,' the huge warrior said. His nose was flat, spread across his cheeks, and his black hair was

45

tied back but left unbraided like a horse's tail. 'Well maybe not hers,' he said, grinning at Valgerd. Like Floki she was being held by two men, only these two were all over their prisoner like dogs on a bone. Having pulled off her helmet they were sniffing her neck and hair, growling filth in her ear, telling her what they would like to do with her. One of them was licking his lips, a silver thread of spittle lacing his beard. That's how much he wanted her. And it made Sigurd burn.

'There is not enough cunny round here to go wasting it when it comes along,' Guthrum's champion said, going over to Valgerd, and with that he thrust his hand under the brynja's hem and grabbed her between her legs. The swords came up at Sigurd because the fury had struck him like a lightning bolt and he had almost broken the choke hold, but then he was held fast again by brawn and blade and could do nothing but watch as the woman he loved was violated.

Valgerd, though, had no intention of yielding to Guthrum's champion and his lust. She jerked like a fish on a hook and slammed her forehead into the warrior's chin and he staggered, clutching his face. He very nearly fell, which would have been good to see, but then he straightened, spat a wad of blood on to the ground and surged forward, grabbing Valgerd round the throat as the other two men let go of her and stepped back.

'Bitch!' the big man bellowed into her face. The arm round Sigurd's throat tightened even more, his head filling with heat. Floki was straining against the men holding him, teeth bared like a wolf, but he could do nothing either.

Valgerd's face was purpling by the flickering lamplight, her bulging eyes full of hate as she thrashed her legs and fought to break the big man's grip, trying in vain to pull his hands from round her neck. The man had lifted her off the ground, even in her mail.

'Put her down, Beigarth,' Guthrum said. 'Before she pisses herself in my tent.' But Beigarth was enjoying himself, his head on one side as he watched Valgerd suffer, the steel gone from her eyes now, replaced by the panic of a body which knows it is dying.

'You're a dead man, Beigarth,' Sigurd snarled. 'I swear it by the Allfather.'

'Beigarth! Put her down!' Guthrum said, and this time the man obeyed him, throwing Valgerd down into the dark corner of the tent. She lay there gasping for breath, rasping like a whetstone on a sword. Sucking life back into her body.

The man who had gone for rope stepped back into the tent and looked down at her, his teeth glinting in the firelight.

'Tie her,' the jarl said, then he turned back to Sigurd. 'What makes you think the Allfather cares for you and your oaths?' He gestured to the tent's entrance and the night beyond. To the hill and the fort sitting upon it. 'Perhaps you thought the gods would favour this bold plan of yours? Even that Óðin would conceal you from my men until your blade was sheathed in my heart? And yet look at you now. If the gods favoured you once, they do so no longer. Your wyrd is mine to cut.'

He gestured to one of his men to tie Sigurd and they wrenched his arms behind his back and bound them. Other men were doing the same to Floki and Valgerd, and as the knots were tied, Beigarth muttered something foul and strode from the tent like a bear from its cave. The jarl followed, leaving four men to guard his prisoners, and Sigurd thought about what Guthrum had said. He thought too about what Asgot had said the day after they had captured the borg through Sigurd's cunning trick with the jarl's war banner. 'You drew Loki's eye, too, with that trick of yours,' the godi had warned him. Asgot was a man who caught the gods' whispers on the breeze. Read their thoughts in the runes. He had advised Sigurd's father where the gods and their capriciousness was concerned, and now he shared his knowledge with Sigurd. The trickster god was part of this whole thing now, Asgot had warned, 'like a man who sits down at the tafl board rubbing his hands at the prospect of the game'. And perhaps the godi was right.

Sigurd thought of Moldof standing there in the borg with his rope, looking out into the night, waiting for them. By now he would be starting to think something had gone wrong. It was possible he had even seen the commotion and the warriors crowding round Jarl Guthrum's tent and he would have no choice but to tell Olaf about Sigurd's plan. If the gods *were* laughing at Sigurd now, the sound of it would soon be drowned out by the sound of Olaf cursing.

'Stay where you are, Uncle,' Sigurd whispered. He doubted Alrik would venture out of the borg, but Olaf? Thinking that Sigurd might be alive and Guthrum's prisoner, Olaf might lead his crew out in some desperate sortie which would have no chance of success.

'When I took this borg, Alrik gave me a silver hoard,' Sigurd called out, knowing that Guthrum, who was talking with his men outside, would hear him. The voices fell silent and Guthrum appeared at the threshold. 'Let us go, Jarl Guthrum, and the silver is yours.'

Guthrum considered this for a moment. 'The man who took my borg is now my prisoner,' he said. 'It seems to me that the luck which has abandoned you, Byrnjolf, is now mine. It has passed from you to me, like a flea hopping from a dog to a wolf.' He pulled his beard through his fist. 'No. I would not give you back to Alrik for a knörr full of silver. With the Allfather at my back, I will attack the borg tomorrow and take back what is mine. When it is done, and if Alrik is still alive, I will carve the blood eagle on his back and give him to Óðin as a token of thanks. I may carve the eagle on your back too, Byrnjolf.'

The threat of the blood eagle was not a thing which a man made lightly, and Sigurd's blood ran cold in his veins at the mention of it. Guthrum looked at Valgerd, who stood tall and defiant again. There was a cut on her forehead which showed how hard she had hit Beigarth with it, and her throat was red against the pale skin around it, from where Guthrum's champion had half strangled her. 'Are you his woman?' Guthrum asked her, nodding at Sigurd.

'I am no man's woman,' Valgerd said. And that was true albeit hearing her say it was an invisible blade in Sigurd's guts.

The jarl's brows lifted and he almost smiled. 'Wrong, shieldmaiden. You are my woman now.'

The look in Valgerd's eyes said what she thought about that much better than words ever could. Then Guthrum turned his back on them and left to make his plans for the next day's assault.

'I would enjoy watching him die,' Black Floki said, spitting after him.

'Then we had better make sure we are alive to see it,' Sigurd said.

CHAPTER THREE

THE NEXT DAY, JARL GUTHRUM ATTACKED THE BORG WITH HIS WHOLE army at his back. They fell upon the east wall in one great mass, taking ladders, hooks and ropes, and even riding their horses up to the palisade and standing on the animals' backs to reach high enough to pull themselves up. Again, Guthrum himself was in the heart of the blood-fray, his best warriors gathered round him as they attacked the gates with axes, hacking at the timbers while others held shields over them.

But before the first insults were hurled, before the war cries and the first blood was spilled, Guthrum had taken Sigurd, Valgerd and Floki up the slope to within a spear-throw of the borg so that the defenders could see that they had failed in their attempt to kill the jarl. To his credit, and to Sigurd's surprise, Alrik offered Guthrum five of his iron bars for Sigurd's freedom. But Guthrum sent his reply in the form of another spear over the palisade, in this way claiming every man in the borg for Óðin.

'Should have told me!' Olaf called to Sigurd, his face hard as a cliff face. The others did not look any happier. Svein would not even look at Sigurd, which said how he felt about being left behind.

'You would have stopped us,' Valgerd called back.

'Aye, and you'd be on this side of the wall instead of that side,' Olaf said.

And that was the end of the talking because it was time for the killing to begin.

Sigurd did not hear what Jarl Guthrum had said to his men that morning but they fought as though they felt the gods at their shoulders, Óðin and Thór, Týr and Vidar, mail-clad and eyes blazing. They threw themselves at the borg as though the scent of the winners' feast was in their noses and the silver lustre of plunder lit the day. Up the ladders and ropes they went, yelling their throats out and thrusting their spears up at the borg men.

Yet, that gods-fevered army broke on Alrik's walls like a wave smashing against a rock. Sigurd saw it all, how Alrik's men speared those coming up the ladders, then used their spears to lever those ladders off the palisade and throw them back. Saw how they let the grappling hooks bite then waited for men to climb before cutting the ropes so that Guthrum's men fell, tumbling back down the bank.

He watched Olaf and Bram, Svein and Moldof slaughtering anyone foolish enough to climb the gates, and he saw Alrik and Knut rallying their men in a desperate and stubborn defence, splitting skulls, staving faces and knocking the attackers off the walls like mussels knocked off a jetty pile.

'This will be a feast for the crows,' Floki said, looking like a crow himself with that black hair, and he was right. The whole thing did not take long. After the time needed to put a keen edge on a blade which is not blunt to begin with, it was over.

They watched as Beigarth had to haul his jarl away from the splintered hole they had managed to make in the gates with their axes. That hole was Guthrum's own work as much as anyone's and by the time his axe had broken through he was beyond all reason, his usual composure replaced with a mad rage. Sigurd saw him drag one of Alrik's men out through that breach and turn him to pulp with the butt of his axe's haft. But even as he was pummelling that man, his own warriors were dying all around him, falling to the spears, rocks and arrows raining down from the ramparts, and had Beigarth not dragged him off, his shield raised over the jarl, Guthrum would have died by that hole he'd made.

The cheer that rose from the borg as Guthrum's men fell back knowing they were beaten must have been a hard thing for the jarl to hear. He did not seem to care that the six shafts sprouting from Beigarth's shield meant there was a good chance he would have been dead if not for his champion.

'He will come over here and cut our throats just because he can,' Valgerd said. But Sigurd did not think Guthrum would do that. It seemed to Sigurd that the jarl was already getting a grip on his rage. He had shrugged Beigarth off and was standing tall again, taking long, deep breaths as he watched his men help their wounded companions down the hill away from the borg; from those walls which had once protected them but against which they had now thrown all their weight and failed.

And yet Alrik had lost his share of men too, warriors he could ill afford to be without, and that night their pyres sent a thick black plume into the wan sky, tainting the air with the smell of burnt flesh. From what Sigurd could see before Guthrum's men led them away, it seemed that his own little crew had survived. He knew that Olaf would have steered them through that fight, not letting them risk themselves unnecessarily, but that did not take the edge off the guilt Sigurd felt for having not been there fighting beside them. In his arrogance he had thought he could do what Alrik had so far failed to do: kill Jarl Guthrum and put an end to this war between them. He had thought that one thrust of his scramasax in the night would make him rich and prove that he was still Óðin-favoured. Instead he had walked into Guthrum's trap like a bear shambling into a pit of sharpened stakes. As if he did not have enough enemies in the world, he was now at the mercy of a new one, a man who owed him a bad death at the very least.

Perhaps the gods were playing with him. Perhaps, as Asgot believed, he had drawn Loki's gaze now as well as the Allfather's, meaning nothing was certain from here on – not that it ever had been.

He cursed as Guthrum's men tied him and Floki and Valgerd to stakes in the ground and left them there as night fell.

Because he had failed.

Through the open door Runa could see that the light was fading. It was not high summer yet and dusk was laying its shroud over Fugløy as the day retreated into the west. And still the woman's child was not born, much to the disappointment of those who had gathered round, drawn to the magic of birthing the way men are drawn to a fight.

'She's never going to spit this bairn out,' Sibbe said with a curl of her lip. If Runa had an enemy on Fugløy, Sibbe was it, though they had not fought with anything other than wooden practice swords since the night the Wise Mother had returned and Runa had knocked Sibbe unconscious. After that they had avoided each other as far as was possible on a spit of an island like Fugløy.

'Why don't we push on her belly?' Drífa suggested, her hands wrapped round the cup of ale which the Wise Mother had told her to fetch. Runa still gripped the tongs she had borrowed from Ingel, though neither she nor the prophetess had put them to use yet because the woman did not seem to want their help after all. 'If we push in the right place it should pop out from between her legs like a ripe pea from the pod,' Drífa went on, which had some of the others shaking their heads and telling Drífa she would be better off saying nothing than talking such nonsense. What did Drífa know of childbirth, having lived her whole life on an island of women who had no men? What did any of them know, Runa thought. Then again, she supposed many of them must have seen new lives being brought into the world, or at least been around labouring women when they were younger, before they had come to this life of sword-craft and solitude.

'Bring it here, girl,' the old prophetess snapped at Drífa.

She had told Drífa to bring ale, the strongest she could find, because she was getting angry with Gudny now. Had been angry for a good while, truth be told, though she had kept the fire of it behind a cold face, perhaps for fear of making things worse. For ever since they had got Gudny comfortably into a nest of fleeces, which had been no easy undertaking, she had refused to spread her legs properly and let the Wise Mother peer inside her or bring the lamplight close enough for a good look. Now and then those bent legs would drift apart, slowly, and it seemed Gudny would let them help her. But then they would snap together again and with the force of a dog's jaws too, so that the Wise Mother had nearly lost a hand on more than one occasion. Certainly the stubborn woman's knees would be bruised like the apples at the bottom of the barrel, as one of the Maidens had pointed out.

'If she does not want our help she should go back to wherever she came from,' Sibbe said.

'*Our* help?' the Wise Mother said, snatching the cup from Drífa, who shrank back as from a flame. 'And tell us, young Sibbe, just how are you helping, hey?' Sibbe had no answer to that and the old witch took a mouthful of ale herself before dragging a claw across her puckered mouth. 'Drink, girl,' she rasped, 'drink it all, you fool. I'd wager you spread your legs easily enough for that man outside.' Gudny's doe eyes gazed at the faces around her as she curled her fingers round the cup which the Wise Mother thrust at her.

'Ale will surely get her legs open,' Signy said, leaning against a roof post, her arms crossed over her chest. 'Two cups and they'll fly apart so fast there'll be a breeze in here.'

'Aye, get it down you, girl,' an older Maiden told Gudny, 'for if you do not want it, I will drink it for you.'

'What is she waiting for?' a woman named Svanloga said. 'I'd wager she must have been up to her tits in ale to let that man out there ride her in the first place.' She nodded towards the door and got a rasped rebuke from Vebiorg who told her that that was no way to talk to guests. For seeing as they had not cast the couple and their stuck bairn back into the sea, then surely it meant they were guests on the island and must be treated accordingly.

'Tsk! He cannot hear me,' Svanloga said, waving a hand which made a nearby lamp flame gutter.

'But *she* can,' Vebiorg said, jutting her chin towards Gudny, who if she was offended showed no sign of it as she sipped at the ale. Vebiorg had been replaced on the bluff by Rinda, who had gone off sulking because she had wanted to see the baby being born. Not that she was missing anything yet.

'I'll not fetter my words for some man,' Svanloga said, loud enough that Varin, who was outside in the dusk, could surely not help but hear. He had been told that a house with a birthing woman in it was no place for a man and that he would only make things worse by standing there all useless, talking of things about which he knew nothing. The man had not needed telling twice and had not shown his face since, though Runa imagined he must have been sweating himself into a lather out there on his own.

'Drink it, girl!' the Wise Mother snapped. 'Don't just wet your lips with the stuff. Drink!'

Gudny drank. And after two more cups her resolve drowned in ale like a cat tied in a sack and thrown into the fjord. Those milk-white legs of hers all but fell open and Gudny let out a thin snickering laugh which had the women glancing at each other, eyebrows arched.

'That ale is not so strong, or is there another stash which I do not know about?' Sibbe said, looking at Drífa, who shook her head.

But the Wise Mother did not wait for further invitation. She had smeared butter on her hand and was up to the wrist in Gudny, whose eyes were round like her mouth. 'So you bled, hey?' the Wise Mother said, her eyes closed as she felt around inside the woman.

'I . . . thought . . .' Gudny winced and drank more ale. 'I thought I was dying.'

By the flickering light of the lamp flames Runa noticed the prophetess's face clench at the same time that her arm went still. She withdrew her hand from Gudny's sheath and wiped it on the fleece beneath her. She stood up on creaking legs, stared at Gudny lying there and then walked towards the hearth, the women parting to let her through the press of them.

'Runa Haraldsdóttir, come here,' she said, and Runa, still holding Ingel's iron tongs, did as she was told, passing through the throng of murmuring Maidens until she stood at the old witch's shoulder.

'What is it, Wise Mother?' Runa asked. She felt a sudden weight in her stomach. Something cold running up the skin of her arms. She looked round to see that the others were watching them, though none had come any closer.

'That woman will squeeze the bairn out soon enough,' the old witch said, turning her gaze from the small hearth flames on to Runa. 'But not tonight. Not by my reckoning.' She chewed on her thin lips. 'The child is there and alive as far as I can tell. Its heart flutters like a little sparrow. See my hand, girl,' she said, holding it in the fire glow. 'Notice anything?'

Runa did. 'There's no blood.'

The witch nodded. 'So what is that on her clothes, eh? Something about these two does not smell right,' she said. 'Her man is still outside?'

'Where else would he be?' Runa said.

'Come with me, Runa Haraldsdóttir,' the old woman said, taking her catskin hat off the nail in the roof post where it hung, 'and we will see where this smell leads.'

*

56

They stepped outside into the dusk and saw men. They were armed with shields and blades and by the faint last light of the day Runa saw their teeth and the whites of their eyes.

She pushed in front of the Wise Mother, pulling her scramasax from its scabbard.

'Drop it, girl, or I'll cut the old hag's throat.'

Runa turned to see two more men looming in the near-dark either side of the longhouse door. One had a fist full of the Wise Mother's hair and a knife against her pale neck.

'It would take just a stroke,' the man warned, pushing the flat of his blade against the witch's flesh, 'and a little tug. Easy as picking a sloe from the bush.'

'Do as we say, Runa Haraldsdóttir,' Varin said, stepping forward to reveal himself to Runa, who hissed a curse at him but threw the scramasax on to the ground beside her. Then Varin nodded at another man who came forward and grabbed Runa round the neck, pulling her against him so that his stink flooded her and she felt the cold kiss of his knife beneath her chin.

'Nice and still now, girl,' this one growled, his foul beard and breath assaulting her. 'I don't want to have to cut a pretty thing like you.'

The others came together, spears and shields raised, some of them facing out into the night while the rest faced the longhouse door through which Varin walked, followed by Runa who went where she was shoved.

'Who are you, then?' Vebiorg asked, she being the foremost of those who stood facing the threshold. Alerted to the danger, the women had grabbed whatever weapons they had to hand, but now they might as well have been rooted in the earth for they stood still as the posts which held up the longhouse roof.

'Careful now,' Varin warned them. 'We don't want any accidents.'

Drífa had her bow raised, its string pulled back to her chin, the arrow aimed at Varin, and Runa knew that she was good enough to put that shaft in any of the pitted scars on Varin's face that she chose.

Yet Varin was confident and well he might be, for whatever his intentions he could not have hoped for it all to be this easy.

'I want a pile of blades there,' he said, pointing his own spear at the long table. 'Every knife, every shield, any silver or iron you have. I want it all on there. Do what I ask and all will be well.' He pointed his spear at Drífa then swung it towards the Wise Mother and Runa. 'Disobey me and we will kill the witch and the girl.'

Runa tried to meet the Wise Mother's eyes but all she saw were the whites as those eyes rolled up into the old woman's head before the lids came down. She was trying to see the future. Or communing with the gods perhaps. Either way she was no longer fully in that room with the rest of them, and Runa was filled with a dread fear that this night was the end which the prophetess had foretold.

Surely Freyja would not have her Maidens' wyrds lead them to this. But what if this were the twilight of the world and Freyja needed her warriors to join her in the last battle between the gods and their enemies? Was Ragnarök upon them all? Runa's mind was knotted with these thoughts and perhaps the other women were thinking such things too. They looked to each other, not knowing what to do.

'If we give up our blades, who is to say they will not slaughter us all anyway?' a fierce-looking, spear-armed woman named Harthegrepa asked the others.

'They're men,' another woman spat. 'If they have come all this way it is not to kill us. Least not until they've had their pleasure.'

Nevertheless, Vebiorg shook her head at Drífa, who eased the tension off the bow and lowered it, though she kept the arrow nocked.

Just then one of Varin's companions appeared in the doorway. 'We've got the others. Gave us no trouble once we made things clear,' he said. 'But the blacksmiths are gone. Hiding in the woods, I would say.'

Varin cursed. 'Keep your eyes open. If they show up meaning to make a fight of it, tell them we'll kill the girl. Her name's Runa. That should keep them out of it.' The other man grinned, nodded, then vanished again. 'Well?' Varin said, pointing his spear at the thirty or so women gathered in the hall. 'Do I have to bleed Runa here to show you that I mean what I say?'

Vebiorg's eyes promised Varin a death she could not give him as she muttered some oath to Freyja and went over to the long table, putting her knife on it. 'Do what he says,' she told the others, who muttered their own dark threats at Varin but followed Vebiorg's lead until the table was covered with weapons whose iron and steel blades and creamy bone and antler hilts gleamed by flickering flamelight. Drífa had been one of the last, but her bow lay amongst the rest of it and now her glare was aimed at Varin, her eyes themselves gleaming like arrow heads.

'Let her through,' Varin said, pointing his spear towards Gudny, who was standing now behind a knot of women who were not ready to let her rejoin her husband, if Varin *was* her husband.

'What is to stop me putting my knife in her belly and skewering the child too unless you let them go?' Svanloga asked, placing the point of her scramasax, which she had kept hold of, against the great swell of Gudny. As for the swollen young woman, she was trembling with fear now that her and Varin's deceit was uncovered and the promise of death hung in the air.

Varin shrugged. 'If it is in you to murder her and the life inside her, do it. I will put my seed in another woman. But I will not give up what we came for. Not for her.'

Runa pitied Gudny then, for all her trickery and the part she had played in Varin's scheme to throw the Freyja Maidens off guard so that his friends could come ashore unnoticed. For there was no doubt in Runa's mind that Varin would stand there and watch Svanloga sheathe her blade in the woman's unborn bairn rather than see the stitching of his plan come undone. Svanloga saw this too, and with a hiss like that of the swan after which she was named she stepped aside and told Gudny to go. 'I hope that bairn splits you like a mallet and wedge,' she spat, going over to lay her scramasax on the table with the other war gear, and the brooches, silver rings, iron keys and amulets spread upon it.

'Wait outside,' Varin told Gudny, who nodded, swiping away her tears as she waddled past Varin out into the night. 'Asvald, Iarl, get in here!' Varin called, and when those two came into the house Varin had them gather up what was on the table and carry it all outside, which took them three trips each, and all the while Runa seethed inside, hateful of these men and angry at herself for being fooled by this Varin and his whale of a woman. The weapon hoard on its own was plunder men such as these could only dream of.

'On your knees, all of you,' Varin ordered them. 'You!' he barked at four women who stood at the far edges of the room where tapestries hung by the beds. 'Here with the rest. All of you, down.' He walked over to the Wise Mother and added his spear point to the long blade at her throat. 'Now!' he said, and the Freyja Maidens went down on their knees in the rushes and straw. 'Good,' Varin said, then he called to his companions outside to bring in the women they had rounded up, who were made to kneel with the rest, so that the only three missing were Gæierlaug and Ingibjorg, and Skuld Snorradóttir. Rinda had taken over Vebiorg's watch up on the bluff overlooking the bay, and Runa feared for her now, for surely she would have warned them about Varin's crew if she had been able to. And where was she now? Ingibjorg was over on the west side of the island at the beacon overlooking Flea Rock, because there was another sandy beach there which was kind to ships' hulls and so had to be watched.

As for Skuld, she was under the cloak and so with the gods.

'Are you enjoying this cuddle as much as I am?' the man gnarred in Runa's ear. She could smell pig grease on his beard and something rotten in his mouth.

'I'll enjoy killing you,' she said, at which he pressed his groin against her and she flinched at the hardness in his breeks, and was suddenly even more afraid than she had been at the touch of his steel against her throat.

'Ever had a man inside you, girl?' he rasped.

'Have you?' Runa dared, and the man did not like that and so he squeezed Runa's neck in the crook of his arm and suddenly Runa could not breathe. Heat bloomed in her face and head and she struggled against the man's bulk but he was immovable, a great reeking mound of muscle and flesh, and so she went still instead, hoping that his grip would slacken if she gave him no trouble. It did. She gasped for breath.

'We have come to Kuntøy for the silver which King Thorir sent here,' Varin said, pointing his spear at the Wise Mother, whom Varin's man had brought forward so that the women could see with their own eyes how helpless the witch was against the threat of the blade at her scrawny old neck. 'Do not bother telling me that you know nothing of it. I know the skipper of King Thorir's knörr *Storm-Elk*. I know that the day *Storm-Elk* brought young Runa Haraldsdóttir here from Skíringssalr there was an even prettier cargo aboard. A sea chest brimming with hacksilver. With full arm rings and ingots and all of it heavy enough that it took four men to offload it.' He planted the spear's butt on the floor and pointed at Vebiorg with his right hand. 'I know all this, so do not try to spin me your lies.'

'That silver was King Thorir's gift to the Goddess,' Vebiorg said.

'Ah,' Varin said, lifting his chin. 'I had wondered what use you would have for such a hoard. Living here stuck to this island like mussels to a rock.'

'They say Thorir means to buy his way into Freyja's hall,' the man holding Runa growled.

'He would rather spend the afterlife there than in Valhöll?' the one called Asvald asked from the doorway behind Runa.

Varin shrugged. 'I know nothing about any of that,' he said, 'and care nothing about it either. What I know is that there is a silver hoard on this island and I will be leaving with it.'

'You take that silver and you'll be stealing from the king himself,' Vebiorg said.

Varin shrugged. 'There are other kings,' he said. 'With a hoard like that we can go anywhere. Pledge ourselves to another lord.' He grinned and it was the first smile Runa had seen on his face since she had met him on the shore. 'I could become lord of my own hall. Somewhere far from here.'

'If we kill them, King Thorir will never know what happened here,' the reeking man holding Runa said, pressing his cold blade against her neck. Pressing his other weapon into her hip.

'That is true, Gevar,' Varin acknowledged with a nod, 'but they are making this easy for us and I am grateful for it. I will be more grateful still when one of them tells me where I can find that chest that came ashore with young Runa scar-face there.' *He was one to talk about scars*, Runa thought as he swept the spear from Runa towards the women who knelt on the floor, the blade slicing through the smoke which hung above their heads. 'Which of you will tell me?' he asked.

'Were it our silver to give, we would say take it and leave,' the Wise Mother said, her eyes still closed. They were the first words she had spoken since this thing had begun and as Varin turned to her she suddenly opened those eyes on him, making him start a little. Everyone in that room saw it, and Runa knew that for all his swagger the man still feared that the witch might put some curse on him. 'It does not even belong to King Thorir, that silver,' the prophetess said. 'Not any more. Vebiorg was wrong about that.' Those old eyes were in Varin's flesh like fish hooks. 'It belongs to Freyja now.' She grinned and it was as cold and desolate as Helheim. 'I know you are a man, Varin, but even so. Surely you cannot be so stupid as to steal from a goddess?'

'Still your old tongue, crone,' Varin told her, turning back to the kneeling women. 'Where is the silver? Tell me now or I'll cut her throat.'

They glared at him, their eyes full of defiance, none of them wanting to be the one to give the shit what he wanted.

He sighed, then walked back to the Wise Mother and gestured at the man holding her to take his knife from her throat, which the man did. Then Varin brought his spear up and slashed open the witch's throat with the point, tearing apart her skin and flesh as easily as if it had been old sail cloth. Blood welled and spilled as the prophetess's eyes widened then rolled up into her skull again. The Freyja Maidens screeched and clamoured but the men threatened them with their spears and the women knew that to move against them was to die.

Runa strained and fought against the arms holding her but the more she struggled the tighter Gevar bound her.

'You next if you keep this up, girl,' he growled into her hair, his breath hot on her scalp. 'That what you want, eh? Hold still, bitch, or I'll cut you myself!'

'Some seeress, hey,' Iarl said, jutting his chin at the old woman on the floor by Varin's feet. In her catskins she looked more animal than human, but for her grey hair which had spilled from her hat and now covered her face, wicking blood from the pool which was spreading amongst the straw. 'She did not see that coming, Varin.'

But Varin ignored him as he bent to pick up a handful of straw and used it to wipe the old woman's blood off his spear blade. Then he walked over to Runa, who was still staring at the Wise Mother, who was no more. Just like that.

'Did I not tell you all what would happen if you did not share the whereabouts of that silver?' Varin asked. He was looking at Runa. Her eyes slid from the dead witch on to his and she wanted to tell him he was a fool to kill a seiðr-wife, for who could say what curse she had laid upon him as she died? But she did not dare, because if Varin's silver-lust was strong enough that he would cut out the Wise Mother's throat like that, then he would surely do the same to her if she gave him reason.

'Now I will ask again,' Varin said, lifting the newly cleaned spear tip to Runa's face. She wondered what he was doing then realized that the blade was tracing the scar which an arrow had carved from just below her left eye to her ear. 'Where . . . is . . . the . . . silver?'

'Tell us, girl, and be done with it,' Gevar mumbled into Runa's hair. The man was all over her, his face and nose pressed amongst her braids. He was breathing her in, sniffing her like an animal.

Runa clamped her teeth together to stop herself telling these men what they wanted to know. *Let them kill me then*, a voice said in her head, for she would not break now. Her father had been Jarl Harald of Skudeneshavn and her mother had fought until her last breath. Her brothers had been great warriors and the last of them yet living was Óðin-favoured. Of all the women in this hall, she would not be the one to break.

'Well, Runa?' Varin said.

She gave a slight shake of her head, then braced herself for whatever was coming. Varin's own jaw was clenched tight, the muscle bouncing beneath the pitted cheeks upon which no beard would grow. Suddenly he turned and strode over to the kneeling women and put the spear blade to Vebiorg's throat and Vebiorg lifted her chin so that it would at least be done cleanly.

'It's buried!' Runa said. 'The silver. It's buried.'

Varin held the spear still, a layer of wool grease and a piece or two of straw all that was between the blade and the Freyja Maiden's white flesh. 'Where?' he asked.

Vebiorg's eyes told Runa to say nothing, but Runa knew that Varin would let that spear blade drink again unless she spoke up.

'I'll take you there,' Runa said. 'I'll show you where it is buried.'

Some of the kneeling women hissed or murmured their disapproval, but others nodded at Runa as if to tell her that she was doing the right thing given how the night was going so far.

'Good,' Varin said with a nod, lowering the spear and walking to the door. 'Bring her,' he said over his shoulder. 'The rest of you, out.'

'Looks like we're off for a walk, girl,' Gevar gnarred at Runa, shoving her after Varin.

As she went, Runa shrugged at Vebiorg. *What choice was there?* she asked with a look.

'The Goddess go with you, Runa,' Vebiorg said.

And then Runa was amongst seven grizzled, predatory-looking men in the gathering dark. She looked at the Freyja Maidens' weapons piled on a fur on the ground but knew she would be cut down before she could make use of any of them.

Those men must have already known what would happen next, for two of them retrieved several planks of wood along with a hammer and nails which they had piled against the longhouse wall while Runa was inside. They held the planks across the threshold and hammered the nails in while two others defied the night with firebrands, having lit them at the forge.

Where were Ingel and Ibor? Runa did not know whether to be glad they were not here, for what could they do against seven armed men? Or angry because they had not at least tried to fight.

'Gevar and Iarl with me,' Varin said, taking one of the torches from a man with a harelip who could not have been much older than Runa. 'The rest of you know what to do.'

They ayed and grunted and hefted their spears and shields, grim-faced in the golden flamelight of those hissing brands.

'This way,' Runa said, the blood in her legs and arms seeming to tremble as she led the three men away from the longhouses, past the grain store and the smoke house and into the woods on the south-east side of the settlement.

At first there was enough light to see by, what with Varin's flame and the birch trunks which seemed to glow in the moonlight that spilled through their flickering leaves. But soon they left the birch and scrub behind and came among the tall pines, whose lower branches were sparse and brittle but whose upper reaches were thick and black as soot. Here was a darkness which might be pushed back by the firebrand's golden bloom but never vanquished, and no sooner had Varin and his torch passed a place than would the night flood in again.

'How much further?' Varin asked after a while, passing Runa so that he could better light their way. He cursed as a branch caught on his tunic sleeve, ripping the wool.

'A little way yet,' Runa replied.

'A little island walk never hurt anyone, Varin,' Iarl said, using his shield to fend off more branches. 'Not unless it was to settle a matter of honour between the hazel staves,' he added thoughtfully, and Runa knew Iarl was alluding to the hólmganga, when two men would go on to an empty island and fight a duel to settle a dispute.

'I still don't see the point in burying a sea chest full of silver,' Gevar said. 'Strange enough that these women all live here together, never letting a man between their legs, without them going around putting silver in the ground for the worms.'

'Or for the gods,' Iarl said. 'You heard the old woman. King Thorir meant his silver for Freyja. An offering, like a bull or a good ram, only without all the blood and bleating.'

'Without the blood, Iarl?' Gevar said. 'Tell that to the old crone who Varin gave a new ale hole for the afterlife.'

Varin muttered something foul. Perhaps he did not like the thought of having sent the Wise Mother to the afterlife. Perhaps he feared meeting her there when he met his own end. Still, he intended to go there a rich man and he picked up the pace, the flame of his torch whipping and flapping, guttering almost as he strode on.

There was no track and Runa wove them in and out of the pines, having only a vague sense of where she was going. It was dark and she was afraid and she had only been to the place once before. But she pushed on and hoped that the Goddess was with her, and when the going became steep she was sure that one way or the other they would get there.

'So, Runa Haraldsdóttir,' Varin said, stepping over a chiming stream and holding the brand up for the others to see their way, 'who are you and why did King Thorir Gapthrosnir put you on Kuntøy with these Freyja thralls? You are Norse, that much is clear whenever you open your mouth.'

'A long way from home, aren't you, girl?' Gevar said. 'Sick for your kinfolk eh?' Runa saw his teeth in the gloom and despised him. These were desperate men. Outlaws and fugitives, perhaps even escaped thralls. None of them worthy of a sword or a name or a row bench on a good ship. Nithings who did not know what they were getting themselves into.

'You can come home with me. I'm a wealthy man,' Gevar told her.

'Ha!' Iarl blurted.

'Will be soon enough,' Gevar said, 'after this night's work is done.'

'If we ever come to the place where they buried our hoard,' Iarl said.

'Runa would not deceive us, would you, girl?' Varin said, casting his light on some deadfall so that he could see his way over it.

Runa thought about making a run for it, haring off into the dark. She was sure she could escape before they could make a grab for her or put a spear in her, and once she was clear into the mire of the night they would never catch her. But then what? Varin and his companions would make their way back to the settlement and the other women would pay for Runa's actions.

'My father was a jarl,' she said. 'Far from here. He was betrayed by a Norse king. A worm named Gorm.'

'That's kings for you,' Iarl said.

'My father and mother and three of my brothers were killed fighting our enemies,' Runa said, a stick snapping beneath her foot, 'but I have one brother who is very much alive. Sigurd is a great warrior, cunning and skilled and fearless. But what should worry his enemies most is that he is a favourite of Óðin Allfather.'

Runa felt their eyes on her then and she put a little more straightness in her spine. She was being a fool telling them all this. Giving them a reason to take more than just the silver from Fugløy perhaps, for they would surely guess that she was hiding from her brother's enemies here on this island. And Varin was clearly not a man to turn his back on an opportunity, nor was he the kind to let the risk of an undertaking put him off, and so now he might think he could sell Runa to Sigurd's enemies. It would be easy enough to track down King Gorm, not least because the silver Varin was about to own would buy him information and passage on the journey north. *He could have his own longship built for the journey if the weight of that sea chest was anything to go by*, Runa thought, recalling how King Thorir's men had struggled to get the thing off *Storm-Elk*.

Foolish to tell them so much, and yet the telling had filled Runa like the warm glow of strong mead. It had sluiced the fear from her belly and cooled the simmering of her blood. She was Runa Haraldsdóttir and would not pretend otherwise. Not to men such as these.

'And just as my brother is Óðin-favoured, so I am Freyja-kissed,' she said. 'So do not think to lay your filthy hands on me again, Gevar.'

Something rustled in the pine litter nearby and they all stopped, holding their breath, eyes scouring the darkness which Varin tried to chase off with his torch, and even Runa's heart tripped in her chest after all her talk of the gods.

Then Varin shook his head and walked on, and a hand shoved Runa's shoulder. 'Move, girl,' Gevar growled, 'for I do not want to be on this island any longer than I need to be.'

'Aye, and from now on keep your pretty mouth shut too,' Iarl said. 'No more talk of gods if you want to keep that tongue of yours.'

Runa kept her mouth shut and they climbed, forcing a path through brambles and bracken and bilberry bushes, past upended pines whose soil-snarled roots dangled like filthy beards, and past rocks that glistened with moisture and were fragrant with moss.

And they were all puffing like a pair of Ingel's bellows when at last they reached the top of a hill, the highest point on the whole of Fugløy, and Runa stopped because this was it. The sacred place.

'You dragged a chest full of silver all the way up here?' Varin said, arming sweat from his forehead and glancing around.

'Well I am not looking forward to dragging it all the way back to the beach,' Iarl said, leaning his spear against a tree and pulling a hand axe from his belt.

'Why do you think I am here, little man?' Gevar said. Gevar was not Svein-big, but he was a head taller than his friends and his arms were like oak boughs.

'Well, girl? Where do I dig?' Iarl asked, waving that hand axe.

But Runa did not answer. She was looking at something which none of the men had seen yet, a spear-throw ahead of them, standing silent and more still even than the pines all around it.

'What in Óðin's arse is that?' Gevar said, his own eyes having sifted the object of Runa's gaze from the dark, which was more silvered up here on this hilltop without the same dense mass of trees to soak up what moonlight there was.

'That is our sacred tree,' Runa said, aware of the weight of that word *our*. *Then I am one of them now*, she thought, looking at the post which had once been a tree like any of those around it, but which had been stripped of branches and bark and carved with modest skill into the likeness of Freyja Giver.

'Not the post, girl!' Gevar said, pointing, the whites of his eyes glowing. 'That! What's *that*?'

Varin lifted his firebrand, which was half its original length now, so that he must have been starting to worry for his hand.

Runa's blood suddenly iced in her veins. There, on the ground a few feet from the base of the Freyja tree, was a figure, hunched beneath a simple shelter made of sticks and animal skins. It would have been easy not to see it at all, and yet at the same time Runa wondered how she had missed it. But then anything was possible where Freyja the seiðr goddess was concerned.

Varin started forward, the flame from his torch flapping.

'No, Varin,' Runa hissed.

He stopped. Slowly, he twisted his neck to look back at Runa. 'Why?' he asked, his voice low, his pitted, pocked face clenched and his hand on the hilt of the scramasax sheathed at his waist. He was nervous. They all were.

'You must not disturb her,' Runa hissed. 'She is with the gods.'

'Fuck this place,' Gevar muttered.

'Who is she?' Varin asked. He had not taken another step towards the figure, whose back faced them, though there was a glimpse of long red braids in the glow of Varin's fire.

'The High Mother,' Runa said. A tendril of white smoke curled up from a ring of stones beside Skuld, who was as still as a stone herself, so that it was not impossible to imagine that she must have died up there on that hill, or frozen solid even though it was summer.

Varin seemed torn as to what he should do, his hand still clutching the grip of his long knife.

'Leave her be, Varin,' Iarl rasped. 'Bad enough what we did to the old crone back at the house. Leave her be. I don't need some god's curse hanging round my neck for the rest of my days.'

Gevar said nothing, which Varin took to mean that he agreed with Iarl, and he nodded, sweeping the firebrand back towards them to let the darkness claim the High Mother once again.

'Where is it, girl?' Varin asked, his voice still low, as though he feared waking Skuld from her sleep or drawing the eye of whichever of the Æsir she was communing with.

Runa pointed to the ground by her feet, which was soft with the rotting remains of an old tree. Iarl grunted and shoved her

70

aside, then knelt and began to hack at the earth with his hand axe. No sooner had he broken the ground than his axe thunked into the wooden lid of the chest which the Freyja Maidens had buried as best they could given what little soil there was up there.

'It's here,' Iarl said, grinning at Varin and Gevar.

'Of course it's here,' Gevar said, but Varin, it seemed, needed to see the chest with his own eyes and he came and dropped to his knees across from Iarl, his grinning face cast in the copper glow of his flame.

'How will we see our way back?' Gevar asked, nodding at Varin's torch. The flame was faltering now, guttering as it crept down the two staves, the tar-soaked rags and rope having all but burnt away.

'If I had known it was this far I would have brought another torch,' Varin said, cursing as another scrap of burning cloth fell from the brand.

'Who needs fire?' Iarl said, grinning. 'We will see our way by the silver glow.'

'What about her?' Gevar said, pointing his spear at Skuld who still had not moved a muscle, so deep was she in the weave of the utiseta.

Varin looked back towards the crude shelter and the woman beneath it in body if not in mind. He laid a hand on the sea chest. 'First we get this out,' he said. And as his face turned back towards Runa, she struck, throwing herself at the firebrand and pushing it into Varin's face. She heard the crackle as his hair, eyebrows and moustaches caught, and he screeched and threw himself back, dropping the torch, which Runa snatched up, spinning and sweeping it at the other two men.

'You're dead!' Gevar yelled, coming for her with his spear, and Runa threw the guttering brand at him and it struck his forearm with a spray of flame and sparks and he yelled again. But Runa was moving. She ran to retrieve Iarl's spear from the tree against which it still leant, then turned and held her ground, relishing the feel of the solid ash shaft in her hands.

71

shoulder and the blade passed all the way through him, the resistance of muscle and flesh vanishing suddenly as it burst from his back.

'Bitch!' Gevar spat, spittle lacing his beard, and Runa let go the shaft and stepped back on unsteady legs as her enemy stood there not knowing what to do now that he was skewered on that spear. Not that he *could* do much with half his face flapping around like a fish in the bilge, and while he stood there Runa picked up Iarl's hand axe and placed herself in front of Gevar so that he could see her, with one eye at least.

'I told you I was your death, Gevar Corpse-Breath,' she said, and he muttered some filthy curse which was cut short as Runa planted the axe in his forehead with a crack that echoed off the surrounding pines. Gevar's legs gave way and he dropped, but before he hit the ground something barrelled into Runa almost snapping her neck and she flew and struck the earth and the weight landed on her, driving the air from her lungs.

Varin's face was like some monster's from a story. The fire had crisped his skin and even burnt away his eyelashes and their lids, so that his eyes were bulging and hideous as he screamed at her, his drool falling on her face and in her mouth as she gasped for breath. But she could not breathe because Varin's hands were around her throat and Runa knew she was going to die.

'I'll kill you! I'll kill you!' Varin screamed, his raw, bloody and blackened face warped in pain and savage fury, and Runa wanted to scream her defiance back at him, wanted to tell him that she would not die here on this hill and that he was a cursed nithing. But Runa could not breathe. The night was getting even darker and then she saw her mother Grimhild standing before her, tall and proud and beautiful.

I'm coming, Mother.

Then the weight was gone.

Runa heard herself gasp. She hauled the night air into her lungs, the night which was brightening as if dawn was already here, and she felt another's hands gripping hers.

She was being lifted, pulled up from the cold ground. She could breathe again and so she drank deeply of the sweet night air. Then the fog cleared and her sight sharpened and there standing before her, holding Runa's hands in her own, was Skuld Snorradóttir. The High Mother's eyes looked like black pools and it seemed to Runa that the woman was looking through her; that part of Skuld was still with the gods, wherever that was.

'Runa,' Skuld said. Just that. Nothing more. Runa looked down and saw Varin lying there, face down, Skuld's scramasax buried up to the hilt between his shoulders.

The other men lay where they had fallen. *Blood offerings for the Goddess*, Runa thought to herself. She bent and pulled Skuld's knife from its flesh sheath and gave it back to Skuld, who looked at it vaguely and so Runa slid it into the scabbard at the High Mother's waist. Then Runa saw something else and knew that they would not need a flame to guide them home. Through the trees and rising above them into the black sky was a molten iron glow.

'They are burning it,' she said, a new horror flooding through her. Pain was seeping in now too. From the cut in her head and the gash in her side which she pressed a hand against, trying to stem the blood. Her neck felt as if it were on fire and other injuries were beginning to announce themselves, but they would have to wait.

She went over to the dead and pulled Iarl's axe from Gevar's head and robbed Gevar of his long knife. She also took up the big man's spear because the one she had put through him would take too much getting out. Then, threading the sheathed knife on to her own belt, she turned back to Skuld, who was watching her every move.

'We must get back, High Mother,' Runa said, pointing the hand axe in the direction of the fire glow in the sky.

Skuld blinked slowly. Then a shiver seemed to go through her from her feet to her scalp, and Runa wondered if that was the High Mother shrugging off the veil of it all. She had been alone up here for days and Runa wondered if she had eaten in that time or whether some seiðr had sustained her.

'Are you still with them? The gods?' Runa asked.

Skuld seemed to consider the question. 'No,' she said.

Runa nodded. 'We must go.'

Skuld's hand dropped down to the hilt of her scramasax and there was a flash of something in her eyes.

'Can you run?' she asked Runa.

Runa touched the gash in her head. The bleeding seemed to have slowed, the oils in her hair helping it to clot. But the wound in her side needed stitching and she knew that blood would spill from it all the way back. Perhaps too much blood.

'I can run,' she said.

Then, leaving the Freyja tree to watch over their corpse-gifts, they loped off into the pine wood. Towards the fire.

Two of the three longhouses were ablaze. Great flapping flames stretched up into the black, roaring their anger at the night sky and spitting torrents of swirling copper sparks. The third longhouse was beginning to burn too, crackling now as hungry young flames worked into the staves and the knots in the pine logs and set the thatch smoking like a beast belching foul yellow breath at the gods. And the Frejya Maidens of Fugløy could not get out of that doomed place because Varin's men had nailed planks across the door. But those men had their own lives to think of now because Ingel and Ibor faced them and the blacksmiths were dressed for war with helmets and brynjur, shields and swords. One of Varin's men already lay dead and by the light of the burning buildings Runa saw that Ingel's sword was bloody.

'Give me your spear, Runa,' Skuld said, so Runa did, relieved to see that the High Mother seemed to have shed the seiðr which had clung to her like a sea fog and her eyes were clear and bright.

'We're with you, Ingel!' Runa called as she and Skuld ran to stand with the blacksmiths against the three men who faced them. Gudny cowered in the shadows nearby, her arms wrapped protectively across her belly.

'They must have killed Varin and the others,' the one called Asvald said, lifting his shield as the three of them drew together.

Ingel glanced at Runa and in that heartbeat his face betrayed his horror at the sight of her.

'I'm fine,' she said, knowing that she must look far from fine, her face sheeted in blood and her kyrtill more red than blue now. 'Ibor, get them out,' she told the older smith, gesturing at the longhouse inside which the Freyja Maidens were trapped. Above the roar of flame she could hear the cracking and splintering of wood and knew that the women were trying to break out.

'We kill these whoresons first,' Ibor said. But the longhouse was burning well now and those inside must be choking on the smoke.

'Do as Runa says, Father,' Ingel said. 'We can deal with these cowards.'

Ibor nodded and ran off towards the fires.

'Ready?' Skuld said.

'Kill them,' Runa said, striding forward, the axe in her right hand, Gevar's long knife in her left.

Asvald came to meet her, thrusting his shield at her, but Runa had known he would do this and she jumped back and swept the axe down on to the top rim of that shield and pulled, tilting it towards her so that Asvald's face was exposed. In the same movement she punched the knife into his eye which was wide with the shock of how easily he had been killed.

Runa looked over to see Ingel slam his shield into his enemy's, the man yelling at the impact though he managed to lift his shield again. So Ingel rammed him again, his smith's strength behind that well-made, iron-reinforced shield and iron boss, and this time the brigand staggered backwards and tripped over his own feet to fall on his backside.

Ingel's sword slashed down and finished him.

'Don't kill me!' the last of Varin's men said, but even as he pleaded for his life he must have known that it was wasted breath and so he turned and ran and Skuld's thrown spear missed him but the arrow did not. It took him in the neck, spitting him, and yet he ran a good four or five spear-lengths even so, before the bones in his legs turned to water and he dropped into the mud by the pig pen.

Runa turned to see Drífa, her face cast in shadow by the burning longhouse behind her, the bow still raised in the wake of that arrow. The other women were spilling out through the splintered planks of the threshold beside which Ibor stood doubled over, gasping from the effort of having hacked a hole big enough for them to escape through. They came coughing into the firelit night, heads turning this way and that as they gathered up their swords and spears and took in the terrible extent of the brigands' handiwork.

'What happened up there?' Ingel asked Runa, his gaze swinging between her and Skuld, who was herself watching the buildings being eaten by flame, knowing it was far too late to try to save them.

Runa's sight was failing her. She saw Sibbe strike down Gudny and spit on her, while another Freyja Maiden was yelling at Sibbe for killing a woman so swollen with child. But a rising tide of sickness eddied inside Runa now and she thought she would vomit. She was cold and her legs had no strength in them and she dared not look down at the cut in her side which felt as full of fire as the night.

'What happened, Runa?' Vebiorg now. Or was it Drífa? The darkness was seeping in like seawater between the strakes.

'Runa killed them,' Skuld said in a voice loud enough to challenge the roar of the flames and the crack and spit of the burning timbers. 'Our sister slaughtered them and left their corpses for the Goddess.' This stirred up a murmuring amongst the smoke-choked, eye-stung Freyja Maidens.

Runa could no longer make out the faces around her, but she could feel all their eyes on her and the weight of that was terrible, yet she bore it, keeping her knees locked as the sea-sickness swirled and eddied in her belly and in her skull.

I must look like the walking dead, she thought, slathered in blood and cut like meat for the wolves. Yet I am alive.

'I've got you,' a man said, and for a cold heartbeat she fought against the arms that held her, fearing it was Gevar and that she had only imagined killing him. 'It's me, Runa. Ingel,' he said. And she let herself slacken against him.

'Bring her into the light. Quickly! We need to stitch her,' someone said.

'I'll fetch water,' another said.

'High Mother, what did the gods say?' a woman asked.

'Yes, what did Freyja tell you?' That was Drífa, Runa was sure of it. 'Are we to leave Fugløy? Or must we stay?'

'Come, Runa,' Ingel said, leading her away.

Runa braced against him. 'Wait,' she said, for she was no less eager than the others to hear what Skuld Snorradóttir had learnt under the cloak.

'Tell us, Skuld,' a Freyja Maiden demanded. 'What did the gods say?'

The flames from the burning buildings stretched into the darkness, thrashing like the sail from a god's ship ripped in a storm. Like tongues they flapped wildly, telling of the end which was surely coming, just as the old prophetess had warned. They spat tiny embers of flame, those tongues, sparks and cinders beyond counting which swirled and soared and were carried off on the fire's breath, and Runa imagined each one took with it word of what had happened here on this island.

'What does it matter?' Skuld said.

The flames whipped and the sparks soared.

And Runa let Ingel take her.

CHAPTER FOUR

_____

TWO DAYS AFTER THE BATTLE, AFTER GUTHRUM HAD DEALT WITH HIS dead and his army were still licking their wounds, Olaf himself came out of the borg to meet with the jarl. Guthrum's men had begun to disassemble their camp within the shadow of the borg's palisade, but if Alrik thought that meant Guthrum had given up, he was mistaken. Guthrum simply moved his camp back down the slope to flatter ground and there set up as before, with smaller bands of warriors stationed at various places along the perimeter to ensure that none of Alrik's men, or Alrik himself, could drop over the wall and make a run for the woods.

It was Beigarth who brought news to Guthrum that one of Alrik's warriors was asking to speak with the jarl, though Guthrum, still wearing his dark mood like a cloak, was in no mind to speak with anyone. That was to say not until Beigarth explained that the man was one of the brynja-clad, helmeted Norsemen who had thwarted his attack on the gate with their unbreakable skjaldborg. One of those who had thinned Guthrum's war host with their spear-craft and sword-work.

'He's part of the same lot as them,' Beigarth had explained, nodding towards Sigurd, Valgerd and Floki, who were tied to stakes on the edge of the camp within sight of those on the borg's ramparts. 'Those boasting bollocks with all the shiny war gear,' Beigarth said.

This was enough to catch Guthrum's attention and he turned to look at his prisoners. 'I will hear what the man has to say,' the jarl told his champion, 'but he must come alone. And he will bring me a gift in return for hearing him out.'

'Something in particular?' Beigarth said.

'Silver. Iron.' Guthrum rolled his left shoulder, a grimace flashing in his big fair beard. Some or other ache, probably from swinging his axe at Alrik's gate like a mad man. 'I will have it all back anyway, but if this man wants to speak to me now he will pay for the privilege.'

Sigurd watched Olaf come down the slope. When he was halfway between the borg and the outer edge of Guthrum's camp Olaf stopped and carefully laid his shield, spear and sword on the ground beside him. He even pulled off his four silver arm rings and placed them on his shield. This was his way of showing that he came under an oath of peace, sworn upon his own weapons and warrior rings, and that were he to break that oath those same weapons would turn against him. This wordless declaration made, he walked no further. Guthrum would have to come to him now. The jarl would have to meet him halfway.

Sigurd could not help but smile to see that.

'Who does this man think he is?' Guthrum asked the knot of warriors standing with him.

'Some strutting Norse fuck,' said one.

'Goat-swiving fjord-spawn,' another rumbled into his beard.

'Still, he has bigger balls than Alrik, for at least he dares set foot outside that wall,' a big warrior pointed out, which got some reluctant *ayes* from Guthrum's men.

'Maybe he has come to pledge his sword to you instead of Alrik,' the first man suggested, thinking he had hit the rivet true with that. 'Maybe he will open the gates for us one night. That would be helpful given how things have gone so far.'

And perhaps Guthrum had the same thought in his head, which was why he, a Svearman with a torc of twisted silver at his neck and an army at his command, set off up the hill towards some waiting Norseman who was too stubborn to walk all the way down the hill.

'Beigarth, bring young Byrnjolf,' Guthrum called over his shoulder. 'It will not hurt to let the man see that I do not mutilate my prisoners.'

And so Beigarth untied Sigurd and hauled him after his jarl, whose ill mood, it turned out, was not helped by the fact that Olaf had not brought him a gift.

'You will get nothing from me, Jarl Guthrum, while you keep my friends tied to posts like dogs,' Olaf said when Beigarth asked him why he had come empty-handed.

'Your friends came to murder me in my sleep. If I treat them like dogs it is better than they deserve, Norseman,' Guthrum replied, gesturing at Sigurd. Olaf gave a nod as though ceding this point. He was careful not to look at Sigurd and for his part Sigurd avoided his friend's eye too. If Guthrum knew they were as close as the rings of a brynja he would only exploit it to his advantage.

'So who are you?' Guthrum asked.

'Olaf Ollersson.'

'And you are oath-sworn to Alrik?'

Olaf shook his head. 'No.'

'And yet you fight for him. Who leads your crew?'

Olaf shrugged. 'We are a fellowship. We all play our part. Oars, tiller, mast and sail, a ship needs all of these else it is dead in the water. It is the same with us.'

Guthrum frowned at that. Perhaps he wondered why Olaf and his Norsemen were still holed up in that hill fort fighting for their lives if they were not even sworn to Alrik. But it made sense of why Alrik had let Olaf come out of the borg under truce to speak with his enemy. The warlord had no choice in the matter, this Norseman being his own man.

'But you fight for Alrik's silver.' The jarl flashed his teeth then. 'Most of which is mine anyway, as it happens.'

'Who it once belonged to is no concern of ours,' Olaf said.

'I know you have not come to offer me silver for my prisoners, for you already know I will not sell them,' Guthrum said.

'That was before you sent your men to a mauling that will feed the crows until they are too fat to fly,' Olaf said. 'Could be you have changed your mind.'

Guthrum did not like that. 'The answer is the same,' he said.

'So be it,' Olaf said.

'Either you have come to offer me your swords, or else you hope to negotiate safe passage away from here. For you and your Norsemen know that I will have this borg and kill every man within. Alrik has brought this end upon himself and all that are fool enough to follow him.'

Olaf shook his head. 'By the time you take this place, if you ever do, I will be a toothless old man and more than ready to drink with my brothers in Óðin's hall,' he said.

'You can drink the Allfather's mead this very night if you want, Norseman,' Beigarth said, not needing to touch his sword's hilt to edge that threat.

Olaf looked at the jarl's champion, taking stock of him from his boots to his black beard and his black hair which hung loose but for two braids which would keep most of it out of his eyes in a fight. 'You're a brave man and a good fighter, lad,' Olaf told him. 'I've seen you in the blood-fray, watched you shield your jarl in the hail of arrows when shafts were striking you. What is your name?'

The man lifted his chin and that massive beard with it. 'Beigarth,' he said, as if Olaf should have heard of him. 'I am the man who killed Jarl Esbern at Baldr's rock. And Fridlef Ox-Neck at the ship fight off Björkö. And Thuning Thuningsson who men called Snake Arm because he was so fast with a sword. That was before I cut off his sword arm and his head too.'

Olaf shook his head. 'I have never heard of any of them,' he said, 'but I am not from these parts, and if you say they had reputations, who am I to argue?' He raised an eyebrow at the man. 'Well then, Beigarth, you might make a name for yourself one day. But not if you throw threats around the place like a man scattering hen feed.' That said, he looked back to the man's jarl, ignoring the scowl on Beigarth's face which would have made an onion cry.

'Look, Jarl Guthrum, we'll not slope off and leave Alrik now, much as you'd like us to.' Olaf thumbed back up the hill to the borg. 'We are comfortable in there with our hearth and our beds. More comfortable than you sleeping out here night after night.'

There were faces up there above the gates, looking out of the fort, and one of them was Alrik's.

'So you *did* come thinking you would buy my prisoners.' Guthrum turned to Sigurd. 'It seems your friends are keen that you should all die together when I take this fort,' he said.

'It could be that,' Sigurd admitted. 'Or it could be that they want us to feast and drink with them when one of them takes your head from your shoulders.'

Beigarth yanked Sigurd towards him and backhanded him across the face so that when Sigurd smiled again he tasted the blood on his teeth.

'Again, I say my prisoners are not for sale, Olaf Ollersson,' Guthrum said.

Olaf shrugged at Sigurd as if to say no one could claim he hadn't tried. 'What will you do with them?' he asked Guthrum.

'Do not waste a moment thinking about it, Norseman,' Guthrum said. 'All I will tell you is that Frey, the best of the gods, has spoken and I have heard him. Now go back to Alrik. He is lucky to have a man of your honour fighting for him.' He raised a hand. 'Know this, though, Olaf. If I find your corpse at the end of all this, I will make sure it is treated with respect. You can tell Alrik that I will not afford his corpse the same. I will geld him. I will stuff his cock and balls in his mouth and I will put out his eyes. He will wander the afterlife blind and prickless.'

'Now fuck off while you still can,' Beigarth said, unable to resist one more little poke.

Olaf turned to the bigger man. 'What did I tell you about making threats?' he asked. He was scowling now, and Sigurd knew Olaf well enough to be sure that his hackles were raised. 'Are you slow-witted, Beigarth? Did your mother drop you on your head when you were a mewling, tit-clamped bairn?'

Beigarth grimaced.

'Go, Olaf,' Guthrum said, flicking a hand towards the borg.

But Olaf did not go.

He stood there.

'Do you want to fight me, Beigarth?' Olaf asked.

'It has been a while since I killed a Norseman,' Beigarth said. 'I have missed the way you people squeal when the blade goes in.'

'It is easy to throw threats at an unarmed man who comes under truce, you big sack of horse shit,' Sigurd told Beigarth. The man yanked the rope again but Sigurd was ready for it this time and had set his feet so that he did not get pulled anywhere. Annoyed, Beigarth strode up to him and hammered a fist into the side of his head, sending white-hot light shooting through Sigurd's skull like a lightning strike. He staggered but did not fall, then straightened and squared his shoulders to the man.

'These men you boast of killing, Beigarth,' Olaf said, pointing at Sigurd, 'were they all tied up like him?'

That was quite the insult and Beigarth dropped his end of Sigurd's leash and strode towards Olaf, drawing his sword as he went, and Guthrum said nothing, perhaps because he thought one dead Norseman here was one less to fight in the days to come.

'Pick it up,' Beigarth demanded of Olaf, pointing his own sword at Olaf's which lay in the grass beside his shield.

'If I do that I break my own oath,' Olaf said.

'If you don't you'll die without a blade in your hand,' Beigarth threatened and with that he moved faster than Sigurd would have thought possible for his size, slamming his sword's hilt into

Olaf's temple. Olaf reeled, blood spilling from his head on to the grass, and when he pulled his hand from his head it was red.

'Kill him, Uncle,' Sigurd said.

'Pick it up,' Beigarth said again, nodding at the sword on the ground.

Olaf glared at him but did not move. So Beigarth stepped up again and threw his left fist into Olaf's cheek, and there was enough weight behind that punch to make Olaf stagger to his left though he did not fall.

'Enough!' Guthrum told his champion, his own sense of honour threatened now by Beigarth's shameful behaviour.

But Beigarth could smell blood and would not be stopped now, not by words. 'I expected better, Norseman,' he spat, coming again, but this time his fist did not connect with Olaf's face because Olaf blocked with his right forearm then hammered his own fist into Beigarth's nose. Beigarth must have had a thick skull for that punch should have come out the back of his head, yet he was rocked back on his heels, blood flowing from both nostrils down his black beard.

When Guthrum's champion came at Olaf again he did so with his sword, scything it so that Olaf had to twist out of its reach or else get dizzy from his head rolling down the slope.

The men up at the borg were clamouring at Olaf now, telling him to pick up his sword and fight, and Beigarth's next swing saw his sword's point scrape along the rings of Olaf's brynja because the Norseman had jumped back just beyond its killing range. Then there was a flash in the sunlight and Beigarth stood still for a moment.

In Olaf's hand was his scramasax, which he had pulled from its sheath behind his back, and even at that distance Sigurd saw the blood on the blade. Beigarth's sword fell from his hand and a heartbeat later he was on his knees, still facing Olaf. A low hum came from the borg as people began to realize what was happening.

'Get up, man!' Guthrum yelled at his champion.

Beigarth couldn't have answered even if he had wanted to. Not with a gash like that in his throat. Olaf walked up to him, grabbed a handful of Beigarth's thick black beard and ran his scramasax through it to clean the blood off.

Down the hill, some of Guthrum's men wanted to come up and kill Olaf for his humiliation of their champion. But most looked as if they thought Beigarth had brought that bad end upon himself.

'Stay where you are,' Guthrum called down at them all, thinking it would be unwise to heap humiliation on humiliation. Besides which, it was not as though Olaf had broken his own oath. His shield, spear and sword, which would have turned against him if he had used them under truce, still lay in the grass where he had left them. As for the long knife with which he had cut Beigarth's throat, Olaf looked at that now for the last time, then threw it and it turned end over end before landing near Guthrum. It would have been better if it had landed blade down, stuck in the earth so that its bone handle offered itself to the hand, but it landed flat. *You cannot have everything*, Sigurd thought.

'You wanted iron, Jarl Guthrum? There is your iron,' Olaf called, and the men of the borg must have heard that for they cheered. Beigarth did not hear it though, which was a shame. He was still kneeling in the grass, back straight, arms by his side, but his head was slumped over now and he was as dead as it was possible to be.

Olaf had killed that mouthy fool without raising a single bead of sweat. Now he turned his back on Jarl Guthrum and gathered up his shield and weapons, taking his time as he slid the four silver rings back up his arms and closed them until they were a snug fit again. Then he strode back up the hill and if he was worried about one of Guthrum's men sending an arrow arcing into his back he did not show it.

Only when Olaf had passed back through the gates did Guthrum send his men to collect Beigarth from where he knelt in the grass as if waiting for some god to breathe life back into his body so that he might resume his quest for a reputation. When two big men took Beigarth under his arms and dragged him back down the slope, Sigurd got a good look at the mess. Beigarth's face was white as chalk but his brynja was sheeted in blood, so that you would have thought its rings were made of some red steel. Sigurd grimaced when he caught a whiff of the mess Guthrum's champion had made in his breeks, but a dead man could not help such things. A cruel truth that, that the body gives up and has no care for honour even when the spirit yet lingers.

'He stinks like a rotting cow,' Sigurd told Guthrum anyway, but the jarl ignored him. It seemed Guthrum had other things on his mind as he glared for a long moment at the men, or rather at Alrik, up there in the borg. Then he tossed his cloak over his sword's hilt and walked back to his camp, muttering to the gods as he went.

Jarl Guthrum burnt Beigarth on a hero's pyre, which was a generous thing to do given the way the man had got himself killed. Sigurd had to assume that the way Beigarth had died was not in keeping with the way he had lived, and that he must have been telling the truth about those men of reputation he had killed. He must have earned that pyre long before he had ever laid eyes on Olaf. Or else perhaps Jarl Guthrum honoured him in that way so as to keep up his men's spirits, which were lower than a snake's belly what with this siege business dragging on as long as it had and all their assaults having come to nothing. A hero's pyre told men that reputation was still important. It reminded them that they could win their jarl's favour through courage and sword and spear-work.

Or perhaps Jarl Guthrum simply wanted the smoke from the pyre to hide him from Alrik's sight as he turned his back on the borg and left, heading north even as the hungry flames consumed Beigarth's body and those left behind complained that it was not proper, saying farewell to a brother-in-arms without ale or mead enough to get blind drunk.

The jarl took Sigurd, Black Floki and Valgerd with him. He and ten of his hirðmen were mounted on ponies whilst another twenty spear-armed Svearmen trudged behind, keeping the prisoners at the heart of the column, almost protectively, which Valgerd noted with a grim expression, saying that such a thing did not bode well for them.

'She's right,' Floki said. 'You might even think we were worth something to him.'

Having been stripped of their war gear they walked unburdened while Guthrum's men sweated, but that hardly made them feel better about their situation. Nor could they expect help from Olaf and the others or even from Alrik, for it was likely they were not yet missed. And even if the borg men had seen them go, Jarl Guthrum had left more than enough warriors surrounding the fort to deter Alrik from letting any of his men trade the safety of the borg for a fight out in the open.

They made camp only when it became too dark to see where they were walking, and slept in the open under skins and fleeces. Then they set off dew-damp and shivering, when dawn was little more than a silver glow at night's hem in the east. Guthrum led them at a pace which had the horseless men grumbling and slung shields thumping against backs hard enough to leave bruises. He drew them northward as if his life depended on it, as if the gods themselves were beckoning him.

And perhaps they were.

It was on the third day that they realized where they were bound. And it was Valgerd who laid it in front of them, like a wind which comes out of nowhere, dispersing the sea fog and revealing the rocks poking out of the dark water before the bow. Sigurd had woken to a kick in the ribs from one of Guthrum's men, which was far less painful than the cramping in his shoulders and arms brought about by sleeping with bound ankles and wrists. Though at least their hands were tied in front of them now and not behind their backs as before.

The camp was stirring awake, men pissing and hawking phlegm, drinking water from a nearby brook and pulling combs through hair made damp by a night sleeping on the forest floor.

The first shafts of dawn light were threading into the glade, the red glow sliding slowly up the coarse trunks of the pines and the wool-clad bodies of Guthrum's men who for the most part lacked mail and steel helmets. Valgerd and Floki were already awake, talking in low voices which was good to see. Rolling on to his side, Sigurd dug his elbows into the forest litter and pulled himself over to them, thinking that his near-bursting bladder could wait until he had learnt what had the shieldmaiden and the former slave scheming like a couple of jealous wives.

'If you have come up with an escape plan I would like to hear it,' he said, levering himself upright so that he was between them. Unlike him they had had their ankle bonds removed, though their hands were still tied.

'I know where we are going,' Valgerd said.

Sigurd glanced at Floki. 'Not as good as an escape plan but worth knowing in any case,' he said, looking back to Valgerd.

For long enough to increase Sigurd's discomfort, she said nothing, her gaze riveted to his, and there was something in the shieldmaiden's eyes that Sigurd had never seen before.

'Well?' he said. 'Are you going to make me wait until we get there?'

'Ubsola,' Valgerd said, shivering with the word.

The shieldmaiden had turned her back on the gods when they blighted and withered and eventually took the völva from her. And yet she had spoken that name in awe, and no sooner was it in Sigurd's ear than he knew she had the right of it. *Ubsola.*

Even in faraway Skudeneshavn, where Sigurd had spent his childhood listening to fireside tales in Eik-hjálmr, his father's hall, they had heard of Ubsola. It had ever been a place where the Svear kings ruled, but it was for three great kings in particular that Ubsola was known: Aun, Egil and Adils of the Yngling line who had claimed kinship with Frey, God of Fertility, whom men also call Yngve-Frey. And these kings were buried at Ubsola, which all men knew to be a sacred place of mysterious rites, blood seiðr and the gods.

Sigurd gestured at Jarl Guthrum now, who was holding a gourd full of water for his pony to drink from. 'When he went to meet Olaf, Guthrum said the gods had told him what he should do.'

Valgerd nodded. 'I have seen him talking to the gods,' she said. The dawn painted her face with crimson and pale yellow and Sigurd could only wonder at her own dealings with the gods when she had lived as the guardian of the seeress and the sacred spring up in the Lysefjord. All gone now, her old life, just as his old life was gone. And yet he still strove to please the gods, while Valgerd despised them.

'Guthrum thinks the gods have turned against him,' she said. But it was not the light across her face which held Sigurd spellbound. It was that look in her eyes. Not fear exactly, but close, and it made Sigurd feel uneasy. He wanted to hold her but knew he could not, even had his hands not been bound.

'He is right,' Floki said. 'The gods *have* turned against him. How else can you explain how he has failed to kick Alrik out of that place with four times the number of spears to call on? He has made a bad job of the whole thing and now he runs off to the gods like a slapped child running to his secret hiding hole.'

If Guthrum has lost the gods' favour he is not the only one for so have I, Sigurd thought. Still, what Valgerd and Floki said made sense and he told them so. Guthrum had lost his borg, his silver and iron and far too many men in this fight with Alrik. He had even lost his champion in what no one could call a real fight, so it was not as though he lacked reasons to suspect his luck was out.

'At this time of year there is probably a market at Ubsola,' Sigurd said. They had all seen the two nestbaggins stuffed with hacksilver which the jarl had slung over his pony's back when they left the camp below the borg. Perhaps he simply had not dared leave so much silver behind with his men, in case they should steal it, or, unlikely as it might seem, Alrik got his hands on it. Or perhaps he intended to bring supplies back from Ubsola; food and ale enough to keep his men happy.

'Or it could be that he means to hire new men, more meat to put in his shieldwall,' Sigurd said.

'More heroes to burn,' Floki spat through his teeth.

'Legs,' a Svearman said to Sigurd, coming over and dropping to his knees to untie the rope, during which Sigurd and the other two held their tongues. The man yanked the rope out, burning the skin on Sigurd's ankles, then moved away.

'You are missing the point,' Valgerd said, her eyes on Sigurd's. 'Why do you think he is taking us with him? Why do you think we are still alive at all?'

For a moment Sigurd just stared back at her. Then the answer hit him square in the chest, like an anvil stone dropped from a height. His blood ran cold in his veins as he looked into Valgerd's eyes, the shieldmaiden waiting as he wove the picture in his mind. For as well as being the seat of the Svear kings for the past four hundred years, Ubsola was a place of bloodletting, of strange rites and sacrifice, where the gods were ever present and men bought their goodwill with the flesh and blood of the dead.

'When I was twelve or thirteen summers old some men came to pay their respects to my father,' Sigurd said, glancing from Valgerd to Floki. 'They had travelled from the north and were bound for Ubsola and my father hosted them well because they brought him seal skins and walrus ivory. They were going to Ubsola for the great blót.'

'The Dísablót,' Valgerd said, for unlike other sacrifices, which are made so that the gods may grant a good harvest or victory in battle, this one at the beginning of winter was dedicated to the Dísir, those goddesses who guide a man's seed and help life to quicken in the womb.

Sigurd nodded as the childhood memory flooded him. 'They were full of the seiðr of it all, these northerners, and it spread amongst our people. When they left us, my father sent them on their way with a very fine sword and scramasax. His offering to the temple at Ubsola, for he said he would likely never go there himself.' Valgerd raised an eyebrow. 'He had done so much raiding amongst the Danes and the Geats,' Sigurd explained, 'and knew that he would likely never make it to Ubsola in one piece.'

'Well I have never heard of the place,' Floki said. 'What was so special about this Dísablót?'

'On your feet, scum!' one of Jarl Guthrum's men growled, kicking Floki, who looked up at him as though making a thing of remembering his face.

'I need to piss,' Sigurd told the man, who nodded and gestured to the trees.

'Be quick,' the Svearman said. 'We need to get where we're going.'

But Sigurd took his time because he could already feel the gods nearby, which meant they would soon be at Ubsola. Yes, the gods were close.

And they were thirsty for blood.

CHAPTER FIVE

OLAF DID NOT LIKE THE WAY MEN LOOKED AT HIM THESE DAYS. NOT HIS own crew mates but Alrik's men. It was as though they expected him to get them all out of this mess with Jarl Guthrum, or else challenge Alrik for the leadership of the borg men. Alrik did not help matters in this regard, for as much as the man needed every able warrior he could get – and the Norsemen in particular, the way Olaf saw it – he nevertheless did a bad job of trying to hide his suspicions. Envy too, though Olaf couldn't say what the man was envious of.

He knew that Alrik had not liked it when he had walked out of the place to talk with Jarl Guthrum. But that was the Svearman's problem not Olaf's. The trouble was that nearly every man in the borg had watched Olaf kill Guthrum's champion, Beigarth, and with such apparent ease too. They had been in awe of him ever since. They straightened their backs and squared their shoulders when they thought Olaf was looking, and perhaps they grew bigger balls in the fighting when he was beside them. No harm in that. Apart from when one young man, trying to impress him, had pulled down his breeks and bared his arse at Guthrum's men. That young fool was dying in agony because although they had pulled the arrow from his arse, the wound rot had come.

Still, Olaf had no intention of challenging Alrik, not least because then the responsibility for the survival of every man in that fort would rest on his shoulders, and truth be told he did not have any schemes or strategies at all that might help them beat Jarl Guthrum's army or see them vanish one morning like dawn mist. All Olaf cared about was that Sigurd was Jarl Guthrum's prisoner. It gnawed at him like rats on a rope and every day that he and the rest of Sigurd's oath-sworn crew did nothing about it, his frustration grew.

'The arrogant bloody fool,' he muttered now, looking south from the borg's ramparts over the tents of Guthrum's camp towards the trees beyond.

'What's done is done,' Bram beside him said, and Olaf realized he'd spoken aloud.

'It's Asgot's bloody fault,' Olaf went on. He might as well now. 'He's filled the lad's head with all this stuff about being Óðin-favoured. Sigurd thinks the Allfather walks next to him with a bloody great shield.'

'Maybe he does,' Bram suggested with a shrug. 'The lad's still alive, or at least he was last time you saw him. Which he had no right being, seeing as Jarl Guthrum found him in his own tent ready to cut his throat like a prize bull.'

Olaf gripped the hilt of the sword at his hip. '*This* is what keeps Sigurd alive. What keeps any of us alive. The moment you start thinking you're some god's golden boy is the moment you trip over your own damned gut rope because some growling fuck has opened your belly with an axe.'

'I say we put our shields together and walk out of here,' Svein said. He was looking south too, one arm resting on the head of his long-hafted axe. 'If those turds out there have the stomachs for a fight, so be it. But I am thinking that without their jarl here they are more likely to let us go on our way.'

'And suffer Guthrum's wrath when he returns and finds out one hundred men let a half crew of Sword-Norse escape like a fart on the wind?' Olaf said. 'I don't think so, Red. And anyway, where would we go?'

'Maybe the gods will tell Asgot where Guthrum has gone. Maybe they will speak to him through the runes,' Hagal said, getting in on it like a dog wanting a gnaw of the bone.

Olaf grunted. 'If the gods are playing with us then they cannot be trusted and are as likely to tell Asgot that Guthrum is halfway across Bifröst when in reality the whoreson is taking a shit in the woods not five rôsts away.'

'I have an idea,' Moldof said, which at least got Olaf's attention, because Moldof did not waste words and if he said he had an idea then chances were it was worth listening to. 'One or two of us go out there and grab one of Guthrum's men. One of those little sods who've been sneaking up at dusk to take pot shots.' He nodded towards a bowman who was sitting in the grass on the edge of the enemy camp fletching an arrow. 'We persuade the little prick to tell us where his jarl has gone.' He turned to Olaf. 'At least that part will no longer be a mystery.'

But before Olaf could say that at least there was an idea worth a try, one of the borg men called to Knut that men were coming up the hill.

They spilled from the tree line to the south and came under a banner which no one in the borg seemed to recognize: a black boar's head on a yellow cloth. Nor did Guthrum's men know these newcomers by the looks of it, for their camp burst into frenzied life as men shrugged into mail coats if they had them, and grabbed shields and weapons and tried to look like warriors.

'Not friends of yours then?' Olaf said to Alrik who had come with Knut to see what was happening.

'Wish they were,' Alrik said, a little too earnestly for Olaf's taste.

There were some fifty warriors under that boar's head banner and they looked serious enough, though there was clearly a bit of cock swinging going on, as Bram put it, what with them trying to make an impression on those already gathered on and around that hill. Whoever was giving the orders made them stop just over a spear-throw short of the borg's gate, and Guthrum's men, who had done nothing to stop them, just stood there scratching their arses waiting for someone to tell them what to do.

'It's us this new lot are interested in, then,' Knut said, as they watched one of Jarl Guthrum's warriors walk across and up the slope alone, his hands raised to the newcomers to show that he meant them no harm. Though what harm he thought he could do to those fifty men, even if he'd had a sword in each hand and a flaming firebrand sticking out of his arse, was a mystery.

A big man in a helmet and mail greeted him, then pointed at the borg with his spear. They did not talk for long and after the time it takes a hungry man to empty a bowl of pottage the newcomer and one of his companions strode up to the wall, Jarl Guthrum's man following some ten paces behind.

'Lord Alrik! I mean you no harm.' This was a good start at least, Olaf thought, as Alrik stepped up to the stakes and straightened his back.

'I'm Alrik. Who are you?'

'I am someone who wants no part in this dispute you have with Jarl Guthrum,' the mailed man said, and Svein murmured that here was another Norseman far from home. 'From what I have heard, this feud of yours is a ravenous bitch, eating men the way the ocean swallows them in a storm.'

Alrik seemed to consider this, as if looking for the insult in it. But in the end he must have found only the truth. 'Then what do you want?' he asked. 'And why is my man standing at your shoulder when he is supposed to be here with the rest of us?'

All eyes on the borg's ramparts flicked across to the second man.

'Thór's hairy sack,' Svein growled.

'Knew that dog would come back to bite us,' Aslak said.

'Who is it?' Solmund hissed because his eyes were not what they had been.

97

'Trouble, that's who,' Olaf said, for there was Kjartan Auðunarson who had slipped away before they'd had a chance to put a knife in him. He stood there looking quietly smug, with a face that just begged to be smacked and those two long beard ropes hanging from his chin.

Kjartan nodded at Alrik. 'If I had stayed I'd be feeding the worms now, lord, and not because of Jarl Guthrum's men.'

Alrik waved a hand as though wafting away a bad smell. He would not do that nithing Kjartan the honour of asking any more about it. Instead he looked back to the other man. 'So who are you? Or if you won't tell me that, what do you want?' He spread his arms wide. 'As you can see, I am busy not letting those goat-fuckers steal my iron and silver.'

Olaf looked at the war band waiting in their skjaldborg across the hill. They were well armed, many of them wearing helmets and mail. At the centre of their line, standing beneath that boar's head banner, were five men who were adorned with war gear easily as fine as anything Sigurd's crew owned. There was a boy too, no more than twelve years old and even he was ring-coated, which was some expense to go to for a boy who would be grown out of that brynja in a summer or two.

Olaf nodded towards those men. 'See the one with the pretty helmet?' he asked Bram, Svein and the others standing with him. 'That's a jarl's torc at his neck.'

No one disagreed. Some growled curses.

'There is a man fighting for you, Lord Alrik,' the mailed man – who Olaf now realized was merely this new jarl's voice – said. 'A young Norseman who thinks he is Óðin-favoured. I am not interested in the outlaws and dregs he has with him, but that strutting, golden-haired son of a flea-bitten whore will make himself known to me now.' He conferred with Kjartan and nodded. 'Wears the name Byrnjolf these days.'

'An enemy of yours then by the sound of it,' Alrik said, to his credit not even glancing at Olaf or the other Norsemen. 'I cannot see why I would hand over one of my men just because you want him. Particularly a man whose courage and war-craft helped me take back this borg from Jarl Guthrum.'

The Norseman looked across the hill at Jarl Guthrum's men who were still waiting patiently, spear blades pointing at the blue sky, probably sweating by now in their wool which was layered thick because most of them lacked for a brynja. 'You look like a man who does not need any more enemies,' the Norseman told Alrik.

'And you sound like a man who is far from home,' Alrik said, which was true enough because he was a Norseman in a land of Spear-Svear. Then Alrik raised a hand. 'But let us not make trouble where there does not need to be any. The man you seek is not here.'

'I have silver for you, Lord Alrik. A sackful of it.' The Norseman pointed back to the trees, meaning that as well as those in the shieldwall behind him, he most likely had friends waiting out of sight with the horses and silver and whatever else they had brought with them. 'Just give me this Byrnjolf and the silver is yours.'

'I am not lying, Norseman. The man you want is not here.'

'Then where is he?' the Norseman asked.

'Jarl Guthrum has him. He's Guthrum's prisoner along with a shieldmaiden and another young man who is one of the best fighters I have ever seen.'

The Norseman frowned at this. 'So where is Jarl Guthrum?'

Alrik shrugged. 'You tell me. The arse-welt disappeared days ago. Perhaps he has heard that his wife is swiving every stinking thrall in his hall. Or maybe he is just homesick.'

'Do you have any of that silver for the man who tells you where Jarl Guthrum is?' This was from Guthrum's man who had followed the Norsemen like a dog waiting for scraps.

The Norseman nodded. 'That information would be worth something, yes,' he said.

Guthrum's man looked nervous then. Suddenly he was not sure he should be saying anything about it. 'And you will pay my jarl the silver you offered Alrik . . . if he agrees to sell you his prisoner, this Byrnjolf?'

The Norseman nodded. 'Jarl Guthrum will have plenty to go around,' he said, which was the best way of putting it to an oath-sworn man such as this, who relied on his ring-giver.

'Here we go,' Solmund gnarred.

'My lord Guthrum has gone north to Uppland. To the temple at Ubsola.'

A hiss escaped from Asgot at that, but Olaf was watching the Norseman, who cursed under his breath and glanced at Kjartan before turning back to Guthrum's man. 'Why?' he asked.

'That is my jarl's business,' Guthrum's man said.

'I'll tell you one thing, that doesn't bode well for Sigurd and the others,' young Thorbiorn said and Olaf looked at him because being the son of King Thorir at Skíringssalr the lad likely knew more about the Svear and the goings-on at Ubsola than Olaf or any of his westerners. But for Asgot perhaps. 'Men go there to appease the gods. Blood offerings and such,' Thorbiorn said. He looked almost amused but had the sense not to smile.

The Norseman opened the purse on his belt and pulled out some hacksilver; half an arm ring, or just under half. He tossed it to Guthrum's man, who caught it, his face beneath the beard flushing red because he felt like a traitor, though not enough to turn the reward down.

'Whose banner is that?' Knut asked, which was as well because Olaf had been about to ask the same question even if it meant drawing attention to himself. Not because he didn't know, but because he wanted to hear it said aloud.

'Do not concern yourself with it, friend,' the Norseman said. 'As Lord Alrik pointed out, you are busy keeping hold of your silver and iron. Besides, we will be on our way and you will not likely see us again.'

'I know whose banner it is,' Olaf said under his breath. 'It's bloody Hrani Randversson's.'

'I told you I had seen that Kjartan Auðunarson at Örn-garð!' Crow-Song said, recalling one of his visits to Jarl Randver's hall when he had been a skald. Nowadays he was just a fighter like the rest of them.

'What do *you* want, Crow-Song? An arm ring?' Olaf said. 'For knowing you had seen him before but not knowing where until it was too late to do anything about it?'

'I told you the day before he sloped off,' Hagal protested, scowling.

'Aye, you did,' Olaf admitted. 'Well, I would have saved us a lot of trouble if I'd cut Kjartan's throat that first day I smelt something off about him.'

'Which is why you can't blame the man for slithering off the way he did,' Moldof rumbled. 'Knew he was dead if he stayed.'

He had a point. But Kjartan had done more than vanish to save his own skin. Who knew why the man had left Hinderå in the first place and come east as far as the Baltic Sea? As one of Jarl Randver's hearthmen perhaps he was no friend of Randver's son Hrani, who now wore Randver's torc at his neck, and left of his own accord. Or perhaps he had offended Jarl Hrani in some way and got himself outlawed. Whatever the reason, rather than wake up dead with Sigurd or Olaf's knife in him, Kjartan had seen an opportunity. He had packed his sea chest and taken the news of Sigurd's whereabouts back to Örn-garð and what better way was there to fix things with the new young jarl than that?

'We will be on our way then,' the Norseman said, but before he turned away he asked Alrik if there was any message he wanted delivered to Jarl Guthrum. He was barely able to keep the curl of a smile from his lips as he asked it.

Alrik was twisting one strand of his drooping moustaches between his finger and thumb. 'Tell Jarl Guthrum that there is no point begging the gods for help, for they do not like to see jarls throw their men's lives away like he does. Tell him that the gods have already turned their backs on him.'

The Norseman nodded and he and Kjartan turned and walked back towards where, if Olaf was right, Jarl Hrani Randversson waited in his pretty helmet under his new boar's head banner. Guthrum's man was already halfway back to his own camp, no doubt hoping his fellows had not seen the Norseman give him that piece of hacksilver.

'Kjartan!' Olaf called, unable to stop himself, and both men turned back, their eyes on Olaf.

'Tell your jarl that if he goes after Sigurd I swear by all the gods I will kill him.' The way Olaf saw it there was no reason to hide Sigurd's identity now. And there was every chance that Hrani had heard that threat with his own ears from where he stood with his warriors.

'From here it does not look like you are in a good position to swear such things, Olaf of Skudeneshavn,' Kjartan called back.

'Jarl Randver thought the same thing before Sigurd's scramasax opened his throat and we dumped him over the side,' Olaf shouted. 'I think he changed his mind about it as he sank to the sea bed and the fishes came to peck at him.' Perhaps it did not mean much, yelling threats and insults from behind a wall, but it felt good. 'If young Hrani wants to wear that torc for a few more years yet, he would be wise to piss off back to Norway.'

The other Norseman growled something to Kjartan and turned away. And Kjartan went with him.

'So I am not the only one with enemies,' Alrik said, grinning at Olaf.

'That's the trouble,' Olaf said, watching that yellow war banner flap in the breeze. 'You kill one and another pops up like a damned toadstool. Take my advice, lads,' he said for the benefit of anyone within earshot. 'When choosing your enemies try to pick men who have no sons. It'll save you no end of misery.'

Svein came up to Olaf, his forehead furrowed. 'So, Uncle, what do we do now?'

Olaf was still watching the war band and their leader with the helmet that looked more gold than grey. Someone gave a command and the whole lot of them, some fifty very well-armed warriors, slung shields on their backs, turned and headed for the woods.

'You know very well what we're going to do, Red,' Olaf said.

They went over the wall on the borg's north side, one after another down the same rope until they all waited on the slope beneath the palisade, hearts hammering, ears straining for any sound which would warn them that they had been spotted by one of Jarl Guthrum's men.

They had let three nights pass since Jarl Hrani had come, hoping for a night on which the moon was cloud-veiled because Olaf decided the risk of waiting was worth it for a better chance of slipping away unseen. At this time of year they could not hope for a pitch-black night, nor anything like proper darkness, but it was as dark as it was going to get and they had been ready. Now all they had to do was make it to the tree line, which would have been far easier had there not been a group of warriors camped round a fire halfway down the hill.

Aside from the main camp there were such knots of men positioned all around the fort, each within shouting distance of another, so it was not as if Olaf really expected that they would be able to pass through the ring unnoticed, like ghosts leaving their burial mounds to walk amongst the living. Which was why he was not surprised when the first shout went up.

'Suppose we'd better run then,' Solmund said with the sort of disgust you would expect. For no Norseman worth his sword enjoyed running from his enemies, but an old Norseman, whose knees ached with the rain and whose neck creaked like a rusty hinge, liked it even less.

Olaf did not answer. He was already running.

They didn't care about the noise of shields scraping on brynjur or thumping against helmets, or buckles jingling or even their own breathing, which sounded like a load of forge bellows all feeding the fire. They just ran, because that was hard enough given the war gear, furs, cloaks, ale skins and nestbaggins full of food weighing them down. They had also divided the silver hoard which Alrik had given to Sigurd between them and Olaf thought that these pieces of silver clinking together made the loudest sound of everything.

'They're coming,' Thorbiorn called, risking a backwards glance which could easily see him trip on the uneven ground. Moths flew out of the long grass before them and now and then a ground-nesting bird clattered up hooting or squawking into the night.

'Course they're bloody coming,' Bram said. 'Arseholes can hear our silver singing to them.'

'Let's . . . put . . . a few down,' Svein managed, thinking that two or three dead Svearmen would discourage the rest. Or perhaps he just wanted to catch his breath.

'And give the rest of them time to catch up?' Olaf said. Which was all the answer Svein was going to get because Olaf didn't have the breath to waste. No man did who tried running in mail.

The shouts from behind them were getting louder. Guthrum's men were gaining, unencumbered as they were. An arrow streaked through the grey above Olaf's head. He thought he saw another from the corner of his eye but realized it was a bat, as the darker mass of the pine woods loomed before them, its sweet scent hanging on the air.

Then they were amongst the trees, where it actually felt like night time, the strange half-light shafting through the woods only so far before it could penetrate no further. And at least there was a good enough reason to stop running, because running face first into a tree trunk was something no one wanted to have to live down.

'They won't follow now. Not in here,' Olaf said. 'Not worth the risk.'

So they waited a while, catching their breath and listening, but for Moldof who was panting like a netted fox and telling the others that they should try running with only one arm and see for themselves how much harder that was.

'So that's that then,' Solmund said when he had got his own breath back and they were walking north through the woods, satisfied that Guthrum's men had given up and gone back to their fires and the easier task of surrounding men who had no intention of going anywhere.

'That's that,' Olaf agreed. 'Alrik will have to manage without us.'

It wasn't as though they had jumped over the wall and buggered off without telling Alrik or Knut. They would have done if it came to it, but in the event Alrik had asked to speak with Olaf shortly after Jarl Hrani had led his men off through these same woods.

'You'll be wanting to go after your friend then, now you know where Guthrum has taken him,' Alrik said.

Olaf had nodded. 'I will.'

'I'd rather not lose you and your Norsemen,' Alrik said, 'for it will be much harder to hold this place without you. I am not too proud to admit it.' He glanced at Knut, who nodded, then he fixed his eyes on Olaf again. 'We would give you another silver hoard in return for your swords. And your oaths.'

Olaf shook his head. 'Not going to happen,' he said.

Alrik could not hide his disappointment, but he nodded. 'I understand these things. These bonds. What are we without them?'

'Sigurd is kin,' Olaf said. 'Or as good as. And I am sworn to him. We all are.' All but for Moldof and Thorbiorn Thorirsson, that was, but there was no need to get into all of that.

Knut raised an eyebrow. 'If you catch up with Jarl Guthrum, do us a favour and put a spear in his belly, hey. That would be helpful.'

And perhaps that was why Alrik gave Olaf his blessing even though he was losing eleven of his best warriors. If the Norsemen killed Guthrum, the jarl's men who ringed Alrik's borg would most likely give up and go home, or else seek service with another warlord.

Or perhaps Alrik was letting Olaf go because really he did not have a choice in it. It did not matter now anyway because they were out. The woods were empty. Or at least, wolf, bear, fox, boar and elk were keeping out of sight, and Olaf and the others could see their way well enough in the gloomy half-light.

'Should make four or five rôsts before dawn,' Olaf said as a vole scampered across his path and into the shadow beneath a fallen old pine.

'Well I am glad to be out of that place,' Svein said. 'Not for me, feeling trapped like a fish in a pool when the tide has gone out.'

'You see,' Solmund said to Crow-Song, 'even Svein is more of a skald than you these days.'

That got some chuckles, even from Hagal, which was a good sound in an unfamiliar forest at night. And they glimpsed enough of the stars through the pine canopy above to know that they were going north.

To Ubsola.

'That one is Thór's. That one is Óðin's,' a warrior named Asgrim said, pointing with his spear at two of the three great mounds which rose some thirty feet above them, dominating a landscape which was fairly flat, albeit that flatness was interrupted here and there by some hills and rocky outcrops. Good land, Olaf would have said. Rich soil, lush grazing for horses, cows, sheep and goats, and even a lake full of fish, and all of it looking as inviting as it ever would, cast in the warm evening sunlight. 'And in that one with all the yellow flowers lie the bones of Frey,' Asgrim went on, thrusting his spear towards the third and last mound. 'Frey who is the lord of rain and sunshine and peace, and who decides if a man will be rich or poor.'

He had said the last bit more quietly, shooting a glance at Jarl Guthrum, who everybody knew was a poor jarl these days what with Alrik sitting on his silver and iron and having taken Guthrum's hill fort too. But Guthrum was busy combing his beard and checking the comb's fine bone teeth for lice and seemed to be somewhere else in his mind.

There were countless other grass-covered humps all across the site, perhaps as many as three thousand in one massive grave meadow, but it was these three which had the hairs standing stiff on Sigurd's arms and on the back of his neck. It was as if the warm breeze was the breath of the gods. As if the faint scent of woodsmoke was a memory of their hero pyres which yet lingered after all those years.

'See how they dug the earth out between the mounds to make them look even bigger,' Valgerd said, and even she, who had turned her back on the gods, seemed as much in awe of the place as Sigurd himself was.

Jarl Guthrum had led them through a forest of fir and pine, then amongst sun-dappled woodland of birch, alder and the occasional oak, and it had been clear that every man felt the seiðr of Ubsola even before he had laid eyes on the parts of it those who have been to the place talk of.

They touched amulets and rings and the pommels of their swords, muttering greetings to the gods and being less in love with the sound of their own voices than they had been previously.

'If I did not fear to dishonour them,' Asgrim went on, meaning the gods buried in those mounds, 'I would like to come in the night and dig into the east grave to see what weapons lie there in the cold earth. Perhaps Thór's hammer Mjöllnir is just lying there waiting for a great warrior to come and claim it.'

Asgrim was Jarl Guthrum's new champion and he made Beigarth look like Baldr the Beautiful. His mouth was warped like an old timber, his nose was all twisted gristle and his eyes bulged in their sockets, and all this did nothing to improve a head which was too big even for his muscle-bound body. It seemed to swell here and there, that head, so that there were bald patches amongst long strands of lank hair, and his two front teeth had been knocked out by someone, which never helps a man's appearance, as Valgerd pointed out.

Floki had suggested that the reason Asgrim had not been Guthrum's champion before was because the jarl would not like to have to look at him all the time, for Guthrum was handsome and vain enough to baulk at a sight like Asgrim. And yet his new champion kept his brynja free of iron rot, his sword sharp and his helmet – which he had inherited from Guthrum's former champion – burnished so that it could blind a man when the sunlight was on it. Besides which, apart from his strong limbs, broad shoulders and bull's neck, anyone could see that Asgrim was a killer born and a warrior made.

'Don't listen to him,' Jarl Guthrum said, coming to stand beside Sigurd while one of his men readied his banner and the others made sure they were looking their finest. 'Asgrim is a man who would believe that the sea is Freyja's tears and the clouds in the sky are the Æsir's sheep wandering in search of good grazing.' Guthrum shook his head at Asgrim, who may have been angry or may have cared not at all; it was hard to tell with that face of his.

'There are no gods buried in those haugar,' Guthrum said, 'but there are kings. The first kings of the Svear.' He looked at Sigurd and it was clear that the jarl did not think these mounds any less important for their not holding the bones of the gods.

'Kings Aun, Egil and Adils,' Sigurd said, not to impress Guthrum with his knowledge of the Yngling rulers, but because those ancient kings' names came unbidden to his lips with the bronze and copper-glow memories of fireside tales.

Even so, Guthrum was impressed. He smiled, for a brief moment shrugging off the misery he had worn since deciding that the gods had forsaken him, and he turned back to his new champion whilst thumbing at Sigurd.

'You see, Asgrim, even this Norseman knows more about the line of our kings than you do.'

Asgrim made a deep *hoom* in his throat. 'If you'd wanted a know-it-all skald for your prow man you should have said so,' he rumbled, which had Guthrum's men chuckling into their beards and the jarl himself nodding in appreciation of the man's point.

'It will be a shame killing him,' Floki murmured. About Asgrim not Guthrum. For the jarl's new champion had treated them well so far. He had even knocked a man called Halvdan on to his backside when Halvdan had cracked his spear's butt across Sigurd's head for no reason other than because he could.

'They are Jarl Guthrum's prisoners not yours, Halvdan, you sheep's prick,' Asgrim had snarled down at the man who sat in the grass rubbing his chin. And Halvdan had not laid a finger or stave on Sigurd or the others since.

It could have been his sense of honour which made Asgrim treat them fairly, but Sigurd suspected it was more likely that the man associated him and his Norse companions with his own rise. If Olaf had not killed Beigarth, Asgrim would still be a nobody, just another bone-sack in Jarl Guthrum's shieldwall. Now he would earn silver and fame as an ambitious lord's champion, and he owed that, in a roundabout way, to Sigurd.

Not that Sigurd, unlike Floki it seemed, could see how they were going to get the chance to kill the man. Ever since they had learnt they were bound for Ubsola Sigurd had looked for the opportunity either to escape or to get a blade to Jarl Guthrum's throat and force the issue, but Asgrim knew his business and Guthrum had not become the warlord he was by being a fool. And if he *was* a fool, then what did that make Sigurd for getting himself caught by Guthrum like a wolf in a snare?

'Being a prisoner gives a man too much thinking time,' Sigurd muttered to Valgerd while they waited in the gathering twilight. Because it was dusk and because Ubsola was even these days under the control of some or other Svear king, Guthrum had sent a man ahead to announce his arrival and ask permission to bring his thirty warriors along the processional way which led north-east past the three huge burial mounds to the hall beyond. That hall's shingle roof could be seen between the second and third hill, as could the plumes of several cook fires, the slate-grey smoke darker than the sky would get all that summer night. And the relief on the jarl's face was clear for all to see when the man returned, grinning from ear to ear, to say that Jarl Guthrum was welcome in Ubsola and would be met with honour in King Eysteinn's hall.

'The king himself is not there. He's off fighting some karls in the north,' the man told his jarl, who was disappointed to hear that, though he pretended not to be.

'What do I care whether King Eysteinn is at his hall, fighting farmers or fishing in some lake?' he announced after a moment. 'I have come to honour the gods.' He threw his arms wide in recognition of the place's spiritual richness, which none there could deny, and Halvdan felt brave enough to punch Floki in the back with his shield's boss as Guthrum ordered the party to walk on.

The well-trodden path, its grass matted here and there with flattened sheep droppings, took them past the kings' burial mounds, and when they were almost past the first of them Floki hissed at Sigurd to look up. High above its summit, in a sky which was purple and dark blue but hemmed in the west with a band of rust, a golden eagle soared. Its wings outstretched, the magnificent bird searched for prey down amongst the long grass, and Sigurd knew what Floki was thinking, that perhaps Asgrim was right and Jarl Guthrum was wrong. That the Allfather's bones, nothing but ashes now, *were* buried in that mound from the time when he walked amongst men, for another of Óðin's names is Arnhöfði which means Eagle-Head.

'So you are still watching me, Allfather,' Sigurd whispered to the eagle as it made its great sweeping circle in the dusky sky. And then the creature called back to him, a thin, high yelp which had Sigurd's guts rolling over themselves. Valgerd and Black Floki looked at him. He felt the weight of their gaze but did not take his eyes from the path ahead, and the hog-backed shingled roof of the hall that waited for them beyond the great mounds.

CHAPTER SIX

———————

KING EYSTEINN'S HALL WAS NOT LIKE ANY OTHER HALL SIGURD HAD EVER seen. There were no long tables around which warriors could feast and drown themselves in mead. There was no high seat for the king himself, nor benches for men and women to sleep in, nor high lofts at either end where the children could hide or a man and woman could go if they did not want everyone else's eyes on them. No flames flapped in the hearth, no dogs lay in the straw which was spread thickly upon the earthen floor, and nor was the place crammed with folk, as such halls almost always are. It was a huge hall, as big as Jarl Hakon Brandingi's up in Osøyro, where they had hidden from the winter and their enemies who were looking for them. But it was silent, this hall, and would have been empty but for they three, Guthrum and the ten hirðmen he had brought in to the place, the jarl having left his other Spear-Svear waiting with the horses by the ting mound outside.

No one else moved through the scented smoke, which rose from several dishes of smouldering herbs to hang thick as a winter pelt just above their heads. This fragrant emptiness would have been the strangest thing of all, if not for the gods.

They sat there, those gods, at the northern end of Eysteinn's hall, silent and watchful. Each was the height of two men and old, older than the hall itself, for they had been carved from three oaks, perhaps in the time of the first Yngling kings, and the hall had been built around them. Their roots were still deep in the earth, the lumps and bumps of them making the floor uneven in places.

Óðin, with a cavernous, empty right eye socket worn smooth by folks' fingers over the years, sat there gripping a spear in one hand and a cup in the other. Beside him sat Thór, all beard and drooping moustaches carved as sleek as the curling sternpost you might see on a fine ship. His hands rested on the haft of his great hammer Mjöllnir, the head of which sat between his feet. But the third god was Frey and even were he not the god which it seemed most of the Svearmen loved best, he would have drawn any man or woman's eye because of the huge cock standing proud between his legs. It was long enough that there was only a finger's width of a gap between it and the point of his beard, and his eyes bulged as if even he was shocked by the eagerness of his own member.

Sigurd could not help but glance at Valgerd to see what she thought of it, but the shieldmaiden seemed more interested in something else, something which Sigurd could not see for Guthrum's men who were in the way. They stood there unarmed and in awe, as though a horde of Valkyries might swoop down at any moment and sweep them all up to Valhöll the way an angry gust will pick up leaves and swirl them into the sky.

Sigurd's eye was drawn in a different direction. Where the hearth would normally be there *was* a table, just not the sort around which men would sit drinking and boasting and hurling insults at each other. It was six feet long and so dark as to be almost black, so that who could say what kind of wood it had been carved from with such skill? Its wide apron was adorned with scenes of Ragnarök, depicting the fates of these temple gods. Thór was wrestling with the Midgard Serpent whose jaws were wide, gaping and inevitable. There was Fenrir Wolf about to swallow Óðin, and Surt the mighty giant with his sword raised about to strike down Frey beloved of the Svearmen. Upon each stout leg was carved a writhing, twisting, knotted serpent, but strangely the legs at one end were slightly shorter than those at the other, so that the table sloped, which struck Sigurd as odd.

'Welcome back, Jarl Guthrum.'

It was a voice which sounded like it would do better for a cup of warm milk and honey, but when the body it belonged to emerged from the smoke Sigurd was surprised the man could speak at all.

'Solmund would have liked to be here now,' Floki said, 'to see someone even older than he is.'

That earned him a knuckle hammer to the back of the head, from Asgrim himself this time, as well as an ice-cold look from the crook-backed, cowled old man, who then turned his glare on Guthrum as if to say he expected the jarl to keep his prisoners on a tighter leash.

'Mead for the jarl and his men,' the old man called, wheezing with the effort of it, and in the flame-flickered dark behind him another figure moved through the smoke leaving a swirling grey wake. 'And make sure it is the strongest and best.' Inside that cowl the man's eyes were like boring awls in Guthrum's own. 'I think Jarl Guthrum is in need of it,' he added, touching the little carving of Frey that he wore round his neck, for he was a Freysgodi, a priest of Frey.

Perhaps there was some seiðr behind the priest's last words, and Sigurd wondered if he had peered inside Guthrum's thought box and seen the jarl's doubts gnawing at him. Could the old man know that the jarl believed his wyrd had soured like milk left in the sun?

Or perhaps there was no seiðr in it at all, for this was not the great mid-winter Dísablót which all kings and jarls and the most powerful of the hersirs were expected to attend, and if a jarl like Guthrum was here now, in high summer, it was because he needed a favour from the gods. And a man did not need the gods' help if his wyrd was stretching out before him like a golden hair from some young beauty's head.

'You want *them* watered too?' the priest asked Guthrum, running those watery eyes across the three prisoners standing there bound and unkempt amongst the rest. And yet the old priest was not so old that he did not fill his eyes with Valgerd when they latched on to her through the herb fog. The tip of his tongue slid like a slug on to his cracked lip and Sigurd could almost hear the creak of his old trouser snake stiffening. There was no doubt that Frey, and not Óðin, held sway in this place.

'I am sure they are thirsty,' Guthrum said and the priest nodded, calling to make sure enough mead was brought out, and that was when Sigurd caught sight of what had held Valgerd's attention before. To their right, mounted on pegs that stuck out of the wall timbers, was a spear. A massive boar-hunter by the looks, but bigger than any spear Sigurd had ever seen. Its ash staff was three feet longer than the spears most men carried these days, certainly over eleven feet all told, and much of its length was bound in iron for protection in the chaos of the blood-fray. The blade itself was typical of the sort which most of the Svearmen favoured, being a broad leaf shape, and by the flickering light of a nearby lamp he could see the intricate runic inscriptions which gave such weapons power.

'Gungnir,' Asgrim rumbled in Sigurd's ear. 'The Swaying One. Óðin's own spear. A gift from the dwarfs whom men call the sons of Ívaldi.' Sigurd nodded, all but open-mouthed, for such a thing could not belong to anyone else but the Allfather whom men called the Spear-God.

'You have come to make an offering, Jarl Guthrum,' the priest said. A statement rather than a question.

The jarl nodded. 'Two offerings.'

This confused the old man but he nodded. 'Not thralls though,' he said.

'Enemies,' Guthrum said without looking at his prisoners. 'Worthy of the god.'

'And yet this is not the time for a blót,' the priest rasped, throwing an arm wide. 'You would need King Eysteinn's blessing and he is not here.'

Guthrum said nothing to that and so the old man took it up again. 'Assuming they have not offered themselves to Frey's knife,' he said, not looking at Sigurd and Floki, 'we would need to know who they are and the nature of their offence or crime.'

'They are Norse,' Guthrum said, and the old man's face twitched. 'They have wet their spears in Svear blood. They have made many widows. They tried to kill me in my sleep,' he added, making them sound like nithing would-be thieves and murderers. 'But it is not my wyrd to die in my bed.' The jarl glanced at the three gods sitting there, as if hoping they might give a sign to confirm his own prophecy.

'Will you allow me to honour the god and this temple?' he asked, turning back to the priest.

The priest looked at Valgerd and it was hard to tell if he was relieved or disappointed that she was not one of those on Jarl Guthrum's platter to be served up to the god. But the shieldmaiden was looking at Sigurd, her eyes cold and flint-sharp with this confirmation that Guthrum had come to Ubsola to make sacrifice. Not that any of it came as a surprise now.

'Young blood for the god. Hmm . . .' The Freysgodi pushed back his cowl in a cloud of dry skin which showed in the dusk light arrowing through the door. Like flour blown off a quern-stone. His white hair was cropped short and there was not much of it, so that the runes and whorls etched into his scalp and filled with greenish blue pigment were clearly visible, though their meaning was to Sigurd as unfathomable as the voices of the fish in the sea. 'I will ask the god if he is willing to accept your offering, Jarl Guthrum,' the old man said at last. Then he frowned. 'You have silver for the temple?'

'Of course,' Guthrum said. There was plenty of silver just in that torc round his neck.

'And for King Eysteinn?'

'Yes.'

'Then we will see,' the old man said with a nod.

'I left a fight to come here, priest,' Guthrum said, 'and I have not brought the god a bull or a ram, but men who are in the prime strength of their lives. I hope Frey will allow me to make the offering.'

The old man did not like that. It was not a threat but it uncloaked the issue about how decisions might be made in this temple, and as if to push the point Guthrum took a thick silver ring off his arm and handed it to the priest.

'For the mead,' the jarl said, and the old man kept his face straight as a spear but nodded again, accepting the payment. He had been a Freysgodi long enough to act as if that beautiful twisted silver ring was fair payment for fourteen cups of mead.

And neither was that mead anything special when it at last arrived, though that did not stop any of them from drinking it as if it had come from the Allfather's own barrel. Asgrim held a cup to Sigurd's lips and then did the same for Valgerd and Floki because of their hands being tied.

'Take Jarl Guthrum to the grove,' the priest told a boy whose hairless head was adorned with symbols and raised scars similar to the old man's. 'He can wait there until I have the god's answer.'

Guthrum seemed happy enough with this and they were being led to the place when Halvdan pushed his way through the other men to get close to Sigurd.

'Not the death you foresaw, hey?' he gnarred into Sigurd's ear with a grin that screamed to be knocked through the back of his skull. 'Thought you were special, didn't you? Strutting around up on that hill, safe behind a wall.' His breath smelt like rancid meat. 'Now look at you.'

'I'm not dead yet, Halvdan,' Sigurd said. 'It might be that the god does not want anything from your lord. Frey knows that Jarl Guthrum is too deep in the mire of his own fetid curse now and any favour will be as a drop of clean water in a lake of piss.'

Halvdan grinned. 'You saw what the jarl just paid for that ball-sweat mead,' he said. 'So we both know the old man will give Guthrum the right answer.'

A warrior called Hrok jutted his chin at Sigurd. 'At least he will find himself in Asgard with the Æsir,' he said, 'for that is where priest-killed men end up. Which of us can be sure of the same?'

'Hrok is right,' Asgrim said. 'Whereas I am certain to carve a reputation killing Jarl Guthrum's enemies, it would not surprise me if you fell off a cliff or shat yourself to death, Halvdan.' His warped mouth twisted into what was as close to a smile as he could manage. 'Ha! It would not even surprise me if you fell off your mead bench and cracked your skull open so that your brains leaked out in the floor rushes.'

'Well, I'd make sure they soaked your shoes, you ugly arse,' Halvdan said.

'And what about her?' another man put in, gesturing at Valgerd.

'Seems our jarl is keeping her for himself, which is a shame if you ask me,' Hrok answered as they came round the far side of the ting mound where meetings were held. 'I am thinking we should have earned more than piss-tasting ale fighting Alrik.'

'Tell Jarl Guthrum that,' Asgrim said, but of course Hrok was not going to do that and so that was the end of it as they followed a track down towards an enormous and ancient yew tree which filled their eyes. Its girth was more than fifty feet and its gnarled and twisted branches writhed off from the great contorted trunk in all directions, so that no one said another word as that yew tree, this place's very own Yggdrasil, filled the world and the sky before them.

'This is the sacred tree of Ubsola,' the boy said when they came under its reaching boughs and all of them turned their faces up to the dark green canopy. Even the boy seemed to be looking at the tree as if for the first time, and his pride and awe reminded Sigurd of himself one day many years ago, when his father had taken the great silver jarl torc from his own neck and put it around Sigurd's to let him feel its weight.

'It is not so heavy, Father,' Sigurd had said with all the swagger he had learnt from his father's warriors in the seven summers he had been alive.

'Then you will be a better jarl than I, for I find it heavier than a mountain,' his father had said, and Sigurd had not understood that then. He understood it now. Or at least he was closer to understanding, because warriors had sworn themselves to him and what had he given them in return? And now it seemed he would never wear the torc as his father had done.

'Have you ever seen a tree like it, Jarl Guthrum?' the boy asked, and Guthrum said he had not. 'If you had been here for the last blót you would have been greeted with a sight you would never forget,' the boy went on. 'All the jarls and chiefs of the Svear were here for the great Dísating, the Assembly of the Goddesses, and for nine days we celebrated with feasts and much drinking.'

'Ha!' one of Guthrum's men blurted, 'you must have been drinking your mother's milk the last time the Dísablót was held, lad!' But the boy took no notice for he was in spate now, gushing with it all.

'Each of the nine days a man was sacrificed, his blood given to the gods, along with many other male animals, until by the end of it seventy-two offerings were made.' He pointed a stick-like arm at the sprawling yew, some of whose boughs were still ringed with old frayed rope. 'In these branches and in the grove yonder were hung men, horses, dogs, rams and even a bull.'

By the mutterings they made it seemed some of Guthrum's men did not believe that about the bull, but the boy pushed on.

'This old tree creaked with her cargo while songs were sung and skalds told stories of the old times and men said they could hear the gods breathing because those lords of Asgard were here among us.'

'I have already hung in a tree for the gods and will not do it again,' Sigurd growled to Valgerd beside him, as the boy led them off towards the sacred grove. Once amongst those trees Jarl Guthrum fell to his knees, along with some of his hirðmen. Seven or eight other men could not stay there more than a few heartbeats and retreated in a way that would have been shameful had it been in the face of an enemy.

Sigurd might have left too if he could, for the grove was like no other place he had ever been. If a place could feel heavy, that grove did. It was silent and strange, the air still as clotted blood, and the trees, spruce and birch mostly, were undoubtedly imbued with the spirits of those beings which had been left hanging from their branches. Rotting a little more day by day.

For who could say how many years those trees' roots had fed on soil rich in human flesh, had drunk the rancid fluids of the dead? And they owned some power because of it.

Bones lay everywhere, too. They carpeted the ground, fragments of human skulls mixed with those of horses and a dozen other types of creature, and now the boy said nothing at all because there was no need.

Asgrim lifted his chin to Sigurd. 'If I ever see your friend again, the one who killed Beigarth, I will tell him where your bones lie,' he said in a voice that was a low rumble. 'So that he can come here to honour you and your young friend.'

Sigurd did not want to speak in that sacred place but words came to his lips anyway. 'I cannot say what the Norns have spun with the threads of Jarl Guthrum's wyrd, or even yours, Asgrim,' he said, 'but this I know, that if you meet Olaf again he will kill you. Guthrum too. So if I were you I would not waste my time telling him about bones or Ubsola or anything else.'

Guthrum hissed over his shoulder at them to be quiet and then they stood – or knelt – amongst the strangely divine trees and shades of the men who had hung in that darkening grove. And eventually the old Freysgodi himself came to deliver the god's verdict to Jarl Guthrum.

*

They slept in tents or under furs beneath the stars by the ting mound east of the kings' mounds. Not that Sigurd slept much. Nor did Valgerd or Floki, who watched Guthrum's men like a hawk, waiting for one of them to stray from his spear or axe. But there were always two men watching the prisoners and Sigurd began to think it would take the intervention of the gods themselves to stop their deaths come the next full moon. For that was when they would be sacrificed and their blood given to appease the gods and turn Guthrum's luck from sour to sweet.

'Frey will grant you his favour in return for the blood of these young warriors,' the Freysgodi had said, his old wet eyes slipping from the jarl to Sigurd and Floki, and Guthrum had let out a sigh of relief, his shoulders softening as though he had shrugged off a great burden.

There had been tears in the jarl's eyes when he arranged to deliver his gifts of silver to the temple and to King Eysteinn, and for his part the priest sent more skins bulging with mead to Guthrum's men who took their ease, sensing their lord's lightened mood and happy at the prospect of a few days lying around in the summer sun not having to fight anyone.

That day, traders from the village beyond the ridge to the south of the mounds arrived in dribs and drabs to hawk their wares to the strangers camped by the ting mound. They brought amber and leather, bone, cloth, glassware, sacks of wool and a hundred other types of thing which were of no use to a war band who were mostly travelling on foot and would have to carry whatever they bought. But they also brought food: cheeses and meats and fresh fish and strong-flavoured spices, and in this produce they did a brisk trade, Guthrum's men gorging themselves and making the most of their jarl's generosity.

Two days later another new face appeared in Guthrum's camp. Sigurd might not have noticed the young man had his ears not pricked up when the man introduced himself to Jarl Guthrum, saying he was a horse trader come to Ubsola to do business with

King Eysteinn. It was not the man's trade which caught Sigurd's attention but that he was clearly Norse, though he said he had been in Svealand now four summers. The man's thrall waited nearby, struggling to hold the reins of eight sturdy-looking ponies, and Jarl Guthrum told the Norseman that whilst the beasts did him credit he would be better off waiting for the king to return because Guthrum would not pay him what the ponies were surely worth.

'Besides, you do not have enough animals for all my men,' the jarl said. 'Even if I bought all eight from you, I would have to put up with plenty of moaning from those who still had to walk.'

The Norseman, whose name was Storvek, accepted this graciously but admitted that there was another reason why he had sought Jarl Guthrum out. 'I heard that you have some prisoners with you,' he said, fighting the urge to glance over to where Sigurd, Floki and Valgerd sat in the grass.

'Here we go,' Sigurd said under his breath.

'What of it?' Guthrum asked, his suspicions aroused now.

This young Storvek seemed embarrassed, scratching his thin beard as if having second thoughts about having brought the thing up at all.

'The truth is they are not my ponies but my father's,' he said. 'He is up in Vaksala, no doubt selling more than me, which he will be sure to crow about when we next meet.'

'Ah, so you're off proving yourself,' Guthrum said with a smile. He was already a different man since the news that he would be allowed to make his offerings to Frey.

Storvek nodded. 'I had two thralls until recently,' he said, thumbing over his shoulder. That would make more sense, Sigurd thought, glancing at the thrall who was being all but pulled off his feet by all those ponies. 'Well, they also belong to my father,' the young man admitted. 'And that is the problem.'

With a look Asgrim asked his jarl if he should throw this Storvek out of their camp but Guthrum shook his head at the champion and gestured for the Norseman to continue with his little saga.

'The thrall that you do not see was a wretched creature,' Storvek said, 'and one night I woke to find him having his pleasure with one of the mares.' He nodded towards the ponies. 'That chestnut one at the end.'

'Well who can blame him, for she is prettier than some women I have known,' Hrok said, grinning at Asgrim and Halvdan and some of the others who had one ear turned towards the conversation between their jarl and this Norseman.

'I was angry of course, as any man would be,' Storvek told Guthrum. 'I hit the thrall. I hit him hard.' He glanced at the others, bringing them in to his tale, and some of them nodded, agreeing that hitting the man was the right thing to do. Storvek shrugged. 'Next morning he was gone.'

'It sounds like you are better off without this horse-swiving thrall,' Jarl Guthrum said, which got some *ayes*.

'Else one day you might wake up to find he is riding you,' Asgrim put in, raising a laugh or two, though Storvek did not find it funny.

'My father will not be happy to be a thrall short. He will blame me,' he said, 'which is why I was hoping to come to some arrangement with the king. But he is not here and nor is there to be a slave market hereabouts for some weeks yet.' Now the young man's eyes flicked across to where Sigurd, Valgerd and Floki sat in the long grass. 'When I heard that you were travelling with prisoners I thought you might be willing to spare one of them, for a fair price.'

'That pretty chestnut mare perhaps,' Halvdan called, bringing upon himself a flurry of good-natured insults.

Storvek pointed at Sigurd. 'The one with the fair hair looks strong and capable,' he ventured. 'I am certain that my father would approve of him as a replacement for the thrall I lost. I dare say he would be an improvement, so long as he kept his snake in his breeks and not in our stock.'

Jarl Guthrum shook his head. 'They are dangerous, Storvek,' he said, 'even the woman. That fair-haired one would cut your throat while you slept. Don't ask me how I know this.'

'But—'

Guthrum had raised a hand to stop the man. 'I will not sell him to you,' he said. 'He and the black-haired one will be swinging from the branches of that tree soon enough. So you see I cannot help you.'

Storvek accepted this and thanked the jarl for hearing what he had to say, then turned and walked back to his ponies and his one thrall and that was that.

'Just think, you could have been a horse trader like him,' Black Floki said to Sigurd.

'And you could have been a king,' Sigurd replied. They both grinned then despite the ropes binding their hands, and the threads of their wyrds which led towards that great ancient yew tree whose evergreen branches had borne so much corpse-fruit since before the time of the first Svear kings.

And four days later Guthrum himself came to his prisoners with bread and cheese and a sense of the occasion which fitted him like that long brynja of his. Asgrim came too and crouched by the crackling fire, leering from that ugly face of his though there was no malice there. Not even Halvdan had any insults or blows for them this morning and it seemed all of Jarl Guthrum's warriors respected Sigurd and Floki for what they would soon endure. Even men such as they, who would put a spear in Sigurd's belly without a thought in a fight or just because their jarl ordered them to, saw it altogether differently if a man was to be lashed to a bench and slaughtered like a beast. And if furthermore all that was to be done in the sight of the gods and with ceremony and in cold blood.

'Will you face it like men?' Guthrum asked, warming his hands above the flames for the sun had yet to rise above the rim of the world in the east. Perhaps he was worried that they would ruffle the waters and embarrass him in front of the old priest and Thór,

Óðin and Frey. In front of his own men too, who were bound to have their doubts about following Guthrum these days, after how things were going at the borg against Alrik.

'I have told you, Jarl Guthrum, I will not die today,' Sigurd said.

'Which means I will not die today either,' Floki said, nodding at Sigurd, 'for I will die when he does.' This might have been funny had Sigurd's guts not felt like water, were his thoughts not being tossed like small boats on an angry sea. And even in the midst of that fear he could not get his mind fully off the spear mounted on the temple wall. Óðin's own spear from the time when he walked amongst men. Gungnir.

'You both spend too much time wondering what the gods have in store for you,' Valgerd told Sigurd and Guthrum. She was already eating the food Guthrum had put down before them, dipping the bread into a cup of ale to soften it. 'But the gods do not care. We are nothing to them.'

Not for the first time Sigurd wondered if Loki the trickster had had a hand in his falling in love with this woman who despised the gods. Who was as intent on ignoring them as Sigurd himself was on getting their attention. 'You are wrong,' he said. 'They watch us. They watch to see if we are worthy of our ancestors. The Allfather and Freyja, who is also the Lady of Battle, watch to see which of us will join their hirð in the afterlife to fight beside them at Ragnarök.'

Valgerd smiled but it was cold as a blade. 'If they watch us it is because they enjoy seeing us suffer. They sing when we are in pain. They laugh when we mourn.'

Guthrum visibly shuddered at her words and he was not alone. It was one thing to speak of the gods that way in a crowded meadhall, the words drowned in the drunken clamour of folk, but to say such things at an assembly place beside a Svear temple of such reputation? Sigurd wondered if Valgerd had just doomed him right then and there. If he were not doomed already.

'Well you are the lucky one, Valgerd,' Jarl Guthrum said after a moment's consideration, 'for let us be plain, you have seen how things have not gone well for me recently, what with that brigand Alrik proving to be like a wound that will not heal. But when this is done, and the god is appeased, you will be at my side to see my fortunes rise like an eagle into the sky.' Sigurd remembered the eagle he had seen in the sky above the kings' mounds and wondered if Guthrum had seen it too. The jarl used his knife to flick a charred stick back into the fire. 'Perhaps then you will swear an oath and become my hearthwoman,' he said without even looking at Valgerd.

'Do you want me in your shieldwall, Jarl Guthrum, or in your bed?' Valgerd asked him, and even a big jarl like Guthrum did not have the power to stop his cheeks flooding red. Asgrim grimaced, keeping his eyes on the flames. 'I am already sworn,' the shieldmaiden went on, 'and will not lay one oath upon another as if the words are no more than floor rushes, the new laid upon the old.'

'To whom are you sworn?' Guthrum asked, looking at her then.

'Does it matter?'

'No,' the jarl admitted, then he stood and tightened his sword belt. 'Though you may think differently about it by the end of the day.' *When your friends are corpses and their blood is pooled on the altar* is what he left unsaid.

'Funny how folk can smell blood even before it's spilled,' Asgrim said, changing tack for everyone's benefit, his ugly great head turned towards a knot of men and women who were trudging along the well-worn path towards the temple.

'The word is out then,' another of Guthrum's men called from the other fire around which most were gathered.

'Why wouldn't they come? It's not every day you get to see two men butchered for the Lords of Asgard,' another warrior said.

Sigurd looked back towards the eastern mound, his eyes searching the dawn sky which was thick with cloud the colour of unwashed wool. He was looking for the golden eagle, hoping for one more glimpse of it that would tell him that Óðin was still watching him. So Sigurd would know that he had not been forgotten.

But all he could see was cloud.

The temple was not full by any means but it was more than halfway to being so. As well as Guthrum and his thirty hirðmen there were two dozen local folk from the village beyond the ridge to the south of the mounds. They came in to the place wide-eyed and buzzing like swarming bees and almost trembling with the prospect of the sacrifice they had heard was to take place.

'We should kill them all if we get the chance,' Floki muttered when a fleshy-faced man and his wife proved brave enough to step up and press hands on him, wanting perhaps to touch what would soon be with the gods. 'Deal with Guthrum first of course, then every one of these other shits. We'll see how they stare then.'

The air was even thicker now than before, herbs and leaves smouldering in soapstone dishes all around the place, the scented smoke stinging Sigurd's eyes and clotting the room but at least masking the stench that always haunts a hall with so many bodies in it. Perhaps it was also meant to hide the copper tang of blood and the foul reek of the sludge which sometimes oozed from a man's bowels in death. The only light came from three lamps: iron bowls mounted on three legs and filled with fish liver oil from the smell of it, each of them with three wicks of twisted moss and all of them burning well. Three gods. Three priests. Three golden glows in the sweet-smelling murk.

Three sacrifices.

Sigurd did not know who the other victim was or what was his offence, but he looked as though he did not fully grasp what was going to happen to him. He was small and weak-looking and his beard was full of spittle but his eyes were not bright and sharp with terror as Sigurd would have expected. Instead they looked dull, dark and swollen as ripe bilberries, and Sigurd would have wagered that he had recently eaten those mushrooms which give men visions, and he remembered his own spirit journey when he had given himself to Óðin in the fetid swamp and Asgot had poured potions down his throat.

For the hundredth time Sigurd pulled, fighting the bonds which held his wrists tightly together, and for the hundredth time the rope proved too strong.

'Jarl Guthrum, you have come to the sacred temple at Ubsola to make an offering,' the old priest began in a voice stronger than he looked. No talk of Eysteinn's hall now, then. Perhaps the king had another place, a brighter hall where things lived rather than died.

'We have heard the will of Frey and you are welcome to make your offering,' the Freysgodi said, 'though only the god can say whether he will deem it worthy.' He frowned at Jarl Guthrum, who stood in his fine war gear, that brynja and that helmet with the eye guards which was so like Sigurd's own, wherever that was now. Guthrum and his men were unarmed, though, because the only blades allowed in the temple belonged to the men who looked least able to use them. For another cowled priest, a man thinner than mist, stood before the great statue of Frey, running a rune-bladed scramasax across a whetstone and muttering to the god while he worked. A third squatted in the corner, casting rune stones across an earthen floor scraped clear of straw.

'At least the knife will be sharp, hey Norseman,' Halvdan said, nodding towards the thin priest, to which Sigurd had a reply on the edge of his tongue, but then the boy-priest began a tune on a bukkehorn. Played it well too, the sound pure as spring water and sad as a hero's pyre in the rain.

'You understand this? That the god may yet refuse your offering, Jarl Guthrum?' the priest asked him.

Guthrum appeared to consider this for a while, and it seemed to Sigurd that the colour had drained from the jarl's face. Perhaps he was suddenly fearful of what might happen if, once given, the offering was rejected. Deemed unworthy. If that happened Guthrum might as well run and jump from a cliff's edge, his luck being what it was these days.

Eventually he nodded at the priest. 'I understand,' he said, lifting his voice above the horn music.

The priest spoke to the villagers then, some speech about Frey and the harvest and those folks' duties to their king who was off fighting to make peace as Frey would want it. Sigurd missed most of it because he was more concerned with his own wyrd and the very real, very sharp-looking knife which would soon cut it shorter than he had thought the Norns had in mind. He thought of his brothers Thorvard, Sigmund and Sorli waiting for him in Valhöll. He could see them in the eye of his mind, gathered round in the heroes' mead benches, laughing and boasting and filling a horn to overflowing for their little brother who would soon be with them. He thought of his father and hoped the jarl would not be disappointed with him, and he saw his mother's face too, and perhaps it would not be such a bad thing to be with them all again. To taste the afterlife for himself.

But then he thought of Runa who would soon be alone in the world, the last of their blood. He had promised he would not leave her. She would be so angry with him. And he thought of the oath-breaker King Gorm and how he would grin when he learnt that Sigurd was dead. That was the sourest of all the thoughts that swirled in his head like rotten brine amongst the ballast stones. If that priest's knife cut Sigurd's life thread now, he would never have his revenge.

The smoke wreathed round the roof support posts and billowed up in the rafters. It clogged dark corners and it filled Sigurd's lungs as he drew it deep inside with each long breath, trying to calm the trembling which had already announced itself in his knees and the big muscles of his thighs. He would not scream when the knife went in. Not because he feared to shame himself in front of these Svear priests and the nobodies who had come up from the village to watch him bleed, but because he knew that his father and brothers and all the other great warriors who used to drink beneath Eik-hjálmr's smoke-blackened beams would be watching too. Men such as Slagfid, his father's champion, and Svein's father Styrbiorn who had been an awe-inspiring warrior, as good as Slagfid on his day and when he was not too drunk to stand.

His mother, who had been the equal of any man alive and the better of most, would be watching too.

'Priest,' Floki called and the old man turned and scowled, for Floki had shouted over the man's incantations to the god, which he did not like at all, and neither did the other men and women in that hall judging by the intake of breath which sucked half the smoke from the place. 'You are old and feeble,' Floki said. 'Do you think the Allfather has need of a half-rotten worm like you?' Floki was grinning, which was strange given what was about to happen to him. 'Well you will find out this very night if there is a place for you in Óðin's hall,' he added as a murmur spread through the hall, and Guthrum nodded at Asgrim who twisted Floki's crow-black hair around his fist, yanked his head back and growled at him to hold his tongue.

'Do no damage,' the Freysgodi warned Asgrim, 'it would insult Frey if the offering was bleeding before the rites have properly begun.' Asgrim gnarred something else in Floki's ear, then stepped back, holding up a big hand to show he had not laid it on the young man.

'You already insult the Spear-God, priest!' Sigurd announced. 'You old fool. I am Óðin-favoured.'

That struck the godi like a stone to the forehead, but he recovered and looked at Jarl Guthrum, who had removed his helmet which he now held under his left arm. 'We do not have these problems at the Dísablót, Jarl Guthrum,' the priest said, 'though now and then men will throw an insult or two around. They think it hides their fear.'

129

'I am not afraid, priest,' Sigurd lied. He was very afraid but he hoped it did not show. 'I am not afraid because I am Óðin-favoured and this is not the night of my death.' The small prisoner whom Sigurd did not know gave a snickering laugh then, his neck twisting as those bilberry eyes followed an invisible bird's flight through the hall. He was off somewhere with the fairies that one.

Sigurd glared at the old man through the smoke, then turned his eyes on all the Svear folk gathered there and at the boy-priest who stood round-mouthed as a fish in the thwarts. The other priest, the one who had been sharpening the knife in front of the wooden gods, had stopped his work and was watching Sigurd now, but the godi on the floor with the runes was casting and gathering up, over and over again, his face the colour of cold hearth ash.

'No more from you, Norseman,' Jarl Guthrum shouted. 'Hold your tongue and face your death like a man. For your own reputation and that of your people.'

Sigurd laughed and people shrank back from it. 'Guthrum, you are like a ship whose sail has been blown out and whose steering oar has broken off,' he said. 'Every decision you make is wrong and your men die because of it.' Sigurd shook his head. 'And yet it is not your fault. Perhaps you were a great jarl once, but the gods have turned their backs on you. No, it is worse than that, they want to see you destroyed.'

'Enough!' the Freysgodi rasped, but Guthrum raised a hand to silence him and you would have thought that the old man had been slapped around the face with a cod fish, such was his expression at being told to hush in his own temple.

'Look around you, Norseman,' the jarl said, 'and tell me again which of us is doomed.'

It was a fair comment but Sigurd knew he must answer it.

'I am Sigurd Haraldarson. My father was a great jarl and my mother killed the man who tried to carry her from her home. I have killed more men than stand in this hall. One of them was a jarl himself. A man as powerful if not more so than you, Jarl Guthrum. I fought him and I killed him.' Sigurd glanced over at Valgerd, holding her eye for a moment, and she gave a slight nod, understanding that Sigurd was asking her to remember this moment in order to give an account of it to Olaf and the others and to Hagal Crow-Song who would make sure to put it in Sigurd's saga.

Then Sigurd turned back to Guthrum, who to his credit was all ears, when Sigurd supposed the jarl could have ordered someone to stuff a cloth in his mouth to hush him. 'Near a place called Tau I gave myself to the Allfather. I hung in a twisted tree for nine nights, starved and half dead.' In truth it had been six nights and it was not a sacred yew tree or a mighty ash such as in the stories of Óðin's own self-sacrifice, but rather a stunted and half-rotten alder. But as Hagal Crow-Song would say, if you're going to tell a good story, the last thing you should ruin it with is the truth.

'I live because the Hanged God wanted it so,' Sigurd told them all. 'Sometimes the gods walk amongst us, for they enjoy being close to death because their own lives are so long and almost never-ending.' He raked his eyes across them all, warrior, farmer and priest alike. 'Believe me when I say that the gods would rather spend a day with one wolf on the hunt than with fifty grazing sheep. And if you believe that I am a killer then let me tell you that my friend here is death itself.' He nodded at Floki, who grinned at them all, which was more effective than saying a word by the look of the hands clutching Thór's hammers and the other amulets which folk wore round their necks. And with that Sigurd dipped his head at Guthrum and then at the priest, as if to say there would be no further interruptions as far as he was concerned.

Jarl Guthrum pulled his fair beard through his fist and cocked an eyebrow. 'I told you my offerings were worthy of the god,' he told the priest, getting some chuckles from his men, as well he might for that was as good a counterstroke as any champion ever made with a sword.

The old man blinked his yellowed eyes and creaked an order at which two thralls came forward and grabbed hold of the small man who, it seemed, would be the first to feel the knife. They were big men these thralls, their thick necks straining against the iron collars, cropped hair like birds' nests, and surely they were more used to building walls, digging peat, spreading manure and herding pigs and goats than hauling men across that hall under the gaze of the gods towards the priest's knife. And yet they did it as if it were the only work they knew, laying the man upon that beautifully carved table which sloped because the legs at one end were shorter by a thumb than those at the other.

They did not use ropes. Didn't need to. The little man lay there gentle as a lamb as the old Freysgodi communed with the Æsir. No doubt men went to their deaths more easily when their spirits were soaring beyond the confines of the flesh, and the priest spoke his words and the Svear looked on in silence because the gods were amongst them. Then the reed-thin godi moved through the billowing smoke and came to stand beside the man's head at the high end of the table, and Sigurd suddenly understood why the table sloped.

Gods that knife was sharp. As it should have been after the time spent on its edge. It went in easily and sliced outwards, cutting open the man's throat just like that. The boy-godi stood at the foot end with a silver-lipped drinking horn and he did not have to wait long, the blood running along unseen channels in the table's surface and out of a hole carved to look like a raven's beak.

They will have to turn him the other way round if they want to fill that horn, Sigurd thought. But he was wrong, which showed what he knew about it. And when it was done the thralls lifted the body off the table and carried it out of the hall where they must have dumped it on a cart because they were straight back in.

We will all be strung up from that old tree together then, Sigurd thought as the thralls went over to Floki.

But the old priest shook his head. 'That one,' he told them, pointing a finger at Sigurd, who lifted his chin and glared at them with all the defiance he could muster.

You would think I was waist-deep in some fjord for how my legs are trembling, he thought, hoping that Valgerd had not noticed them. He would pay a silver hoard for some of Asgot's bitter draught now, or some of the mushrooms the other man had eaten, but then he forced such shameful thoughts from his mind. Let them all see him face the blade like a warrior, for he was no less than his brothers who waited for him in the hereafter. Let these Svearmen watch and drink their fill of it. Fuck them. And if Óðin had forsaken him after everything, fuck him too.

The big thralls took an arm each and Sigurd's feet barely stirred the straw as they carried him over to the table upon which the last man's blood was already beginning to thicken in the smoky warmth. He wanted to tell Floki that he was sorry. He wanted to tell Valgerd other things, things that she might laugh to hear. But he said nothing.

The old priest gestured to Jarl Guthrum for help and the jarl sent Asgrim forward, and the big man took hold of Sigurd's ankles with a grip like Fenrir's fetters. It seemed the Freysgodi had his doubts that Sigurd would accept the knife in his throat as calmly as the last man had.

'Lord Frey, who governs the sun and the rain and all the fruitfulness of the earth. Who brings about the prosperity of men. Lord of peace and plenty, accept this offering given by Guthrum son of Guthfrith, who is a generous lord and a renowned warrior amongst your people.' The old man nodded and hissed at the boy at the foot of the table but he needn't have, because the boy was ready, standing there with another drinking horn. 'Frey, grant Jarl Guthrum your favour in return for this young warrior's blood.' His voce was all rasp, dry as the smoke which had folk coughing and muttering, though no one dared to open the hall's door for fear of breaking the spell which the Freysgodi wove.

Sigurd turned his head to look at Valgerd. If he was about to make the long journey to the afterlife then he would do it with her face in his mind. Yet in his peripheral vision he saw the thin godi come close. Saw that wickedly sharp knife in his hand, sensed the blade coming closer to the bare skin of his neck. His throat.

'Óðin!' he roared and at that moment through the blur of smoke he saw Valgerd kick the iron legs of the lamp stand, saw the air glisten wetly from the impact, then saw the whole thing falling. Shrieks ripped through the smoke as the great iron dish flung its oil and flaming moss wicks across the crowd and then a great flash lit the hall as the oil itself burst into liquid fire.

Sigurd twisted and grabbed hold of the hand gripping the knife, then rammed the whole lot up into the priest's face and pulled it back. Screaming, the man let go the knife and Sigurd slashed it across the nearest thrall's neck, then plunged it into the old Freysgodi's chest and it went in and came out quick as a bird in flight sipping from a lake.

The other thrall threw himself out of reach and then Sigurd's arms were free. So were his legs, for Asgrim had run to help his jarl whose cloak was on fire, and the place was chaos because the men and women were burning and the dry straw was burning and fire was the new god in that temple.

Sigurd was standing now and before him was the boy-priest, still holding the empty drinking horn, rooted to the spot like those old wooden statues, his mouth hanging open.

'Cut the rope, boy,' Sigurd told him, handing him the knife by its pretty bone hilt. More hot light flared. More screams because Valgerd had knocked over another oil lamp and fire hurtled along the straw-strewn ground as far as the Frey statue with its enormous prick which would be a firebrand before long. 'Told you I was Óðin-favoured,' Sigurd said to the boy.

The boy took the knife and a heartbeat later Sigurd's hands were free and he took the knife back and yelled at Floki who turned to him, his face sheeted in blood. On the floor beside him knelt a man grasping at his own neck, trying to stop the blood which was spewing everywhere because Floki had ripped the man's throat open with his teeth. 'Kill them,' Sigurd called, throwing the knife to Floki who caught it easily.

Then Floki was killing.

Sigurd stumbled through the smoke, not towards the door at which folk thronged, shoving and fighting each other to get out, but towards Gungnir, Óðin's own spear, which drew him to it. He reached up and lifted the spear from its mounts, its massively thick ash staff filling his hands like a man's spear in the grip of a small boy. And he turned to face two of Guthrum's hirðmen who had kept their heads in the shrieking, flaming, smoke-filled madness, and perhaps they thought they were heroes.

The first died because Sigurd swept the spear across and its long blade tore open his throat. The other man leapt forward but Sigurd brought the shaft up fast as thought, cracking it into the warrior's chin with a splintering of bones. The man fell and that was him done, and Sigurd turned because the other temple thrall was there like a troll from the mist and he got his big hands on the spear before Sigurd could use the blade against him. He was strong as an ox, this one, and Sigurd knew he could not hold on to the thing. The thrall was grinning because he knew it too, but suddenly Valgerd was there and she threw her bound hands over the thrall's head and hauled back so that the rope caught round his neck and his eyes bulged with the surprise of it. The thrall's hands let go of the spear to reach for the rope, and Sigurd stepped back and thrust the blade into his belly, twisting it before pulling it free of the sucking flesh.

As the thrall fell to his knees clutching his death wound, Sigurd peered through the smoke to see Asgrim beating men aside, ploughing his way through the press to get Guthrum out of that fiery maelstrom. Others were trying to escape Floki who was more dangerous than the flames, stabbing and slashing at anything that moved, plunging that knife into flesh again and again.

'Show me the other way out of here, boy,' Sigurd called, sawing the spear blade through Valgerd's bonds. The boy nodded and led them through the choking gloom past the three statues to the north wall where, in the corner, there was another door. The boy opened the door and it drew the smoke and flame so that for a moment they were caught in a cloud of breathless heat.

'Floki!' Sigurd yelled, then he saw that Floki was beside him, grinning like a blood-fed fiend, and together they followed the boy-priest out into the night.

CHAPTER SEVEN

THE MOON WAS A FLOOD OF SILVER IN THE NIGHT, MAKING IT BRIGHTER than it had been inside the temple, at least before Valgerd's fire had bloomed in the darkness. Valgerd and Floki looked to Sigurd who gripped Gungnir as if he would fight the whole world with it if needs be. But they could hear Jarl Guthrum's men shouting on the other side of the hall, gathering their weapons and looking for those who had turned this night on its head. The village folk were running off into the night, terrified of men and gods and fire.

'You!' someone shouted. They turned to the voice and saw a man sitting on his pony beneath the eaves at the southern end of the hall.

'That horse trader,' Floki said, as the man trotted up to them followed by his thrall, who hurried behind on foot, leading the other ponies.

'Mount and follow me,' this Storvek said.

Just then two of Guthrum's warriors came round the side of the hall, one of them yelling back to the rest that he had found the prisoners.

'The knife?' Sigurd asked Floki.

'In someone's head,' Floki replied, looking at the two men who were striding towards them, spears levelled.

Storvek pulled a sword from the rolled-up furs behind his saddle, slipped from the pony's back and ran at Guthrum's men. The nearer one lunged and Storvek twisted, beating the spear wide before bringing his sword up in an underarm cut which hacked the man open from his left hip to his right shoulder. Before Guthrum's man had fallen Storvek turned and parried the other man's spear, then plunged his sword into the man's belly, doubling him over before hauling the blade out.

'We should go now,' he said to Sigurd, breathing heavily. Sigurd glanced at the boy-priest who stood there staring at him as if Sigurd had just dug his way out of one of those burial mounds nearby.

'Tell Jarl Guthrum that Sigurd Haraldarson is Óðin-favoured,' he said to the boy, who nodded, unblinking. Then all of them, including the thrall, mounted and rode off along the moon-washed path past the kings' mounds, the shouts and bellows of their enemies following them on the breeze.

Storvek led them east along a track beside which some Svear king, many years ago by the looks, had stuck posts in the ground, each eighteen feet from the next. Huge pine trunks they were, like ships' masts, twenty-five feet high or more so that they towered above the riders, dark against the silvery sky. Foreboding too, like giants keeping watch over the land.

'Have you ever seen anything like this?' Valgerd asked, looking up at each one they passed. They seemed to go on for ever, those posts, and Sigurd had lost count somewhere after one hundred.

'Whoever put them in the ground wanted everyone to know his name,' Sigurd said.

'And yet we do not know his name,' Floki pointed out, 'which just goes to show that you can make a better-lasting reputation with the blade than by digging holes and putting tree trunks in them.' No one could argue with that and when eventually they came to the last post they turned off the track towards a pine wood.

There was no sign that they were being followed, which did not come as a surprise because Guthrum's men had not been prepared, their horses being back in the camp, and the five rode on amongst the trees, talking little so that they could listen out.

'Why are you helping us?' Sigurd asked Storvek after a while. It was a good time to ask the question as they had slowed to let their mounts pick their way across a shallow stream. The three spare ponies had followed dutifully, so at least the young man would not get into trouble with his father for losing their stock. If the man really *was* a horse trader. From the way he had handled himself against Guthrum's men, Sigurd suspected there was more to this Storvek than he had let on to the jarl.

'You looked like you needed a friend,' Storvek said, 'since it seems even the gods do not want you. What happened in there?'

Sigurd had no answer to that. Not yet, not until he had given it some thought and unravelled the chaos of it. For Óðin's hand must have been in it, meaning Sigurd had not lost the god's favour after all. *And now here I am carrying your spear, Allfather*, he thought, a sudden shiver running up the back of his neck. He had killed men with that sacred spear which he held couched beneath his right arm, the shaft crossing over the pony's back, so that the animal could see the long blade out of its left eye.

'Besides,' Storvek went on, seeing that he wasn't going to get an answer to his last question, 'if I help you then perhaps it will help me.' He tugged the reins, turning his mount on to what looked to be nothing more than an animal track through the drifts of old bark and pine needles. There were many dead pines scattered amongst the green trees; barkless and pale they gleamed in the silvered dark, like the ghosts of ancestors watching over the living. Something made Sigurd look over his shoulder and from the deeper shadows of the pines a pair of animal eyes glowed orange and green. A bear perhaps, watching these intruders to make sure they did not linger in his part of the forest.

'So where are we going?' Valgerd asked their guide just as Sigurd opened his mouth to ask the same thing.

'I know of a place where we can rest,' Storvek said, 'then . . .' he shrugged, 'then we will see what tomorrow brings.'

Valgerd glanced at Sigurd and he saw suspicion in her eyes. She wore breeks and a long green tunic belted at her waist and her hair was mostly loose but for two golden braids which fell either side of her face. It was no wonder that Jarl Guthrum hoped she would swear his oath and join his war band, that he had wanted to keep her close to him. Not that you would have known she was a warrior at first glance now, and Sigurd knew her well enough to imagine how vulnerable she felt without her war gear: her brynja and helmet, her bow, scramasax, shield and sword. Floki must have felt all but naked too, without the tools of his trade. Without the blades with which he was a master, god-touched himself perhaps and if so by Týr, Lord of Battle, or even some darker, more vicious god.

'Did you see Jarl Guthrum's cloak catch fire?' Floki asked, his face full of awe. 'Must have been newly greased for it went up like the flames from Völund's forge. Now *there* is a man whose luck has gone. I would not like to be one of his hearthmen now.'

'The ones with ambition will desert him,' Sigurd said. 'He is cursed if you ask me.'

'Unlike you, hey?' Valgerd said. 'Sigurd Haraldarson! The man over whom the Allfather holds his own shield! Ha!' She was teasing him and he did not like it much.

'Say what you like but you do not see me hanging from that old tree the Svear love so much,' he said.

Valgerd snorted. 'The reason you and Floki are not bloodless corpses swinging from that tree has nothing to do with the gods and everything to do with me,' she said. 'Who was it that set Jarl Guthrum on fire?'

'You could have set him on fire sooner,' Sigurd said, 'instead of leaving it until I could feel the cold edge of that priest's knife on my skin.'

'Perhaps I was waiting to see if the Spear-God would come down from his hall and kill that old priest for you,' Valgerd said through a curl of lips. She was still teasing him but it got Sigurd thinking. He had certainly killed the old godi and most probably the thin one too, and he wondered at the wisdom of that, for men did not kill priests if it could be avoided.

'Or perhaps it was Óðin who put the idea into your head to knock over that lamp,' Sigurd replied with a smile of his own.

'Ah, so that is what happened,' Storvck said. 'I wish I had been inside that temple to see it. I'd wager Jarl Guthrum did not look so haughty with his cloak on fire.'

'It is a shame in a way for I was looking forward to killing him,' Floki said.

Sigurd knew that if he said they should turn and go back to kill Guthrum and fight his men, Floki would pull his horse round with a grin on his face.

'Not far now,' Storvek said.

Neither was it. Sigurd smelt the smoke before he saw the steading. It stood in a clearing on the edge of the forest with a steep meadow behind leading up to rocks and more trees. The longhouse itself was modest but well kept, the sort of place where you would find a clever karl who knows his husbandry, and his hard-working family along with four or five thralls. There were outbuildings too, all pine-log-built like the house itself and thatched with turf, including a byre for the animals, a grain store and a smokehouse whose hanging treasures had Sigurd's mouth watering from a spear-throw away. With the place smelling as sweetly as that it was no surprise there was a bear living nearby, he remarked to Floki as they rode up to the farmstead, and Storvek told them to wait while he went to speak with the farmer.

'It is only fair to warn the man and his wife that they will be playing the hosts,' the young man said.

'You expect him to be less than happy about it, then?' Floki said, for having dismounted Storvek had taken the sword from its sheath of rolled blankets.

Storvek looked at the sword and smiled. 'Habit,' he said, walking off.

'Still, they will not be happy being woken in the middle of the night and faced with three Norse strangers,' Valgerd said. Sigurd could not disagree, but there would be some way he could repay these folk for the comfort of a bed of furs and a plate of whatever smoked meat he could get his teeth into.

Storvek had barely knocked when someone opened the door, which Floki said was strange given that the husband and wife should have been snoring in their blankets.

'Could have heard us coming,' Sigurd suggested as the door closed behind the young Svearman, for one of the ponies had nickered and snorted softly as they had approached, which had in turn raised a few snorts from the pigs in the byre.

They waited long enough for Valgerd to say she did not have a good feeling about this and that maybe they should ride off now even if it meant stealing Storvek's ponies and repaying him so badly.

Sigurd twisted in his saddle to look at Storvek's thrall. The man's face was white as the moon and he was shaking too by the look of it. Just a slight tremble in his thigh which, along with his white knuckles as he clutched his reins, did not bode well so far as Sigurd was concerned.

'What's wrong with you, then?' he asked the thrall.

The man shook his head.

'Answer him before I rip your tongue out and make it flap without you,' Floki said.

'It . . . it is a trap,' the thrall said, his voice barely more than a whisper. Just then a horn sounded and the door of the house opened and warriors were spilling out.

'Fuck,' Floki gnarred, and Sigurd looked round to see that men were coming out of the cattle byre too, clutching spears or axes but otherwise in their under clothes, the horn blast having woken them.

And in Valhöll the gods laughed.

*

Spear and axe blades held the moonlight as men closed in on them like a knot being drawn tight, and in a matter of heartbeats they were surrounded by thirty or forty warriors.

'Hold,' Sigurd said, for unarmed as Valgerd and Floki were there was no point in trying to fight or even run, yet he gripped Gungnir as though he would sooner be cut down than let go of the thing.

'Thought he'd be bigger,' one of the warriors said, eyeballing Sigurd.

'Don't need to be big when you've got the gods on your side,' another said in a mocking voice, and it was not what they said but the way they said it which made Sigurd growl the foulest of curses. These warriors had been watered by the same rain as he, had grown strong on fish pulled from the same fjords and boar hunted in the same forests.

They were Norsemen.

A big man came forward, parting the others like a dragon ship's bow through the sea, and the silver-panelled helmet he wore told Sigurd everything he needed to know. A boy came with him, all fair hair and a face full of spite as he stared at Sigurd, who would have wagered a helmet of hacksilver on the boy being the man's son.

'Hrani Randversson,' Sigurd said, the name itself tasting like poison in his mouth.

'Sigurd Haraldarson,' Hrani said, removing his helmet so that Sigurd could get a proper look at his moon-washed face. It was Hrani who had brought death to Skudeneshavn, Sigurd's home on the southern tip of Karmøy. And it was on that raid that one of Hrani's men had killed Sigurd's mother. And yet anyone who knew Sigurd or Hrani knew that the hatred between them was mutual. Every man in that clearing could feel it hanging in the air like a cold fog. For Sigurd had killed Hrani's father in a ship fight in the shadow of Jarl Randver's own hall which men called Örn-garð, the Eagle's Dwelling-Place.

'I always knew we would come face to face again,' Hrani said. He was a big man, solid as an oak and every inch a warrior. But men said of Hrani that he had a cruel streak as wide as a fjord is deep, which was something they never said of his father Jarl Randver.

'So you are jarl now,' Sigurd said. Hrani nodded. 'Then you should thank me for cutting your father's throat. The crabs in your fjord should thank me too for giving them a feast.'

Hrani's teeth flashed in his beard but he kept a hold of his temper. 'When we heard that you were to be slaughtered like a goat at the Svear temple I was disappointed.'

Sigurd's eyes flicked to the man standing at Hrani's left shoulder and recognized Kjartan Auðunarson, who had flown from the borg to take news of Sigurd's whereabouts to Hrani. He had done well by it too, judging from the two silver rings glinting at the ends of his moustache ropes.

'I was disappointed and I was angry because I had always thought I would have my revenge,' Hrani said. 'I drank to it and dreamt of it many times, but the way things turned out I did not think it would be wise to start a war with this King Eysteinn over it. Let the Svear priests butcher you then, I thought. Let them hang your corpse in their tree for the crows.' He lifted his big sword, pointing it at Sigurd. 'So as you can imagine, I am surprised to see you.' With that he pulled a twisted silver band from his wrist and tossed it to Storvek who caught it and flashed a smile. Since he had failed in persuading Jarl Guthrum to sell Sigurd to him, Storvek must have hung around like a fly around blood, waiting for the priests to do their work so that he could at least take news of Sigurd's death back to his lord. And yet he had been wise enough to keep his horses nearby just in case.

'Well here I am, Hrani,' Sigurd said. 'Let us fight here and now. And when I have killed you as I killed your father, your men will let us go.' It was worth throwing that challenge at the man's feet for it would be hard for a jarl not to pick it up with his men watching, and to Sigurd a fighting chance was better than what he expected from Randver's son.

'Kill him, Father!' the boy said, pointing his own short sword at Sigurd. 'Spill his guts and put out his eyes for what he did to grandfather.'

And if words could drip hatred . . .

'As much as I am stiff between the legs at the thought of gutting you,' Hrani told Sigurd, 'I am not the kind of man who wolfs down a meal without tasting it. No, Haraldarson, I will take you back to Hinderå so that my people can watch you die.' He grimaced. His son spat a curse. 'Your reputation has grown. I do not mind that,' the jarl said, 'because by killing you my own fame will swell too.'

'Frey, who is the god most of these Svearmen seem to love even above the Allfather himself, could not kill Sigurd this very night,' Floki told Hrani. 'But you think you can?'

Hrani considered this. Then he walked up to Floki and swung his sword, hacking into Floki's pony's neck. The animal screeched and toppled and Floki fell with it, then scrambled clear of the thrashing beast whose blood pumped on to the ground in great hot gouts.

'Tie him,' Hrani said, pointing his gore-stained sword at Floki. 'The shieldmaiden too.'

Some of his men pulled Valgerd from her mount while others took hold of Floki and another warrior ran off to the byre where he said he'd seen some rope. Then Hrani walked back to where Sigurd still sat on his pony, the enormous spear across him.

'Where did you get that?' the jarl asked.

'He came from the temple with it,' Storvek said, filling the silence which Sigurd left. 'The Svear folk say it once belonged to Óðin.'

Hrani's eyes grew wide at that. Of course they would, for there was not a jarl alive who would not want to own a spear which men believed was in some distant time wielded by a god.

'Give it to me,' Hrani said.

Sigurd threw a leg over the pony's back and slid down, and Hrani's men bristled, bringing their own weapons up in readiness for some madness. Sigurd lifted the spear to his shoulder and felt the muscles in his arm bunch and swell in readiness to launch that great weapon. If Hrani wanted it then he would give it to him. He would plant it in the jarl's chest and that would be the end of Hrani Randversson.

'No, Sigurd,' Valgerd said.

His heart was thumping and the sound in his ears was like the roar of the surf against a craggy headland. He turned and hurled the spear with all his strength and it flew as if from the hand of a god and even if Kjartan Auðunarson saw it coming he could do nothing about it. The long blade cut straight through Kjartan's chest, taking the man backwards with its flight so that he fell but did not hit the ground. Instead he hung there with a foot of shaft in him, pinned by the spear, his back a hand-span from the dry earth and his arms flopping uselessly either side.

If Hrani was impressed by the throw he did not show it as he walked over to the pinned man, crouched and sawed the ends of Kjartan's moustache ropes off because he would have those silver rings back. He took back the newly given arm ring too. Then he stood and showed them to Sigurd. 'I never liked that man,' he said. 'He left my hall for Svealand because he did not think I should wear the jarl torc. Whoreson soon came running back when he saw a chance to get rich.' He nodded. 'You have saved me some silver there, Haraldarson.' He kept the arm ring but handed the hair and smaller rings to another man, telling him to work the silver from the braid, then ordered his men to bind Sigurd's hands nice and tight, which they did. Then Hrani sheathed his sword, went back to his pinned hearthman and, taking hold of the spear's shaft, put his foot on Kjartan's chest and shoved the body down to the ground before pulling the blade from earth and flesh.

'I have never seen such a spear as this,' he said, 'not even in my grandfather's day when men liked their spears longer. Thank you for bringing it to me, Haraldarson.'

'I hope you can run with it,' Sigurd said, 'for when this Svear king, Eysteinn, learns that a Norse war band has the thing, you will be haring back to your hall if not lying in a worm-ridden grave pit with your hirðmen.'

'The Ubsola folk will have sent word to their king that the spear is stolen,' Storvek told Hrani. He nodded at the three prisoners. 'And Jarl Guthrum will be looking for them, if he is not burnt to death,' he added, glancing at Valgerd. 'Once the Svearmen see that we have them, they will surely know that we have their spear too.'

A man with a huge belly and a long-hafted axe shook his head at his jarl. 'It would be a bloody thing to fight our way back to the sea, Hrani,' he said. He was old enough to see little glory in being savaged all the way back to the coast and was not afraid to speak his mind. He tilted the axe head towards Sigurd. 'I will do it gladly for the sake of taking that troll's turd back to Örn-garð, for I as much as any man want to see your father avenged. But what need have we for that spear?' No doubt he had been Jarl Randver's man before Hrani's, and it surely chafed the new jarl that these voices from the past still lingered.

'You have grown soft, Bjorgolf,' Hrani said, 'which we can all see for ourselves.' The warrior glowered at that but held his tongue. He knew that Hrani, who was a warrior in his prime as well as his jarl, would have the better of him in a fight. 'But I am not a fool, Bjorgolf, and do not intend to start a blood feud with this Svear king. Nor would it be clever to risk the Allfather's anger, for if this spear belonged to Óðin he is likely to make sure no good comes to the man who steals it from the Svearmen.' He lifted Gungnir high so that all of his warriors could see it well, its blade catching the moon glow. 'I will sell this spear back to them. To King Eysteinn or the temple priests or even to Sigurd's friend Jarl Guthrum. Any man with a brain in his skull will choose to trade rather than fight us for it.'

And that was true, Sigurd thought, because now it seemed all of Hrani's men had gathered in the clearing and there must have been fifty of them. And they were not farmers either but hardened Sword-Norse, men who had stood in the shieldwall and soaked the earth with the slaughter's dew. Such a war band was not to be taken lightly, even by a king.

Hrani's boy grinned. Clearly he was proud of his father's great wisdom.

'Come, Randver, let us drink some ale to celebrate,' Hrani said to the lad. *Named in honour of the crab-feast jarl then*, Sigurd thought, knowing he had yet another enemy in that boy, albeit one not yet old enough to sprout down upon his cheeks. 'I want a proper watch set until daybreak,' Jarl Hrani announced, then turned and walked back towards the longhouse, the Óðin spear resting on his shoulder and his boy walking behind.

'I am beginning to think Asgot was right when he said that Loki the mischief-monger has joined this game,' Floki said, watching Hrani walk away.

Sigurd tested the rope which bound his wrists. There was no give in it and the knot would have kept a longboat at its mooring in a storm. He cursed the Æsir under his breath, not caring if Thór hurled a spear of lightning down to pierce him as he himself had skewered Kjartan.

Because the gods were playing games and he was a prisoner again.

They stayed at the farmstead another four days and in that time Sigurd never caught sight of the karl who owned it nor his family nor even the dogs you would expect to see around the place, sleeping in the shade or sniffing for deer and boar.

'I'd wager they are all buried together in a hole in the woods,' Valgerd said when Sigurd brought it up, which seemed a reasonable assumption given who was sleeping in the farmer's bed, eating his smoked meats and drinking his ale.

But it was not for these home comforts that Jarl Hrani had decided to stay there a few days more. Rather it was because he wanted to let the Svear folk miss their sacred spear awhile before he gave them the chance to see its return, and it was Storvek whom he tasked with going back to the temple ahead of them. The young man would tread gently to discover who out of some godi or king's man, or even King Eysteinn himself if he were thereabout, would pay the most to get the spear back.

Then at dawn on the fifth day Jarl Hrani's patience snapped like a hemp line and hook snagged on the sea bed. 'Storvek has had enough time to find a buyer,' he announced to anyone in earshot.

They emptied the smokehouse of the last of its tasty treasure and put it into sacks along with the salted meat from the animals they had slaughtered themselves. The ale was long gone and so was the cheese and skyr, but they went about milking the cows, goats and sheep until bucket after bucket was filled before being emptied into the ale skins which bulged by the end of it. All of this was loaded on to the ponies and they set off southward through the forest to Ubsola.

They were fifty men in all their war-gear glory. Twelve owned brynjur and more wore steel helmets than hardened leather skull caps and all carried painted shields or had them slung across their backs. They walked through that Svealand forest with the assured swagger of men who have little to fear. Even little Randver Hranisson carried himself like a champion-killer, so that Sigurd wondered what kind of man he would grow to be, if he survived into manhood. And yet, confident as Hrani was in his hirð's ability to deal with any threat that they might encounter, he was not so arrogant that he neglected to send two men ahead on ponies to make sure he did not walk into some other war band, either Jarl Guthrum's or the king's or that of some hersir with a thirst for plunder and fame. So when those riders came trotting back through the pines with faces as white as marsh-grass flowers and Thór's hammer amulets warm from the clutching of them, Hrani put his beautiful silver helmet on and waited for the bad news.

'Jarl Hrani, there is something on the track less than one rôst from here,' one of them said, glancing over his shoulder like a man who fears his own shadow.

'A trap?' Hrani asked.

The other rider shook his blond braided head. 'I don't know, lord. I saw no one.' He glanced at his companion. 'No one alive, anyway.'

'But someone knows we are coming,' the first man said. 'And knows the course we are taking through this forest.' He was breathing hard, too hard for that little trot, and the hand which was not on the reins was on the little silver Mjöllnir hanging upon his chest.

'So what is it?' the jarl asked, nodding into the forest beyond the mounted men.

'It is better if you see for yourself, Hrani,' the man said, 'but if you ask me there is some seiðr at work. Perhaps we have angered the Allfather,' he dared, though he did not mention the spear in his jarl's hand. He did not have to.

'You two have forgotten your fathers' faces,' Hrani said, 'to be shaking like old hounds about something you do not even have the balls to talk about. I should have sent my son ahead, for he would not be pissing in his breeks like you.'

Some of his men laughed at this but the two riders did not, as Hrani ordered his men to form into a column two abreast and with shields up and spears ready. 'If it is a trap whoever set it will know we have seen it and must surely expect us to take another path through the trees,' Hrani said. 'So it is on that other path that they will be waiting.' He shook his head. 'But I do not think it is a trap. We will keep going this way and we will see what has got Bild and Erlingnar's arses singing like a pair of bukkehorns.' He pointed at Sigurd, Floki and Valgerd, who were near the front of the column. 'Whatever happens keep your eyes on them. Haraldarson will not wriggle off my hook as he did Jarl Guthrum's.'

There was no talking as they moved along the track, their eyes searching the forest and their guts looser than they had been before, as is the way of it when men half expect a fight.

'Guthrum?' Valgerd said under her breath.

'Doubt it,' Sigurd said. 'Not without help anyway. He doesn't have enough spears.'

'Thirty can beat fifty if the fifty are not expecting it,' Floki said, 'but this lot are ready for Ragnarök.'

They knew they had reached the place when they heard a clamour of *kowws* and a murder of crows clattered off through the trees. It was a sound to chill a man's blood, the song of the slaughter field after a battle.

Jarl Hrani raised the Óðin spear to halt the column, his neck twisting and that beautiful helmet glinting in the shafts of sunlight filtering through the trees as he turned this way and that, looking for the ambush that wasn't there. His men were mumbling curses and invoking the gods' protection. Some were spitting in disgust or shaking their heads and all gripped spear shafts and axe hafts with white hands. Twenty feet away a stake had been stuck in the ground and on it was rammed a man's head, the mouth and eyes open as if in shock. The crows had not yet ruined the eyes but the flies were feasting. They swarmed thickly around the severed neck and fed on the congealing dribbles that had cascaded down the length of the stake. It was Storvek's thrall, or at least it had been. Sigurd had not learnt the man's name, not that it mattered now.

The rest of the thrall was scattered amongst the pines: an arm hanging here, a leg there, and all of that flesh buzzing with flies so that you only had to let your ears follow the hum to find another bit strung up amongst the sweeping green boughs or the brittle brown lower branches.

'Show yourself!' Hrani roared into the forest. 'Where are you, coward?' His voice was swallowed in the shady gloom and the only reply he got was more crowing from the unseen birds who were waiting to resume their meal. The fact that there was no answer from a human mouth did nothing to dispel the men's fears that some god had had a hand in this scene of slaughter.

'We keep moving,' Hrani said, hoisting Gungnir, and with that they set off, giving the thrall's head a wide berth because no one wanted those staring eyes to fix on their own. They walked on, all but peering over the rims of their shields as if they expected a hail of arrows from the forest at any moment, and soon Hrani raised his spear again and the column stopped.

This time it was Storvek himself, though unlike the thrall he was alive. Naked as a newborn bairn he was tied to the base of a tree, ropes round his legs, waist and chest with another round his face and in his mouth to keep him quiet. There was a strip of cloth blinding him, but he could hear all right, for his stomach was pumping like forge bellows because he knew his jarl had come.

'Let me cut him free, Father,' young Randver said, moving forward until his father, who was growling foul things under his breath, grabbed a handful of the sword belt across the boy's shoulder.

'Stay here,' he told the boy, then turned to the two men at his back. 'You two, with me. You see anything move, you so much as smell a fart on the breeze, you shout.' Both warriors nodded grimly as the three of them went forward to help Storvek.

'Cut him loose,' Hrani said, and one of the men thrust his spear into the earth and drew his scramasax and had no sooner bent and put the blade to the rope around Storvek's legs when a man dropped through the lush boughs and put an axe in his back. There was a scream and in the same heartbeat another man fell from the pine and threw an arm round Jarl Hrani's neck while bringing a blade up to his throat.

'Move and I'll bleed you like a pig,' Bjarni told the jarl, who still gripped the massive spear. Bjarni's brother Bjorn stepped in front of him, his axe threatening the third man, who stood there not knowing what to do.

Hrani's champion, a man named Hadd whom men called Hog-Head, though he was only half as ugly as Jarl Guthrum's champion Asgrim, growled and moved forward, spear levelled.

'Not another step!' Bjarni yelled at him and Hog-Head stopped, but little Randver didn't, which meant he was either stupidly brave, just stupid, or Týr, Lord of Battle in disguise.

'No, Randver!' Hrani managed even with Bjarni's arm crushing his windpipe.

'Get back here, lad!' one of Hrani's men growled, but young Randver had a legend to make. He pulled his arm back as if to hurl his spear at Bjorn, then he yelled 'Óðin!' in a screechy voice, but before he could launch the spear a man burst from a tangle of thorns nearby and ran across the path, grabbing the boy the way a sea eagle scoops up a fish. It was Thorbiorn Thorirsson and Sigurd realized that what Thorbiorn lacked in war-craft and experience he made up for in speed, and now he stood off to the side amongst the trees, holding the son the same way Bjarni held the father.

If Hrani Randversson had not looked afraid before, he looked very afraid now with some stranger's knife at his boy's throat. Though he tried to put some steel in his eyes when he saw the big man walking towards him from the forest, because he knew now who he was dealing with.

'Olaf Ollersson,' Hrani spat.

Olaf strode forward looking like a war god in his brynja and helmet, his bright-painted shield and gripping his big boar spear. The others came from the trees too and Sigurd whispered his thanks to the Allfather at the sight of them. Svein, Bram, Aslak, old Solmund, Asgot and Hagal Crow-Song and even Moldof Wolf-Joint. They were all there, had somehow dug their way out of that mess at the hill fort and come north to Ubsola to find him.

'Hrani Randversson,' Olaf said, greeting the jarl with a nod. Hrani's men were silent and watchful, their expressions alone betraying what they thought about having been lured into this trap by their enemy and a Norseman at that. 'You all right then, Sigurd?' Olaf asked. 'I heard a rumour that the Svearmen tried to cut your throat and give you to the gods but the gods didn't want you.' He was grinning, as were Svein and Aslak and the others.

Sigurd grinned back. 'No thanks to you, Uncle. While you have been sitting around scratching your arses we have been dragged from here to there like dogs on the leash.'

'Untie them,' Olaf demanded of Hadd Hog-Head, but the man did not move. He was waiting for Hrani to tell him what to do. Hrani, though, was like a man with one foot on the boat and one on the jetty and he did not know which way to jump, so Thorbiorn Thorirsson made it easier for him.

'I will prise out your boy's eye like a clam from its shell,' he told the jarl, putting the point of his knife to the skin just below Randver's left eye. For his part young Randver did not beg nor say a word, so that Sigurd found he was starting to like the boy, but Jarl Hrani was not about to watch his son earn himself the byname One-Eye.

'Do as he says,' Hrani told Hog-Head, who thrust his spear into the ground, drew his scramasax and cut the rope binding Sigurd's wrists.

'Lucky shit,' the champion muttered, then freed Floki and Valgerd. They went to join Aslak and Hagal who gave them each a spear and scramasax so that they were at least armed. Sigurd walked over to Thorbiorn and the king's son nodded at him, pushing young Randver towards him because he knew what was coming.

'Now then, Hrani,' Sigurd said, taking the scramasax which Thorbiorn offered him. 'It seems I am going to earn myself quite a reputation with your kin, being the man who killed your father and your son.' He wrapped the boy's hair round his fist and pulled his head back to reveal the delicate white throat which did not yet boast a man's throat stone. 'My brothers will pour you a man's measure of mead when you get to Óðin's hall,

Randver,' he said, locking eyes with the boy's, which were wet now though still he did not beg for his life.

'No, Sigurd!' Hrani said.

'Shut your mouth before I cut your tongue out,' Bjarni growled at the jarl, tightening the grip round his neck.

'You know I have to do this, Hrani,' Sigurd said, 'but I will make it clean and quick because none of this is the boy's fault. He did not ask for an overreaching snake as a grandfather or a woman-killing nithing for a father.'

'I did not kill your mother,' Hrani managed, choking now thanks to Bjarni.

'You did not stop it,' Sigurd said, then bent to Randver's ear. 'Are you ready, boy?'

'Please!' Hrani gasped. 'Let the boy live.'

'And have him stick a blade between my ribs one day when he is full grown and I am old and slow?' Sigurd shook his head. 'That would not be very clever of me, Jarl Hrani.'

But Sigurd knew that he and his own men were the ones walking a knife's edge there and then in that Svealand forest. If he killed the son and Bjarni killed the father, Hrani's men would go berserk and Sigurd and his crew would be cut down in a frenzy of blood. So he would dangle the hook a little deeper in the hope that Hrani would catch the glint of it. Before the pines around them drank the slaughter's dew.

'What would you do in my position?' he asked the jarl. Hrani's eyes were bulging now, his face pale, so Sigurd gestured at Bjarni to loosen that iron grip of his to let the jarl speak.

The first thing Hrani did then was plunder a lungful of air, the gasp of it loud in those quiet woods. 'We could make an agreement,' he said. 'Your lives in exchange for my boy and me.'

'Try again, Hrani,' Olaf put in and Hrani curled a lip at him.

'You know my men will kill you all if I tell them to. Even if I am dead, they will avenge me,' Hrani said.

Sigurd shrugged. 'You still get to watch your boy die before you do,' he told him. 'Besides which, you must know I cannot let you live after everything that has happened.' He looked at young Randver, then brought the knife's point away from the boy's face and used it to scratch his own neck. 'Unless,' he said, letting that word hang there like hope for Jarl Hrani, 'unless you join me.'

Hrani Randversson was not as handsome as his father had been, yet he still boasted looks that gave a skald something to work with, and his grin then was one which must have had girls wet between the legs when he flashed it back home in his hall. 'You are mad, Haraldarson,' he said. 'We are sworn enemies and everybody knows it.'

'Everybody?' Sigurd said. 'You think we are more important than we are, Hrani, if you believe everyone is talking about us and our feud. These Svear warlords have their own feuds. I know this because I have been tangled in one myself.'

'I'd sooner die than join you,' Hrani said.

'I would hope that is true,' Sigurd said with a nod, 'but would you sooner watch your boy die at the hands of the same man that killed your father? Would you watch that rather than join me, Hrani Randversson?'

Hrani wrestled with that question, though everyone in that forest knew what the answer was going to be even if he did not. It was in his eyes, clear as runes carved in a rock.

'What are you suggesting?' he asked Sigurd.

'Join me,' Sigurd said. 'Swear an oath to fight at my side.' It seemed to Sigurd that someone else was speaking, for how could his own mouth craft the words that would see him become allies with Hrani Randversson? The muttering from some of his own men, including Svein, did not help him to believe he was doing the right thing, but making war against jarls and kings was more like playing a game of tafl than wrestling. Besides which, there was only so much war he could make with just his half crew around him.

'I am a jarl,' Hrani said. 'Why would I swear to be your man? What are you but a wolf on the loose? An outlaw with a handful of followers, fighting for some Svear warlord in return for the food in your bellies and the ale in your cups. You have no hall.' He had to say all that, what with his men's eyes on the whole thing like sailors watching the waves and the ship's vane to know where the wind was blowing. 'You have nothing.'

Sigurd grinned. 'I have your son,' he corrected Hrani, and he could not help but nod at Olaf in thanks for that. 'And while it is true that you have picked up the jarl torc which your father dropped, that is not the same thing as earning it.' Hrani could have been the greatest warrior standing in that forest that day but it would not have made Sigurd's words any less true. And they all knew it. 'Fight with me, Jarl Hrani, and swear an oath, and in return I will help you become much more than you are now.'

Clearly Hrani was confused by this, as were other men judging by the frowns amongst the trees. Some were murmuring amongst themselves. Others loosened shoulders and necks as if readying to fight Sigurd's hirðmen who had planted themselves across the track before them looking magnificent in their war gear.

'How would you like to be King Hrani Randversson?' Sigurd asked. 'You know I am going to kill Gorm oath-breaker and so you already know you cannot both swear to me and remain loyal to him. But when we have killed that goat-swiving whoreson you will be the one to take his high seat and sit there on the hill at Avaldsnes squeezing silver from every ship which sails past.'

Hrani's eyes became slits. 'You don't want to be king?' he asked.

'I don't want to be king,' Sigurd said and it was the truth; he did not want to be king, though he was not sure why not. 'Your son lives, you live, your men live and you become King Hrani. You will live in the oath-breaker's hall and with all that silver sailing into your hands you pay half a dozen skalds to sing about what a great man your father was but how you are even greater.'

'You'll want them to be better skalds than Crow-Song here,' Olaf said, nodding at Hagal, 'which shouldn't be a problem seeing as how you'll be richer than Fafnir.'

For a while then Hrani stood there thinking about it all, as though he had a choice. Then he nodded, at which Sigurd told Bjarni to let go of him, which must have pleased Hrani for he could at last straighten his spine and stand like a man.

'If you swear to help me be king, I will swear to fight with you, though I will not let you throw away my men's lives.'

Now it was Sigurd's turn to consider what he had heard and he made a show of scratching his beard as he weighed it up in his mind.

'Agreed,' he said at last and there was a low hum from Hrani's men because they were relieved that their jarl was going to live, and the only person who looked unhappy with the way it had turned out was Floki, who spat a curse in Hrani's direction and glowered like a boy who is made to go to sleep when he would rather be playing.

'No sword then?' Olaf said to Sigurd, for if Hrani was to swear an oath properly the words should be spoken over Sigurd's sword. But Troll-Tickler was amongst Jarl Guthrum's loot now.

'The spear,' Sigurd said, pointing at the Óðin spear which was still in Jarl Hrani's hand.

'That's what it is!' Olaf lifted his bushy beard. 'I thought it was one of those posts from the side of that track near Ubsola.'

'It's from the Svear temple,' Sigurd said.

Olaf frowned. 'I know,' he said. 'I just hope *you* know what you are doing by stealing it. Not from the Svearmen, I couldn't give a shit about that, but from the Allfather. If it really *was* his favourite boar-sticker.'

Bjarni held his blade close to Hrani while his brother Bjorn took the spear from the jarl and carried it to Sigurd, appreciating the weight of the thing in his hands.

'Tell them about this spear, Asgot,' Sigurd said, turning to the godi, who had tied some new bones into his hair and beard since Sigurd had last seen him.

'Gungnir, the Swaying One,' Asgot said. 'Fashioned by dwarfs from Yggdrasil's sacred ash, it never misses its mark.' The godi talked about how the Allfather had pierced his own flesh with Gungnir as he hung on the ash, sacrificed to himself, and of how he would use the spear to fight Fenrir Wolf at the twilight of the gods. And while he talked, men listened and Sigurd ran his fingers over the runes carved into the spear's shaft, and on to the strange shapes etched in the massive blade itself, wondering what they meant. 'Óðin himself carved the runes on it,' Asgot explained, 'just as he carved them into the teeth of his horse Sleipnir.'

'We all like a good story,' Hrani interrupted, 'but if we are going to make some agreement here instead of making a slaughter then let us get on with it.' This earned him a hiss from Asgot, not that he noticed. Even with his life and his son's life in his enemy's hands Hrani was still a jarl and could not help speaking like one.

He had a point too, Sigurd thought, because Asgot had not got to the part Sigurd had been waiting for. 'Hagal, tell Jarl Hrani why the spear has a part to play now,' he said, and Crow-Song smiled because he knew the old stories inside out, upside down and back to front. And as a skald he had spent enough time around jarls and kings to know which bit of the Gungnir story Sigurd wanted, just as a shipwright knows which tool to use for each part of a boat build.

'An oath made on the Allfather's spear can never be broken,' Crow-Song said, simple as that, and that was all he needed to say.

'I don't see how it can be Óðin's spear,' Svein mumbled. 'For a start, even though it is the biggest spear I have seen, I would expect Óðin's to be bigger still. And if this really is Gungnir then what spear is leaning against the Allfather's high seat in Valhöll at this very moment, while we stand around making friends with men who we ought to be killing?'

'Shut your mead hole, Red,' Bram growled, 'you'll ruin the moment.'

Svein shrugged, pushing such questions to the back of his thought chest because he knew they were about to watch a powerful jarl swear an oath of loyalty to Sigurd.

It did not take long, because Sigurd did not make each of Hrani's fifty men swear on the great spear. Every man amongst those pines knew that as the jarl himself was saying the words, and thus binding himself to Sigurd, then so they were bound also for they were already oath-tied to Hrani.

The jarl spat the words more than said them, but that was only to be expected, him hating Sigurd as much as he did, but once it was said it could not be unsaid and from that moment every fighting man there loosened like the weave of a sail after a blustery crossing. Swords were sheathed and shields were slung on backs. Hadd Hog-Head introduced himself to Moldof because being a prow man, but the younger of the two, Hrani's champion had heard stories of Moldof's fights. He had envied and respected the king's champion in equal measure and now took the opportunity to meet him properly and as equals – if not in some ways as Moldof's better, Moldof being nowadays an ex-champion and wolf-jointed.

'This I never thought I'd live to see,' Solmund told Sigurd as they watched the two hirðs come together like the confluence of two streams, admiring each other's war gear, comparing swords and boasting of the craftsmanship that went into pommels and lobes, hilts and the patterns in the iron which men talk of as the breath in the blade. As if a sword is a living thing.

'It is not an easy thing to swallow, my friend,' Sigurd said, knowing how the old helmsman must feel what with him having fought Hrani's men, been half killed by one of them too, when they had attacked Sigurd's village. 'But what we have done here is navigate through the skerries and arrive at the Jól feast.'

Solmund was too old to pretend that he would not rather have seen that Óðin spear in Jarl Hrani's belly than in his hands as he spun the oath to Sigurd, but he nodded anyway. 'You are learning the game of jarls and kings, Sigurd,' he said, 'and I knew your father well enough to be certain that he would be proud.'

The weight of that made itself known on Sigurd and he held the old man's eyes a moment, remembering how he had sewn the wound in Solmund's chest himself when he had found him pale as a corpse amongst the dead of Skudeneshavn.

Then a peal of laughter turned their heads towards a group of Hrani's men gathered in front of Storvek, who was still tied to the tree, even after the whole oath-swearing thing.

'You've had your fun, you rancid shits!' Storvek said. 'Bild! Erlingnar! Untie me, you grinning arses.'

'Looks like we've got ourselves a proper war band,' Olaf said, slapping Sigurd's back as they watched Hrani's men cut Storvek loose while the jarl himself spoke with his most important hirðmen, no doubt dealing with their concerns about being enemies now of King Gorm. For by swearing an oath to Sigurd, Hrani had just pissed on the oath he had sworn to Gorm. But then the oath to the king had not been made on Gungnir.

'It is a start,' Sigurd said. 'But we will need more than this.'

'Aye, I expect we will,' Olaf said.

'And I want my sword back. My brynja too.'

'Guthrum's got them?'

Sigurd nodded. Olaf grinned. Because they were now more than sixty warriors: Sword-Norse who fed the wolf and the raven and whose ears had so often rung with the din of the sword-song.

And they were going to find the Svear jarl who had thought he could buy the gods' favour with men's blood. Because Sigurd wanted his sword back.

CHAPTER EIGHT

THEY FOUND JARL GUTHRUM AND HIS MEN STILL CAMPED AT THE FOOT OF the hill to the east of the kings' mounds, his axe banner fluttering in the warm breeze. Storvek had assured Sigurd and Hrani both that King Eysteinn was still nowhere to be seen, having yet to return from whatever fighting he was up to his neck in, which was good news as it meant there would be no other war band getting mixed up in things.

It turned out that having arrived at Ubsola Olaf and the others had recognized Guthrum's banner and kept watch from a safe distance while Asgot had gone to the temple to speak with its priests. Two of them being dead, it had been the boy-godi who explained what had happened and how the two would-be sacrificial offerings and a fierce woman warrior had escaped, stealing the sacred spear as they went.

'When Storvek rode into the place telling anyone who would listen that they could see the spear returned for the right price, we knew all we had to do was put a blade to the lad's throat to find out what he knew, then use him as the bait on the hook,' Olaf explained.

Now Jarl Hrani's boar head banner was revelling in the wind as his Norsemen climbed the ting mound and formed a great shieldwall upon it to deny Guthrum the high ground. They had come round from the north of Ubsola and come at speed too so that Jarl Guthrum was caught completely by surprise, his own men not expecting to be faced with a fight of any kind, much less with a force outnumbering them two to one.

'I can see you've made yourself known around here, lad,' Bram said to Sigurd, grinning at the sight of the temple, or King Eysteinn's hall if that was what the Svearmen called it, for it was still standing but half of it was black and charred and you could smell the burnt timbers on the same breeze that made Guthrum's and Hrani's banners dance.

'Not my doing, Bram,' Sigurd said, looking at Valgerd. 'She is the bravest of us all for she thinks nothing of burning down a temple even if it belongs to a king or the gods themselves.'

Bram grinned at Valgerd who denied none of it. They were standing in the pre-dawn gloom at the top of the hill, waiting for Guthrum's men to notice them, which they just had by the look and sound of it. Down in the camp amongst the shelters and the cook fires men were shouting and pointing and others were running towards Guthrum's own tent in which he was still sleeping.

'I wonder if the statues burnt,' Floki said.

'They didn't,' Valgerd answered.

'How do you know?' Floki asked.

The shieldmaiden smiled. 'Because if that Frey statue had caught fire it would be burning still, what with the size of his cock.'

That raised a few laughs as Sigurd watched Jarl Guthrum emerge from his tent, shrugging himself into his brynja as he looked up to see the army gathered in a wall of flesh, iron and wood upon the crest of the ting mound.

'So what is he like, this Guthrum?' Jarl Hrani asked. Sigurd had to admit that Hrani looked formidable in his war gear. If he was anything like his father Randver he possessed war-craft and courage and a combination of those two was something you would sooner have in an ally than an enemy.

163

'He is brave enough,' Sigurd said, 'and he hates to lose men, though he has been doing a lot of that recently.'

'His weakness?' Hrani asked, which was a good question because one weakness in an otherwise impressive warlord could be enough to sink him, like one sprung strake in a ship which lets the water gush in.

'He is certain that the gods have abandoned him,' Sigurd said. 'He feared it before but after what happened at the temple he must be sure of it.'

Hrani nodded because he heard the sweet music in those words. 'Then he is as good as dead,' he said.

Which was not quite true, Sigurd knew, for a healthy man did not die until someone put a cold blade in his flesh and tore his heart or lungs or caused him to bleed out like a slaughtered beast. There was also the question of Jarl Guthrum's men. They were his best warriors, his hearthmen, and Sigurd did not want to see his new war band whittled away in a fight which had nothing to do with him having his revenge on the oath-breaker king.

Below, Jarl Guthrum's champion Asgrim was bellowing orders, setting up his own skjaldborg and calling for someone to bring him his jarl's axe banner from where it stood near Guthrum's tent.

'Want me to claim them?' Svein asked Sigurd, lifting his spear. He meant he would walk down that hill and hurl the spear over Guthrum's shieldwall and by doing so claim those warriors for the Allfather. Guthrum himself had done that at the borg and his spear-throw had been good enough to have men talking about it for days after. Which was no doubt why Svein wanted to throw his spear now. To prove he could throw further.

Sigurd shook his head. 'I don't want them dead if I can help it.'

'So you've some other Loki trick to make Jarl Guthrum swear the oath to you as I have done,' Jarl Hrani said through a grimace.

Standing side by side with Sigurd still felt like an ill-fitting brynja to him, as it did to Sigurd.

'No tricks,' Sigurd said. 'I'm just going to kill Guthrum and see what happens then.' Floki stepped forward but Sigurd shook his head before Floki had the chance to ask. 'I'll do it myself, Floki,' he said, 'but you can come. You too, Valgerd.' The shieldmaiden nodded and grinned and together they walked down the hill, none of them in mail or helmets but each armed with sword, shield and spear, Sigurd's being Gungnir which he turned so that the rune-marked blade caught the first pink light of the rising sun.

Floki also had a hand axe tucked into his belt and Valgerd had a long scramasax sheathed against the small of her back, and Sigurd hoped that seeing the three of them again would anger Guthrum enough that he would accept Sigurd's challenge to single combat.

They all carried their shields above their heads to show the Svearmen that Sigurd wanted to talk, and Jarl Guthrum and Asgrim came forward to meet them at the foot of the hill.

Sigurd had wondered why Guthrum was not wearing a helmet. Now he knew. The jarl's face was a mass of raw, weeping flesh, glistening with pus and red as a wound. His golden beard was gone and in its place was a shiny wet-looking scar upon which no bristles would ever grow again. Much of his fair hair had been burnt away too so that his scalp was one horrible sore, and it would have been further agony to wear that helmet of his with the eye guards. Nor was he wearing his silver torc, for the skin on his neck was oozing yellowy liquid.

Sigurd lowered his shield and the others did the same. 'I am Sigurd Haraldarson whom men call Óðin-Favoured,' he announced loud enough for Guthrum's warriors to hear as they stood there looking grim as granite cliffs.

'You know who I am,' Guthrum said, 'albeit I have lost some of my good looks.'

If Guthrum was in pain, which he must have been with that fire-eaten face, he did not show it.

'I know you, Guthrum the cursed,' Sigurd said, and the jarl could not hide the pain at hearing that. He nodded up towards the top of the hill.

'They are your men?'

'They are,' Sigurd said. 'But there does not have to be a fight here today. Your men do not have to die.'

'You want to fight me yourself?' Guthrum asked.

'You would have watched some Freysgodi cut my throat,' Sigurd said. 'Then you would have hung my corpse in that tree over there.'

'That is true,' Guthrum admitted.

Sigurd nodded. 'I want to fight you,' he said, taking in the pitiful sight before him. 'Can you fight?' He looked at the jarl's right hand which he noticed was also red raw, and should still have been bound in clean cloth, but perhaps Guthrum had not wanted to appear hurt in front of his men.

'I can fight,' the jarl said, putting all of his considerable height into his legs and spine then. Beside him Asgrim's ugly face twitched. What a sight those two made together. The troll and the burnt jarl. It would make a good children's story.

'I can fight well enough to kill you, Sigurd Haraldarson,' Guthrum said, and there was a spark in the eyes of that flame-ravaged face. 'And when you are dead I will kill him,' he said, glaring at Floki, 'and you too,' he added to Valgerd and there was real hate there then because she had tipped the burning oil on to him which had stripped him of those Baldr good looks.

Sigurd nodded. 'So we will fight and either your death or mine will settle things between us. There will be no more blood spilled after.'

Jarl Guthrum thought about this, as well he might knowing as he did that not only were the gods against him but they favoured Sigurd. Still, he was a brave man for all that because he knew that if he did not accept Sigurd's challenge it would come to a fight between the two skjaldborgar which his own men would certainly lose.

'I will fight you, Sigurd Haraldarson,' Guthrum announced, 'but only on equal terms. Halvdan, fetch this man's brynja. His sword too. When he is dead and I meet him again in Óðin's hall I do not want him saying that I only won because he was not using his own familiar war gear.'

That was well said and got growls of approval from those grim-faced men at his back, and even Floki, who would as soon bury that hand axe of his in Guthrum's head as listen to him any more, nodded because the man was acting like a proper jarl. And the battle thrill was beginning to announce itself in Sigurd's marrow and muscle. For now it was the flutter of moths' wings in his blood. Soon it would become a trembling in his thighs and in his hands, and the saliva in his mouth would sour.

Then Asgrim pulled his scramasax from its sheath, took a step and ripped out his jarl's throat with it, spraying blood into the rings of Guthrum's brynja and across the grass at Sigurd's feet, some of it spattering Sigurd's boots.

For his last few heartbeats Jarl Guthrum stood there staring at Sigurd as his lifeblood gushed away, then his great body toppled like a felled tree and his hand flapped like a fish then went still on the grass and he never moved again.

Asgrim bent and wiped the blade of his scramasax on the hem of the dead jarl's tunic, then straightened and pushed the blade back into the sheath at his waist.

'That's that then,' he said to Sigurd, who was still staring at Jarl Guthrum, unbalanced by what he had just seen, like a boat heeling in a sudden gust.

'Why?' he asked Asgrim.

The champion, who was in fact no one's champion now, shrugged his shoulders, put a thumb to one nostril of that nose which was spread across his face and shot a wad of snot on to the grass. 'What was the point in you two fighting?' he asked. 'The fire ruined his hand so he could not grip a sword properly.

Not well enough anyway,' he said. 'None of us who have fought with him a long time needed to see him humiliated today.'

'He might have won,' Sigurd said.

'And if he had, then what?' Asgrim said. 'We would still be following a man whom the gods have forsaken.' That warped mouth of his twisted though it could not be called a smile. 'Whereas you, Sigurd Haraldarson, have the look of a man who is weaving his own saga.' He swept a big arm back towards his Svear brothers who stood behind their shields waiting for other men to decide their futures. 'If you will treat us with the respect due to those who have stood up to our knees in the wound-sea and never run from our lord's enemies—'

'We saw you run from us when you fucked up that attack on Alrik's walls,' Floki interrupted him.

Sigurd expected Asgrim to be furious at that, but the big warrior simply shrugged again. 'Sigurd was atop that wall,' he said, eyes boring into Sigurd's own, 'so we were fighting the gods too. A man needn't feel ashamed for running from the gods' fury once in a while.' He pointed at the great sacred spear in Sigurd's hand, whose butt rested on the ground so that its massive blade accused the crimson sky. 'You have the Allfather's favour and now you have his spear. So as I was saying, if you treat us as you would your own hirðmen we will follow you and swear an oath.'

'I am no jarl,' Sigurd said.

Asgrim's thick lips spread to reveal the cave where his front teeth should have been. 'Not yet,' he said.

'Then it will be as you say, Asgrim,' Sigurd said, laying his shield down on the grass then striding forward to grip the warrior's outstretched arm. 'I will be honoured to fight with you and your Svearmen.' He glanced down at the dead jarl and wondered what Guthrum had done to earn himself the gods' displeasure. But then Asgot always said that the gods are fickle.

'An ale horn in one hand and a scramasax in the other, lad, that's what you can expect from the Lords of Asgard,' the godi had told Sigurd after King Gorm's betrayal of Jarl Harald.

'So what are we going to do with him?' Valgerd said, gesturing at the jarl's corpse.

'We will honour him with a hero's pyre,' Asgrim said.

'That will have to wait,' Sigurd said, pulling his sword from its scabbard. 'I want his head.'

Asgrim pulled his own head back as if he'd been hit with an oar blade. 'Why?'

Sigurd bent and moved one of Guthrum's arms, placing it under his neck so that the dead man's head was off the ground. Then he lifted the sword and brought it down with enough muscle behind it to all but sever Guthrum's head from his neck. 'We are going back to the borg and I want Alrik to see that the jarl is dead,' Sigurd told Asgrim, using the blade to saw through the last bit of gristle and skin until the head came away. 'I want Guthrum's men to see it too.'

'If they recognize that burnt face,' Floki pointed out.

'You could have just shown them his jarl torc,' Asgrim said unhappily. 'It is in his tent with his other things.' He did not like seeing his jarl's head separated from its body, which was understandable. A man should go to Valhöll in one piece if he can. *Not that the Allfather would want Guthrum drinking in his hall all the days till Ragnarök,* Sigurd thought, or he would not have let the jarl's luck piss away like that.

'I could have shown them his torc,' Sigurd agreed, grabbing what was left of Guthrum's hair to lift the head. The eyes were open, which was probably a good thing for the sake of folk recognizing whose head it was. Sigurd looked into those eyes and could not help but think it was a bad end even for a man who would have sacrificed him in the Svearfolk's temple. Yes he could have just taken the torc and let Asgrim burn the jarl as was befitting for such a man. But nothing convinced people that a man was dead quite so much as his head being somewhere other than on the end of his neck.

'Have your men ready to leave by midday, Asgrim,' Sigurd said. 'I will have their oaths on the way but we should be gone before King Eysteinn returns to Ubsola.'

'We'll be ready,' Asgrim said, then turned to walk back to those warriors who had just watched him murder their jarl yet seemed not to have a word to say about it.

And Sigurd, Floki and Valgerd climbed back up the hill to Jarl Hrani and the men waiting up there.

'If you go on like this, Sigurd, we will die of old age without ever having to fight at all,' Olaf said when Sigurd had told him and Hrani and the rest what had happened and that the Svearmen were joining them. Olaf was grinning and Hrani was getting a good look at Guthrum's head because jarls are always interested in other jarls, even dead ones.

'Let us see if we can give you one more good fight then, Uncle,' Sigurd said as Solmund came forward with a sack for Guthrum's head, 'before you hang your sword in some hall and spend the rest of your days watching your boys grow and telling stories to anyone who will listen.' The head went in and Solmund tied the sack and Sigurd was glad not to have to look at that burnt face any more.

'Whose hall will that be then?' Olaf asked, smiling, 'for you have already given away King Gorm's to Jarl Hrani, which is generous of you and a little bold seeing as that oath-breaking weasel shit is still living in it.'

Sigurd thought about this for a moment, not that Olaf, a warrior in his prime, would be sheathing his sword for the last time any day soon. But still it was a good question.

'Well I will need my own hall,' Sigurd said, 'and you can live there wherever it happens to be.' Sigurd did not know where he would live when this feud was over, but he did not think it would be Skudeneshavn where his father's hall had stood.

There would be too many ghosts there. Too many ghosts and too many memories to drown in.

Then again, perhaps this blood feud with King Gorm would never be over and Sigurd would never have the chance to lay roots into the earth and raise his own hall. Or maybe he would be killed in the blood-fray, sword-hacked, spear-gutted or arrow-shot. A whitening corpse amongst a pile of corpses, dead and never to be avenged.

'We will follow the threads of our wyrds and see where they lead, then, Sigurd,' Olaf said and Sigurd nodded, slinging the sack with its heavy contents over his shoulder, the Óðin spear in his other hand.

For they were going south back to Fornsigtuna and Alrik's hill fort, then back across Løgrinn and west to Norway and to the reckoning that would decide it all.

On the third day, when they had put plenty of thick forest between themselves and Ubsola, Guthrum's men swore the oath in front of the rest. Asgrim was the first to do it and the others followed and even Halvdan, who had made a nuisance of himself when Sigurd, Floki and Valgerd had been Guthrum's prisoners, spoke the words as though he meant them and was proud to do it. Though this clearly nettled Floki who had been looking for even half a reason to kill the Svearman.

'Sword and shield, flesh and bone, I am your man, Sigurd Haraldarson. As long as the sun shines and the world endures, henceforth and forevermore,' he said as the others had done.

'Gjöf sér æ til gjalda,' Sigurd said to each of them. A gift always looks for a return. 'I will be a ring-giver and a raven-feeder. As long as the sun shines and the world endures, henceforth and forevermore.'

When it was done, Sigurd shared a look with those who had been with him since the beginning. Olaf, Svein, Solmund, Asgot, Aslak and even Hagal Crow-Song stared back at him, each with the same look in his eyes. It was enough to unnerve Sigurd because he knew what they were thinking, even though none would say it aloud. He was thinking the same. They had come a long way in a short time, grown from a half crew to a very powerful war band of ninety men, and not farmers who do a little raiding here and there either, but hearthmen, warriors who live to feed the wolf and the raven. Men with good blades and mail or tough leather armour. Men with pride in their war prowess and who lust after reputation.

Sigurd recalled the words the witch had spoken to him the previous winter before they had left Jarl Burner's hall at Osøyro.

'Who are the two who ride to the ting?' the witch had asked him. 'Three eyes have they together, ten feet, and one tail: and thus they travel through the lands.'

'Óðin and Sleipnir his eight-legged steed,' Sigurd had answered.

'His passing raises such a rush and roar of the wind as will waft away the souls of the dead. And with it Haraldarson,' the witch had said, pointing at him, aiming her warning like an arrow nocked to a bowstring. She had said he could not escape the wings of the storm and yet he did not want to, whatever the risk. He had a war band of oath-tied men and their expectations lay heavy on him, yet he thrilled to the burden like the palm to the touch of the hilt. He was soaring despite it. He was the eagle which sails on the draughts high above the world tree Yggdrasil, and his talons were now sharp enough to rip flesh.

'The lad is not sworn,' Svein reminded Sigurd, nodding at Thorbiorn Thorirsson who was sitting on the other side of the fire. There were three fires in that camp by a moss-fringed stream above which clouds of gnats swarmed. One for Hrani's men, one for Guthrum's, and one for Sigurd's original crew. It was to be expected that they would keep to themselves for a while at least, for men who have fought together are bonded by blood. Besides which, for all that they could understand each other well enough, the Norse tongue sounded strange to the

Svearmen's ears and it was the same the other way round. 'We should make him swear it,' Svein said, teasing a comb through his red beard which he had freed from its braids so that he could hunt for lice.

'He is the son of a king and cannot swear loyalty to another man,' Sigurd said.

'Not even you?' Svein said, grinning.

'Not even me,' Sigurd said.

'Well, King Thorir owes us for making a man out of his son. That I do know,' Svein said.

Looking at Thorbiorn now Sigurd agreed with Svein about that. There was little sign of the preening, cunny-chasing young Dane they had met in the king's hall at Skíringssalr. In his place was a warrior who had earned himself one or two boasts. It was Thorbiorn's fleetness of foot when grabbing Jarl Hrani's son Randver which had delivered the jarl and his men into Sigurd's hands.

'He might be pretty enough to be your sister but he deserves his place in the skjaldborg, I'll give him that,' Olaf put in, turning his face away from Thorbiorn so that his beard all but swallowed the words, 'but don't be telling him that yet. Praise can go to a young man's head faster than ripe mead, and we all know that fighting with a skin full of mead can get a man killed.'

'Aye, but you die happy,' Bram put in, drinking ale from Guthrum's men's stash. The warriors around those cook fires might be mixing like fish oil and water but at least they were sharing what food and ale they had.

And that is a start, Sigurd thought. Soon enough they would make the spear din together. They would soak their shoes with the slaughter's dew. For Óðin was the Wild Huntsman tearing through the sky on his fearsome steed. And the raging winds from his passing were the wings of the storm.

They came to Fornsigtuna on a grey day with their banners hoisted above their heads: Guthrum's white battle axe in a sea of black, and Jarl Hrani's black boar's head on a yellow cloth, trembling in the gusts which brought spits of rain from the west.

'I want a banner, Uncle,' Sigurd said. They were moving not abreast like a loose shieldwall or in a spear-like column, but rather in one great mass, sweeping amongst the trees like the shadow of a wind-blown cloud, war gear clumping and fittings jingling and men's voices merged in a low continuous hum.

'You can have Guthrum's after today,' Olaf said and meant it. 'He has no use for it now, for the worms or the flames won't care who he is.'

But Sigurd shook his head. 'I want my own banner.'

'I would have an axe,' Svein said.

'And have the same banner as Jarl Guthrum?' Solmund asked him.

Svein shrugged though he must have known that was not one of his better ideas.

'A ship,' Solmund said, puffing as they trudged up a slope whose long grass shared its dampness with their breeks, 'for it shows you are a raiding man and someone who gets off his arse to go and see the world.'

Sigurd liked the sound of that and said so, moving the Óðin spear on to his other shoulder as he did now and then to share the weight of it. His shield was slung over his back and it felt good being in his brynja again, Troll-Tickler at his hip. He had his helmet back too.

'A ship?' Moldof said, unimpressed. 'Well that will make your enemies shiver with fear and shit in their breeks, won't it?' He shook his head.

'Well then maybe we should put your head on a pole instead of a banner,' Valgerd told Moldof, 'for that would scare the birds out of the sky and have grown men crying for their mothers.' For what King Gorm's former prow man lacked in his right arm he made up for in his monstrous size and troll's face.

Olaf ordered tongues to be still now. The wood was thinning. Soon they would emerge from the trees on to the meadow upon whose hill Jarl Guthrum had built his borg, and they did not want to announce their arrival just yet.

'A wolf,' Floki said, breaking the new silence. 'Just the head but make sure the teeth can be seen.' He did not say more because he did not have to. A wolf's head banner needed no explanation.

'A wolf,' Sigurd said with a nod, seeing the banner in the eye of his mind. It was perfect, and even Svein, who would still have preferred an axe, could not disagree.

And soon they came to the edge of the woods, where their noses filled with the tang of a war host's encampment, with woodsmoke, thyme and onions, the sweet scent of butchered meat, the stink of burning iron from the forge, the melted beeswax with which the smith coated the finished blades, and the reek of shit from the pits and from the pigs and sheep pens. Sigurd halted the war band there, telling Asgrim to be ready just in case, then went closer with Olaf and Hrani, the three of them keeping to cover as best they could.

Beyond the animal pens and the men's tents, looming over the camp on a hill not much bigger than the largest of the kings' mounds at Ubsola, stood the borg. Alrik's borg these days, anyone would have to admit, and it looked as unobtainable as an aerie, its timbers scorched black in places, repaired here and there, but solid enough and as defiant as when Sigurd had last seen the place.

Olaf pointed out Knut who was standing on the ramparts above the main gate, watchful as ever even though Sigurd doubted Guthrum's men would have risked their lives in another assault without their jarl. Warriors such as those whom Guthrum had left behind were more inclined towards brave or reckless acts when their lord was watching because he might reward their efforts.

'Like pigs in a bloody sty,' Jarl Hrani said, taking it all in.

'Aye, but rich pigs,' Olaf reminded him and Hrani nodded, because for all that he was unimpressed with Alrik for allowing himself to be trapped, his eyes had lit at the talk of all that silver and iron stashed inside the borg.

'Not so rich soon,' Sigurd said.

'So we're going to take this place?' Jarl Hrani said, not seeming against the idea even though he knew Guthrum himself had tried and failed.

'No,' Sigurd said.

'We'd break too many teeth trying to get the marrow out of that bone,' Olaf said. 'Seen it happen.'

'There is an easier way to relieve Alrik of some of his hoard,' Sigurd told them, looking to the west to see how long it would be before the sun boiled the distant sea. He smiled because it would be night soon. 'A much easier way,' he said.

And there was.

The nights now were more like proper nights. It was as dark as it was going to get, and still, barely a breeze to stir an old man's beard, so that the smoke from the fires inside and outside the borg hung in the sky like low cloud. And again Sigurd could not help but wonder if the Allfather's hand was in the game, because he had made it to the walls unnoticed. He had walked between the fires of Guthrum's men and climbed the hill and no shouts of alarm had punctured the still night. He was invisible. He was a ghost, passing through the night as a draugr can pass even through solid rock or the timbers of the hall in which it once drank and feasted with the living.

He waited a while at the foot of the wall, cloaked and crouching, the scent of charred timbers in his nose as he hissed like a cat until one of Alrik's men above peered over the edge and saw him. For a heartbeat the man's eyes bulged and his mouth opened as if to yell that the borg was under attack, but his mind was quicker than his mouth and he realized that Sigurd was alone and one man did not an attack make.

'It's the Norseman, the one Jarl Guthrum took off to Ubsola,' another man said, leaning out over the palisade beside his companion.

'What are you doing back here?' the first man hissed down at Sigurd.

'Throw me a rope,' Sigurd said, looking over his shoulder to make sure none of Guthrum's men were coming up that hill to kill him. For some reason Alrik's men seemed reluctant to haul him over the wall. No doubt they were surprised to see him again, for they would have expected him to be a rotting corpse by now. But still. 'Do it now,' he growled up at them, 'unless you want to spend the rest of your days trapped here like rats in the rain barrel.'

The two men looked at each other and shrugged, then one of them disappeared and Sigurd decided that if Alrik's man had not gone off to fetch a rope he would burn the place down himself.

'Up you come then,' the Svearman said as a rope thumped against the timbers and more faces, one of them Knut's, appeared in the gloom above. Sigurd climbed.

'I never thought to see your face again, Byrnjolf,' Knut said, scratching the nub of gristle which was all that remained of his left ear. 'Or should I call you Sigurd these days?' He had been wolf-lean before but now he was sunken-cheeked and looked ten years older than when Sigurd had seen him last, and looking at the others too it was clear that Alrik's men were starving. 'Better go and see Alrik then,' Knut said. So they did.

'My name is Sigurd Haraldarson. I killed Jarl Randver of Hinderå. I vow to kill King Gorm of Avaldsnes whom men call oath-breaker.' They stood by the gates, Sigurd, Knut and Alrik himself, along with some forty of his men who had come from their beds to see Sigurd for themselves and hear what news he had of Jarl Guthrum.

'Even when you were Byrnjolf Hálfdanarson it was clear to me that you were an ambitious man,' Alrik said, 'and indeed you must be to have made enemies of jarls and kings.' You could say one thing for Alrik, and that was that he had not pecked away at some secret store by the looks but had hungered with the rest of his men. The skin of his face was taut and the veins beneath his eyes showed like mould in cheese. 'But it is also clear that you are a difficult man to kill, Sigurd Haraldarson, so whoever this Norse king is I would advise him to make friends with you even if it costs him a sea chest of silver or a pretty daughter.' Still, there was suspicion in the warlord's sunken eyes for all that he was trying to be patient and let Sigurd unfurl this story in his own time.

'So are you going to tell us how you escaped from that turd Guthrum?' Knut asked so that his lord would not have to appear too eager. 'And why if you were a free man and could go anywhere in the world, you would climb back into this trap again, for it is not as though you are oath-sworn to my lord.'

Sigurd nodded. 'I will come to all of that later, Knut,' he said. 'First I want to agree a price with Lord Alrik.'

'A price for what?' Alrik asked, his eyes all but disappearing in a suspicious squint.

Sigurd let a smile come to his lips, not that he could have stopped it. 'What will you pay me to make those men out there vanish?' he asked, then turned to Knut and fluttered fingers at him. 'Vanish like smoke in a strong wind.'

Alrik laughed but there was no mirth in it. 'And how would you do that, Norseman?' he asked, a hint of scorn in *Norseman*.

'What would you pay me?' Sigurd said again, ignoring the man's question. 'How much of your silver and iron hoard?'

'Who does this Norseman think he is?' one of Alrik's men rumbled, stirring a few insults and complaints, which Sigurd did not mind for he knew he was coming close to treading on their pride with his talk of saving them, like Beowulf saying he would save Hroðgar and his Danes from the monster which was preying on them.

'I don't know what has happened to you since we saw you last, but we in this borg are not so fond of riddles these days,' Knut said, and there was an edge of threat in it, but Alrik nodded, having decided to play Sigurd's game if only to see how it ended.

He gestured to the unseen enemy beyond the walls. 'If you took this noose from my neck I would give you half of it,' he told Sigurd.

Sigurd looked at the lean faces of those gathered there in the firebrands' copper glow. 'You will give me half of your silver and iron hoard if I make Jarl Guthrum's men disappear so that you may fill your bellies again and come and go as you please.' He said it loud enough for all of them to hear, for he needed witnesses, for all that Alrik looked angry now because he suspected Sigurd was somehow making a fool of him.

The warlord nodded. 'You did not tell me you were a famous godi, Sigurd Haraldarson, for this will have to be some powerful seiðr,' he said, forcing a smile.

'Powerful and fast-working too,' Sigurd said, 'as you will see tomorrow at dusk when you look out from the ramparts and see only smoking ashes and sheep droppings where there was a war host before.'

Knut and Alrik looked at each other, two hungry men, tired from this feud with Jarl Guthrum, spirit-weary from keeping their constant vigil from the walls lest their enemies come to steal their silver and iron. They did not like this game Sigurd was playing but if there was any chance at all that he could do what he promised, then these Svearmen would raise their hopes to the wind and see where they blew.

'So your friends found you then? In Ubsola?' Alrik said, seeking to draw more from Sigurd with this other approach.

Sigurd looked at the night beyond the flickering bloom of the flamelight. The sooner he got back the better. He turned to the two men who had helped haul him over the palisade.

'Come with me. You are going to lower me back over the wall.' They did not even look to their lord, but nodded without a word. Sigurd turned to Alrik. 'Tomorrow then, Lord Alrik,' he said. 'And as well as ridding you of Guthrum's men I will have six pigs brought to the gate. You look hungry.'

Now it was Alrik's turn to nod, the warlord not knowing what to say to this young Norseman who promised to do the impossible. Then Sigurd left them standing there and climbed the bank up to the ramparts, and the two men followed with the rope.

Guthrum's war host surrounding the borg barely had the chance to shrug themselves into brynjur, tie helmet thongs and pick up their shields before it became clear to them that there would be no clash of shieldwalls to greet the dawn. They recognized their jarl's champion Asgrim and Halvdan and their other sword-brothers coming across the meadow under their lord's axe banner. Doubtless they were surprised to see those men walking beside the Norsemen who had shown up at the borg those few weeks previously, their own boar's head banner rippling in the wind which had begun to stir when Sigurd had returned from his talk with Alrik.

'I cannot say I will miss the stink,' Svein said through a grimace as Sigurd walked out ahead of his war host with the sack containing Guthrum's head. Asgot had covered the dead face with honey, smearing it across the eyes and the gory, gristly mess of the severed neck, saying that it would slow the rot, but Sigurd had not set eyes on the head for a few days now and he hoped it did not look as bad as it smelt. Asgrim went with him and Sigurd could tell from his silence and the set of his jaw that the champion was at the least uneasy and perhaps even afraid. Sigurd liked him all the more for it, too, because it was no small thing for a man to murder his own jarl and it was good that Asgrim knew that. But the big man did not know how Guthrum's war host would take the news. A man's reputation could rot quicker than a severed head if his sword-brothers turned against him.

Asgrim might not know what was going to happen, but Sigurd did. He had spun the whole thing of it in his mind and he approached these Svearmen as if he had already spoken the words and they the reply.

But it was Asgrim who would speak first.

'Brothers!' he called, as the Svearmen came to gather round. They were surprised to see Sigurd, but more interested to know where their jarl was. 'You all know that Jarl Guthrum lost the favour of the Æsir,' Asgrim said. 'It had run from him like water down a rock face.' He was no skald, Asgrim, which was just as well. Who would want to watch that face as a good story and pretty word pictures poured out of it?

'He was lucky once,' one of the older warriors said; 'he could be lucky again. Men lose the gods' favour and then earn it back.'

Asgrim shook his head. 'Not Guthrum,' he said.

'So where is he?' another warrior asked, lifting his spear in agitation. 'He has left us here like we are shepherds watching the sheep.'

'He did not have much choice,' Sigurd said, thrusting the Óðin spear's shaft into the earth and opening the sack, trying not to screw up his face at the stench that hit him. He plunged his hand in and took hold of the hair that was sticky with honey, then hoisted it up so that all could see. A murmur rose from the warriors, punctuated by curses and mutterings and the hum of men spreading the news to those at the back who could not crane their necks quite enough to see the head for themselves. 'When one of your own men cuts your head off, well then you know that your luck is never coming back,' Sigurd said and Asgrim glared at him because that was not how the champion had planned on putting it.

'I killed Jarl Guthrum because if I had not, we would all have followed him to a bad death. He would have led us to it because he was cursed and you all knew it.' Asgrim stood tall and strong. Little things like the way a man stood mattered at such times and Asgrim knew it.

'So what has the Norseman to do with it?' a voice called from somewhere amongst the throng. Men were staring at the head in Sigurd's hand and though his arm was beginning to shake with the weight of it, for a man's head is a heavy thing, Sigurd kept it up there because he needed them all to know, to be sure that it was in fact their jarl's for all that it was green now and somewhat shrivelled and of course half burnt.

'This is Sigurd Haraldarson, the son of a famous Norse jarl,' Asgrim announced, 'and he will lead us towards fame and reputations which will shine long after we have met our deaths in the sword-song and the red war.'

'You'd have us follow a Norseman?' a warrior asked, turning to spit but finding there was no room to do it.

Sigurd pulled the spear from the ground; the spear upon which men would swear loyalty to him. 'I will be your ring-giver in exchange for your oath,' he said, keeping it simple because he did not think he needed to oversell it, for what else were these warriors going to do? Go back to their homes with nothing to show for their time with Jarl Guthrum? Sell their swords and their helmets and become farmers to be ruled by the soil and the seasons?

'The Allfather's favour shines in him brighter than the lustre of this helmet of his,' Asgrim said, gesturing at Sigurd in all his war glory, his mail and helmet, the Óðin spear in his left hand. 'And that spear he is holding is Gungnir, which once belonged to the Allfather whom we call Spear-God. Here is a lord of war favoured by the god of war. Do not tell me you cannot see it.'

And they could see it, too.

'When we have gone to Valhöll what will we leave behind for our children and their children if not a shining reputation?' Asgrim asked them. And now they were murmuring again but this time it was because they were agreeing with their champion and so Sigurd dropped Guthrum's rotting head because it had served its purpose.

And Sigurd thought that maybe Asgrim was a half-decent skald after all.

CHAPTER NINE

THAT WAS NOT THE END FOR JARL GUTHRUM'S HEAD AS IT TURNED OUT. Of the remaining one hundred and fifteen warriors of the jarl's host, only twelve did not swear the oath to Sigurd. Six were in ill health and said they did not have it in them to follow Sigurd back to Norway. Four were so disgusted by Asgrim's murder of the jarl that they wanted nothing to do with him and said they would rather fight for any king, even a king of a cave, than for a treacherous prow man and a Norseman they had never heard of. Asgrim wanted to kill these rather than let them go out into the world pouring scorn on his name, but Sigurd overruled him, saying their honesty had taken courage. 'Besides, Asgrim, they will spread our names, which can only be a good thing for there are always fighters looking for men to fight for.' Asgrim still did not like it but was clear-thinking enough to see that killing men he had campaigned beside would not go down well with the others.

As for the last two who refused to take the oath, they were grey-bearded, life-weary warriors for whom thoughts of dying with the spear din ringing in their ears were no longer as warming as thoughts of a hearth and hounds and a comfortable bed, and no one begrudged them gathering their things and tramping off east.

But when the rest had spoken the words over Sigurd's sword Troll-Tickler, and had then broken camp and made ready to turn their backs on the hill fort, Sigurd took up Guthrum's head once more and carried it up the slope in full view of Alrik and all his men, who were wide-eyed at this turn of events.

'Jarl Guthrum has given up his claim to this borg,' Sigurd called up to Alrik, lifting the rotting, half-burnt, honey-slathered head. 'His men are now my men, and I have no quarrel with you, Lord Alrik.' He gestured back to his war band of one hundred and ninety-three warriors, an army now by even a king's reckoning. 'As you can see, I have fulfilled my side of our bargain.' Three of Guthrum's former warriors were driving six pigs up the hill and at Sigurd's words the suspicions filling the heads of those warriors on the ramparts flew off like starlings from a thatch fire and cheering rose from the borg.

'You have done all that you said you would, Sigurd Haraldarson,' Alrik said, unable to keep a grin off his face at the sight of his enemy's severed head. Guthrum's face had haunted Alrik's dreams long enough that the warlord knew it even with the scorched skin and the green pallor. 'I will have half my silver and iron brought out to you. And no one can say you have not earned it.'

Jarl Hrani had suggested that they try to persuade Alrik to join them and swear to Sigurd. 'Better men than he *have* done,' Hrani pointed out, but Olaf said Alrik would never do it, and Sigurd knew that was true. At last the borg was truly Alrik's. He and his men had suffered for it and now there was no way he would abandon it to go off fighting somewhere else. Thór's balls but he would not even come out of that gate – for all that he must have wanted to spit on Guthrum's rotting head – just in case this was some scheme of Sigurd's to take the borg and the whole of its silver and iron hoard for himself.

'I will want carts and the horses to pull them,' Sigurd said.

'We've eaten the horses,' Alrik said, 'but you can have the carts.'

That would have to do. He had enough men to take turns pulling the carts. It was not all fame, silver and skald-song this being a warrior.

'We're going to need a bigger boat,' Solmund grumbled, looking at the mass of them all as they got the measure of each other, these Norsemen and Svearmen, and Guthrum's men who had been left behind asking the others what had befallen their jarl at Ubsola. 'Even with Jarl Hrani's *War-Rider*, which is a good spear-length longer than *Reinen*.'

'Probably,' Sigurd said, 'but there are good problems to have and there are bad problems. Even you must agree this is one of the good ones.'

Solmund muttered an *aye* and Sigurd turned to Asgrim who had come up to him, his face, which would surely frighten his own mother, clenched like a fist.

'I will have Jarl Guthrum's head now, lord,' he said and there was not much of a request about the way he said it.

'You know that if you put his head back together with the rest of him there is a chance he will make it to Valhöll, so my godi tells me,' Sigurd said, tossing him the head which he caught without so much as a grimace that wasn't already there. 'Like a man coming to the feast through the back door, but even so. I think he was a good and brave enough warrior in former times to be useful to Óðin come Ragnarök.'

'If we meet again in the hereafter we will be friends as we once were,' Asgrim said, though he did not look convinced. 'If not,' he went on, looking into those dead, shrivelled eyes, 'then so be it.' With that he turned and that was the last time Sigurd saw or smelt that stinking head, other than when the smoke of the jarl's pyre reached his nose that dusk when the rooks and crows clamoured off to their roosts.

'If you ever burn me, do it when I'm still warm, not reeking like a rancid turd,' Olaf told Sigurd as they set off at the head of the war host.

'A hero's pyre? For you, Uncle?' Sigurd said, an eyebrow arched like Bifröst. 'I think we will save the wood for our meal fire, hey, Svein!'

The red-bearded giant grinned. 'Aye, or even for a new ship,' he said, lifting his chin to Solmund. 'What do you think, old man?'

The old helmsman smiled. 'At last some sense from the bairns,' he said, and the rooks' *craaw*ing was drowned by a war host's laughter.

They knew they had come to Alrik's camp on the shore of Løgrinn before they could see it, because of the woodsmoke in the air and the constant rhythmic *thwock* of axes cutting trees as the timber men encroached ever deeper into the forest. But even without these signs, the midges dancing in brown swarms amongst the trees, making men slap exposed skin, scratch heads and beards and curse, told them they had come to the lake. Not that it was really a lake, of course, seeing as men said there was a channel in the east which led out into the Baltic Sea. But Birka sat on an island in Løgrinn and it was that famous trading centre which drew ships and crews into the great bay like crows to a newly sown field. It was from Birka that Alrik recruited most of his warriors, enticing young men and old growlers with promises of riches in exchange for their spear and sword arms. That was where Alrik's man Knut had recruited Sigurd and his crew, and now they were returning to the camp at which they had stayed before marching to the borg. The camp where, one rain-flayed night, Sigurd and Valgerd had given themselves each to the other, so that he felt the weight of that on him now and wondered if she did too.

They came up to the palisade with their shields above their heads to show that they came in peace, for the men of the camp would be more than wary of such a large sword-host, more so if they recognized any of Jarl Guthrum's men. Bram had thrown Guthrum's axe banner into a fire, which was less subtle than

quietly burying it as Olaf had suggested, and those who had
served the jarl watched it blacken and burn, their faces grim and
betraying what a heavy thing it was to see that. Not that Bram
cared.

'What?' he said, answering glares with a shrug. 'You watched
your jarl's luck go up in smoke. Now you can watch his banner
do the same.'

But some of Guthrum's men still had the axe painted on their
shields and there was a good chance someone in the settlement
would spy them and raise the alarm, believing that Alrik was
beaten and Guthrum had come to finish them or hurl them back
to the sea.

'That head would have come in useful again now, even stinking
as it did,' Olaf said, but as it turned out the men watching from
behind those sharp stakes recognized Sigurd and his crew, not
least Valgerd who Sigurd made sure was standing with him, with
her golden braids lying over the swell of her mail-clad chest.
They recognized Jarl Hrani too and his boar's head banner,
for the jarl had paid a man acting as harbour master to moor
War-Rider there and keep her safe while he tramped inland on
Sigurd's trail.

Sigurd had allowed Hrani to keep that banner not out of
respect for the jarl or as a first act of generosity to a man who was
now oath-tied to him, but because it would not hurt for other
jarls and lords back in Norway to hear that Hrani Randversson
was now allied with Sigurd Haraldarson. *Let the oath-breaker hear
it too*, Sigurd thought, *so that he might feel the icy worm of betrayal
looping over itself in his guts.*

If they had turned heads the first time they had walked
through that camp on the shore, it was nothing compared with
this time. It seemed that the whole place went still. Women came
out of the houses and stood planted there, hands on hips as they
eyed the war host in all its grim glory. Men could not help but
put their hands on spears and sword grips; much good it would
do them if Sigurd meant the place harm. Only the hens and the

beasts in the byres and the pigs in the pens seemed unimpressed, clucking and snorting as normal, and of the craftsmen who had been about their daily tasks only the blacksmith did not stop, his hammer ringing like a bell because he was in the middle of a forging and to stop now was to ruin the blade.

Neither did the folk there need to see beneath the skins covering the carts which the sweating men were pulling to know what lay beneath, and they must have wondered how Sigurd had got his hands on the hoard which their own lord had set out to pillage from Jarl Guthrum – though none had the balls to come up and ask him, and the only man who saw opportunity rather than danger was Trygir, who had given Sigurd's crew their allotted two skins of ale each day when they had stayed there before.

Sigurd was drinking in the sight of *Reinen* when Trygir came up to him, getting his attention by hawking and spitting a gobbet into the mud. He nodded at *Reinen* sitting still and graceful and full of quiet promise on the water, which was as flat as the whalebone plaques which women used with smoothers to get the creases out of linen.

'You'll be wanting supplies if you're off,' he said. 'I can get you plenty of ale, some mead too. Meat, bread, cheese. Fish of course. Got some eggs and plenty of bilberries. Crowberries too if you want them.'

Sigurd nodded. One hundred and ninety-three warriors needed a lot of food. That was one thing to consider now that he was responsible for them all. You could not expect them to row, fight, or fuck for that matter, with empty bellies, and he would have to be careful – even as rich as he now was – not to see that pile of silver and iron shrink. Which was why he decided he would not pay for the supplies which Trygir had gone off grinning to find. No point telling Trygir that though. Neither would he hand over any silver for *Kráka*, Alrik's ship, which he was going to fill with those men who could not fit aboard *Reinen* or *War-Rider*.

'She's a pretty thing,' Olaf said, looking at the sleek karvi and knowing exactly what Sigurd was thinking. 'It's not as if Alrik will miss her either, what with him clinging to that borg like a shipwrecked man to a rock.'

'We'll make an enemy of him,' Sigurd said.

Olaf said nothing. Later, when the checks to the ships were done, the provisions stowed and the crews were climbing aboard to take their places, the men of the settlement gathered together. They had come in small groups, twos and threes, spear and axe-armed, and now there were some sixty men arranged in a half-decent skjaldborg though they kept a safe distance from the wharf.

'You think they've got it in them?' one of the men asked Asgrim who with thirty bristling Svearmen had made a defensive line with their backs to the ships, their blades threatening death to the settlement men. Asgrim muttered something into his beard but Jarl Hrani, who had come to get the measure of Alrik's men, said he did not think they would be wetting their blades that day, even though Trygir was hurling insults at them, yelling at Sigurd and Olaf that they were men without honour, for all their shining war gear, nothing more than whore-born thieves and pale-livered, dog-tupping Norse scum.

'They are not going to die for the sake of one karvi and the food we've stowed,' Jarl Hrani said and that was Sigurd's take on it too, for they were leaving Alrik with his other boats: three broad-beamed knörrs, that other karvi and, most importantly, his big snekke, a warlord's ship with high curving prow and stern, a sturdy but shallow keel and room for twenty-two oarsmen on each side. Solmund had wanted them to take that ship instead of the karvi. The old sea-wolf could not help himself. He was weak at the knees for a beautiful ship the way even warriors of reputation weaken in the presence of a pretty girl.

'She will sit well ploughing a furrow beside *Reinen* and *War-Rider*,' he had said, his mouth close to Sigurd's ear, trying to convince him. But Sigurd shook his head.

189

'We'll take *Crow*,' he said, 'for she will serve us well enough and it is a theft which Alrik can choose to ignore if he wants to. We take his best ship and his honour will leave him no choice but to bring his little fleet west to repay us in blood.'

'Burn his little fleet then,' Solmund suggested, 'apart from her of course,' nodding at the snekke.

'We take *Crow*,' Sigurd said, ending the discussion before his mind was changed, and Solmund had accepted that and gone aboard the karvi to make sure she was still as seaworthy as she had looked when they had followed in her wake from Birka into this bay.

'We are ready,' Sigurd called to Asgrim now and the big man nodded and growled at the warriors in his shieldwall to walk slowly backwards, keeping their shields up in case one of the settlement men chose to make a point by lobbing a spear or loosing an arrow. As it was, those men came forward bit by bit, the way nervous dogs will edge closer to the boar they have trapped, but it was little more than a gesture because they knew that if they attacked they would die and Alrik would lose much more than some supplies and a pretty boat with room for sixteen pairs of oars.

Sigurd went aboard *Reinen*, and his crew, which now included twenty-five Svearmen, pushed off with their oars to turn her bows into the west and the other crews did the same so that all three ships glided out into the bay. And being on the water again, albeit more a glorified lake than a real sea, was a joy which had men singing bawdy songs as the oars bit and pulled, bit and pulled, and the three ships slid across the flat water like a small skein of geese crossing the sky.

'Ah but this feels good,' Olaf announced, standing at the prow upon which Svein had mounted the great reindeer antlers. 'How do you like this life, lad?' he asked Thorbiorn Thorirsson who was grinning as he pulled his oar. 'Better than wasting your days in your father's hall, rutting the hours away with the women's burbling in your ears all the while.'

'I miss the rutting part,' the young man said, 'but I will get even more of that done when I return a hero.'

'Is that so?' Olaf said, winking at Sigurd.

'Well we will find out soon enough,' Sigurd said, for after Birka they would go back to Skíringssalr in Viksfjord, because Sigurd was a warlord now and a rich one too. And he had a proposition for King Thorir and his Spear-Danes.

The sun hung in the west in a purple sky and their prows followed it, the oarbanks beating steadily like eagles' wings. Then, as though the Æsir themselves thirsted for the blood and the crop of warriors that this feud was bound to reap, a gust gathered from the east to agitate the water. At first it ruffled the lake but soon it furrowed it, even whipping spray from the small waves and giving the crews enough reason to stow the oars and haul the sails up.

'This will do us,' Solmund said, standing at the tiller and keeping their course as straight as an arrow's flight. 'Aye, this will do us just fine.'

And Sigurd felt as light as a leaf dancing in the wind. He wanted to shout with joy, to call out the names of his brothers who awaited him in Valhöll. He was out for vengeance and there was nothing in this world that could stop him.

He was going to war.

They did not stay long in Birka. Nevertheless, two days was enough time to pick up a handful of landless, lordless men who might have ended up serving Alrik or some other Svear warlord had they not been drawn to the harbour like dogs to meat as word of the three new ships spread through the town. Three were grizzled, growling, big-bearded men who, to look at them at least, any jarl or king would be pleased to have in their skjaldborg. They had assumed Olaf or Jarl Hrani would be the man receiving their oath but to their credit they made no fuss when Asgrim pointed out that it was Sigurd to whom they would bind themselves.

'He's young, I'll grant you,' one of them, an Irishman named Niall, said in a fair mix of Norse and Svear, 'but if he already has the oath of all these then who are we to question it?' He nodded at Asgrim. 'I would rather fight for a young man on the rise than an old man on the fall.' He did not have any disagreement from Asgrim about that.

The other five were young men out for adventure as much as silver, and they spoke the words with trembling voices and such grave solemnity that it was obvious this was their first oath-taking. Still, all the rest had long enough memories of their own beginnings along the warrior's road and did not tease these nervous new beards too sorely about it.

'You know that we are off to fight a king?' Sigurd asked them as the first young man put his lips to Troll-Tickler's pommel. 'And not just some little king of some unknown valley but a powerful king, the lord of Avaldsnes and master of the North Way.'

The young men looked at each other, grinning. 'We will fight anyone you want us to fight, lord,' one of them said as if it were all the same to him.

Olaf scowled and nodded at Sigurd as if to say *They are willing, man! So by Thór's arse get on with it before they grow brains!* So Sigurd got on with it.

The kaupang at Skíringssalr seemed a different place than the one Sigurd remembered from when they had come to it in the deep of winter. It had been a silent land sleeping under a blanket of white. A place pressed upon by the low, dark sky and choked with the smoke from the hearthfires around which folk gathered and spent their days.

Now the bay was full of fishing boats, the sky was filled with the shriek and whirl of gulls and the marketplace was buzzing with trade. Beyond the market the nearest slopes bristled with barley and rye and the far-off hills were dotted with cows and sheep between the many burial mounds, and Sigurd knew what

Olaf was thinking as they dropped the sail and took the oars out
to row up to the jetty.

'We will make him a generous offer, Uncle,' Sigurd said.

'We'll have to,' Olaf said, for he was thinking that this trading
place and all this good farming land rich in beasts and milk and
crops would be earning King Thorir plenty of silver. Tempting
such a rich man away from a comfortable life would not be easy.
But Sigurd wanted Thorir. Wanted the king's Spear-Danes to
join his raging host against King Gorm's army.

'A prosperous place then,' Jarl Hrani said, viewing it through a
raider's eye. The store houses and workshops which had been
boarded up in winter were all open to the world and busy as
women's mouths round a loom, as Moldof put it. 'Maybe we will
come back here one day, boy,' he said to little Randver who gave
his wolf grin, and Sigurd could not help but think what a fine
thing it must be to have a son.

'Well let me give you some advice if you do come back here,'
Sigurd said, even now thinking how strange it was to be talking
to Jarl Hrani whom he still hated, oath or no. 'If King Thorir
challenges you to a wrestling bout, say you have a crick in your
back or the shits or a splitting skull from too much ale, but do
not accept.'

'Jarls and kings do not roll around in the rushes, Haraldarson,'
Hrani said through a twist of lips.

'Jarls are not supposed to break their oaths to kings and swear
to outlaws either,' Sigurd said, 'and yet you have done both
these things, Hrani Randversson.'

There was nothing Hrani could say to that and so he turned
his gaze back to the shining hall for which Skíringssalr was
named. He, his son Randver Hranisson, Sigurd and Olaf were
standing on the wharf admiring the place and enjoying the sun's
warmth on their faces. They were waiting for Thorbiorn who
had gone up the hill to his father's hall along with several Danes
who had been watching the ships turn into the bay, scattering

the færings. Some had already run off up to the hall at the first sighting, their warning calls echoing out across the bay, and one man was still hammering a piece of iron which hung on a gibbet and made a clamour like the smith god Völund working in his forge. But the Danes who had stayed by the jetty had recognized Thorbiorn standing up on *Reinen*'s sheer strake, hanging on to the stem post now that the prow beast had been stowed to show they came in peace, and they had waved to him as if he were a long-lost hero returned from doing heroic things. Which was of course how young Thorbiorn thought of himself anyway.

Now the young man strode back down to the wharf and invited the others up to speak with his father the king. For all his hatred of Hrani, Sigurd wanted to watch the jarl's face to see what he made of King Thorir's blazing, golden hall as they were ushered into the place. They left their weapons with the king's steward outside, but for the Óðin spear, which Sigurd had not offered up and which the steward had not tried to take from him.

'Skíringssalr,' Jarl Hrani muttered, looking up. The shining hall.

The hearth was lit but it was only a small fire now, not the great flapping flame that had greeted them last time when they had stepped out of a white world into a golden one. But the thralls had been busy lighting lamps and candles again by the looks and there seemed as many small flames flickering as there were stars in the night sky. These little flames did not so much light the darkness as banish it so that the golden cloths hanging from the roof beams, fine as a goddess's breath and shimmering in the draughts, were wondrous to behold.

'They are silks, Jarl Hrani Randversson of Hinderå,' King Thorir boomed from his high seat, as proud as ever of his possessions and as thrilled as ever to see their effect on new guests. Beside him sat his wife the queen and behind them stood four burly, spear-armed, mail-clad Danes. 'From lands you can only dream about,' the king said.

There were some two dozen of the king's hirðmen in the hall, half watching, half playing dice or tafl, most drinking. A cat curled round Sigurd's leg and many more sat or lay here and there, preening or sleeping. One lay in Queen Halla's lap, being fussed to death and purring.

King Thorir swept an arm across his hall and his men. 'We are friends with the Goddess here, Jarl Hrani,' he said, as if that explained everything, including all the cats. 'Well then, Sigurd, we meet again.' The king stood from his seat and held out his hand and Sigurd stepped forward to grip him arm in arm, the warrior's way.

'It is good to see you again, lord king,' Sigurd said, the smile on his face as genuine as his words. There was something about this Danish king that he liked. 'And you also, Queen Halla,' he added, dipping his head at her, and the queen smiled with her eyes because she liked Sigurd. If she could she would have Sigurd in her lap instead of that cat, he knew.

'Sigurd jarl-killer,' she said, those dark eyes of hers shining like the fist-sized gold brooches which boasted of their position on the swell of her bosom. 'I thank you for bringing our son safe home with all his limbs still attached.'

'Aye, we thank you for that,' added King Thorir, appraising the young man beside him, 'but it seems to me you might have made a man of him too.' He grabbed Thorbiorn by the shoulder and shook him. 'I swear you've put on a bit of muscle, lad. See here, wife! The boy might be on his way to growing a set of shoulders to have the women dewy.'

'Father!' Thorbiorn said, no more embarrassed than he should have been.

'He's fought then?' the king asked, looking from Sigurd to Olaf. 'And I mean properly. In the shieldwall or out of it.'

Sigurd nodded. 'In the blood-fray, lord,' he said.

'Some of the men have started calling him Thorbiorn Fleet-Foot,' Olaf said, recalling the lad's grabbing of little Randver Hranisson.

The king frowned at that because it could easily be the byname of a man who runs from a fight. 'Fast-Blade is better,' he said.

Olaf's lips pursed and he nodded.

'He has fought well and bravely, lord king,' Sigurd said and Thorir's grin was almost as wide as the one which had earned him his own byname of Gapthrosnir, which meant one gaping in fury.

He punched his son's shoulder this time and there was enough muscle behind it to knock Thorbiorn back a step. 'So you've been wetting your sword instead of your cock for a change. Good lad!'

'I've killed six men, Father.'

'Six! You hear that, wife? Six!' The king winked at Olaf. 'And I'd wager at least one of them was a full-grown man too.'

Thorbiorn scowled at that but said nothing.

'And my sister?' Sigurd said, unable to hold the question back any longer. Gods but he missed Runa now. He thought of her often, it was true, but this shining hall, this beautiful place, put her in his mind like a stone in a plum.

'Young Runa is thriving with the Freyja Maidens,' King Thorir said, 'so I am told. I can tell you no more because as you know we have little to do with the warrior women and they have even less to do with us.'

Relieved, Sigurd nodded, taking what he could even from that threadbare news.

'But what I want to know is how come you are friends with Jarl Hrani here? For if my memory serves, the jarl you killed was this man's father.' He looked at Hrani suspiciously, clearly wondering how a man could seem to be contentedly standing beside someone he ought to have killed if he were any sort of son at all.

'All that is behind us now, like bubbles in a ship's wake,' Sigurd said, making less of it than how it really felt in his chest. 'Jarl Hrani is going to help me kill the oath-breaker. In return I will support his claim to King Gorm's high seat at his estate in Avaldsnes.'

'And what claim is that?' King Thorir asked, knowing full well that it was ambition and not kinship that was the fuel in the flames. Sigurd did not see any reason to go into how the agreement had come about. King Thorir might not like that he had threatened to kill the handsome boy who stood there now in his golden hall as though he had seen it all before. As though he were born to be the ring-giver of just such a place.

'I will make a good king,' Jarl Hrani said, knowing that was hardly justification for turning on an oath but not really caring either.

King Thorir raised an eyebrow at him. Sigurd dreaded to think what Runa would say when she learnt of this alliance with Hrani. She had been in Skudeneshavn when Hrani, no jarl then, had brought death to the village. But she would have to understand how things were. How they had to be.

'Let's have a proper look at it then,' Thorir said with a flap of his hand, and Sigurd knew Thorbiorn must have already told his father about Gungnir. He stepped forward and handed the great spear to the king, who gripped it in both hands as though he would run them all through.

'Suits me, don't you think?' the king said, admiring its weight in his hands and its rune-carved blade, and for a terrible moment Sigurd thought Thorir meant to take the spear for himself. But then the king laughed and handed it back to him and Sigurd's fingers curled round that smooth ash shaft as though they would never let it go again. 'The Goddess would only be jealous were I to make too much of a fuss about the Allfather's spear,' Thorir said. 'Now give me a horn full of Freyja's golden tears or a feather from her cloak and I will light a fire such as your people or mine have never seen and pay a hundred skalds to sing the tale of it.' His brow furrowed then. 'But tell me, Sigurd jarl-killer . . .'

Better if he does not call me that in this company, Sigurd thought, seeing the frown on little Randver's face.

'. . . tell me why you are back here again so soon. For I will not believe you have made a hero of Thorbiorn already. Even a

197

good meal takes time to prepare, as any woman will tell you.' He pointed through the beeswax-scented air towards the hall's door. 'Last time you came with barely half a crew, puffed up and arrogant standing there on my jetty, but half a crew all the same. Now you come with three ships and two hundred spears. It seems to me that even an eagle cannot rise so high so fast.'

'I want you to join me in this fight,' Sigurd said. 'Many others have, as you can see from looking down into the bay.'

But the king waved a hand and shook his head. 'I have already told you that I am comfortable here and do not need a slice of the glory you have your heart set on.'

'Sigurd is rich, Father,' Thorbiorn said, grinning. 'Very rich.'

'Is he now?' the king said, that long beard rope of his polishing his brynja's rings.

Queen Halla's lips curled like the cat in her lap. 'Just think, husband, we would no longer have to feast those wretched men who come trying to win us for their king Karl and his white god.' She would have spat were she a man. 'I am sick of playing their games.'

'You could buy candles to light the night sky,' Olaf said, 'and tell this king Karl and his god to sail off over the world's edge together.'

'You could have a statue made of the Goddess,' Sigurd said, 'but not like the ones in Ubsola which are of wood,' *or were of wood*, he thought, imagining them burning, 'but of silver, which would be the envy of jarls and kings and would earn you Freyja's favour for long enough to see your sons and their sons become great men.'

'I do not know you, King Thorir,' Hrani said while the king pulled his silver beard rope through his fist, 'but you do not strike me as a man who is over the hill of his own greatness yet. Or a man who means to die a straw death with no good songs about his own war glory filling his ears.'

The king was thinking and thinking hard. It was all over his flame-washed face and in his small grey eyes.

'We do have many untested young men here,' he said. 'Lads who have yet to wet their spears or know what it is to stand in the skjaldborg against other men who are trying to spill their guts in the grass.' He looked at Olaf. 'We have had peace in these parts for years now,' he said, as if he felt guilty about it. He thumbed behind him, then pointed out several of the hirðmen around the hall, who were all listening now that there was talk of war. 'Many of these men have sons who, like my own, have much to learn,' he said. There were some *ayes* and grunts of agreement at that. 'But I do not want to tie myself to a sinking ship. I will only fight if we cannot lose.'

Sigurd smiled and lifted Gungnir. 'The Allfather has given me his own spear. We have the Lord of War on our side, King Thorir. How can we lose?'

The king went over to a knot of men who from their arm rings and general bearing looked like they had done their fair share of fighting over the years, though perhaps not for a while judging by their paunches and lack of fresh scars. For a while these men talked with their lord but there were enough nods for Sigurd to be hopeful when Thorir walked back up to his high seat and sat down facing his guests. 'My men and I still have some talking to do, Sigurd Haraldarson,' he said, 'and of course we would have to agree exactly how much silver my help is worth to you. Good Spear-Danes come at a price,' he added, nodding at his men, who grunted their approval at that. 'But if you stay here tonight and drink my mead I will have my answer for you in the morning. I will have food and drink taken to your men at the wharf. You understand I cannot feast them all here.'

'Of course,' Sigurd said. 'We would be honoured to share your mead and your hall.' He flashed a smile at Queen Halla because it could not hurt. And she smiled again, wise enough to know his game but vain enough to let him play it.

'And I'll tell you what, Jarl Hrani Randversson,' the square-shouldered king added, thumping the arm of his chair. 'If you can beat me in a wrestling bout I will fight beside you even if the rest of my men do not.'

Jarl Hrani looked at Sigurd. Sigurd shrugged.

'I have a bad leg, lord king,' the jarl said, touching his right thigh. 'I fell. From my horse.'

The king's grin vanished like mist and a frown took its place. 'That is a shame,' he said, clearly unimpressed. Then he looked at Sigurd. 'It seems as though we will just have to drink, Norseman,' he said, and even in that there was a challenge.

And so they drank.

The boar was not even fully grown. A juvenile, its stripes still clear enough to see by the dimming light.

'And that is how we know that the gods love you, my king,' Hreidar said as they strode up to the skewered beast, around which the flies were buzzing. 'You still have a throw that Thór himself would raise a horn to.' The champion was grinning. 'Just as well, too, for he was about to come at you like a lightning bolt.'

King Gorm said nothing. He took hold of the shaft and pulled it from the creature's chest just inside the left foreleg. It took some pulling too. *Just a youngen though,* he thought. A squeaker no more than three moons ago. That he had brought the creature down with a good throw was nothing to boast about, for he knew, just as Hreidar knew, that the boar had been about to run, not towards him but away. It had been a heartbeat from turning and tearing off into the forest, screeching in terror at being caught by a hunting party that had managed to get down wind of him. But that did not make for a good story to tell when they got back to the king's hearth and Hreidar knew it.

'Ah, well done! A fine boar! But I am sorry I missed the kill.' Jarl Arnstein Arngrimsson of Bokn, whom men called Twigbelly on account of his massive stomach, came puffing out of the pines behind them, his own spear blade as clean as it had been when they had set out that morning. Truth be told Gorm had been trying to shake the jarl off all day, but Twigbelly was surprisingly – and annoyingly – determined and seemed to have the vigour of a man half his size.

'I should have let him go,' Gorm rumbled. 'He is barely worth the effort of carrying and skinning.' Not that he had done either of those things himself for many years.

'You get them while you can, lord king,' Twigbelly said, dragging an arm across his sweaty face. 'Let them grow too big and you risk things not going so well when you next meet.'

Gorm turned to the man, searching his face for a sign that Twigbelly was mocking him, bringing up this whole Sigurd business when he should know better. But the jarl just looked hot and out of breath, bent over now, fat hands on his shapeless legs as some of the hunting party caught up. *At least I can still out-hunt the rest of them*, Gorm thought, proud of himself, or ashamed of the others, or both. To be king you had to have iron in your bones and Óðin's mead for blood. Start letting other jarls and ambitious hersirs beat you to the prey and you might as well give up the high seat and drink yourself to death. A king must not show any weakness, for other men are like wolves sniffing for blood or disease amongst a herd of deer and they will be upon you before you know it.

Deer. Those were the days. When in these very woods you could sometimes bring down a monstrously big bull elk, a creature so magnificent that it made your breath catch in your chest just to behold it. The sort that skalds put in their tales to make their heroes sound even bigger. You could hunt such creatures with worthy men, too, not just catch-fart jarls and hersirs who only accepted the king's invitation because they feared offending him. Feared the flat rocks in the strait below the royal manor at Avaldsnes upon which Gorm chained his enemies and watched them slowly swallowed by the rising tide. Upon which he had chained his beautiful young wife Aesa years ago because she had made a fool of him. So he had made a crab-picked corpse of her.

Jarl Harald was one of those worthy men, Gorm thought now, watching two thralls tie the boar's feet together and thread a couple of spears through the legs to carry it off back to his hall and people as if it were some fabled, man-eating beast slaughtered at last by the warrior king. Yes, Harald had been a proper jarl. *My equal perhaps*. And perhaps that had been the problem, why in the end Gorm had to kill him. *Perhaps? Ha! Of course it was.*

Didn't see elk like that in this forest any more. Didn't see jarls like Harald at his shoulder either.

'We will have the light a little longer yet, lord,' Hreidar said, pulling some bristles from the dead boar's haunch as it hung there between the thralls, blood dripping rhythmically from the spear wound which had gone deep enough to kill it, tearing its heart, Hreidar had said. The champion lifted his fist and dropped the bristles and they fell more or less straight to the forest floor. 'No wind,' he said. 'Shall we cut west and see what else we can find?'

Gorm looked at Twigbelly, who tried his best not to look unenthusiastic about the prospect of walking further and into deeper, thicker forest instead of returning to the king's hall for mead, meat and women.

'Aye, on we go. We'll find some full-grown beast,' the king said, 'and we'll not go back until we do.' This got some murmurs of approval from his hirðmen, who knew their king well enough to prefer his company when they had speared something decent. *And fuck Jarl Arnstein Arngrimsson*, Gorm thought. Let him drown in his own sweat. The fat swine had only come up to Avaldsnes because he wanted to ask the king's permission to raid in the south as far as Mandal. Everyone knew the man was losing the respect of his people and hoped a good bit of booty-taking and blood-letting would keep the Bokn folk contented. So Gorm would let him raid, but he'd want a third of the loot. And the soft-bellied, red-faced toad would have to keep up with him now for another three or four rôsts at least, until they found some prey worthy of the king's spear.

'Someone's coming, lord king,' Otkel said, pointing his own spear north in the direction of Avaldsnes. Three riders. Coming noisily through the trees, kit and fittings thumping and jangling, breaking twigs as they came.

Twigbelly will be pleased if this is the end of the hunt, Gorm thought.

'Fools will scare off every creature between here and Snørteland,' he growled. 'Whoever it is I will flay them alive.' His hirðmen nevertheless drew together, hands falling to sword grips until they knew who this was who cared nothing that they risked ruining the king's hunting and his mood too.

'It's Alfgeir,' Otkel said and men's hands fell away from their swords at that, though it was only the younger, greener ones who relaxed. The others knew that Alfgeir, being an experienced man who had fought at King Gorm's side for more than twenty summers, would not have ridden six rôsts and risked his lord's anger for no good reason.

Not Kadlin! Gorm asked the gods, pleaded really, struck with the sudden fear that something might have happened to his wife.

'The queen?' he asked even before Alfgeir had dismounted the snorting pony, whose nostrils were smoking in the chill pre-dusk air.

'Queen Kadlin is well, lord king,' Alfgeir said, and the king looked at the other two riders throwing their legs over their mounts' backs. He prided himself on his ability to read men's faces the way clever men could decipher rune stones, and these men were not fearful or nervous. They were excited. Eager to relay whatever news they had for him. Same with Alfgeir albeit he was better at hiding it.

Alfgeir locked eyes with him, then glanced at Jarl Twigbelly.

'Whatever it is, you can say it in front of Jarl Arnstein,' Gorm told him. Twigbelly nodded in thanks for the courtesy. No doubt he was simply enjoying the rest.

'We are betrayed, lord,' Alfgeir said. 'Sigurd Haraldarson has returned from Svealand at the head of a war band. He—'

'A war band?' Gorm put in, unable to stop himself. 'But who would follow that whelp? How many men does he have? Two dozen?'

'Reports vary. Three hundred. Maybe four.' Alfgeir shook his head. 'We do not know, but Sigurd is calling men to his banner. Offering them silver if they will fight with him against you.'

'So he has a banner now, hey?' Gorm looked at Hreidar. The champion spat on to the forest floor, violence simmering in him already.

'More of a charm, lord. Of sorts,' Alfgeir said. 'A spear.'

'A spear?' Gorm looked at Twigbelly now, who was drinking ale from a skin which one of his men had handed him.

'So your former champion did not manage to gut young Sigurd, then?' the jarl said, licking his lips. 'Moldof was his name if I recall. We heard he rowed off to gain the fame and position he lost along with his arm.'

'Ha!' Hreidar blurted, the king's new champion and prow man making it clear what he thought about that.

Gorm ignored jarl and champion both, turning his gaze back on Alfgeir who clearly had more to say.

'Not just a spear, lord, but Gungnir. Óðin's spear. It turns out that Sigurd had made another enemy, some Svear jarl, and this jarl captured him and took him to Ubsola. Meant to sacrifice Haraldarson to the gods.' Alfgeir shrugged. 'He wouldn't know what a lucky shit Sigurd is.'

Lucky? Gorm thought. *Why don't you say Óðin-kissed, for that is what everybody thinks. And rich now, too, if he has managed to draw three or four hundred men to him.*

'Sigurd escaped, the gods know how. And he pilfered the spear from the temple. It's a big 'un, this spear,' Alfgeir went on, holding the imaginary weapon in his hands.

'I've seen it,' Gorm said.

'Of course,' Alfgeir said, and well he might seeing as he had travelled with the king to Ubsola for the last Dísablót. Five years ago? Or six? When the blood had flowed like ale at the Jól feast and the sacred trees had groaned under their corpse-burdens. And the crows had fed till they near burst from so much flesh.

'Well, the crows will feed again soon, when Haraldarson and his pack are put down,' Gorm said, getting odd looks from those around him, for they had not been inside his head to see those memories of the blood rites. 'So he has come back to settle this feud then. Good.' Gorm nodded, looking at his hearth warriors, beginning to feel the same tremble in the blood that had got into these three messengers, making them ride hard through the forest to find their king. 'He has enough ships to face me in the Strait?' he asked Alfgeir. He would be surprised if so. Men were relatively easy to come by. Ships were not.

'No, lord,' Alfgeir said. 'It seems he wants a land fight.'

'Does he?' Gorm said. *He means to end this thing one way or the other then*, he thought. No beating of oars to fly if things were going badly. Just the clash of shieldwalls. The spear din until the issue was decided.

The red war.

'Who would be mad enough to join him against you, lord?' Twigbelly asked, pushing the stopper back into the ale skin and swiping the drops from his moustache bristles. 'Even with a magic spear he cannot hope to beat you. Beat us,' he added just in time. 'No one of worth would join him.'

'Betrayal, Alfgeir,' Gorm said, remembering how this conversation had started. 'You said betrayal.' He could not have been talking about Sigurd, for they were already enemies, since long before Haraldarson had refused the jarl torc which Gorm had offered him. Since his own betrayal of Sigurd's father if they were getting to the nub of it. Even so, who would have thought that Harald's last living son, the pup of the litter at that, would survive so long and grow such fangs?

'Yes, lord, betrayal,' Alfgeir said, frowning, and his next words seemed stuck in his throat.

'Well?' Gorm snapped.

Alfgeir cleared his throat. 'There is another banner alongside this Óðin spear. The white axe on black.'

Gorm almost laughed. 'No, Alfgeir. Some mistake.'

'No mistake, my king. It is Jarl Hrani Randversson's banner. He is with Sigurd.' Alfgeir took a step towards him. 'There are whispers,' he said, his own voice barely above a whisper, 'that Jarl Hrani has even oath-sworn himself to Sigurd.'

If that boar hanging beneath the spears had been an adult male, all bristling fury, and had it charged him at full speed the blow could not have struck Gorm like those words did.

Gorm shook his head, trying to dispel the very idea of it. 'Jarl Hrani hates Sigurd as much as I do,' he said. 'Haraldarson killed his father. No, Randversson would never swear to him. Nor would he turn against me after all I have given him. He would not wear his father's torc if I had not put it round his neck. As I put it round Randver's neck before him.'

Alfgeir thumbed back in the direction of Avaldsnes. 'The men who brought the news have no reason to lie from what I can see,' he said. 'But I have told them that they cannot leave until you have heard with your own ears what they have to say.' He shrugged. 'And yet even if they are mistaken about Jarl Hrani Randversson, what they say about Sigurd is likely to be true. The strutting shit is coming and he wants a fight.'

And by the gods I will give him one, Gorm thought. 'Jarl Arnstein, how many spears can you bring?'

The fat jarl considered the question. 'Thirty hearthmen. As for the levy,' he chewed his lip, 'sixty or seventy and all spear and shield-armed.' Gorm grinned. That was at least ninety just from this one jarl who was sworn to him. There were eleven other jarls whom he could call on to bring their hirðmen and bonders to his banner. Gods but he could raise five hundred spears from his own lands!

'Ride back, Alfgeir,' he said. 'Send word to Jarls Leiknir, Baugr, Vragi and Tósti. The others too. Tell them I have raised my banner. Tell them to muster their fighting men. All of them. If any refuses, he shall be my enemy.'

Alfgeir grinned and nodded and walked back to his pony and the two others, who were also grinning. For war was coming, a war which they could not lose. And in war men make their reputations. They make themselves silver-rich too.

Gorm turned back to Hreidar. 'So we will go that way,' he said, pointing his bloodied spear first westward and then at the hanging boar around which the flies swarmed. 'This piglet must have a father or some big brothers hereabouts.'

Hreidar grinned and nodded and the thralls and his hearthmen prepared to set off again, buzzing themselves with the talk of war.

'But . . . lord king . . .' Twigbelly began, again swiping sweat from his forehead. There were plenty of flies around the jarl too, Gorm saw. 'Surely we should be getting back. You will have much to prepare. I myself will need to get word to the outlying farms.'

'Not at all, Jarl Arnstein,' Gorm said, batting the man's concerns away with a big hand. 'We did not come all this way for one little boar. Besides, if you are like me you do your best planning with a full belly.'

The jarl forced a smile and nodded. 'Of course, my king,' he said, lifting his spear purposefully.

Maybe we will drown you in your own sweat, you hog, Gorm thought, spreading his lips with a smile as he walked off into the trees with Hreidar beside him.

Some decent prey for their spears and then back to the hall to talk of the coming steel-storm. For Sigurd was back and this time he would not slip through the net. *Perhaps I can catch him alive,* Gorm thought, the very idea of that flooding him like the first waves of drunkenness. *I could chain him to the rock and invite everyone to come and watch him drown. Make a feast of it.*

But first to spear something for the table. And remind this fat jarl what kings are made of.

CHAPTER TEN

'STRANGE BEING BACK HERE LIKE THIS,' OLAF SAID.

And it *was* strange. Sigurd looked over at Jarl Hrani's high seat, the seat in which Sigurd himself had sat when it had belonged to Jarl Randver and Sigurd had come to Örn-garð to kill him. Now Hrani was the power in Hinderå and he and Sigurd were allies, which was the Norns spinning men's wyrds after too much mead in Solmund's opinion. And he wasn't the only one.

'This man killed your father, Hrani,' one of the hall's white-beards reminded everyone, as if they needed reminding. He had forgone the *jarl* or *lord* or any other term of respect in order to press the point that until very recently it had been a better man's backside polishing that beechwood seat which sat halfway along the east side where the wall bowed outwards. 'And now you would have us *feast* him? Share our meat and mead . . . with *him*? This . . . shit from Skudeneshavn who sent our lord to the crabs and denied him a jarl's pyre.'

There were plenty of low mumbles at that from those who thought the old warrior had spoken boldly and well, albeit the sound was deadened by the pelts and skins that covered the wall's dark timbers.

But Hrani was their jarl now and it seemed to Sigurd he knew how to be one too, for he held his anger out of sight like a blade in a sheath, his eyes doing all the steel-work instead.

'If you are going on a long sea journey, Athulf, do you eat all the food in the first day or two just because it feels good having a full belly? Or do you ration it so that it will last until you reach your destination or else can raid for more?'

This did not of course need an answer and Athulf swallowed whatever it was he had been about to say then.

'I am thinking about more than just the sweet pleasure there is to be had from revenge,' Hrani added, turning to all his people who had gathered in that old hall which was as chokingly smoky as Sigurd remembered it. 'I am thinking about the whole journey, not just the first crossing from shore to shore, because that is what a jarl must do. A jarl owes his people more than blood. More than a few arm rings and slaves. For those can be snatched away by some other raiding band and we can all be left grinding acorns for bread and watching our children go hungry. We can be called away from our crops to fight for a king who will not risk his own hearthmen because he has others to do the dying for him.' Hrani had steered that so that every man and woman there was thinking of King Gorm without their jarl having spoken the king's name aloud. 'I have put aside my right to vengeance, my blood-duty to my father, in order to raise us all,' Hrani said. 'Would you rather wheel like gulls behind a fishing boat, waiting for fish heads and guts, or soar like eagles, choosing your prey?'

'Speaks well when he needs to, I'll give him that,' Olaf muttered beside Sigurd as a hum rose from the people of Hinderå. Still, it was on a knife-edge this thing, and Sigurd doubted even the Norns knew which way it was going to go. As for King Thorir, he looked bored already, standing there waiting for someone to refill his cup, clearly underwhelmed by the hall which, compared with his golden, Freyja-lit hall, was like a smoky cave. 'Black as

Hel's arsehole,' he had growled when they had first been led inside.

'How? How will wading into a hard fight against our king raise us?' a knörr-breasted woman called out, hands on hips, her elbows creating space around her even in that crowded place, 'because I never feel like some soaring eagle when I am burning one of my sons or stitching their flesh back together.' Her large silver brooches and the keys hanging from her belt marked her as a rich karl's wife and Hrani paid her the respect she was owed by nodding and holding up a hand to hush the crowd so that he might answer.

'In return for helping Sigurd Haraldarson have his revenge on King Gorm,' the jarl said, cleverly hinting that Sigurd was, unlike him, a short-sighted man, 'I will become king.' There was a gasp at that, followed by the beating of cups on tables by those of Hrani's warriors who were already invested in their jarl's ambition. 'Together, Sigurd Haraldarson, King Thorir of Skíringssalr and I will roll King Gorm down his hill at Avaldsnes. I will be king and we will live there and grow rich on the taxes from all the ships going up the Karmsund Strait.'

'And the hall we are building at Skudeneshavn?' a man asked. A carpenter probably, who had downed his adze and his augers to return to Örn-garð to hear for himself the news of this strange new alliance between his jarl and his enemy. 'We are at head height with the walls already and the turf for the roof is due to be cut by the next moon.'

'We will finish the hall at Skudeneshavn but I will not live there,' Jarl Hrani said. 'It will belong to Sigurd Haraldarson and his people, as did Eik-hjálmr before it.' Some did not like that by the sound of it, but Hrani took no notice. 'Those of our people who wish to stay here may do so, but those who wish to come with me to Avaldsnes will be given farmland so that they might start again. We will all be rich after this fight, and that is before all the ship taxes that will come to us,' he held out his cupped hands, 'pouring in like rain.'

'And the gods are with us!' Hadd Hog-Head said, lifting his cup high towards his jarl. The champion then waved his ale in Sigurd's direction so that Sigurd, who had been quiet until now, knew that it would soon be up to him to tip the scales in their favour. 'We have Gungnir, Óðin's own spear, to poke those Avaldsnes men with,' Hog-Head called, grinning from ear to ear. 'How can we lose?'

All eyes turned to Sigurd, not that there hadn't been plenty of eyes on him from the very beginning because of his fame amongst these folk. Hrani's younger brother Amleth was staring at him from behind the jarl's right shoulder and Sigurd wondered what was in that young man's mind, for Amleth had once been set to marry Runa and celebrate in this very hall. But Sigurd was never going to let that marriage take place and rather than bringing his sister's dowry to the wedding he had brought mayhem and slaughter. Instead of moaning with the pleasure of the rut on what should have been his wedding night, Amleth had moaned with pain because Floki's axe had cut into his shoulder deeply enough that bone had gleamed in the wound.

But now the wind had changed and Sigurd must set the sail accordingly. Now an alliance, not war, was what was needed with Hrani's people, and it was up to Sigurd to convince them of it.

'Some of the men in this hall, some of you standing before me now, came to my village with fire and the sword,' he said. A fact rather than an accusation. 'Some of you killed my friends. My kin. One of you, a man named Andvett, tried to dishonour my mother, though he is dead now because Grimhild had no patience for a drawn-out feud and gave Andvett his death wound there and then, before she herself was slain by another Hinderå man.'

'You were our enemy!' someone shouted from the throng.

Ayes at this, but Sigurd continued. 'Even now some of you wear my father's knives, or his arm rings, or the silver hammers which Jarl Harald had pulled from the necks of men he had slain in battle. You have the balls to stand here in front of me owning things which were taken from my father's sea chests and from the corpses of his people. I am sure the women here are wearing brooches your husbands pulled from the Skudeneshavn women after they forced themselves upon them like beasts, spilling their seed in anything that moved.'

'Who does he think he is?' a man gnarred.

'Aye, enough of his talk,' Athulf put in, for no men liked hearing this sort of dark thing by the light of the hearth, even if they had been up to their balls in it on some or other raid.

'But I answered these offences,' Sigurd said. 'I came to Hinderå and I fed the raven. I killed Jarl Randver and many of your best men lay dead at the end, even your champion Skarth, who was no match for Olaf here.'

They looked at Olaf then but with respect not hatred in their eyes, for no one could argue with the way Olaf had taken Skarth down, like an experienced man felling timber.

'Our blood-worms drank deeply,' Sigurd said, touching the hilt of Troll-Tickler, which Hrani had allowed him to wear even under Örn-garð's soot-stained roof, a sign of the new trust between them, 'and the scales between us were balanced.' He took a step forward and lifted the great spear high. 'Now that we are friends, your people and mine, you have the chance to make Hrani Randversson king. And with Gorm's power broken and no other jarl strong enough to challenge the new king at Avaldsnes, you will have years of peace if you want it. You can sit on your arses getting rich off the taxes from those crews passing through the North Way. You will sell those same crews your crops and your meat, for they are always in need of supplies. Pick and choose a raid or two each summer if you wish, for new slaves and the adventure of it.'

'And what'll you get out of it, Haraldarson?' the knörr-breasted woman asked, those silver brooches gleaming fierce as dragon's eyes.

Sigurd felt the grimace come to his face before he had the time to put it there himself. 'I will have my revenge on the oath-breaker,' he said, the words themselves sweet as mead in his mouth. 'Seeing that goat-shit Gorm's bloodless corpse lying at my feet is enough for me.' He would have *Sea-Eagle* back too, his father's second-best ship, which King Gorm had stolen after his men had cleared Jarl Harald's warriors from its blood-soaked deck in the Karmsund Strait. But no point in bringing that up now. 'I swear I shall see him dead.'

Some of them nodded. A few touched the Thór's hammers at their necks because they knew a solemn and self-binding oath when they heard it.

That would have been a good end to it all, and only a skald would put a better shine on it by having Hrani's people cheering and clamouring for the fight. As it was, there was no cheering but they seemed content. Perhaps in their minds some of them were already spending the silver paid by skippers who as yet had not even provisioned their ships for a sail up the Karmsund Strait. Others were no doubt imagining how else their lives might be improved by their being the king's own people.

But this was real, not some skald's tale. And that big-mouthed, big-breasted karl's wife had no flair for the poetic. They were not done yet.

'So what has he to do with any of it?' she asked, pointing at King Thorir, which was not really the thing to do even though the man was a Dane in a Norseman's hall. 'This is not his fight. Who is to say he will not want Gorm's high seat for himself when Sigurd Haraldarson stands crowing on Gorm's corpse?'

For a heartbeat or two King Thorir looked as if he might challenge the woman to a wrestle, and that might have been something to see, but then he lifted his chin with its long silver beard rope and threw back those massive shoulders of his. 'I have come to my own arrangement with Sigurd,' he said, 'and am in this up to the hilt.' He grinned at his sons, who were all there with him, and they all grinned back. 'My Spear-Danes will win this little fight for you and then we will be gone before the crows have had their fill. No offence meant, Jarl Hrani,' he said, glancing at his host, 'but as you well know, my own hall makes this place look like a dung heap.' Hrani did not like this, but he wasn't about to make a thing of it. 'So you can all be sure that we will not be staying around here, or in this Avaldsnes place, any longer than need be.'

'Still,' Sigurd said, picking up the thread from where he had left off, 'it will not be a little skirmish.' He let his eyes roam across the faces of those gathered in the acrid flame-chased dark. 'As you all know, King Gorm has many warriors. He knows we are coming and even now will be calling in the levies and bringing other jarls to his banner. But as word spreads, more fighters will flock to my own banner too. To this spear,' he said, lifting the thing again. 'For this will be a fight to tell your grandchildren about. A fight for warriors and skalds.' He grinned and Svein beside him grinned too. 'The gods are watching,' he said, 'so let us make sure we are worthy of it.'

'Óðin!' Olaf roared.

'Óðin!' Svein echoed. And then the other warriors in that hall, Sigurd's crew, Hinderå men and Danes alike, took up the chant, their blood coming to the boil with the thought of war and booty, the sword-song and fame.

'Óðin! Óðin! Óðin!' they called, hammering the boards, caught up in the moment.

'This is how you will tell it, skald,' Sigurd said to Hagal Crow-Song, who was grinning like a fiend.

'Óðin! Óðin! Óðin!' Like the beat of oars. Like swords on shields.

'This is how I will tell it,' Crow-Song agreed. 'But I think I will add some thunder and lightning.'

They came to Rennisøy on a sleeping sea, sails furled on the yards and oars chopping the still water as neatly as a jackdaw's wings in flight. *Reinen, Crow, War-Rider, Sea-Eagle* and King Thorir's two most impressive ships, *Sea-Shaker* and *War-Pig*, which was a strange name for a boat in anyone's ears but they were both named after Freyja and her battle swine Hildsvini. And by a Dane, as Solmund had said, as if that explained it all. They came more or less together, crews bantering at each other across the smooth water, insulting each other for their ships, their rowing, their beards and anything else they could come up with, such as how busy the men in other boats were in the bilge with the bailing buckets. Always a well-spring for taunts, that.

'Ha! She leaks like a cracked egg!' one of the Svearmen in *Crow* called over to *Sea-Shaker* which was being skippered by King Thorir's son Thidrek. Brine was being flung over *Sea-Shaker's* side so often that Moldof muttered he would be surprised if the sea level did not rise around Rennisøy with water from the Svealand coast.

'At least she is a real ship and not a fishing boat,' one of the Danes yelled back, as another man, who was not needed at the oars, jumped nimbly on to the sheer strake, pulled his breeks down and showed the Svearmen his arse. Lucky he didn't get it slapped by an oar, with how close they were, like a skein of geese across the sky.

And all of this was good to see because insults were better than silence. 'A bit of banter does no harm. Can be the glue that binds men before the slaughter,' Olaf said as *Reinen* slid up to her mooring and men jumped off with ropes while the others shipped oars, the staves clumping as they stowed them across the oar trees.

'So long as we save some good 'uns for that goat's turd king and his haughty buggers,' Solmund said, and in his life he must have heard every insult a man could weave, though he'd likely forgotten plenty of them.

Rennisøy had been Jarl Hrani's idea. 'Neutral ground,' he had said simply, looking from Sigurd to Olaf. Olaf and Hagal nodded, seeing the sense in choosing the island, which lay due east as the crow flies from the southern tip of Skudeneshavn. Long ago the strongest jarls of Haugalandet, Rogaland and Ryfylke had agreed that Rennisøy would belong to no man and that pact stood to this day.

'If we go to Avaldsnes, we'll be fighting on the king's ground,' Olaf said. 'To other men we'll look like dogs turning on our master.'

'And it will seem that Sigurd is only after the king's high seat on that hill overlooking the Strait,' Crow-Song added.

'We could fight him at home,' Svein had suggested, meaning Skudeneshavn. *Not many left who would call it home any more*, Olaf's eyes said to Sigurd. 'Why go to an effort?' Svein went on. 'Let the mighty king march his arse down to us and die tired.'

Sigurd shook his head and not just because he did not like the idea of fighting in the ashes of his childhood home, with all those ghosts watching. With those memories of defeat hanging there like heavy black clouds. Like swarms of midges, biting him every which way he turned. 'Let the king come to us at Skudeneshavn and he'll trap us,' he said. 'His shieldwalls in front of us, his ships at our backs. No, Svein.' He looked at Hrani. 'Jarl Hrani's idea is a good one.'

This being most of the Svearmen and the Danes' first time this far into the north-west, they had no opinions one way or the other and were content to let the others decide how they would play this game.

'We go to Rennisøy,' Sigurd confirmed for them all. 'We find a good place to raise our banners and we let him come to us there, but in the meantime we spread the word so that others may join us if they too want to see the oath-breaker laid low.'

'Aye, there must be others who would feed that rancid piece of gristle to the wolves and the ravens if they could,' Solmund said.

And so here they were, unloading spears and shields, tents and food, barrels of ale and sheaves of arrows, and all of them thrumming with the thrill of being part of something. For this was an army now, a great rebellious horde. Certainly a big enough affair, this thing, to draw skalds like crows to carrion.

'You see this, Sigurd?' Asgot asked him now, his head on one side as he watched him, making Sigurd uncomfortable with the weight of it. 'Do you see what you have done?'

'I have done what I must if we are to pay the oath-breaker back for his treachery,' Sigurd snapped. He felt judged. Felt the burden of so many men's lives about to be weighed in the scales of his ambition.

'You have called the storm down from the skies,' Asgot said. He lifted his staff as if half expecting Thór to strike it with a bolt of lightning. 'I hope you are ready.'

Sigurd did not answer this. He turned his back on the godi and watched the men coming ashore, spilling over the rocks in a tide of leather and iron. Sword-Norse, Svearmen and Spear-Danes. It was, he thought, like forging a sword. Like taking iron bars and twisting them together, making them into a single blade which he would wield against the hated enemy. All those he had lost, his kin – they were the pattern in the iron, the ghost in the blade. And they would drink of Gorm's blood too.

'So this is a sight, hey!' Svein said, stopping beside Sigurd and Asgot and resting a brawny arm on the head of his long smiting axe.

'Our fathers would have liked to be a part of this, Svein,' Sigurd said. They had climbed up to the higher ground from where they could look out across the Boknafjord for King Gorm's ships, though they knew it would be some days yet before he was ready to set sail. Below, Jarl Hrani was bellowing at two of his men who had dropped a barrel which they had been unloading from *Sea-Eagle*. It had sprung a stave so that ale was spraying out across the rocks. The jarl was furious.

'If my father were here now he would take their heads off for wasting good ale,' Svein said with a smile. 'And then he'd be on his knees lapping it up.'

That was a little too close to the truth to be funny, but Sigurd smiled anyway, wondering where he would be without Svein at his side. Without Solmund and Olaf and the others too. Perhaps

Harald had felt the same way about Svein's father Styrbiorn, until the drinking ruined him.

A loud croak had them turning to see a raven, all black gloss and bill, on the rock behind them.

'So the Allfather is here, anyway,' Svein said. Which was just what Sigurd himself was thinking. Svein knew him well enough to know it too, which was probably why he'd said it. *Doesn't make it any less true*, Sigurd thought, watching the bird pick up a mussel in that heavy beak and smash it against the rock to get to the meat.

Hugin or Munin? Sigurd wondered which of his ravens Óðin had sent to keep an eye on him. *Thought or Memory?* For himself memories lay heavy on him now. Weighty as his brynja. Memories of his brothers and of a simpler life in Skudeneshavn.

Simpler? Back then? Hah! What could be simpler than now, living only to wreak vengeance against your enemies?

He was struck then with another memory. It came unbidden to his mind, bursting through his thoughts like a drowned corpse rising to break the surface, all bloated and refusing to be ignored. It was a memory from his boyhood, of the elk hunt he had gone on with his father and King Gorm in the woods near Avaldsnes. They had tracked the magnificent beast for days, a lifetime for a boy gripping his first man-sized spear. But in the end, when they had caught up with their prey there had been no glory in the killing. The once noble beast had been rotting alive, writhing with maggots, and the sight had sickened Sigurd and tainted the summer. And now he wondered at this blood feud and his hunger for it. Gorm the oath-breaker needed killing. Nothing could change that. But then what? The whole thing was already tainted, as the boy's summer had been, by the faces of those he had lost. The friends and sword-brothers and the kinsmen who were no more. What awaited him now at the end of this hunt? Despair? Maggots squirming in his flesh? Death?

'Not before the debt is settled,' he muttered, remembering how, at the feast after the hunt, the king had praised him for his patience. In front of his father and all the honoured guests in his hall. If only the oath-breaker had known then that of all his enemies, even those who were not enemies yet, the seven-year-old boy at his feast table would be the one he should have made sure to kill.

Well it would be over soon. One way or another. If all went to plan, King Gorm would come to meet Sigurd's challenge. He would have no choice. Pride would force his hand and oars would drive his ships towards Rennisøy and there would be such a fight as the islands had not seen for a generation.

'Shame it won't be today,' Svein said, intruding into the spell which the bird had woven around Sigurd.

Sigurd looked up. Blue sky. Not many clouds and those that there were drifted lazily, no rain in them, like hulls out for a raid, their holds empty.

Thought or Memory?

Thought would be more useful now, for King Gorm would come at him with every spear he could muster. Every jarl, hersir and powerful karl who owed him fealty would be sharpening their swords and rounding up their own young men. But it would not be about the numbers alone. The oath-breaker had fought wars before and knew the art of it. The craft. And in the thick of the fight there would be decisions to be made. Sigurd would need to think hard and think well, because the lives of these men spilling ashore would depend on it.

'Ah, there is his mate,' Svein said as another raven landed beside the first with an agility that belied its size. It began a loud rhythmic call, a *toc-toc-toc* which had Svein touching the silver hammer that he wore on the chest of his brynja.

Thought and Memory both, then.

For years beyond counting, men had come to Rennisøy for the first three days after each full moon to buy and sell slaves. Now they would come for the sword-song. For the spear din.

'Come then, oath-breaker,' Sigurd said, looking out to the north-west towards Bokn and beyond, where the king's estate at Avaldsnes sat above the Karmsund Strait which carried ships north the way a big vein carried blood to the heart.

Let us finish this.

Sigurd looked up to the top of the hill as he had done a dozen times since the dawn had begun to rise in the east like a tideline, wicking into night's hem inch by inch. The man up there was moving and for a moment Sigurd's stomach rolled over itself and his breath caught in his throat and he watched to see if the sentry would light the beacon fire. But the man got halfway to the pile of wood, stopped and went still.

'Just pissing,' Olaf said in a low voice because most of the men were still asleep.

Let them rest. This may be their last sleep. Or wake them because this might be their last sunrise?

'He'll come when he comes,' Olaf said, spitting on his helmet and rubbing it. Not that his war gear could shine any more than it did already.

'What about them?' Bram said, nodding over at a group of newcomers as he poured himself a cup of ale. 'Think they're any good?'

They looked across at the thirty men who had come from Mekjarvik, some of whom were sitting round a fire as their companions snored and farted in their nests of fleeces and skins.

Olaf shrugged. 'I think they all have spears and axes,' he said, 'which makes them welcome here if you ask me.'

Their leader was a one-eyed, bushy-browed hersir called Erp who had sailed for Rennisøy the day after hearing from a fisherman that there was going to be a fight. Some years ago King Gorm had killed Erp's brother over a disagreement about taxes.

'The sheep-swiving fuck invited my brother up to Avaldsnes to air his grievance,' Erp had told Sigurd as his men disembarked from a flotilla of færings and row boats, as excited as women going to a wedding. 'We never saw Enar again. Mother dreamt that Enar had a drowning death.' Erp's big brows had knitted together with those terrible words. 'Perhaps he did. Perhaps he didn't. But she has a way with dreams,' he said.

Erp had been waiting ever since for a chance to repay the king. Now that chance had come.

Others had come too. Twenty-nine men had rowed over from Sandnes, fierce-eyed warriors all, who looked to a godi called Thokk as their leader. It was the Óðin spear which had lured them in, and they watched Sigurd as if half expecting him to transform into a wolf or an eagle or even the Allfather himself. There were whispers that these Sandnes men were berserkers and whether or not that was true, the others avoided them. Avoided Thokk too, but that was nothing unusual. The godi, who went by the name of Far-Flyer, had raven or crow feathers tied into his black hair and a stare that could turn water to ice.

Sixteen spearmen, young and old, had come from Jæren with their lord, a tall, silver-haired karl called Hastin. No one knew what Hastin's grievance was with King Gorm, or why he had come, but he looked a steady man and all of his warriors had tough leather armour and seemed eager for the fray.

There were some forty others who had sailed or rowed to the island, some in small groups, others alone, and each for his own reasons. Sigurd welcomed them all with ale and food. He let them touch the sacred spear and he asked each man his name, telling him that he would earn a fair share of the plunder when the fight was won. When these new men were added to Asgrim's one hundred and thirty-three Svearmen, Jarl Hrani's ninety Sword-Norse, and King Thorir's seventy Danes it made a total of four hundred and twenty-eight men.

And it would not be enough.

'I expected more,' Sigurd said on the fourth day, when it seemed no one else was coming no matter how hard he looked out to sea. There was still no sign of King Gorm and his ships, which was in itself disheartening because it meant the king was still gathering his war host. Sigurd all but shivered to think of it.

'Gorm has bought off or threatened every jarl within a hundred rôsts of his high seat,' Olaf said. 'He's been getting fat in every bugger's hall within fifty. What else has the prick been doing while we were off fighting and you were getting yourself half sacrificed in some Svear temple?'

It was true of course, and everyone knew it. Only Olaf would say it.

They were watching Hastin and his Jæren men practising for war. The karl had got them into two shieldwalls and these two skjaldborgar faced each other, the men for now throwing insults, not spears, across the gap between.

'We've got a war host here,' Olaf said. 'Gorm will have a bigger one. That's kings for you.'

And it was.

There was a cheer and Hastin's skjaldborgar slammed together, men leaning into their shields, digging their feet in, trying to push their opponents back to the marks scraped in the ground behind them. It was a simple pushing match – no blades – to see which wall was the stronger. Nothing to lose but pride. Nothing to gain but bragging rights.

Folavika. Named for the inlet in which *Reinen*, *War-Rider* and all the other boats sat rocking gently at their moorings. *So this will be known as the battle of Folavika then*, Sigurd thought, looking down at the ships now, hoping he had done the right thing in choosing to fight a land battle rather than inviting the oath-breaker to a ship fight.

'When we leave our ships what is to stop this king blocking them in at their moorings and burning them all?' King Thorir had asked, and everyone agreed it was a fair question.

But that was before they saw where Sigurd had chosen to plant his banner. From here at the northern tip of the island they would see Gorm's ships coming from the west. Those ships would put into the first, smaller bay to the west of Folavika because Sigurd had men waiting there with horns to signal the king and tell him to do just that. Sigurd's messengers would assure the king that he would not suffer a single arrow or thrown stone while his men disembarked.

No reason a fight shouldn't begin honourably, even if it ended in blood and screams and piss-drenched breeks.

'And if he has his own ideas?' King Thorir's son Thidrek had asked.

'We will be ready,' Sigurd replied. For if King Gorm's ships sailed past that first bay and on past Sigurd's position, intent on destroying his boats in the water, Sigurd would know about it. He would send crews hurtling over the rocks down to the bay and those crews would take the ships out into the fjord before the king had a chance to swoop down upon them. 'But it will not come to that, Thidrek,' he said.

He had laid his challenge out to the oath-breaker for all to see, like a fur trader showing his last pelt to the crowd. King Gorm was coming. Of that there was no doubt, and Sigurd bargained on him seeking to end this feud with one clean strike, rather than going for Sigurd's ships and risking some of them flying the coop with his enemies aboard. No. Gorm needed one battle, shieldwall against shieldwall. He needed to kill Jarl Harald's last living son and put out the fire he had started.

'He'll have the spears but we'll have the ground,' Sigurd said to Olaf now, looking at his banner planted a stone's throw away at the crest of a rise amongst a sea of long grass. Half an arrow-shot in length, this ridge fell away to bumpy uneven ground upon which a large body of men would find it difficult to hold a tight formation. And where there were gaps in a skjaldborg there was death, because men would force a way through like an arrow or the slenderest spear point piercing a ring in a brynja.

At their backs would be rocks: big, high, awkward rocks, a formidable enough obstacle to prevent anyone coming at them from behind even if they got down the flanks. And behind those steep rocks it was a careful climb down or a leg-breaking drop to the shore. A good place to set up for a fight. A good place to plant your first banner.

There was a light rain blowing in from the west but it had not yet soaked the half-circle of cloth enough to stop it bristling below the blade of the Óðin spear, whose butt Svein had thrust into the ground until it hit rock. A black wolf's head on a green field, the beast snarling at the sky. A wolf because Sigurd was a wolf. Hunted, homeless, the last of the litter but the most dangerous of them all. Embroidered by King Thorir's wife, Queen Halla of Skíringssalr, and drenched in Asgot's magic. A powerful thing then, his new banner, with enough seiðr of its own perhaps to keep it stirring even if rain lashed down in a hissing fury.

The next day the rain came properly, sweeping east across the bluff in grey swirling clouds which slapped their shelters and drummed on helmets and shields and had men squinting their eyes against it as they looked west, ever west. It was that very same wind which would bring the king to Rennisøy.

But first it brought two men.

'Blacksmiths the pair of 'em,' Solmund said the moment he saw them coming over the bluff, and to be fair that was before he laid eyes on the tools, the hammers, tongs and bellows, which they later brought up to the camp. A man had come to Sigurd to say that a small boat had beached on the shingle and two Danes, with war gear which frankly deserved a much better boat, had come ashore to fight for him. Big men both, heavily muscled, with big hands and coal-blackened breeks. Father and son clearly, the younger man, Ingel, still boasting good looks which age had tempered in Ibor, though neither sported forelocks or much in the way of eyebrows, those having been singed away by the forge.

'We cannot swear the oath for we are already King Thorir's men,' Ibor told Sigurd. 'But we'll set up hereabouts and make ourselves useful.'

'We're glad to have you, Ibor,' Sigurd said, shaking both men's hands. And he *was* glad too. The smiths would be busy day and night, fixing or replacing broken brynja rings, hammering dents out of helmets, straightening swords and making arrow heads.

'I've heard a rumour that you've a little iron around here,' Ibor said, lifting one of his non brows. His son Ingel looked sheepish for all his shoulders and brawny arms. But then Sigurd had a famous name these days, as well as a war host, and all this while not even being jarl. And then there was the Óðin spear. It was no surprise that men could act flea-bitten around him.

'I found some iron on my travels. One or two bars,' he told the smiths, watching their eyes light up at that, the way Svein and Bram's did when mead was mentioned. 'You will earn a share of it if you work hard for me.'

Ibor nodded, then exchanged a look with his son before setting off back to the bay to fetch his tools. 'Make it quick, lad, we've work to do,' he called over his shoulder to Ingel who lingered, pulling at his short beard so that it was clear to everyone that he had something he needed to say.

'Well, lad?' Olaf said. 'Spit it out or swallow it.'

Ibor looked from Olaf to Sigurd. 'I have news from your sister Runa, lord,' he said.

Sigurd's heart leapt like a salmon but he kept his face spear-straight as Olaf nodded at Solmund and Svein and the others that they should busy themselves elsewhere.

'You've seen her?' Sigurd asked Ingel when they were alone on the bluff but for the wheeling gulls above and a colony of gannets at the cliff's edge, their incessant *rab-rab-rab* calls cluttering the day.

'Yes, I've seen her,' Ingel said, colour flushing cheeks already chafed by the heat of the forge. 'My father and I have been living on the island of the Maidens. Working,' he added a little too hastily.

'I thought no men were allowed there,' Sigurd said.

Ingel cleared his throat. 'King Thorir sends us, lord.' He shrugged. 'To help where we can.'

Sigurd imagined what it must be like for two handsome, capable men on an island teeming with women. Then he cleared his mind of that thought, afraid of where it led. 'Runa is well?'

he asked and to his great relief Ingel nodded, almost smiling for the first time.

'Your sister is well, lord,' the young blacksmith said. 'King Thorir sent news to Fugløy of your uprising. He wanted Skuld the High Mother to know that he was coming west to fight, bringing young men to blood them against some Norse king.' Now came the grin and it made Ingel instantly likeable. 'When my father heard that you had come into possession of the Allfather's spear, I knew we would come. He is curious to see how the blade is forged, for Ívaldi's sons who made Gungnir were the greatest smiths to ever pick up a hammer.'

'Then tell your father you may both handle the spear and learn its secrets when there is no more work to be done,' Sigurd said, at which the young smith smiled again, resigning himself to never laying hands on the sacred weapon.

'So are you going to let your father unload your boat all by himself?' Sigurd asked, glad to have news of Runa but thinking that there were other tasks which needed his attention, such as telling four hundred warriors one more time where they could and could not shit.

Ingel looked itchy again. 'There is something else, lord,' he said. 'Something which Runa told me to tell you and you alone.'

This man loves my sister, Sigurd realized then with sudden, breath-catching certainty. Realized actually that he had known it from the first time those forge-cracked lips had spoken Runa's name.

He took a breath, wondering what he had done by letting Runa out of his sight. His beautiful, golden, Freyja-kissed sister.

'I am listening,' he said.

The oath-breaker King Gorm, whom men still called Biflindi, Shield-Shaker, though not in Sigurd's hearing, came in nineteen ships. A great fleet led by *Storm-Bison*, the king's own ship, sweeping past the north-west tip of the island, riding Rán's white-haired daughters which beat past the rocky coast, driven eastward, wind-whipped and relentless. It was a fleet buoyed by its own importance, revelling in the strength of the pack, each ship rejoicing in the wind which filled its sails and sang on its stays like the promise of fame.

That wind whipped the spume off the rolling grey furrows and Sigurd imagined the king standing by *Hríð-visundr*'s prow beast, the salt spray soaking his face, beading in his beard, crusting his lips which were pulled back from his teeth in a wolf's grin. Because Gorm had assembled a great war host, the greatest of all his days, and he was coming to crush his enemies the way a man takes a spade to a nest of rats.

'It's not too late, Sigurd,' Olaf said, the first words either of them had spoken for a long time as they stood together on the grassy bluff, looking out to sea. Watching.

Sigurd had never seen so many sails spread to the wind, so many hulls ploughing the grey fjord, and from Olaf's long silence he knew his friend had not either. Now, with those words Olaf was offering him a way out of this. Though not really, of course. It *was* too late and they both knew it. Every man on Rennisøy knew it. Even if they hared down to the big bay now and got aboard their boats they would have to row them out before they could catch the wind in their sails and by that time Gorm's fleet would be upon them.

'Some of us would get away,' Olaf said.

'Perhaps,' Sigurd said. But neither of them moved. Nor did any of the others who had come up to the bluff to watch, their beards bristling in the gusts, their eyes round as oar holes at the sight. So many carved beast heads chasing across the fjord, all snarl and stare. So many tallow-stinking sails swollen with the gathering wind, the strakes trembling beneath men's feet, whispering into their limbs like the thrill which comes before the blood-fray.

Perhaps it was worth fighting a battle you could not win, to have seen nineteen proper ships, plus a dozen smaller craft, given to the wind, offered up to Njörd, Lord of the Sea and god of wind and flame.

The crews of the lead ships were working hard now, reefing, robbing the wind of wool so that they could drive their tillers over and turn into the first bay, to take Sigurd up on his invitation to moor there. Those not working the ship would be gripping the sides, clutching spear shafts and shields and the little hammers at their necks. They would be trying to ignore the rumbles and gurgles in their guts and their dry mouths and the creeping fear. They would be telling themselves that this was not their death day. Others will bleed. Others will be ripped open by sharp blades. Others will die screaming in pain, drowning in fear, shitting themselves, suddenly stripped of the honour and courage which they had worn like a cloak since they had first wanted to be like their fathers. A thin garb, that, when the end comes.

'Well if we're staying, we should probably go and get ready,' Olaf said, turning his back on the scene and walking off.

'Aye, it's not every day you get a visit from the king,' Solmund said. He was braiding his grey hair so that it would not blind him in the fight. Gods be with him, that old man who was never happier than when out in the fjord at the helm of a good ship. That skipper who had never rejoiced in battle but who would stand beside Sigurd no matter what.

'Thought you said we couldn't lose,' King Thorir said, coming to watch the first of Gorm's ships beach on the strand or drop anchors into the shallows. As for the other vessels, now that they were coming closer, bows turning across the rolling furrows, everyone up on that crag could see that each was crammed with spear-armed men. Warriors from scores of villages, islands and farmsteads, who owed allegiance to the king at Avaldsnes and had been reminded of that.

'You must have wrestled with men who were bigger than you, King Thorir,' Sigurd said, watching *Storm-Bison* for sign of the king himself.

'Careful, lad,' Thorir said, for he was short, a head and a half shorter than Sigurd. 'What of it?'

'Yet you have never lost,' Sigurd said. 'Even though these bigger men must have thought they had the beating of you.'

'True enough, lad,' King Thorir said, knowing where Sigurd was going with this. King Gorm had ridden *Storm-Bison* up on to the shingle now and men were spilling over her sides and forming a shieldwall on the beach in case Sigurd had planned an ambush. But Sigurd would not fight him there. 'It'll be a rare fight all the same,' King Thorir said. 'And I'm glad my boys are here to see this. Might not see its like again in their lifetime. A fleet like that. A bloody swarm like that.'

Other ships were slewing on to the beach, using the wind's momentum and their oars for the final push, sinew and muscle driving them up the foreshore which had been made smooth by countless hulls before them. They disgorged their spear- and axe-armed cargo and those men came with yells and banter and the thumping of blades and staves on shields because they were already rousing themselves to the coming violence, like water coming to the boil. The wind carried the din of it up the craggy rocks to where Sigurd waited, and for a while he let it wash over him, let it feed his own war beast which was stirring inside him now.

Then he turned and went to make his stand beneath his snarling wolf banner.

CHAPTER ELEVEN

SIGURD DID NOT LET HIS ENEMIES HAVE IT ALL THEIR OWN WAY. WHEN Gorm was arraying his host on the uneven ground to the west of their position, Sigurd sent Erp and Hastin down the slope with those of their Mekjarvik and Jæren men who had bows and slingshots. Shieldless and light as shepherd lads they went down in loose order, half running over the bumps and tussocks to harass the king's men, to sting them with arrows and smooth stones. Some arrows came back, darting over the king's skjaldborgar like swifts, but none of his Sword-Norse wanted to waste their muscle and breath running up the hill to chase those fleet-footed men off. Instead, the king's men kept their shields up and their heads down. Even so, one or two of them died who did not see death flying towards them. More were hurt badly enough that they were put out of the fight before it began. It was nothing in the scheme of things but, as Asgrim said, it can never be a bad thing to blood the enemy before he bloods you.

'Just another seven or eight hundred and things will start to look good for us,' Moldof rumbled, attaching a shield to the stump of his half arm.

'Perhaps you are beginning to regret joining me, Moldof,' Sigurd said, remembering that freezing day when Moldof had come to kill him but had ended up joining them instead. How King Gorm's former champion had even saved Sigurd's life at the borg when a man from Alba, perhaps sent by King Gorm, had tried to murder Sigurd in the stinking dark of a cattle byre. Moldof had proved himself in a dozen fights since then. Gorm's loss had been their gain.

'Aye, you could be down there combing your beard with the king,' Svein told the one-armed warrior, watching the hordes below order themselves into smaller groups and crews, cousins and kinsmen drawing together because a man always likes to know the man either side of him in the skjaldborg.

'I would rather fight the fettered wolf,' Moldof said, perhaps bringing up Fenrir because all men knew that Týr had lost an arm too, Fenrir having bitten off the limb when he realized that the Æsir had deceived him. Or because Týr was the Lord of Battle and Moldof had a high opinion of his own sword-craft even being an arm short of a whole man as he was.

'It cannot be easy being a king's former champion,' Floki said, which was bound to sting Moldof's pride like a wasp's barb in some tender part of the flesh. Floki grinned at Svein and Sigurd knew Floki well enough to be sure that he would still take Moldof's other arm for the fun of it.

'What is he like, the oath-breaker's new champion?' Olaf asked. Sigurd's crew stood together in the front row of a shieldwall three men deep and fifty men across, along the spine of high ground running north-south. Behind them the rocks and then the sea. In front, uneven, sloping ground more suited to goats and sheep than men, for which the king was no doubt cursing Sigurd now. Not steep or rocky enough to make Gorm refuse the fight, but difficult enough to cause his men problems when it began.

'His name is Hreidar and he is a brainless ox,' Moldof said.

'Big then?' Svein said.

'They're always big,' Bjorn said, half glancing at Svein who was Sigurd's champion in as much as he was his prow man and put the fear of the gods into his enemies with his fiery red hair and beard and his massive smiting axe.

'Always brainless too,' Bjarni put in. 'Big and brainless.' He shrugged. 'Big so that they catch the arrows and blades meant for their lord, and brainless so they don't notice when they're dead but keep on fighting.'

'Turd,' Svein muttered.

'Hreidar will notice when I put my sword in his belly,' Moldof said.

'I would like to see a king or jarl have a normal-sized man as his champion, just for once,' Bjarni said.

'You hear that, Sigurd?' Svein said. 'Bjarni wants to win this fight by making King Gorm laugh himself to death.'

This had Sigurd's crew chuckling amongst themselves so that the others in the shieldwall around them must have wondered what could be so amusing given the number of men coming to kill them.

King Gorm's main shieldwall was four men deep and half as long again as Sigurd's, albeit a little ragged by comparison because of the hummocks and rocks breaking out of the ground. His best-armoured men were in the front. They were not his own hearthmen but those of other oath-sworn lords, men like Jarl Baugr, Jarl Vragi, Jarl Tósti and Jarl Arnstein Twigbelly. And Jarl Otrygg, whom Bram had recognized by his men's shields which were all painted red with the black rune Laguz because Otrygg thought of himself as a great sea jarl, which was a joke as far as Bram was concerned.

'That fat toad hasn't gone raiding for years,' he told them all, 'unless you call fishing raiding for silver.'

Behind these well-armed men, about a third of whom wore mail, were those with good leather armour and skull caps and shields, axes and spears, and behind those were the men who lacked good war gear: men who wore several layers of wool and who must have been drowning in sweat and stinking but who hoped those layers would prevent a blade from biting, though it might still break the bones.

The king's own hirðmen were at the rear with their lord, a mass of grey and bright painted shields, each boasting brynja and helmet and burdened with the tools of death. And it was not cowardice on Gorm's part, him being back there behind a bulwark of flesh and iron and oath. Just good sense, for if he took a wound early on his jarls might take the decision to withdraw, even under the pretence of getting their king safely away, and Gorm knew it would take weeks if not another season to assemble such a host again.

'You know that's where you should be too,' Olaf said to Sigurd. 'At the back. Out of the way.'

Sigurd did not answer that. For his part in the oath which bound him to his men, Sigurd had sworn to lead them into battle, but that was not the reason why he stood at the front now. Even the warriors who had received his promise would understand the need to keep him alive. Simple good sense which stood clear of any oath like a rock breaking the sea's surface. No, he stood at the fore because he wanted the oath-breaker to see him there. Simple as that. Sigurd wanted that worm to see that he was hungry for the fray, for the revenge which he owed to his family.

Sigurd looked left and right now, drawing strength and courage from the wall he had built. *If hatred was a blade the oath-breaker would be dead already*, he thought, looking at Svein and Solmund and Olaf, at Hastin and his Jæren men and those other men whom he did not know but who had come to stand with him because of some feud they had with the king.

'You've done what you can, Sigurd,' Olaf said, mistaking Sigurd's neck-twisting for misgivings about the way he had set his own host up, or about the ground he had chosen.

At either end of the main shieldwall were two smaller skjaldborgar, wings comprising three rows of twenty-five men each, which sloped back right up to the rocks so that the king's men would not be able to wrap all the way round their position and come at them from the rear. Not that they would need to. With their numbers they could just keep hammering away at

Sigurd's wall, replacing their front rank over and over until they punched a hole through. Then it would be a savage melee, a chaos of blades and blood, but in the end there could only be one winner.

Behind Sigurd's main shieldwall was his reserve, some ninety men including Thokk Far-Flyer and his twenty-nine from Sandnes. Most of those with bows who were now ranging down the slope stinging the king's men would join the reserve when the fight properly began. They would clamber up on to the high rocks behind and from there nock and loose into the enemy masses until their arrows were gone. Then they would take their places in the wall of flesh and iron as other men fell, like new caulking thumbed between strakes to keep the sea from sinking the ship.

A murmur travelled through the line and Sigurd turned to see men touching amulets or rune-carved blades. He heard them whispering to the gods and he knew the reason for it. Asgot. The godi was coming and Sigurd welcomed the chill which ran like ice water down his spine.

'Let's see how the oath-breaker likes this,' Olaf gnarred, a grim smile nestled in his beard, as the men shuffled aside, shouldered into their neighbours to make a channel through which the godi could pass, hefting the gift he had prepared for King Gorm. It was a níðstang, which men called a nithing pole, if they spoke of such things at all. The staff was of hazel and the head mounted upon it was that of a horse, freshly killed so that its blood was running down the shaft to redden Asgot's hands and arms and clot in the rings of his brynja as he carried it forward. It was heavy by the looks, but the godi was well aware of the seiðr he was weaving and he carried the thing high for all to see, its neck skin flapping in the wind, its dead eyes staring and its bottom lip hanging down revealing its teeth, as if the dead head was giving one final and everlasting nicker against its fate.

And Asgot carried the cursing pole to a clump of rocks a little way down the hill, where all the king's men could see it.

'Here I put up this níðstang!' he called, for those in front and behind. And above. 'And this curse I turn on King Gorm the oath-breaker.' He turned the horse head to the left and the right. 'I lay this curse also on those of you who fight for the oath-breaker this day, for you follow an unworthy man and this makes you less than men yourselves.' He turned the grim head to the centre of the enemy line again, where the king's banner flapped wildly. 'Gorm son of Grimar, I curse you and promise you a bad death. No fame in the wake of your life. It will be as though you never drew breath. Not for you the Allfather's hall. Just everlasting torment.' With that he thrust the pole down into a cleft in the rocks and he must have already tested it earlier in the day because it stood straight and solid even in that wind which had the dead beast's mane flying. Sigurd could see that the godi had carved the bones of that curse into the hazel pole, which made it as real and enduring as the rock behind and the sea beyond. It was a terrible, horrible curse and down there at the foot of that slope King Gorm must have felt as sick as if he had eaten a plate of rotten meat.

Without wiping his bloody hands on the grass Asgot turned and walked back to take his place amongst his crew, and Sigurd nodded to him to say it was a job well done, for all that the nithing pole seemed to have cast an even darker cloud over the day for everyone.

'Here it is then,' Sigurd said to himself. He could see now what Gorm intended. Not one single shieldwall, for that would soon be broken up by the ground over which it moved, but many separate skjaldborgar, groups of fifty to eighty which would hit Sigurd's line at different times, like separate hammer blows or storm-tossed waves in the suck and plunge of a rocky outcrop. And one of those smaller shieldwalls was on the move now, marching up the slope to the beat of their own spear staves against their shields.

'They're either all mad or they've been at the ale all night,' Olaf said, watching as Erp and Hastin yelled at their bowmen and slingshot men to retreat back up the slope in the face of this oncoming wall of wood and spear blades, albeit this shieldwall came alone. The other shieldwalls remained rooted to their positions, awaiting their king's order to attack.

'I am thinking that they would rather die good and quickly than drag it out,' Svein said, leaning on his long-hafted axe as if he were on a jetty on a summer's day, watching the tide creep up the piles.

A gust whipped the enemy's shield din up the slope and some of the men to Sigurd's left yelled insults back into the wind.

Jarl Hrani came over and stood beside Sigurd, a half grin on his face. 'You know who that is?' he said, nodding down the slope. 'Jarl Leiknir from Tysvær.' At that moment the men trudging towards them lifted their shields and held them above their heads, which was their way of telling Sigurd that they came in peace.

'Ha!' Solmund blurted. 'Maybe Asgot's cursing pole has them pissing in their breeks already.'

'Jarl Leiknir and I have an understanding,' Hrani said, which was doubtless the real reason why those men were holding their shields above their heads and why Sigurd's grin matched Hrani's own. For Tysvær sat within a day's sailing of Jarl Hrani's own hall, and Hrani being the more powerful jarl, Leiknir could not afford him as an enemy. It was still a risk of course, choosing the rebels over the king, but who could say what other factors had tipped the scales in Jarl Leiknir's mind?

Jarl Hrani strode forward and Jarl Leiknir broke from his men to grip his hand, the two of them binding their fates in a handshake while those king's men left at the foot of the hill bellowed insults and called them traitors.

'Put them in the reserve?' Olaf suggested.

Sigurd shook his head. 'Rather not have them behind us,' he said, thinking that he did not know or trust Jarl Leiknir enough to have him out of sight. 'Put them on the left. Thicken the line there. Let Hrani keep an eye on his friends.'

Olaf nodded and went to speak to the Tysvær jarl as Hrani's men greeted Leiknir's men, telling them they had made the right decision and that today they would make their fame. But all this was cut short by the clamour from a dozen or more horns on the wind, riding the gathering gale, some sounding deep as a bull's bellow, others thin as grass blown between pressed palms.

'Here we go then,' Bram said. Behind them the wolf-head banner flapped beneath that great, rune-bitten blade. It sounded like a wind-whipped fire.

'We'll sleep well tonight,' Aslak said.

Sigurd looked at Olaf and Svein. They nodded. Grim now. Ready to do what must be done. Sigurd looked at Floki. The young man's lips pulled back from his teeth. Not a smile. Something else.

Below, the king's host was on the move, washing slowly across the rough ground like a dark tide.

'Svein, have you a saga-worthy throw for me?' Sigurd asked.

Svein nodded, lifting the spear in his hand. Testing its weight and balance. 'You will want to see this, Crow-Song,' he said, walking forward, 'and stay alive today so that you can put what you see into a song,' he called over his shoulder.

'Make it count, lad,' Olaf growled into his beard, watching Svein walk down the slope as far as the nithing pole which stood there cursing King Gorm with its dark seiðr. Sigurd expected Svein to roll his left shoulder in its socket, make great circles with his arm to loosen the sinew and muscle, to make ready.

He did none of these things.

'Sigurd Haraldarson claims you for Óðin!' he roared down at the men coming towards him now, some of whom were loosing arrows which Svein ignored as if they were flies as he pulled his brawny arm back and launched the spear. It flew in a great arc, as if over Bifröst the shimmering bridge which joins the worlds of men and gods, and passed over the heads of their enemies, whose faces were upturned as they watched it soar. Right over the whole host it flew, landing blade first in the ground far behind the king's banner.

And up came the king's men, beating their shields, summoning the courage they would need. The fury. The animal which lives inside all men. And the battle began.

Shieldwall. War-hedge. Slaughter-bed? Left foot forward, shoulder turned slightly towards the enemy so that your shield overlaps the man to your right. A rampart of limewood, each shield braced by two men. Leather-rimmed edges kissing dented metal bosses. Swords and spears beating in rhythm against the planks, a din meant to bolster their own courage as much as sap their enemies'. A living thing. A bulwark only as strong as the will and the fear-soaked strength of the men behind it. A shivered wreck when it breaks, a shield-ship with its belly ripped open and destined for the sea bed.

'Hold!' Olaf bellowed. 'Hold them, you whoresons!'

Thunder as the shields clash. Screams too, thin as cold fjord water. Pathetic and shocking from those big grizzled men.

'Hold!'

'Fucking kill them!'

'Keep tight! Tight as a good cunny.'

The weight of the enemy as a whole. The stink of them. The breath of the man leaning into his shield, leaning on you, doing his bit, trying not to die. No room to swing sword or axe. Just rooting yourself to that small patch of ground. A statement of intent. I shall not be the one to move backwards. I shall not yield, not with my brothers around me. They might not see but they would know.

'Hold!'

Olaf roars and men drink in his voice like mead, for they know he is a god of war.

'You fucking give them the ground and I'll kill you myself! Hold!'

Spears jab over men's heads, thrust from those in the second row, seeking anything soft, looking to slake a thirst. One scrapes off Sigurd's helmet. It will come again, he knows, but what can he do about it?

'Heads down!' Olaf calls, and Sigurd thinks they are for him, those words. 'The rancid shits will tire before us. Lazy-arsed fucks.'

Not everyone in Sigurd's shieldwall was fighting. Or pushing. Only some of the enemy skjaldborgar had struck, those jarls and crews most eager for the fame of breaking their king's enemy perhaps. Fools if they thought it would be over so quickly, that they would start the route that begins when a shieldwall is breached.

Sigurd glanced to his left. A spear-throw along the line he could see Jarls Hrani and Leiknir, braced for the attack, striking their sword pommels against their shields, roaring insults into the teeth of the wind. *I would not like to attack Jarl Hrani up this hill*, Sigurd thought. *He's a fighter. Like his father was.*

Arrows hissed over their heads, shot by men on the rocks who were trying to put a shaft in King Gorm's face or neck. Worth a try, that, to end this thing before it began. But then, Sigurd hoped the king's shield men were about their business because he did not want a lucky arrow to rob him of his right. Gorm's death belonged to Sigurd and he would have it.

A thunder of shields and yells, made distant because of his helmet, announced that another of Gorm's skjaldborgar had struck the line, somewhere to the right, near where Asgrim and his Svearmen were. That clash might as well have been another battle for all that Sigurd could influence it, yet he knew that Asgrim was granite-hard and that those coming up against Jarl Guthrum's former champion were dead men sooner or later.

That spear blade again, hitting his helmet square this time, thrusting his head back on his neck so that his brain rattled in his skull. Some ambitious turd, that one with the spear, wherever he was. Sigurd locked eyes with those peering over the shield rim opposite. Greying brows above those calm eyes. Not a young man but someone who had done all this before, more than once too. He was biding his time, this front-ranker, taking no risks, keeping his shield locked on his neighbour's and trusting to the spearman behind to prise the enemy wall open like a knife tip into a clam.

'Svein,' Sigurd called, nodding towards the grey-browed man.

'Aye,' Svein on his left said, knowing exactly what Sigurd wanted of him. Taking his own opponent's weight on his shield and gripping his long-hafted axe one-handed, Svein lowered the axe head so that it was between his own hip and Sigurd's. Then he thrust it beneath their overlapping shields, hooked the bottom rim of the shield pressed against Sigurd's and pulled, and Sigurd let his own shield go with it.

Grey brows got a face full of his own shield and then those eyes, which knew death when they saw it, widened as Sigurd brought Troll-Tickler up and rammed it forward, its point finding the recess of the eye socket, its edges splitting the bone as Sigurd pushed a foot of steel-edged iron into the man's face, into the brain until it erupted from the back of the skull.

Sigurd hauled Troll-Tickler back and the man fell, revealing that whoreson with the spear, who had not expected to be forced into the front line so soon, and he died with Troll-Tickler ripping out his guts in a reek of blood and shit.

'Hold! Hold, Haraldarson's men!' Olaf bellowed, for it was not time to force that breach. Not yet, with the king's men as thick on that hill as flies on a gory corpse.

Another crash, this time to the left, distant as the crack of mountain ice in spring. Jarl Hrani was in the fight, then. Good. Let the oath-breaker bleed his men on Hrani's Sword-Norse, on Hadd Hog-Head and those proud Hinderå men. Perhaps Sigurd should have put himself at the rear so that he could watch the ebb and flow of the thing. From the rocks he would see it all. He could throw reinforcements into the fray where they were needed.

It floods his guts with sourness, this sudden doubt, and he wonders if his pride will cost him. Will cost them all.

But they are holding. He doesn't need to see it to know it. It is as certain and tangible as the sweat-soaked leather sword grip in his hand.

'Oath-breaker!' Sigurd called. 'You cannot win!' He did not know if the king could hear him. Doubtful in that clamour of cursing, straining men, but it felt good to say it anyway.

'Come, maggots! Are you so afraid?' This was King Thorir's voice, carrying over the shield din from the far right of the line near the wing which sloped back to the rocks. 'Fight me, you whore spawn! What are you waiting for, a roast pig and mead bench? Here I am! Fight me!'

His Danes were the only ones not in the pushing match now and King Thorir did not like that at all, not when others were in the thick of it. Perhaps King Gorm's jarls had purposefully avoided these strangers under their unfamiliar banner, not having their measure and preferring to make their fame against better-known men, but Thorir was inviting them to come at him, almost begging them to.

'Danes are mad,' Solmund gnarred, jabbing his sword over his shield to *tonk* against a man's helmet.

'He'd wrestle them one by one if he could, that mead-soaked little growler,' Moldof said, not caring that Thorbiorn Thorirsson was beside him.

'He would,' Thorbiorn agreed, grinning behind his shield. Thorbiorn who had become a warrior himself and deserved his place beneath that wolf-head banner flapping on the spear which Óðin himself had once wielded.

A spear blade streaked over Sigurd's head to take a young man in the shoulder, making him curse as well as a man who had seen twice as much life. To Sigurd's left, Floki somehow managed to reach over and plant his hand axe in a man's skull, his eyes wild with the thrill of it, and to Floki's left Valgerd, who had been holding her own against a growling bear of a man, suddenly gave way so that the bear all but fell forward, impaling himself on her scramasax which she then hauled across to open his belly. His gut string sprang free, fast as rope after an anchor into the depths.

'Fight me, you Norse shits!' King Thorir bellowed at Gorm's shieldwalls, which still held back or else took the fight to those either side of the Danes and their banner, which was a triangular piece of the same golden fabric that hung from his roof in Skíringssalr.

An arrow streaked by Sigurd's cheek and he heard the thump of it embedding in flesh followed by the shriek of the man whose life thread it had severed. And yet still there was not much proper killing being done by either side, not in that stinking press of bodies, in that battle din which was being swirled about by the wind and carried up to Asgard to the gods' ears.

'Bollocks!' Olaf exclaimed, and Sigurd looked over to see that King Thorir, sick of waiting now, had broken from the line. He was taking the fight to the Norsemen and his Danes were following him. 'Somebody bring him back!' Olaf roared, but King Thorir's advance was already reverberating through the great skjaldborg he had left behind, like wind in the rigging.

'Hold!' Asgrim yelled at his Svearmen, for some of them had taken a few steps down the slope, eager to follow King Thorir and get their taste of the fight.

'The fool will drag us all down with him,' Sigurd growled, working with his sword through the gaps, quick thrusts to keep his enemies on the defensive. King Thorir's sally had scattered a loose horde of men who were in his path, but now a well-formed shieldwall was advancing to meet him, slanting across the hill to take the Danes in the side like a wave slamming a ship abeam.

'Twigbelly,' someone said. Hagal probably, for few men were as good at recognizing jarls and crews as Crow-Song, if only because he had drunk their mead and put them in his mediocre saga tales to pay for it.

'The Danes'll carve that fat hog up,' Svein said, but Sigurd was not so sure. He knew that the oath-breaker, wherever he was, would be watching, would know that Sigurd's skjaldborg was, if not broken, then vulnerable, and he had not become a powerful king without having his share of war-craft.

'He'll send more than Twigbelly against them,' Olaf said, as if he had heard Sigurd's thoughts. 'I would if I were him.'

'I'll go,' Thorbiorn said, leaning to lock eyes with Sigurd from behind his shield. 'Please, lord, let me go. I'll bring him back.'

Sigurd nodded. Thorbiorn arranged it with Moldof and the man behind, who slipped neatly into the space which the young Dane had occupied a heartbeat before. Then he was gone.

'Think the king will listen to the lad?' Olaf said.

Sigurd did not. But at least Asgrim had stemmed the flood, holding his Svearmen in check and bringing the right wing across, closing the gap where Thorir's Danes had stood before.

I need to see, Sigurd thought. *I need to know what is going on.*

'We're blind,' Olaf said, again seeming to fish Sigurd's thoughts from his head. 'Go, lad,' he told Sigurd. 'Floki, go with him.'

Floki nodded and he and Sigurd prepared the men around them, then stepped out of the line and Sigurd felt suddenly unbalanced, his arm feather-light because the weight was gone. He strode back through the knots of men waiting in reserve, shaking some life back into the limb, then clambered up on to the rocks to stand beside the bowmen. And he cursed when he looked over to the right to see King Thorir up to his wide neck in the blood-fray, laying about himself with his heavy sword, cleaving shields and earning his byname Gapthrosnir, one gaping in fury. No shieldwalls there, just chaos now, and the Danes were making a slaughter, no doubt, but Gorm was throwing more men into that maelstrom and the tide would have no choice but to turn.

'Bring him back, Thorbiorn,' Sigurd said, hoping it was not already too late.

'Danes,' a silver-haired bowman beside Sigurd said. As if that explained the whole thing. And perhaps it did.

'Should we send Far-Flyer's men?' Floki asked, nodding down towards the godi and his Sandnes men, who were purple-faced, ale-soaked and working themselves up, growling and snarling and slamming their shields together, roaring curses and frenzying. Many were bare-chested, having stripped down to their breeks, even discarding shoes and boots, whilst others were putting on wolf pelts or bear skins, tying them round their necks, channelling those creatures' fierce spirits, and they looked as though they were about to kill each other where they stood.

Sigurd turned back to the fight. King Thorir and his sons Thidrek and Thorberg were shoulder to shoulder, the king's hearthmen around them, holding the enemy swarm off. More than holding them off, they were carving a path through them, smashing shields, staving skulls and lopping limbs. Those Danes were in the grip of the blood madness. They were making a name for themselves, carving their fame in wood and flesh the way a skald or a godi etches runes in a rock.

But the brave fools were dying too.

'They should have stayed,' Sigurd said. Pouring more men into that storm of swords to help the Danes would weaken the shieldwall. Even if they drove those Norse jarls back they would be making the right wing vulnerable to a counter attack. Too early in the day for that throw of the dice, when they still held that spine of land and King Gorm had yet to expose himself.

King Thorir took a man in the neck then broke another man's shield so that Thorberg's axe could find its mark and they were almost through to Jarl Arnstein himself, who was screaming at his Bokn men to put these Danemen down.

Thorbiorn had wriggled and squirmed and shoved his way through the press to get to his father and Sigurd could see him yelling at Thorir to retreat back up the slope, to have his men lock shields and withdraw. But the king was deaf to his son's advice and Sigurd saw Thorbiorn spitting fury.

'If they stay they die,' Floki said, pointing his blood-slick axe across the slope. A wave of death was coming for the Danes. At least two jarls judging by the banners, and as many as two hundred spears. Not a shieldwall as such, they were moving too fast across uneven ground to have their shields locked rim to boss, but a flood of blades with fresh arms behind them.

Asgrim had seen the danger too and he turned and looked at Sigurd and Sigurd shook his head.

'Hold!' Asgrim bellowed at his Svearmen who were leaning into their shields, stabbing at King Gorm's men from behind their rampart. 'We stay here!'

'You are lost now,' Sigurd told King Thorir under his breath, watching those new jarls slam into the Danes. A spear took the king's son Thidrek in the shoulder but Thorir cut the spearman down. Then a massive warrior planted an axe in Thorberg Thorirsson's head, for Thorberg had lost his helmet, and he went down like a stone even as the king thrust his sword through the huge warrior's side. And then the Danes were swallowed by the tide and Sigurd lost sight of Thorir and his sons.

And Asgrim held his Svearmen on the ridge.

The horns called King Gorm's host back and they went in good order, shields up, heads down, leaving a tideline of dead and dying, broken and torn men before Sigurd's skjaldborg. And yet perhaps only a third of the oath-breaker's men had fought so far that day, whereas almost every one of Sigurd's men, other than his small reserve, had wet their blades or at least blunted them.

'Whoreson has weighed us in the scales and now knows what it'll cost him to beat us,' Bram said, which they all knew was the truth of it as they watched the king's men regrouping beneath their respective banners. Everywhere men were examining the damage done to their shields and fetching spares if they thought they were too far gone to take another battering. Norseman, Svearman and Dane looked to their blades, cursing at the nicks in the edges, working with whetstones to restore their bite. Some were out looting the dead, stripping corpses of good war gear, taking keepsakes from fallen friends. Bowmen were out scavenging for arrows. Some young men were puking after their first taste of the shieldwall. Some were buzzing with the thrill of it. Others were silent and pale and still, like the living dead.

Unseen, the Valkyries were already swooping.

'It is bad about the Danes,' Svein said.

King Thorir lay down there. Somewhere amongst that corpse pile. Thorir Gapthrosnir of Skíringssalr, who had fought Sigurd's enemies for silver and gold and won only death for himself and his sons. Perhaps he had already been borne to the afterlife, was even now with his daughter Hallveig in Sessrymnir, Freyja's hall, challenging other heroes to wrestle with him.

'He was a fool,' Olaf growled, even given the company. For not all of Thorir's sons had died in that welter of blood. Somehow, Thorbiorn had survived the final slaughter. He and a handful of Danes, most of them the untested young men who had not yet lived long enough to know they should have died in piles round their king as Gapthrosnir's hirðmen had done. Instead they had put their shields together and ploughed a furrow back to the ridge.

'A brave fool but a fool,' Olaf said, and Thorbiorn, spattered with gore and wild-eyed, did not disagree. He was angry with his dead father and brothers for ignoring his pleas to resume their position beside Asgrim on the higher ground. Even at the end they had not taken Thorbiorn seriously. And yet who was wearing the bull-necked king's silver torc now? Who had pulled it from his dead father with men being butchered all around? Thorbiorn had and it gleamed at his neck now and no one questioned it.

'What now then?' Valgerd said. She was running a whetstone along the edge of a broad-bladed Svear-looking spear she had found. Sigurd thought that spear suited her as well as the torc suited Thorbiorn.

'They'll come again. And again,' Sigurd said. 'And the oath-breaker won't care how many of his men die on our spears.'

'Aye, he'll keep sending them and eventually they'll break through,' Olaf said.

Svein shook his head. 'We'll hold, Uncle,' he said, his fierce red bristles being buffeted by the wind. 'Shits won't break us.'

'Asgrim won't break,' Moldof said. 'Or if he does I'll be surprised.'

'Neither will Jarl Hrani, the arrogant swine,' Solmund put in, hating Hrani as much as ever.

'At least that fat snot Twigbelly is dead,' Olaf said. 'Shame to have missed that for it would've been worth seeing.'

Sigurd had not seen Jarl Arnstein die either, but Thorbiorn said his brother Thidrek had given the man his death wound. Said Thidrek had hacked into the jarl's belly and men had been amazed by the foul gush which had come out, appalled by the yellow fat flapping everywhere in the spray of silver brynja rings.

'Must have been some muscle behind the blow to get through all that blubber,' Olaf said, thinking deeply about it.

'I wonder if Jarl Otrygg knows I am up here,' Bram said. 'And I wonder who his new champion is. Probably some walking beard who hasn't wet his sword for the last five summers.'

'I can guess what happened to his last champion,' Olaf said, raising an eyebrow at Bram.

Bram scratched amongst his beard. 'Aye, well I'm not proud of that,' he said, getting Olaf's meaning. 'Brak was a brave man and good in his day. I blame bloody Otrygg for letting Brak and the rest go to seed. That's them down there, see?'

But Sigurd wasn't interested in this Jarl Otrygg and he let the others' voices fade in the distance like the murmur of the sea. He was watching the oath-breaker's banner, that black prow beast on red cloth, chosen because King Gorm held the keys to the north and grew rich on taxes from the crews of all manner of craft who sailed up the Karmsund Strait in the shadow of his hall perched on that hill.

The oath-breaker wants me and I want him, Sigurd told himself now, ignoring every other warrior on Rennisøy, every man who would kill or die trying to grant Sigurd or Gorm their burning wish.

'Where are you?' Sigurd whispered, searching for the king amongst those beneath his banner.

'They're getting ready to come again!' someone over on the left of the line called. The archers scuttled back up on to the rocks clutching their shafts. More archers would be good, Sigurd thought, more shafts to rain upon those king's men who lacked helmets and mail or good leather armour. He looked north, then east over his shoulder, telling himself that he would make do with what he had.

Somewhere over to the right, near Asgrim, a group of Svearmen were passing the time by singing a song about Óðin's nights on Yggdrasil. Those brave warriors would be fighting again before they got to the Allfather's ninth and last night hanging on that mighty ash.

Behind him Thokk Far-Flyer's men were sharing cups of only the gods knew what, while Thokk decorated them with painted runes and symbols, charms against the enemy's blades. Or perhaps he was dedicating that ale-drowned crew to the Spear-God. Who could say?

Solmund was watching those strange warriors too and he shook his head. 'Sandnes men,' he muttered, knowing no more needed saying.

Sigurd looked back down the slope. He had yet to lay eyes on the oath-breaker but he knew he was down there. Surrounded by big men with big beards dressed in good mail. How many on both sides would have to die before Sigurd could get his hands on that treacherous piece of troll shit?

'So, they'll come again and we'll beat them off again. And then we'll cross the next fjord when we come to it, hey,' Olaf said. There were mumbles of agreement. What else was there to do?

Unless, Sigurd thought. *Unless* . . .

'Thorbiorn!' he called.

'He's off with the Danes, what's left of them. Fetching his dead kin,' Bjarni said.

'I want him here now,' Sigurd said, and Bjarni nodded, stalking off to find the young man.

'What's on your mind?' Olaf asked, keeping his gaze fixed on the king's skjaldborgar, some of which were on the move, the men in them thumping hilts and blades against shields. The sound of it was like thunder on the wind.

'Well, lad?' Olaf all but growled it, not liking being in the dark where Sigurd's ideas were concerned. He still hadn't quite got over the whole thing of Sigurd hanging himself from some tree in that stinking swamp, as he was keen on reminding everyone.

Sigurd let him wait, kept his lips sealed as his own mind chewed the idea for a bit.

Hrani Randversson stood there showing no fear of the king he had betrayed, even though he must have feared for his boy at least and what would happen to young Randver if they lost this fight. Randver who stood there at the rear of his father's shieldwall looking like a little god of war, all four feet and a knife hilt of him, in his own brynja and a helmet that was too big.

'What's he doing bringing a boy to a fight like this?' Olaf had said, unimpressed, perhaps thinking of his own boys Harek and little Eric who were both safe with their mother in Skudeneshavn.

Sigurd had shrugged. Not his problem, for all that he quite liked the lad for some reason.

Other things to think about now though.

The Svearmen sang. The Sandnesmen drank. The oath-breaker's host came up that rock-strewn slope. And Sigurd told Olaf what he planned.

Gorm wanted Sigurd dead. He needed it. He hungered for it like he had never hungered for anything, not even power. Well perhaps that, for a great man cannot ignore his appetite for power.

That lust, that hunger is a beast which writhes barely below the surface, shaping every waking thought and shading dreams too. It spawns such ravenous ambition that it makes a man want to be more than a man, yet in reality it makes him less of one because he cannot enjoy the simple pleasures of life. A row to a deserted island. Skating on an iced lake. Good ale with good friends. A woman's love.

He looked up at that banner. A wolf, said one of his men who had been up there twice already, and twice come back down again because the skjaldborg on that ridge was stubborn. Gods flay them!

A banner? When did Sigurd Haraldarson decide he was worthy of his own banner? Arrogant turd. *A pain like a toothache, this golden lad, for the son of a dead nithing jarl,* Gorm thought to himself as he watched that wind-whipped wolf and the grim-faced men below it. Men such as Olaf Ollersson, as good a warrior as had ever come out of the fjords. And that red-haired giant with his smiting axe, who if he was anything like as good as his father Styrbiorn had been, would take a fistful of Gorm's hearthmen with him to the Spear-God's hall by the end of the day. And Moldof.

'Moldof.' Gorm said the name under his breath, tasting the rot in it. That was a betrayal which hurt, seeing his old champion and prow man up there, even if the man *was* an arm short of the warrior he had once been.

'You must think you have done well, Haraldarson,' he muttered into his beard, ignoring the askance looks he got from Hreidar, who had taken Moldof's place at *Storm-Bison*'s prow. A good fighter, Hreidar, as good as a two-armed Moldof perhaps, but carrying too much unearned swagger.

He supposed young Haraldarson had some right to feel pleased with himself. After all, not so long ago he had been able to boast of nothing but a half crew of nobodies and a child's lust for vengeance. Did the fool not know that life is more complicated than that? Than the need to poke out someone's eye because they poked out yours. Not even yours! Someone you share kinship with. Bloodfeuds were for petty men.

'Power is not about friendship, boy,' he growled.

Does the tide seek the shore's friendship before it submerges it?

Look at him up there. Thinking he can challenge me. Even if he has somehow got himself a war host. Taken strakes from here and there and riveted a skiff together. A skiff to take on a sleek-prowed, snarling beast of a dragon ship. Ha!

That Jarl Hrani was up there with the young fool was almost impossible to believe, and yet there he was, his own banner flapping like a fish in the bilge. Gorm could not imagine how that arrangement had come about, though he'd heard it had something to do with Hrani's boy. The boy's life for an oath. Randver, like his grandfather, wasn't it?

Gorm expected better from Hrani. A man can make new boys but he only betrays his king once. Well, young Randver would be dead by the end of the day. They all would.

'Shall we go again, lord?' some jarl called. Was it Baugr? Or Jarl Vragi? No matter.

'Of course, man!' Gorm yelled back. 'We are not here for the market!'

Baugr or Vragi or whoever in Heimdall's hairy arse it was grimaced and turned back to his men and gave the order to advance. Three times they had attacked that wall of limewood, iron and flesh, and three times they had failed to break it. But this time would be different because that fool Haraldarson had moved men over to the right of his line to fill the gaps left by that even bigger fool of a Danish king who had thrown his life away. Though they had killed too many before they fell, those Danes. Not that Gorm would miss that fat hog Jarl Twigbelly, for all that he had died well, better than Gorm expected.

'It takes time to learn war-craft, Haraldarson,' Gorm said, feeling a grin come to his lips. 'What could you possibly know of war, other than how to lose like your father and brothers?'

'Lord?' Hreidar said, thinking the king had meant the words for him.

'You'll enjoy killing Moldof, won't you?' Gorm said, tightening the helmet strap beneath his chin and loosening his sword in its scabbard in case he got carried away and ran to join his men for the final slaughter. He hadn't swung his sword in the blood-fray for some years now. Nothing like this anyway, but he would be ready just in case.

Hreidar grinned. 'I will take his other arm before I do him the honour,' he said, sharing a predatory look with Otkel, Ham and Alfgeir, all of them in helmets and mail and feeling like war gods, knowing that today was a day which skalds would sing of. Wanting their names and deeds to be in those songs.

Fine warriors, Gorm thought, enjoying the glow of confidence which was spreading through his veins like wine in the blood. *Wine would be good now*, he thought, but called for mead because that's what he had. It wasn't nearly often enough that a skipper came through the Karmsund Strait with good Frankish wine in his hold. He would get hold of some for the victory feast. Rich deep Frankish wine the colour of his enemies' blood-stained tunics and breeks.

'Óðin! Óðin!' he bellowed now, lifting his sword into the grey day, its point threatening the low-slung cloud which raced on the wind. The wind which was gathering in ferocity, lashing banners and hair and ruffling beards and swirling across that island. Gorm hoped his ships were protected in the bay. They would have to wait for the fjord to calm before heading back to Avaldsnes. 'Óðin!' he called again and his men took up the chant. For why should young Haraldarson claim the Allfather for himself? Óðin is a king's god! Stealing some spear from the Svearmen in the east did not buy Sigurd the god's favour. Only a wet-behind-the-ears boy would think it did.

He was trudging up that rocky slope now beneath his own banner. Haraldarson must see his own death coming. *Gods but I hope he doesn't run*, Gorm thought. Up and over those rocks behind him and scrambling down to the bay with piss-soaked breeks. No, Haraldarson wouldn't run. It was not in his blood. *Good. I am getting too old to be chasing men to kill them. Like a man haring after a deer running with an arrow in it.*

This attack was different from the previous two. Every man under the king's rule was going up that hill to kill those who mistakenly thought they were not beholden to him. Every spear which the king could summon was turned on Sigurd and the oath-breaker Jarl Hrani. It was a great killing wave that would first batter the thin skjaldborg on that ridge, then sweep it into the sea.

Unlike in the previous two assaults, when crews and war bands had struck the rebels' line at different times, giving Haraldarson and his men time to bolster the skjaldborg in places which looked vulnerable, this time they would hit together. As one hammer.

There would be no stopping it.

All across the war host in front, banners were tugged ragged by the wind. Men's voices were carried the distance of an arrow-shot one moment and lost in the gale the next. But orders were unnecessary now anyway. His jarls and his warlords knew what was expected of them. His own hearthmen, one hundred warriors and most in mail, knew their business and were salivating like hounds on the boar's trail. In front of the king, a place of honour, was Jarl Tósti and his fifty. No small thing to fight in plain sight of the man to whom you owe your jarl torc. Tósti was a solid sort, brave and thankful for his position, and he would fight well, Gorm was sure. He would likely die attacking Haraldarson himself beneath that wolf-head banner, and his men would be mauled by Sigurd's best. But they would soften the rebel centre, already weakened to bolster the right where the Danes should have been. They would bleed Haraldarson's best men. They would tire their shield arms and their sword arms. They would soak up arrows and spears and then, when Tósti broke, Gorm himself would lead *his* best men in to the carnage to finish this thing.

Gods how he hungered to finish it!

CHAPTER TWELVE

TÓSTI WAS DOING WELL, HIS SKJALDBORG TOE TO TOE WITH HARALDARSON'S, whilst to the left and right, all along the ridge, the battle raged like the storm. Men shrieked and wailed with pain. They bellowed like bulls to the slaughter. Now and then Gorm caught the reek of blood and shit but mostly it was borne off on the wind, thank the gods. Arrows flew and shields thumped and blades scraped other blades or mail or struck flesh. And there was no doubt the skjaldborg on the ridge was weakening as men in the front ranks fell and there were fewer and fewer to take their place.

Gorm saw a spear almost rip into Haraldarson's neck. Saw an arrow glance off the young man's helmet, so that if it hadn't been for the eye guards Sigurd would have had a skullful of shaft. But the golden-haired young shit was still standing before the Óðin spear, that flaming-haired, flame-bearded giant planted beside him like a damned oak tree.

So much for that nithing pole, Gorm thought, watching the seething mass of killing, dying men, waiting patiently for his moment to wade into the fray. No one else had dared cut the thing down, its horse head staring down the slope in echo of the curse which Haraldarson's godi had hurled at them. Asgot who men said had turned himself into a fox and chewed off his

254

own leg to escape the drowning death which Gorm had tried to give him. So much for his seiðr now though. Perhaps the others had been afraid of that níðstang, but not Gorm. He had taken Otkel's axe and, his hearthmen hoisting their shields to shelter him from a rain of arrows, had chopped that pole down like an old birch for the fire. He'd spat on the beast's head as it lay there in the long grass. And that was that.

Gorm saw the man on Jarl Tósti's right fall, his skull split by Olaf's sword. The man on Tósti's left, big, square-shouldered, fur-clad, was bent double, the shieldmaiden's spear in his belly, so said Hreidar, spitting in disgust. Then the jarl himself fell to Sigurd's own sword and Gorm almost cried out for joy because the time had come for him to lead his hearthmen to fame and reputation.

'I am coming for you, Haraldarson!' he roared, knowing that his king's voice drowned out even the wind and the shield din. 'You're a dead man, Sigurd!' He wished he could see the fear in the eyes within that pretty helmet. No matter. Perhaps there would be a moment. Before he gave the upstart his death wound.

Then he felt something. Like a change in the wind. Something most men would miss, but he had fought many battles on land and on sea. His war-craft was honed like an eagle's talons and he felt it.

'Lord!' someone yelled. 'Lord!'

Gorm turned to look down the slope which should have been empty but for the corpses and the dying and the arrows sprouting like summer wheat. Except it was not empty. It was full of half-naked, spear- and axe-armed warriors, painted men in wolf and bear pelts, some bollock-naked, with spittle-flecked beards and wild eyes and all of them screaming.

'Fuck,' Gorm growled, for he had seen berserkers before, though never more than three or four in one fight. Never thirty. And berserkers were killers. They had no fear, felt no pain. The animals barely knew when they were killed. 'Turn!' he bellowed. 'Shields!' he yelled, sensing the fear run through even his hearthmen, his best, as they saw what was coming, those rune-marked warriors who had somehow got down behind them, come down from the right side of Haraldarson's line, shielded from sight by his wing and then the rocks over on that side of the slope.

'Hold!' Gorm cried, lifting his shield, wondering what in the world could stop so many screaming, potion-maddened, ale-soaked, cock-flying warriors.

Not all of them were wolf- or bearskin-clad or bollock-naked, he noticed. Two wore mail. One had hair black as crow's feathers and a wolf-lean face. The other was golden-haired and handsome enough to be considered god-favoured. He was young and full of fury and even in his mail he somehow kept pace with the berserkers.

Gorm did not need to look over his shoulder. No point in staring back up the slope to confirm what he already knew, that the man beneath that wolf-head banner was not his hated enemy after all. He was a stand-in, a young, fair-haired Loki trick. A slice of low cunning that would have the gods themselves laughing into their mead horns.

For Sigurd Haraldarson was coming for him now and he brought death with him.

The Sandnes men flew across that uneven hillock-strewn ground, ravenous for blood, the first two or three of them impaling themselves on the king's hearthmen's spears while others slammed into shields and one or two somehow scrambled over the skjaldborg to be stabbed to death by those behind. Then Sigurd, sword in his right hand, scramasax in his left, was amongst it all, and he slammed his shoulder into a shield, the impact of it rattling his brain in his skull as he threw his right arm up, turning his wrist over to let Troll-Tickler bite what it could. Then a berserker slammed into him from behind, screaming as he hauled the hirðman's shield down with one hand and buried his hand axe in the man's face. On his knees, Sigurd lashed out with his scramasax, slicing across a shin deep enough to score the bone, and all around him berserkers clawed at shields and wriggled between them and clambered over them, shrieking in wild rage.

Floki was already through the skjaldborg, amongst the second rank, his two axes cleaving skulls and splitting breastbones, and Sigurd scrambled up, turning aside a spear blade with his sword then thrusting the scramasax into a neck.

'Hold them! Hold them!' someone was bellowing in a king's voice, as the tide of blood-crazed berserkers overran the mail-clad hirðmen, hacking and carving and screaming. Sigurd saw a big Sandnes man with three spear wounds drive through the enemy like a wedge splitting timber, killing two men before they brought him down. He saw a wolf-skinned berserker clamp his teeth round a man's neck and tear out his throat in a spray of blood. He saw two skin-and-bone Sandnes men pull down a big-bellied king's man and heard his scream as they plunged knives into his groin and face.

A spear blade struck Sigurd's shoulder and slewed off the mail. Another slammed into his side, cracking a rib though it didn't break the rings, and he flailed with his own blades, no skill, just savagery. Just seeking white flesh amongst grey iron. Sometimes sinking his scramasax into meat, sometimes feeling a bone break beneath his sword, lost in his own blood-lust now, consumed by the vicious joy of killing and an animal's need to survive.

'Hold them, you swines!' someone roared, that king's voice edged with fear like an iron blade edged with steel.

'Oath-breaker!' Sigurd yelled. 'Fight me, oath-breaker!' A shield boss cracked into his head and he fell again, blackness coming for him, flooding him, and he thought he would die then without even knowing it as they plunged spears into his body.

No, my son. Not yet. Not yet, boy. Kill them.

'Oath-breaker!' Sigurd screamed, defying the black wave that sought to drown him, forcing it back as he rose, his vision clearing to reveal Floki standing by him, cutting men, killing them, spilling guts amongst the long grass where they steamed and stank, lopping hands which fell and lay there like dead crabs. 'Fight me!' Sigurd roared his challenge as the Sandnes men killed and died in the blade-chaos around him. And there was King Gorm, just a few spear-lengths from him now, peering over the rim of his painted shield, feet planted, sword ready.

Sigurd threw his left arm up, catching a sword on his scramasax, the blow shaking the marrow in his bone as he brought Troll-Tickler round, driving it into a man's belly with enough muscle to pierce the brynja and the leather and the wool, thrusting the long blade through the fat and meat, its edge scraping the bones of the man's spine before erupting from his back. A king's man saw his chance and scythed his sword down at Sigurd but a bear-skinned Sandnes man barrelled into the hirðman and the two disappeared amongst the throng.

Hauling Troll-Tickler free, Sigurd turned, seeking the king, but now there were two warriors in front of him, shields overlapping. One of them fell with Floki's thrown axe in his face but another man took his place and Sigurd knew then that it was over.

Because almost all the berserkers were down. Of the seven or eight still fighting, at least six were wounded and the oath-breaker's men were rallying. Those king's men had been savaged and were reeling with the shock of it, but they were his household men, experienced killers bound by oath and honour, and they knew that with the attack broken all they need do was lock their shields and take the last berserkers apart piece by piece.

Half falling over a tangle of limbs and shield and wolf-skin, Sigurd threw himself at a hirðman who was trying to stand. He thrust his knife into the man's throat and sawed through the gristle of his windpipe and climbed to his feet, blinking hot blood from his eyes and looking east up to where Hrani and his men were fighting for their lives. Where Olaf and Svein, Bram, Valgerd, Solmund and the others were holding their ground.

Then he looked to the west.

Gods but don't come now. Not now.

A king's man took a berserker's head off with one swing of his long axe. Another Sandnes man died on his feet with four spear blades in him. Sigurd looked behind him again and this time saw Thokk Far-Flyer standing there with his arms raised to the storm, calling on the Spear-God while his men were being butchered.

But it wasn't Óðin who waded into the fray then, it was Erp and his thirty from Mekjarvik. They came across from the south, following the ground which Sigurd and the Sandnes men had taken to get round the flank of the oath-breaker's host now it had moved up to the ridge. They came in an ugly skjaldborg, daylight showing between shields and not even three together making a straight line. But they came, just as the last of the berserkers was dismembered and King Gorm's champion finished building his own skjaldborg which, if it had been built on the strand, would prove watertight enough to turn back the sea.

'Olaf sent us,' Erp called above the thunderous beat of king's swords on king's shields.

Sigurd nodded. Locked in the fight on the ridge Olaf had done what he could, but the loss of Erp and his men must have weakened his own position considerably.

'We can't win this,' Erp said. He spat, expecting no answer from Sigurd, his one eye blinking at the sight of the mail-coated horde facing them.

Sigurd glanced over his shoulder to see that Thokk Far-Flyer was down now, on his back in the grass, arms spread either side like wings, an arrow sprouting from his forehead. *Where are you flying to now, godi?* he thought, swinging his gaze back on to the sea of iron beneath that ship-prow banner.

'We can if we take the king,' Floki said, as if it were a simple game of tafl. He dragged an arm across his face but all that did was smear the gore over his skin, making the whites of his eyes glow against the dark blood.

Had night come already? Sigurd wondered. Surely not. Just the storm then. He looked up to see that the sky was almost black, the roof of the world veiled in swaths of fast-moving bruise-coloured cloud. There was water in the wind now too.

'There is no way to get to him,' Sigurd said, glaring at the oath-breaker, his breathing raspy and ragged. Each breath scalded him inside his chest. At least one broken rib, likely two. 'Too many between us and him.'

Don't come now. Allfather, whatever happens, don't let her come now.

'We just have to kill them all,' Floki said. 'Then we will have him.'

'Simple as that eh?' Erp said, as they edged closer to the king's shieldwall, the hersir using his sword pommel to hammer his helmet down so that its rim covered his bushy brows. He grimaced. 'Why didn't I think of it?'

'Close up! No gaps!' Sigurd bellowed at the Mekjarvik men. 'On me!' If there was going to be another clash of shields then they might as well look the part.

'Forward!' King Gorm cried, his sword threatening the shifting black sky. 'Forward!' he roared, and his men were coming, stepping over the mangled, shit- and blood-slick corpses that had been left on the slope like sea wrack above the tideline.

Sigurd took hold of a spear shaft that was sticking up like an offering, its blade lodged between a berserker's ribs, and yanked it free. He was good with a spear. Svein could throw further but further was not what was needed now. Accuracy was, and only Floki could match Sigurd for that. Floki who was god-favoured too, at least when it came to war. Though who could say which dark, blood-lusting lord favoured him?

Sigurd tested the spear's weight as he picked out the oath-breaker, imagining that spear entering the king's open, roaring mouth. Then he hauled his arm back and launched the spear and it flew.

He saw the shaft shudder at the height of its arc, then it fell fast as a swooping hawk towards the king. But another man had watched it too and he shouldered his king aside, throwing up his shield just in time to meet the spear, which went straight through the limewood and impaled him. Sigurd watched the hirðman fall, cursing as the others closed ranks before the king like the sea over a thrown pebble and the oath-breaker was lost from sight.

Sigurd looked beyond the king's hirð to his own wolf banner which was still whipping at the top of Gungnir, though the maelstrom was raging beneath it now and he could hear the clash and roar of it on the swirling, beating wind. Hastin and his Jæren men were shoulder to shoulder, shield on shield with Olaf and the others, each of them knowing that to lose the banner and the ridge was to be crushed against the rocks or driven into the sea.

Over on the right, the Jarls Leiknir and Hrani were still holding firm on the ridge, though they would be outflanked if Olaf's centre was pushed any further back. Sigurd could see Hog-Head smiting men, as full of fury as the berserkers, only that fury was matched with skill. Hrani stood there like a king himself in his war glory, his rich, silver-chased helmet the brightest thing up there on the ridge in the raging grey day.

On the left, though, Asgrim's Svearmen were dying. Asgrim won't break, Moldof had said. But Moldof was wrong. Jarl Otrygg had seized his chance to come round the side and now red rune-painted shields were driving into the line of Asgrim's wing, spilling through the gaps and tearing into the Svearmen's rear, so that Asgrim was fighting on two fronts.

But Sigurd did not have the chance to watch any more of it because the oath-breaker's shieldwall was on him, almost within spitting distance. He could smell the iron and leather, the sweat of unfamiliar men and the grease which coated their woollen clothes and their war gear. He could smell the oil on their shields and the ale on their breath, the sweet juniper and bog-myrtle and the sourness coming up from the stomachs of men who were fearful that this might be their last day.

'You're going to need this, lord,' Erp said, handing Sigurd a shield he had picked up. It was scarred and splintered but still solid enough and Sigurd took it with a nod, sheathing Troll-Tickler and wrapping his fist round the shield's wood and metal grip, feeling the coolness of the iron boss against his knuckles. His scramasax would be more useful than Troll-Tickler in this fight because the shorter blade had its own instinct for finding gaps in the press, holes between shields and opportunities to slide beneath them, to seek the flesh which was never safe. Men's groins. Necks. Shins. Ankles.

'What about you, lad?' Erp asked Floki who had found a spear to replace the axe he had thrown, though he still gripped the other axe in his left hand. But Floki shook his head and Sigurd knew what he had in mind. Floki would do the killing while Sigurd put his shoulder into his shield and held the ground.

This is it, then.

'We hold them as long as we can!' Sigurd called, looking left and right at the men in his pitifully thin skjaldborg, knowing that they could not stop what was coming. Those king's men were grinning because they knew it too. They knew that Sigurd had gambled everything by attacking their rear with those wild, howling Sandnes men, and he had lost.

'They're going to carve us up like the prize bullock,' a man said somewhere to his right.

'Carve us up! Ha! Snot-sucking shits are going to walk right over us, pricking us full of holes on the way back to their bloody boats,' another man answered. And yet they stood their ground, all of them, when they could have turned and run. Not that they would likely get off the island even if they did run, for the king would have men guarding his ships.

'If we can hold, I'll kill them,' Floki said, as if it were as easy as that. And yet it gave Sigurd an idea.

'Men of Mekjarvik, can you make a skjaldhus?' he asked them. 'A shieldhouse that will stand up to a storm?' *Not enough time for that now, lad,* Sigurd could almost hear Olaf saying. *Too late for tricks now.*

Some *ayes* even so.

'How many in the walls?' Erp asked like the good warrior he was, never resigning his men to their blade deaths when there was yet something useful to try.

'Five in each,' Sigurd said, and with that the Mekjarvik men swarmed in towards him, the smaller, weaker men giving their shields to the biggest and broadest so that these men would have two shields each. Sigurd gave his to a bull-necked, big-bearded warrior who held out his hand expectantly, knowing his wyrd had led him to this moment. In return the man gave Sigurd his spear.

Not enough time. They are on you, lad!

'I don't even want the rain getting in,' Sigurd yelled as they formed around him, building that shieldhouse, the sixteen men in the outer walls holding one shield low to cover shins and legs, the other shield high to protect chests and faces. Those eight men on the inside square braced their bodies against the outside wall to add weight to it, whilst holding shields as high as they could, slanting them up like a shingled roof. This left just eight men within this breath- and sweat-stinking skjaldhus, waiting in the dark, their spears poking out through the gaps.

The king's men struck like a rockslide, almost breaking the shieldhouse apart so that the grey day flooded in through the widening cracks. It seemed they would be swept away in a welter of blood. But then the Mekjarvik men roared their defiance, bellowed their war cries, braced muscle and bone and will and held their ground, drawing their shields back together so that they clumped and rattled and the whole thing held.

'Good lads!' Erp yelled in the reeking gloom, proud of his men and rightly so. 'Now hold so we can kill the whoresons,' he told them, thrusting his spear out and getting a shriek as his reward.

'That's it, Erp,' Sigurd said, feeling the wolf's grin on his face as he jabbed his own spear through a hole. The blade hit mail. 'Nowhere you'd rather be, hey?'

It grew dimmer still inside the skjaldhus and someone cursed because the oath-breaker's men were all around them, on every side so that the only light coming in now was at the centre where the smoke hole in a longhouse would be.

Swords and axes hammered on the walls and the roof in a deafening clamour and men grunted under the impact, growling at those who had spears to gut the swines who were battering them.

Between strikes, Floki pulled his spear back inside the shieldwall so that no one could lop it or grab hold of it, and Sigurd saw that the blade was slick with blood.

'Don't come now,' Sigurd whispered, burying his spear in a man's thigh. 'Stay away.' *Stay alive. You are the last of us.*

Then the Mekjarvik man whose spear Sigurd gripped grunted and fell to his knees like a throat-cut bull, blood sheeting his face because the great crescent blade of a long axe had cut through shield, arm, helmet and skull to kill him. So much for wyrd.

Another man went down under a flurry of axe blows, and yet another big man collapsed with a beard full of bubbles and blood and a spear in his lungs, and the skjaldhus shrank as the Mekjarvik men closed the gaps, clinging to each other the way men will hold to an overturned boat.

A spear came in through a crack and took the young man beside Sigurd in the cheek, knocking out his teeth on the way through. The spear pulled back leaving the man on his knees in the dark, gurgling and choking and clutching his ruined face.

'No way to die, this,' Floki spat, his spear blade snaking out and back again, seeking, hungry as a crow.

And it wasn't, Sigurd knew, but at least they were lasting longer than they would have spread out in one flimsy shieldwall. Still, this was not the way his father would ever have died, hiding in the dark like this, killing men – hurting them, anyway – without seeing their faces. And he realized, whilst putting his spear straight through a helmet's eye guard and pulling it back before it got stuck, that his need to kill the oath-breaker was stronger even than the need to die with honour.

For there could be no honour in death, even a saga-worthy one, if that goat-swiving worm of a king got to spit on his corpse when it was done. When Sigurd met his brothers again in the Allfather's hall, would he say to them, 'I tried, brothers, but I could not avenge you. I could not spill the blood which the oath-breaker's crimes against our family demanded'?

No. He would not.

Another of Erp's men died, his high shield cleaved and his arm lopped off at the shoulder, likely by the same king's man with his long-hafted axe.

'That whoreson's got to go,' Erp growled, but no one volunteered to oblige him.

'Where are you, Haraldarson?' the king bellowed, his voice matching the thunder of blades on shields and the roar of the wind itself. 'Come out and die like a man! This is no way to fight!'

'Says him who's been fart-blown by his own men all day,' Erp gnarred.

The man in front of Sigurd screeched, his leading foot chopped in half, then he toppled like a felled tree and was gored with three spears before his head hit the ground, and Sigurd snatched up his shield even as a spear gouged into his back, breaking brynja rings, perhaps half a dozen by the fish-scale glitter of them flying in the grey day. But the leather beneath the rings held and he stood tall, taking an axe on the shield before putting his spear blade through the man's neck.

'I have him!' a king's man bellowed, grinning, lifting his long-hafted axe, and Sigurd would have wagered a silver arm ring on it being the same man who had been taking the skjaldhus down piece by piece.

'Come then, troll,' Sigurd challenged him, wondering how he was going to fight the man let alone beat him without being able to leave the shieldhouse. He knew what that axe would do to him. Had seen Svein sunder men with his own axe, split them from head to groin, shield or no.

'Finish him, Gerbiorn!' a warrior with a scarred face and two beard ropes said, fingering the silver Thór's hammer hanging on his chest because he knew this was a big moment, one for winter nights to come.

'Aye, get your name in a song, Gerbiorn,' another man said through his teeth, and big Gerbiorn lumbered forward, looping that smiting axe so that Sigurd heard the slap of its haft against his palms, once, twice, then up soared the great blade and Sigurd was about to throw his spear even if it meant losing it, when an arrow suddenly appeared in Gerbiorn's shoulder followed by another in his neck. The big troll stood there frowning, as if he could not understand what was happening, and then more arrows, dozens of them, were streaking into the king's men, like starlings flocking to their roosts.

'Shields!' the oath-breaker's champion shouted, raising his own so that it covered more of his lord than himself, which was just as well for Gorm judging by the two shafts it already sprouted.

'Hold here!' Sigurd told the Mekjarvik men in the ruins of their shieldhouse. Not so much a house now as a tumbledown shepherd's hut. But they kept their shields up, rims kissing as best they could because those arrows were whipping in amongst the king's men, *tunk*ing into shields and *thoot*ing into mail and flesh. One flitted past Sigurd's face so close that he felt the fletchings brush his cheek.

'Who is here, then?' Floki said, hardly caring about those terror-sowing shafts, taking advantage of this new chaos and sinking his spear one-handed into a greybeard's leg. Sigurd knew full well who it was. She had come! She was here to give herself to the slaughter. Just as she had told the blacksmith Ingel to tell Sigurd that she would.

Runa!

Sigurd twisted and turned, trying to see what he already knew. There, through the gaps left by Erp's dead and dying men, he saw them. And he had never felt the gods closer than in that moment.

'Runa?' Floki said. 'Can it be Runa?' He was looking south too, as were many of the Mekjarvik men now because the oath-breaker's warriors had drawn together again like fingers into a fist and were trying to make sense of what was happening whilst also being flayed by arrows.

'Fuck, it's a host of Valkyries!' Erp said, looking more terrified than he had all day. His men were muttering oaths and touching their Thór's hammers, peering over their shields with bulging eyes, for there, sweeping across the slope, all shining mail and long braided hair beneath that low black sky, was a host of warrior women. Well, perhaps not a host, but a war band anyway, more than thirty and all of them nocking, drawing, loosing as they came, sending flocks of deadly shafts into the oath-breaker's hirð.

'Are we dead?' a man asked his companions and not one of them seemed sure that they weren't.

And there amongst these shieldmaidens, these terrifying brynja-clad, arrow-shooting women, was Runa, her golden hair bright in the dark day, a shield slung over her back.

Sigurd had told no one what Ingel had told him, because he did not want it to be true, did not want Runa to come to Rennisøy to stand beneath his banner in the storm of swords. There had been no time to send someone to the island of Fugløy to tell her not to come, but at least by not speaking of it, not sharing Ingel's message, he could pretend that there was no more to it than breath on the breeze.

'Tell my brother I am coming,' Ingel had said, careful to use the exact words that Runa had. 'And that I will bring the Maidens of Freyja to fight with him against the oath-breaker king.' The young smith had frowned and half choked over the next part, as if he feared to intrude on things that were between a brother and sister. 'For are we not of the same mother? The same father? Are we not beloved of the gods? Then let us stand together. We are the last but we are enough. Look for me, brother. I am coming to you.'

267

Sigurd had not wanted her to come. Now he was grinning like a moon-mad fiend.

They drew and loosed, drew and loosed, sending arrow after arrow and gods they were good, because those shafts had been finding the parts which even the king's hearthmen in all their fine war gear had trouble protecting: eyes, faces, hands, the lower legs. And most of the women were making these shots on the move, too.

But those Sword-Norse who had halted their attack on Sigurd's skjaldhus had built their own shieldwall again, so that the Freyja Maidens' arrows were hitting shields now and bouncing off helmets. Not that this was much fun for the men beneath them, as Erp pointed out happily.

Sigurd saw and heard one of Runa's arrows *tonk* off the oath-breaker's own helmet and he began to wonder if one of the lords of Asgard was watching over the king.

'Shieldwall!' he yelled and Erp's men moved well, getting into line beside him and overlapping their shields, some of them even hammering hilts and shafts against the limewood to let the Avaldsnes men know that death was coming for them. They knew as well as Sigurd that they must seize this moment, when the king was wrong-footed, while the arrows were raining and his men were cowering behind their shields. From the look of it the warrior women each had two quivers of arrows on their belts, which meant some eighty arrows each, but they would run out fast at this rate, desperate as they were to slay the king and end the battle.

'Ready!' Sigurd called, an order not a question. 'Now!' He strode forward and what was left of Erp's crew, some twenty men, went with him. 'Runa! Behind me!' he bellowed, and Runa heard him above the wind's roar and the battle's din, screaming at her companions to follow her, sweeping around Sigurd's rear. Over the dead they went, across the blood-slick long grass, the lopped limbs and the broken spears and the splintered shields, and then the skjaldborgar struck and Sigurd thought he heard a peal of thunder rend the sky at that same moment as he put his shoulder into his shield and dipped his head.

The Freyja Maidens were with him now and he sensed the battle thrill in them. The warrior behind him was a tall, fierce-eyed, red-haired woman who nodded at him before loosing an arrow at the man whose shield he heaved against. From that distance and with a draw like that, mail was useless, and suddenly the weight was gone and the shield fell and Sigurd was moving forward, as was his whole skjaldborg. 'Just hold the line!' he roared.

'No gaps, you bastards!' Erp shouted, his one eye glaring ferociously, and they knew that their job now was to maintain the bulwark from behind which the women could do the killing, from less than five feet away sinking their arrows deep, every shaft a kill or maiming. And yet they also knew that they could not hold against those sixty hearthmen who yet fought beneath that ship banner. 'Kill them!' Erp bellowed at the Freyja Maidens. 'Put your arrows into the shits! Murder the reeking, pus-filled maggots!'

The bow strings hummed. The arrows whipped and *thunk*ed and the warrior women shrieked with savage joy for every man they killed or put down, and Sigurd knew that their god then was not Óðin or Freyja or some reasoning Asgard-dweller but the fiend of battle which can consume a warrior when the blood is flying.

And then a war horn sounded, thin and plaintive enough to cut through the steel-storm and the wind's howl. And Sigurd looked up at the ridge because he knew that horn meant that Asgrim and his Svearmen had been overrun.

'Olaf can't hold now,' Floki said from behind his own shield, 'not with them coming into his side.'

'He'll hold,' Sigurd said, face against the limewood, still moving forward as the red-haired woman, who was quite beautiful he realized even in the maw of it all, loosed shaft after shaft into the enemy, all the while snarling like some wild creature.

269

'Erp's down!' someone yelled. Someone else cursed and as the line pushed on, somehow driving the king's men back, Sigurd saw Erp on his knees, clutching his side where a tear in his mail revealed a purple bulge which was his guts trying to spring out. Erp riveted his one eye on Sigurd, who held his stare for a heartbeat or two before looking back to his own shield. His shield which had struck rock then, or at least it felt like it. Then the rock pushed back against Sigurd and Sigurd could not hold it, and from the size of the feet which he glimpsed beneath their shields he knew he was in trouble.

'Take him!' he yelled at the red-head, who pulled another arrow from her quiver, nocked it to the bow string, drew and loosed, and cursed because the arrow missed, bouncing off the warrior's helmet from the sound of it.

Then Sigurd's shoulder turned as the man broke through the wall, punching his sword hilt into Sigurd's face and roaring as he came. Sigurd spun, reeling, but saw the big man, the oath-breaker's champion it was, hack the bow from the red-head's hands, and she drew her sword but the warrior's next swing sent that flying with her severed hand still clutching the grip. He was fast, as fast as a man with half as much bulk, and he put his sword straight through the Freyja Maiden and had it out again before you could blink. She fell and suddenly mailed men were pouring through the breach, hacking at the warrior women and spearing them.

'Runa!' Sigurd screamed, spitting blood, scything a hirðman's leg off at the knee then cutting into the spine of another, trying to reach his sister through that tide of the enemy. The Freyja Maidens were dying but not yet beaten, many of them having unslung shields and drawn swords to stab and slash in shrieking fury, almost dancing around their bigger, heavier opponents rather than trading blows with them.

King's men were dying too, because the Maidens knew their sword-craft, but those king's men were hirðmen of many battles and furthermore they now knew that these women could die, that they were not in fact Valkyries riding the wind.

Floki split a skull and hacked off another man's jaw, and Sigurd blocked a wild swing that would have lopped off his head, then scythed his shield into the man's temple, dropping him like a rock, and he could see Runa fighting shoulder to shoulder with two other women but he could not get to her.

'Can you reach her?' he asked Floki, slipping on the wet grass even as he caught a sword on his shield, and twisted, plunging Troll-Tickler into a man's belly. He must have wished he owned a brynja, that man, if he could think of such things with his body ruined and death flooding in. And when Sigurd looked up Floki was gone, carving his way through the oath-breaker's finest warriors like a man scything barley.

There was a roar and a moaning of big war horns and through the chaos Sigurd caught sight of his own wolf-head banner, the green cloth thrashing in the wind, and for a terrible, heart-freezing moment he thought all was lost. That the enemy had captured the banner and the Óðin spear and were bringing it back down the slope to their lord. But then he saw the rearmost of the oath-breaker's men turning to face back up the hill, bringing their shields together and bracing. Screaming at each other to hold. Spitting curses and insults at what was coming. Promising pain and death.

And what was coming was fury. Olaf and Svein and Aslak and the others were walking down the slope, having abandoned the ridge. Having lost the ridge. They came in a swine-head formation, Svein and Olaf at the tip of the snout, Moldof, Bram and Bjarni behind them. Five in the rank behind, seven behind that, Sigurd's crew and Hastin and his Jæren men making up the rest of the svinfylkja.

It was like a ship's prow through the fjord, Crow-Song might have said, Gorm's men rolling off Olaf's like waves before the bow, but really it was nothing so beautiful as that. In truth it was a crude nail driven into a splintering beam. They came at pace, not stopping to trade blows but battering men aside with shields and trampling them under foot, Olaf roaring into the wind, screaming at them to keep going, to not stop even if they were dead. Because Olaf knew he must strike the king's hirð and break them before those king's men they had left on the ridge arrayed themselves into a shieldwall and trapped them like the grain between the quern-stones.

A warrior with a red beard rope came at Sigurd then, thinking to make his fame. He thrust his spear high and Sigurd caught it on his shield and pushed it out wide as he swung his sword across, scything off the spear blade and a foot of ash with it. The king's man jumped back, pulled his sword from its scabbard, then came again and maybe he was very fast or maybe Sigurd was slowing, but he rained down blow after blow, howling in savage joy with each piece of Sigurd's shield which flew.

Sigurd thrust Troll-Tickler but Gorm's man parried it and rammed his own shield into the shivered wreck of Sigurd's and swung his sword backhanded, lopping off all the splintered limewood that was left above the iron boss. But Sigurd still gripped that boss and he stepped forward and hammered it across the man's face, cracking bone, and then as Gorm's man reeled and threw his sword up to meet Troll-Tickler, Sigurd turned the boss and drove a scramasax-sized splinter of limewood into his neck and only then did Sigurd let go of the thing.

The king's man fell to his knees, clutching at the shield boss and the sliver of wood sticking in his neck, his hands fumbling and slipping in his own blood.

'Wait for me in Valhöll,' Sigurd told him, then swung his gaze left and right, looking for Runa. Most of the king's hearthmen had turned to face Olaf's svinfylkja, so the remaining Mekjarvik men who had built the shieldhouse with Sigurd were now bunching together with the twenty or so warrior women who had survived Gorm's counter attack.

'Kill them!' Sigurd roared, striding forward.

'For Freyja!' a woman yelled, and Sigurd recognized that voice if not the fury in it. He glanced over his shoulder to see Runa haul a spear from a corpse and hurl it like a lightning bolt to take an Avaldsnes man in his shoulder where it stuck, making him scream in pain and shock. Then she and Floki were at his shoulder and Floki was grinning through a veil of blood which was not his own.

'They're breaking!' one of Erp's men shouted. 'Whoresons are breaking!' And they were. Olaf and his swine-head had driven deep into King Gorm's horde and in the grey day Sigurd could see the blood misting the air as Olaf and Svein and Bram laid about them with shield and blade, cutting and hacking as they plunged deeper still towards the oath-breaker himself. And the Avaldsnes men could not stop them, not with Sigurd at their backs. Not with Erp's brave Mekjarvik men and a band of shrieking Freyja Maidens spearing them like fish in a barrel because many of them were caught in the press and unable to wield their own spears and swords effectively.

'Stay with me, Runa,' Sigurd said.

'And you with me, brother,' Runa said, grinning savagely, and Sigurd wondered when his little sister had become a goddess of battle.

Then the king's hirð was splintering the way Sigurd's shield had, and it was not because those men were cowards. Sigurd knew they would die on the field for their lord and revel in it too, mouths watering at the thought of the mead they would soon be drinking in the Allfather's hall. But there was no glory in a bad death, perhaps no Valhöll either, and bad deaths were what most of them were looking at now, if they did not escape the crush which Olaf's charge had started like an avalanche down a mountainside.

Floki cut men as they fled, his axe biting necks and shoulders and even cutting hamstrings so that men fell in heaps and lay screaming until Runa's Freyja Maidens filled them with spears or cut their throats.

'The gods are watching now, Haraldarson!' Olaf was yelling, though Sigurd could not see his friend in the bloody heart of the fray. Now and then he caught sight of Svein, though, who looked like his father Styrbiorn as he cleaved shields and hammered helmets, breaking anyone who dared stand and face him.

'Gorm!' Sigurd called. 'Oath-breaker! I have claimed you for Óðin!' He pushed through a knot of Mekjarvik men in the direction of the king, who was on the move surrounded by a dozen hearth warriors. 'Fight me, oath-breaker! Fight me, you nithing pile of troll shit!'

But even if the king could hear Sigurd's challenge above the sword din and the howling roar of the wind which whipped men's hair across their eyes and hurled stinging rain into their faces, he showed no intention of doing anything other than flee the fight.

It was chaos. Olaf's swine array was no more, the formation having fractured now that its momentum was lost, and men broke off to give themselves to the slaughter, to the maelstrom of steel, flesh and blood. Valgerd was there, twisting and turning, lunging with her spear and retreating behind her shield. Bram was insulting men even as he cleaved their shields and split their skulls, and even Thorbiorn Thorirsson looked like a proper warrior in the steel-storm, matching a big hirðman blow for blow, the splinters flying from their shields.

Up on the ridge the fight still raged, with Jarl Hrani, his champion Hadd Hog-Head and Asgrim's surviving Svearmen up to their arses in it with Jarl Otrygg, who had once been Bram's jarl.

But Sigurd did not see much more. He was moving, forcing his way through the throng towards his hated enemy, putting down anyone who stood in his way, and Floki and Runa and a handful of Mekjarvik men went with him.

'He's making for the ships,' Floki at Sigurd's shoulder said. 'The maggot thinks he can wriggle his way out of this.'

'Not today he can't,' Sigurd spat, putting Troll-Tickler through a neck and blocking a sword with his scramasax before Runa's spear streaked out to open the swordsman's belly. Olaf and Crow-Song and some of the others were cutting a swath across the field to get to the king and Sigurd knew that he was not the only man beneath that storm-tossed sky who burnt to kill King Gorm, to send him to the afterlife where Harald and Thorvard and Sigmund and Sorli waited for him.

Then Floki stepped in front of Sigurd and butchered two warriors with axe and scramasax, and it was as if the king felt Sigurd on him like a change in the wind, because he suddenly turned and lowered his shield so that the thick gold torc at his neck gleamed dully against the grey rings of his brynja. He glared at Sigurd through his helmet's eye guards and then he shoved the warrior next to him aside and lifted his sword, pointing it at Sigurd like an accusation, and Sigurd felt himself grinning like a fiend because every warrior on that field, and every lord of Asgard too, knew then that the oath-breaker meant to fight Sigurd man to man.

'Come then, Haraldarson,' Gorm bellowed, his voice as impressive as the thunder rolling across the sky. Rain dripped from his helmet's rim and ran down his sword, and his silver-threaded beard bristled in the wind.

'I am your death, Gorm snake-in-the-grass!' Sigurd yelled. 'My father waits for you in Valhöll!'

'Your father was an ill-wyrded nithing fool, boy! And your brothers were turds that fell from between your whore mother's legs!'

Troll-Tickler in his right hand, his scramasax in his left, Sigurd was already moving, the gusts thrashing rain into his face and against his teeth, and the king's hearthmen stood aside to let him through. And Gorm was coming for him, too, striding across the ground as if his very bones and blood screamed at him to kill Sigurd.

Then up came Gorm's shield and Sigurd met it with Troll-Tickler, the thump of it lost in the clamour of shouting, cheering men, then the king's sword flashed and the steel and iron sang on the wind.

'He's mine!' Sigurd roared at Moldof who was suddenly beside him, but then Moldof's sword scythed down and Sigurd felt it coming and twisted but the blade caught him below his shoulder, cutting brynja and flesh, and Sigurd staggered away from that blow, as Crow-Song flew at Moldof, enraged by this betrayal.

Moldof took the skald's sword on the remains of the shield strapped to the stump of his arm then swiped his sword across, taking the skald in his side, and Sigurd could not have been the only one who heard the snap of ribs, but then Moldof rammed his sword into Crow-Song's mouth and that was Hagal's death blow.

'Go, my king!' Moldof roared, turning to fend off Olaf and Svein, but others spilled into the moment then from both sides and Sigurd could only watch as bodies and shields swarmed between him and his enemy. Watch and bleed, for Moldof's sword had carved into him, not that there was any pain yet. There was just rage at Moldof and at himself for having let the wolf-jointed troll play him like a bukkehorn this whole time when really he was still Gorm's man. Moldof had bided his time, even saved Sigurd's life before now, and all so that he could at last kill Sigurd in front of the man who still had his oath. And he had nearly succeeded too. Gods, but Sigurd almost respected the man for his patience, for holding on to his ambition all this time, even one-armed as he was.

Then the king's battle horns sounded and with it a surging roar rose from his men into the wind and rain, and for a moment it seemed they had broken because many of them turned and ran, whilst others who could not turn their backs on their enemies lifted their shields and strode backwards across the blood-slick grass.

A shoulder slammed into Sigurd, almost knocking him down. 'What kind of a king runs from a fight?' Olaf spat, his face a mask of savage horror as he hauled breath into himself and flicked a gobbet of meat off his sword where it had caught on a notch in the steel.

'Told you we should have gutted that one-armed swine-humping shit,' Solmund growled, and even in the midst of his rage Sigurd was pleased to see the old skipper still breathing.

'Thought he was going to gut the oath-breaker,' Olaf gnarred, as close as he would come to admitting that he should have stopped Moldof before the man cut Sigurd.

'The gods want their game to last a little longer,' Asgot said, his face gore-spattered so that the little bones knotted into his beard looked as if they had been freshly pulled from some carcass. The godi speared a man in the back and spat at him as he died.

'Aye but these goat-swivers are on the run,' Bram said. 'You can hear their arse cheeks clapping.'

Up on the ridge Jarl Hrani had somehow won and now Jarl Otrygg's men were scattering like rats before the hounds. The king's men at the foot of the slope had seen this too and they knew that Jarl Hrani would sweep down that hill to join his men with Sigurd's and so some of them were backing away from the bloody snarl of it all.

'Nithings!' Svein yelled at these, hoisting his long axe above his head. 'Fight us, you cowards!'

'Why should they die while their king runs like a river?' Valgerd said, standing shoulder to shoulder with Runa who had picked up a bow and replenished her own quiver with arrows now. The shieldmaiden's question was a good one, because Sigurd caught a glimpse of the king and Moldof and a small knot of men beyond the skjaldborg which those loyal hearthmen were building now so that their king could escape the slaughter.

But there could be no escape for Gorm, and Sigurd snatched up a discarded shield and ran at the skjaldborg, and before he could cleave the shield of the nearest man, an arrow suddenly jutted from the warrior's face and he fell. Then Sigurd crashed into the gap before the Avaldsnes men could lock shields, and plunged Troll-Tickler into a man's thigh and another arrow found its mark and then he was through that wall of men and wood and running still.

He ran down the slope, the wind howling in his ears, past boulders and humps of tufted grass and then joined the path which led down to the bay, above which no gulls soared in this wrathful storm. And when he came round a bend past a stone-built shepherd's shelter he saw all the ships and boats which had brought the king's war host to Rennisøy. They were being tossed in the shallows, those nineteen ships and all the smaller boats, heaving at their mooring lines and bucking wildly. Even Gorm's favourite ship *Storm-Bison* was being savaged now that they had pushed her back into the sea. As if *Hríð-visundr* was the creature after which she was named and she was being beset by wolves which were the white breakers, and no skipper in his right mind would put out into a sea like that.

Unless his king was commanding him to. Or Moldof was. The one-armed giant was bawling orders at the others, even at Hreidar the warrior who had replaced him as Gorm's prow man, and though Moldof's words were lost on the wind, Sigurd could see men taking their oars from the stands and threading them through the ports. He could see others cutting the ropes and still others preparing to haul the sail up the mast and give at least some of the cloth to the wind once they were off the shallows.

Behind him the clamour of battle, the shouts and screams of warriors and the ring and scrape of the sword-song. In front of him the roar of the sea, the grey squall of fjord and rain, and the promise of revenge.

He ran and stumbled, slipping on the scree path and tripping on rocks and roots, and he knew others came after him but he did not stop to see if they were his warriors or the king's. Then he came down to the beach where old men and beardless boys waited with the boats, watching them like hawks because they were the ones who would be blamed if their kinsmen and companions returned from the battle to find their knörrs and longships rolling on the shingle and springing strakes or being carried off across the fjord having been plucked from their moorings.

'Sigurd!'

Sigurd turned and saw Floki and Valgerd, Runa, Olaf and Svein coming down the sea path, Valgerd gripping Svein's long axe as well as her spear because the red-bearded giant carried old Solmund in his arms like a bairn. They looked like Hel's own warriors, all wild-eyed and gore-spattered and full of the battle thrill.

'Óðin's arse, Sigurd! Wait!' Olaf yelled, his voice carrying to Sigurd on the wind, but Sigurd's vengeance would not wait and he was crossing the strand which was all that separated him from the oath-breaker.

Then one of King Gorm's warriors broke off from the others who were climbing aboard *Storm-Bison*.

'Haraldarson!' this warrior shouted, holding his sword and shield out wide to let everybody see – to let Sigurd see – how big he was and how fine his war gear.

'Hreidar Herdísarson,' Sigurd called back, beyond caring that he was about to fight the king's champion, the man who stood at *Storm-Bison*'s prow and hewed down the oath-breaker's enemies. The man who now believed he would cast his reputation in gold by killing Sigurd on that beach.

Behind Hreidar, the king himself was aboard his ship now. He was clinging to the stem post and glaring at Sigurd as *Storm-Bison* pranced and jerked on the spume-crested rollers which threw themselves on to the strand.

'Is this how you saw your death, Hreidar?' Sigurd asked him, stalking towards him with his sword and scramasax, ignoring a voice in his head which warned him that he was bleeding badly from the cut Moldof had given him.

'My wyrd is not to die by your sword, Haraldarson,' the champion said with a smile. Along the beach some of those who had been guarding the boats were summoning the courage to go and stand with Hreidar, but most were unsure because up on the rise were Jarl Hrani and his Sword-Norse and they brought with them the Óðin spear with Sigurd's wolf banner thrashing beneath its blade.

Even Sigurd shuddered to see the jarl up there, his helmet brighter than the day, because had Hrani been Sigurd's enemy, as he was until recently, then Sigurd would surely have lost this battle and the oath-breaker would have pissed on his corpse.

Then Valgerd flew past Sigurd and Hreidar banged his sword against his shield because he knew the shieldmaiden meant to kill him and he respected her for the ambition.

'He's mine!' Sigurd yelled after her, but she was already on Hreidar, probing his defences with her spear and measuring his speed as he swung, trying to shorten that spear by a foot or two.

Olaf and Floki ran towards a handful of greybeards and boys who turned and hared back to their knörr, thinking better of their former plan to continue their king's fight. And more king's men were flying down the sea path to escape Jarl Hrani. They scattered like rooks from the roost, fleeing across the shingle towards their respective boats, screaming at friends and kinsmen to make a shieldwall or to put out into the storm-tossed sea, which showed that the king's great war host was a shattered thing now, that his men would risk a drowning death rather than stay and fight.

'Go, Sigurd!' Valgerd yelled over her shoulder while jabbing her spear at Hreidar's face but striking his helmet. 'That færing with the new strakes. Go!'

Sigurd ran to the high-tide line on to which the sea had spewed its green wrack, and to the abandoned boat lying there in danger of being claimed by the fjord. No more than sixteen feet in length it had a small mast and yard as well as two pairs of oars and Sigurd set his shoulder to it and pushed but it would not move.

'Come on!' he growled, and then Sigurd thought the gods had heard him, for the little boat was moving, its belly crunching on the stony sand.

'You think I'd let you butcher that oath-breaking bollock of a king without me, lad?'

Sigurd looked up and saw Olaf at the other end of the boat, leaning back, hauling the thing towards the sea. Floki and Runa were beside Sigurd too now and the hull kissed the breakers and they jumped aboard but for Olaf who stood in the surf fighting to hold on to the little færing while Svein waded in with Solmund still in his arms.

Sigurd took the skipper from him and put him on the bench at the tiller, earning the old man's thanks and a pained grin but a grin nonetheless. Like all of them Solmund was daubed with blood but in his case too much of it was his own.

'Don't you die yet, old man,' Olaf growled as Svein pushed the boat into deeper water and Floki hauled the yard up the mast and spread her sail to the storm. Sigurd looked back to the beach and saw Valgerd duck Hreidar's wild swing and put her spear in his thigh, heard the champion bellow in fury before swinging again, but this time the shieldmaiden leapt back and sprang forward, supple as a slender yew, jumping for height and thrusting the spear down over Hreidar's shield into his shoulder. The champion cast his shield aside to better see his enemy and Valgerd seized on his stupidity because she had him for both reach and speed and he did not even have a shield now.

'Take him, Valgerd,' Floki growled into the gusts, seeing Hreidar's mistake as he worked the yard and wrestled with it to catch the wind.

Valgerd feinted high and the champion swept his sword up to block, only the spear blade was no longer there. It was in his belly, and Hreidar had been right when he had said it was not his wyrd to die by Sigurd's sword. He was dead by Valgerd's spear. Or would be.

The shieldmaiden's next strike took him in the groin and her last opened his throat and Hreidar kept his feet but Valgerd must have known she had given him his death wound because she turned and ran down the beach and plunged into the waves and Sigurd pulled her aboard, so that the little boat now showed only a sliver of freeboard above the waterline.

'They made it, then,' Svein said, pointing, and they all looked back to see Bram and Aslak, Asgot, Thorbiorn, Bjarni and Bjorn all spilling on to the beach, their splintered shields and gore-stained mail and blades telling their story better than any skald could.

'Here!' Olaf yelled to them, and somehow Asgot heard him through the storm din and lifted his spear high.

But *Storm-Bison* was bearing the oath-breaker westward, her mast bending to the wind even with her sail more than half reefed and her crew fighting as hard as they had fought all day.

There was no time to wait for the others.

'Go!' Sigurd called, turning his back on those on the beach, the wind whipping his hair across his eyes and crusting the blood caught in the rings of his brynja. Floki grinned and nodded, catching that storm in the square sail so that it cracked with the joy of it and the reefing ropes danced.

'Don't lose them, Solmund!' Sigurd called over his shoulder as he peered into the gusting grey veils of rain after *Storm-Bison*, growling at Rán Mother of the Waves that she could not have the oath-breaker because his death belonged to Sigurd.

'Don't need you to tell me how to breathe, lad,' Solmund called back, gripping the tiller as the rest of them clung on to the benches and sides and planted their feet in the waterlogged thwarts and the færing flew into the Boknafjord.

CHAPTER THIRTEEN

AMID THE RAGING STORM, SWATHS OF EVEN HEAVIER RAIN RACED ACROSS the fjord like the shadows of gods, so that the glimpses they got of *Storm-Bison* were few and fleeting. Yet from what they could see, whoever was at her helm was earning his silver, as were those men breaking their backs with the bailers and those who had managed to lower the yard and roll up another few feet of sail before hauling it back up the mast. For *Storm-Bison* had somehow managed to avoid being wrecked on the rocks in the channel between east and west Bokn, and to do that she must have slanted her stem into the wind which is a good way of sinking a boat because it will ship water the way Thór ships mead.

'How can they be afraid of a little færing like us?' Svein called into the wind, wondering why the Avaldsnes men would take such risks in flying from them.

'It's not us he's afraid of, though he should be,' Olaf shouted above the hiss and roar. 'The oath-breaker knows his men have flown. He means to get back up to his hall on his hill.'

'He'll try to raise more spears,' Runa said. She had unstrung her bow and buried the string inside her clothes to try to dry it.

Olaf nodded, rain dripping from his beard. 'Whoreson'll bury his silver too, for he knows that Sigurd and Jarl Hrani will be standing by his hearth soon enough.'

A rush of wind caught the sail wrong and the little boat heeled into a wave so that water spilled over the sheer strake before she righted again, and Sigurd swung his gaze back to Solmund to make sure he was still with them and not already drinking Óðin's mead.

'She's not *Reinen* but she's brave enough for me,' Solmund called to let them all know he was still their helmsman and they should not get any other ideas about it.

Svein was doing his best to fling the bilge water back into the fjord where it belonged.

'There!' Valgerd said, pointing across the white-haired furrows which rolled past Bokn's headland, on towards Karmøy's craggy shore.

There she was, *Storm-Bison*. And she was running wild.

'She's keel-loose,' Olaf said, and Sigurd and Svein cursed to hear it. *Storm-Bison* was planing so swiftly on the surface of the water that she and her rudder had lost their grip on the fjord, meaning neither the king nor his helmsman nor anyone else aboard had control of *Hríð-visundr* now.

This time Sigurd appealed to the Spear-God himself, growling at old One-Eye to let the oath-breaker live a little longer yet. 'He's mine, Allfather,' he gnarred, swiping the rain and salt spray from his eyes, willing *Storm-Bison* to ride out this horror of wind and fjord. 'Do not take him from me.'

Because the king's ship was like a leaf on the wind now. Without its keel and steerboard gripping the water there was a very real chance that *Storm-Bison* could plunge sideways from a wave-top down into the valley in front and then be swamped by the wave from which it fell. If that happened there were not enough bailers aboard to stop her sinking down and down to lie in the grass of the fjord bed.

'Get that sail down, you fools,' Olaf growled at the distant ship, as he and the others clung to that brave little færing and Sigurd all but threatened the gods themselves, and Solmund bled at the tiller.

And then *Storm-Bison*'s sail came down and she continued bare-masted and storm-driven, scudding across the Karmsund Strait, and beyond her prow Sigurd could make out the heather-furred rocks and scrub-covered islands, the shallow coves and the pine-bristled hills of a coastline which he knew better than any other. Though the sight of Karmøy brought him no comfort now, and he almost laughed to think of his wyrd, the threads of which led him back home again after the blood-soaked saga of it all.

A hand clutched at his arm and he turned to look into Runa's eyes. She was still golden, his sister, even on a grey and red day such as this. 'What will happen, brother?' she asked.

'They cannot stop her now for risk of turning into the wind and being tipped out like bad ale,' he told her. 'So her helmsman will look for the best place to beach her.' He grimaced. 'Not that he will have much choice in it.'

And neither did he, whoever was at *Storm-Bison*'s tiller. Not that Sigurd saw much after that because a skein of rain seethed across the wind-flattened water a long arrow-shot off the færing's bow, hiding his prey and the coast beyond.

'He'll be a feast for the crabs,' Svein said, still bailing.

But Sigurd refused to believe that. He clung on to the boat as he clung on to hope, his eyes thirsting for each glimpse of the oath-breaker's ship, as Solmund somehow rode their own little færing through the storm fury which should have swallowed them. Which would have swallowed them had any man but Solmund gripped the tiller. And Sigurd thought that this was what it would feel like to ride Óðin's own grey, eight-legged horse Sleipnir through the sky in the wild hunt.

'Hear that?' Olaf said, flinging another helmet-full of water over the side.

'That's no beaching,' Svein said, for they had all heard it, even above the wind's howl: the terrible snapping of a ship's keel and the splintering of its hull strakes. The screams of doomed men and, dangerously close now, the suck and plunge of the rock-smashed waves, which could have been the eager breath of Rán as she welcomes each corpse into her cold embrace.

Sigurd saw Runa clutch the Freyja amulet at her neck and Svein grip the long haft of his axe now as if an axe would be of any use in Rán's dark kingdom beneath the waves. *Storm-Bison* was no more. Her back broken, she was being dismembered against the rocks, her skipper having missed, if only just, the sandy cove a good spit off her larboard. And the king's men were spilling into the churning swells, screaming as their mail dragged them down. Not all of them, however, and Sigurd caught sight of the oath-breaker amongst a knot of men scrambling from the wreck of his best ship, casting themselves up on to the shore like sodden wrack.

But then the færing bucked and heeled and Sigurd was thrown against the side and blinded by a slap of salt water and he reached out to grip Runa's hand because she had fallen against him and he thought the boat would roll over and that they would sink to the bottom together.

But then the boat righted itself and they were thrown back on to the benches and there was a deafening rasp and scrape of sand and stones against the hull as the færing rode up the beach and stopped suddenly, the water in her bilge flying over the prow and slopping back over her half-drowned crew.

'They are watching, brother,' Runa told Sigurd, the two of them finding their feet as the others gathered their weapons and helmets and stumbled out of the boat. And Sigurd did not know if his sister was talking about their kin up in Óðin's hall, or the gods themselves.

'Well that's going in the tale, you old goat!' Olaf called, he and Sigurd turning back to help Solmund out of the færing which was cast like driftwood up on the strand. 'Bollocks,' Olaf muttered. Sigurd cursed too and felt as though he had been kicked in the stomach, because Solmund lay slumped over the tiller, still gripping it though he had let go of his own life now. His tunic was blood-soaked and so was the bench upon which he still sat, and his face was white as old hearth ash. Somehow the old skipper had held on just long enough to win that last fight against wind and fjord and drive that little boat up on to the shore.

Olaf took the old man's head in both hands and pressed his mouth against the sodden hair. 'Thank you, old friend,' he said.

Sigurd clenched his face against the pain of the wound which Moldof had given him, Moldof who would have killed him if not for Crow-Song. *Alive because of a skald*, he thought, then gripped the dead skipper's shoulder. 'Tell my brothers they will have to wait a little longer for me, old man,' he said, thinking that the gods were surely laughing into their mead horns.

'He is getting away,' Floki said, pointing his short axe up the beach where the king and his surviving hearthmen were making for the birch trees, Moldof himself turning to take one last look at their pursuers before lumbering after his king.

'Oath-breaker!' Sigurd bellowed. And then he was running across the sand, a spear in his hand, and Floki was beside him, they two like predators on the scent of prey, their limbs young and strong and their blood thrumming with the arrogance that made them believe that they were invulnerable, that their wyrds were golden while other men's were only red. Behind them came Runa and Valgerd, Svein and Olaf, and together they were a wolfpack as they loped amongst the trees.

Deeper into the woodland they went, keeping the heaving of the storm-tossed sea in their right ears because that way they knew they were going north towards Avaldsnes and the king's hall. That was where Gorm was bound, of that there was no doubt, for he would have men there, and weapons too, and so Sigurd pressed on, his lungs burning and his heavy brynja rusting on him as he ran, because he would get his claws into the oath-breaker before the worm wriggled back to his hole up on the hill.

Then Floki lifted a hand and slowed, turning his right ear to the north, and the others stopped with him because they knew that his instinct was gods-given. No one spoke, each of them catching their breath as best they could and doing it quietly too as they peered into the dark pine forest around them, wondering what they had missed which Floki had not.

'Be ready,' Floki told them.

The higher boughs of the trees around them were filled with wind so that the tall trunks creaked like ships' masts, and now and then a brittle branch would snap off and fall to the pine litter. Yet for the most part the woods protected those within from the storm and there was a strange stillness which had enough seiðr in it to make the hairs on the back of Sigurd's neck stand.

'The gods are here, Uncle,' he said in a low voice, feeling them in the very air around them.

'The Valkyries too,' Runa said, stringing her bow, and Sigurd shuddered at that because perhaps Runa was right and the strange breezes searching in the trees were draughts from the maidens of death, the choosers of the slain, who swooped and glided unseen amongst them.

Neither was it lost on Sigurd that these were the same woods in which he and his father had hunted with King Gorm those many years ago. Hunted a far nobler creature than the one which Sigurd hunted now.

It was in these same woods too that Harald, and Sigurd's brother Sorli, and so many other good hearthmen fought their last battle and fell never to rise again. Where Harald had taken Moldof's arm in single combat.

Yes, the gods are in this up to their necks, Sigurd thought, watching Floki, who was watching the shadows, and just then men burst from the forest around them.

They came fast and hard and screaming, three big-bearded growlers of many fights, and the first dropped like a quern-stone ten feet from Sigurd with Floki's axe in his skull. Another man's spear would have spilled Sigurd's guts had he not swiped at the blade with his sword, turning it aside, but the warrior behind the thrust came on, bone, flesh and mail hitting Sigurd with enough force to send him flying. He looked up from the ground to see that spear coming again, the blade streaking down, then Svein stepped in, swinging his long axe double-handed to take the king's man in his side, cutting him clean in half and spraying Runa with blood.

'Pick it up,' Olaf told the last king's man, who was slumped on his knees bleeding through the broken brynja rings over his belly. His name was Otkel and Sigurd recognized him as one of the king's closest hearthmen. 'Last chance, lad,' Olaf said, pointing his bloodied sword at the dying warrior's own which lay in the pine litter in front of him. *Lad*, though Otkel was Olaf's age if not older. 'Pick it up now.'

His face all beard and teeth and pain-filled eyes, Otkel reached out and wrapped his fingers round the leather-bound bone hilt and looked up at Olaf who nodded, stepped up and held the point of his sword just inside the warrior's collar bone. 'Tell Jarl Harald it is nearly done,' he said, then he drove the blade down and the man gurgled and shit himself and died.

'We'd best get a move on,' Olaf said, wiping his blade on the dead man's breeches while Floki pulled his hand axe from the skull it was sheathed in.

Still winded, Sigurd nodded and set off, moving with less haste and more care now because he expected more Sword-Norse to burst from the trees looking to get their names in saga or song by putting their blades in him.

'There,' Valgerd said, pointing her spear at a warrior who sat with his back against a pine trunk. He was corpse-pale but still alive.

'His name is Alfgeir,' Olaf said, 'and he's been swinging an axe for Gorm for twenty summers or more.' An arrow jutted from this Alfgeir's neck, its goose feathers as white as his face.

'He did well to make it this far,' Svein said as they came up to the man, who managed to spit a decent insult at the red-bearded giant and at Runa and her bow too, and perhaps it had been Runa's arrow before it was Alfgeir's.

'You deserved better than to be sworn to that spineless shit, Alfgeir,' Olaf told him, meaning King Gorm.

'Do it, goat turd,' Alfgeir growled up at him, blood welling in his mouth and spilling through his lips into his beard. He already gripped his sword in readiness for the long journey and so Olaf gave him his death cleanly out of respect for a warrior who had served his oath-sworn lord well.

'Good,' Svein said, 'I was getting tired of walking,' and Sigurd looked up to see five men standing shoulder to shoulder a stone's throw away. The oath-breaker himself stood at their centre and it seemed the hunt was over. Not one warrior amongst any in that forest carried a shield now and so it would be a quick and bloody butcher's job this, and everyone knew it.

'Stay behind me, Runa,' Sigurd said, and Runa nodded, pulling an arrow from her quiver and nocking it to the string.

'Tonight you drink with your father, boy!' King Gorm bawled and Sigurd knew he was expected to answer this with insults and threats of his own but he would not waste the breath on them. The oath-breaker had already lived far longer than he should have, and so Sigurd strode forward, following the threads of his own wyrd, and his wolves matched him stride for stride.

Steel sang and men shrieked and in less time than it would take to tell it, three king's men were down, but then Svein grunted and staggered forward, a spear in his back, and the king and Moldof were backing off, swords raised before them. Floki ran at the man who had thrown the spear but he turned and fled and Floki chased him.

'Somebody pull it out,' Svein growled, unable to reach the shaft himself.

'Help him,' Sigurd told Runa, as he, Olaf and Valgerd moved in on the king and the one-armed warrior who had come close to earning his sword-fame and a name that would fan the hearth flames for years to come. Close, but not close enough.

'You chose wrong, Moldof Wolf-Joint,' Olaf told him. The world outside was still roaring, howling fury, but amongst those trees the air was heavy and thick and laden with consequence, so that Sigurd found it difficult to breathe. It was all destiny. 'Now I'm going to take your other arm,' Olaf promised, 'and you will have to find your mother in the afterlife so that she can wipe your arse for you.'

'I am the king's prow man, Olaf,' Moldof said, lifting his chin, 'and an oath is not given lightly.'

'You've more honour than your king, I'll give you that,' Olaf told him, at which Gorm spat in Olaf's direction.

'Sigurd!' Runa yelled, and he turned to see her loose an arrow at a man who was running at her with a spear, and the arrow hit him but he came on and Runa had no time. Valgerd made three strides and on the fourth she cast her spear and it flew as straight and true as a spear ever did, taking the warrior in his chest and hurling him back with the force of it. But then Moldof was on Valgerd and she turned back in time to see his face as he thrust his sword into her and pulled the gore-slick blade out and the shieldmaiden fell. Runa screamed and ran at Moldof but Olaf was already there and Gorm's man did well to make three good blocks with his sword before Olaf lopped off his left arm at the shoulder just as he had said he would.

Moldof staggered back and then simply stood there, armless as a post, his new stump spurting and his face warped like an ancient roof beam with the horror of what had become of him.

'Leave him like that,' Olaf growled at Runa, but she was already on him, hacking at his neck with her scramasax and Moldof had the balls to stand still to make the thing more quickly done.

'Crow-Song will be waiting for you in the hereafter, Moldof Stump,' Svein said, still on his feet but now holding the spear which had been sticking in his back. His brynja had taken the worst of the sting out of that throw. His brynja and his pride.

'If the Allfather even wants him now, the worthless pile of dung,' Floki said, striding from the trees and throwing a severed head at Moldof. That head had belonged to the last of the king's men and now there was just the oath-breaker himself, standing there with his sword in one hand, his long knife in the other, and the thick gold torc gleaming at his neck.

Sigurd looked at Valgerd who was lying there curled in on herself, clutching the terrible wound in her stomach but watching him still. Her eyes told Sigurd to finish it while she was still alive to see it.

'Come then, Haraldarson,' Gorm said, beckoning Sigurd with his scramasax. 'Let us see if you are your father's son.'

Sigurd could feel Floki's hunger, his blood-craving, but this was Sigurd's kill and Floki knew it. So did the others, and so they drew closer, just in case, but Sigurd knew that they would not interfere.

Gorm came at him not like a man who had fought countless fights but like a drunken mead-soaked growler who can barely see the man he is trying to hurt. Sigurd caught the king's sword on his scramasax and punched his sword hilt into Gorm's face, knocking out his teeth and sending the king reeling. Then Sigurd strode forward and feinted and Gorm scythed his sword across, hitting nothing because Sigurd was already moving, and he stepped outside and brought Troll-Tickler down on to Gorm's right wrist, taking off his hand which fell still gripping his sword.

The king could smell Valhöll now. He could hear the whispers of his father and his father's father and those of his line going right back to the beginning. Whoreson could almost taste the Allfather's mead. He even swung his gaze left and right then, as though he could sense the Valkyries swirling amongst the trees, closing in on him.

And Sigurd would not give the oath-breaker that.

'Olaf, Floki, we take him alive,' he said, and the king's eyes bulged with horror and he yelled and threw himself at Sigurd, who crossed his sword and scramasax, catching Gorm's long knife between his own blades. Then he stepped forward and drove his forehead into the king's face and heard the crunch of it and then Olaf and Floki had a hold of the king and Sigurd took the scramasax from him.

'You are king of nothing now, oath-breaker,' Olaf spat in Gorm's ear, as the king stood there bleeding from his mouth and nose and from the stump where his right hand used to be.

Sigurd ran back to Valgerd, beside whom Runa knelt gripping the shieldmaiden's hands in hers. Sigurd knelt too, seeing the blood and ruin that Valgerd was trying to hide by folding in on herself.

Runa let go one of her hands and nodded at Sigurd, so he took the blood-slick hand in his and looked into eyes which did not seem to see him.

'We did it, Valgerd,' he said. His whole body was still brimming with the battle thrill, trembling with it. But there was something else too. It was as if one of those unseen maidens of death had reached into his chest and clenched his heart in her icy grip.

Valgerd blinked slowly and there, lasting no longer than the beat of a sparrow's wing, was the glimpse of a smile in the snarl of grimace. And a muttered word.

'What did she say?' Runa asked and Sigurd could feel his sister's eyes on him.

Sigurd swallowed and felt the tears drowning his eyes. The invisible hands squeezing his throat.

'Ikorni,' he said under his breath. 'Squirrel.'

For that had been Valgerd's name for Sygrutha, the völva with whom she had lived by the sacred spring in the Lysefjord. 'Ikorni,' he said again, smiling in spite of himself. Valgerd had loved Sygrutha. He had always known that. And perhaps the shieldmaiden could see Sygrutha now. Perhaps the völva was waiting for her beyond the veil which separates this life from the next.

Sigurd leant in and kissed her cheek which was cold on his lips. 'Thank you,' he said.

But she was gone.

CHAPTER FOURTEEN

THEY STOOD IN THE COOL DAWN SHADOWS BECAUSE THE SUN HAD NOT YET risen above the mountains in the east to flood the hillside below the king's hall with warmth. There was a hum in the air and fog rising from so many mouths as men grumbled and winced and complained about wounds that were still fresh and broken bones and bruised flesh. For all that they were still full of the ale and mead in which they had tried to drown themselves all night, seeking numbness.

'I wish our fathers were here to see this,' Svein said, looking down on to the channel where the rocks showed still above the rising tide.

'The others too,' Sigurd said, thinking of his mother and brothers and Solmund and Crow-Song, Hendil and Loker. And Valgerd.

'Aye. Too many,' Svein said, wincing at the thought of all those who had fallen along the way. The spear had not gone deep into him and Runa had washed and stitched the wound, but time would tell whether or not the wound rot would come.

'They're all here with us now, lad, on this hill,' Olaf said. 'Don't you doubt it.'

And perhaps they were.

'Not long now,' Runa said. 'I will be glad to see it finished properly.'

No one disagreed with that. The storm had passed and the day would be calm by the looks, and there was much to do including burning the dead.

Not that all the dead would be burnt.

Gorm, whom men once called Shield-Shaker, was chained to the flat rock out in the channel below what used to be his hall and his land. Sigurd himself had rowed him out there and put the chains on, and Runa had gone with him, scowling at Gorm who was half gone with fever or pain on account of that missing hand. Olaf had bound the stump good and tight because they had not wanted Gorm to spill all his blood and die before they were ready for him to die.

They were ready now though, and as Sigurd had bound him to that same rock upon which Gorm had drowned so many enemies, and even one of his wives, Runa had asked Gorm how it felt to know that he would never see Valhöll.

'How does it feel to know you will spend the afterlife in the cold dark while better men and women feast at Óðin's table? And at Freyja's,' she added, thinking of King Thorir and all those Freyja Maidens whose corpses were barely cold and stiff.

She got no answer from Gorm. He glared and shivered and said nothing, though the fear came off him like the stink off a wet dog, and Sigurd breathed it in.

'We leave this rotting nithing for the crabs, Runa,' Sigurd said, turning his back on the chained man and climbing back aboard the row boat to take up the oars. He had nothing to say to the oath-breaker. There *was* nothing he could say which spoke louder than the act of chaining Gorm to that rock and letting the tide have him.

But he did hold the oath-breaker's eye as he rowed them back to the shore and all those waiting on the grassy hill upon whose heights the king's hall – King Hrani Randversson's now – sat wreathed in morning mist.

It wasn't until they neared the shore and Sigurd could no longer see Gorm's face that he had noticed the cloth which Runa clutched in her hand. Though he recognized the scene stitched into it.

'The wild hunt,' he said, and Runa had nodded, telling him that the old seiðr-kona had been pushing her threads into that cloth until the day she died at some outlaw's hands.

There, stitched by skilled hands, was a host of gods and warriors sweeping across the sky, led by Óðin who gripped his spear Gungnir and rode Sleipnir his eight-legged steed.

'I don't think she would have minded my keeping it,' Runa explained, running a finger along the stitches of the sacred spear.

'"And his passing raises such a rush and roar of the wind as will waft away the souls of the dead",' Sigurd said, recalling the words the prophetess had spoken to him up in Jarl Burner's hall.

Runa's eyes were fixed on his like rivets in a ship's strake. The old witch had been right about that.

Now there was a sudden gust which seemed to fly north up the Karmsund Strait and it pushed a ridge of water up the channel so that it swept over the rock and the man chained to it.

Not enough to drown him. Not yet.

'Even the gods want to be done with this,' Hrani Randversson said, his fingers going to the thick gold torc which he had taken from Gorm's neck himself. Sigurd had not minded seeing him do it. He had promised Hrani Gorm's high seat. Besides which, Hrani still had enough men left to be called a war host, so there was little Sigurd could have done even if he had changed his mind about putting the man up in that fine hall.

'We all want done with it,' Olaf said, sharing a look with Asgrim, Jarl Guthrum's former champion who had somehow survived the previous day's carnage. Perhaps Asgrim and his handful of Svearmen would stay on with Sigurd now. More likely they would become King Hrani's men, for a gold torc draws warriors like carrion draws crows.

They shivered in their cloaks and were for the most part quiet, as men are who are exhausted and still have the claws of the blood-fray in them. When they are wondering how they are still breathing and full of pains while so many friends and kinsmen have left such things behind.

'Are you going to put that on or just hold it all day?' Olaf said, nodding down at the jarl torc in Sigurd's right hand. Bram had found it in a sea chest up in Gorm's hall, had got to it before Queen Kadlin had the chance to stash it and the rest of her husband's silver too.

'He is waiting for the sea to take the oath-breaker before he puts it on,' Svein told Olaf and Sigurd thought that might have been it, at least in part.

But there was more.

He could not shake off the rest of what the old seiðr-kona had said. It clung to him like wet wool.

And his passing raises such a rush and roar of the wind as will waft away the souls of the dead. And with it Haraldarson too.

The old woman's words tumbled round his head as he looked at the ring of twisted silver that had belonged to his father, which Gorm had taken from the dead jarl's neck back when this whole thing began.

And with it Haraldarson too.

And yet I am alive. I am here while my enemy waits for the sea to spill into his lungs. I will live while he is a feast for crabs.

He lifted the heavy torc and pulled it open enough to get it round his neck and the cold of it on his skin was enough to send a shiver through him.

'So, Jarl Sigurd!' Hrani called. 'When this is done and that whoreson is drowned, we will drown ourselves in his mead, hey!'

This got some *ayes* from Olaf and Svein, from Bram, Bjorn and Bjarni and from Thorbiorn Thorirsson who had surprised them all by turning out to be a proper warrior when the blood was flying. And as they talked of feasts and ale, women and mead, Sigurd laughed.

Jarl Sigurd now, then, he thought. *Haraldarson no more.* That was what the witch had seen. Not his end but his beginning.

Somewhere up on the hill behind him a raven croaked and Sigurd turned to see the bird sitting on the thatch of King Hrani's hall. It croaked again then took off into the brightening sky and for a while Sigurd watched it as it flew into the west.

And in the channel below them the tide rose.

GLOSSARY OF NORSE TERMS

---

the Alder Man: a spirit or elf of the forest

Asgard: home of the gods

aurar: ounces, usually of silver (singular: eyrir)

berserker: 'bare-shirt', or perhaps 'bear-shirt', a fierce warrior prone to a battle frenzy

bietas: a long pole used to stretch the weather leech when the ship is working to windward

Bifröst: the rainbow-bridge connecting the worlds of gods and men

Bilskírnir: 'Lightning-crack', Thór's hall

blood eagle: a method of torture and execution, perhaps as a rite of human sacrifice to Óðin

blót: a sacrifice to the spirits and the land, often in the form of a feast

bóndi: 'head of the household', taken to mean a farmer or land owner

brynja: a coat of mail (plural: brynjur)

bukkehorn: a musical instrument made from the horn of a ram or goat

Dísablót: a sacrifice to the Dísir

draugr: the animated corpse that comes forth from its grave mound

dróttin: the leader of a war band

færing: literally meaning 'four-oaring'. A small open boat with two pairs of oars and sometimes also a sail.

Fáfnir: 'Embracer', a dragon that guards a great treasure hoard

Fenrir Wolf: the mighty wolf that will be freed at Ragnarök and swallow Óðin

Fimbulvetr: 'Terrible Winter', heralding the beginning of Ragnarök

forskarlar: the waterfall spirits

galdr: a chant or spell, usually recited rather than sung

Garm: the greatest of dogs, who will howl at the final cataclysm of Ragnarök

Gjallarhorn: the horn which Heimdall sounds to mark the beginning of Ragnarök

Gleipnir: the fetter which binds the wolf Fenrir

godi: an office denoting social and sacral prominence; a chieftain and/or priest

Gungnir: the mighty rune-carved spear owned by Óðin

hacksilver: the cut-up pieces of silver coins, arm rings, and jewellery

Hangaguð: the Hanged God. A name for Óðin.

haugbui: a living corpse. A mound dweller, the dead body living on within its tomb.

haugr: a burial mound

Haust Blót: autumn sacrifice

hei: 'hello'

Helheim: a place far to the north where the evil dead dwell

hersir: a warlord who owes allegiance to a jarl or king

Hildisvíni: the 'battle boar' on which Freyja rides

hirðmen: the retinue of warriors that follow a king, jarl or chieftain

hólmgang: a duel to settle disputes

hrafnasueltir: raven-starver (coward)

Hugin and Munin: 'Thought' and 'Memory', Óðin's ravens

huglausi: a coward

húskarlar: household warriors

Ívaldi [sons of]: a group of dwarfs who created treasures for the gods

jarl: title of the most prominent men below the kings

Jól feast: winter solstice festival

Jörmungand/Midgard Serpent: the serpent that encircles the world grasping its own tail. When it lets go the world will end.

Jötunheim: (giant-home) the realm of the giants

karl: a freeman; a landowner

karvi: a ship usually equipped with 13 to 16 pairs of oars

kaupang: marketplace

knörr: a cargo ship; wider, deeper and shorter than a longship

kyrtill: a long tunic or gown

lendermen: managers of the king's estates. Nobles.

merkismaðr: standard-bearer in a war band

meyla: a little girl

Midgard: the place where men live (the world)

Mímir's Well: the well of wisdom at which Óðin sacrificed an eye in return for a drink

Mjöllnir: the magic hammer of Thór

mormor: mother's mother

mundr: bride-price

naust: a boathouse, usually with one side against the sea and a ramp down to the water

nestbaggin: knapsack

Nídhögg: the serpent that gnaws at the root of Yggdrasil

Niðstang: 'curse-pole', a pole inscribed with a curse, mounted with a horse's head turned ceremoniously towards the intended recipient of the curse

Niflheim: the cold, dark, misty world of the dead, ruled by the goddess Hel

nithing: a wretch; a coward; a person without honour

Norns – Urd, Verdandi and Skuld: the three spinners who determine the fates of men

Ragnarök: doom of the gods

Ratatosk: the squirrel that conveys messages between the eagle at the top of Yggdrasil and Nídhögg at its roots

rauði: bog iron ore, related to rauðr meaning red

rôst: the distance travelled between two rest-stops, about a mile

Sæhrímnir: a boar that is cooked and consumed every night in Valhöll

scían: an Irish fighting long knife

scramasax: a large knife with a single-edged blade

seiðr: sorcery, magic, often associated with Óðin or Freyja

seiðr-kona: a seiðr-wife. A practitioner of witchcraft.

Sessrymnir: the dwelling place of the goddess Freyja

skál: 'cheers!'

skald: a poet, often in the service of jarls or kings

Skíthblathnir: the magical ship of the god Frey

skjaldborg: shieldwall

skjaldhus: shield house (term most probably invented by the author)

skyr: a cultured dairy product with the consistency of strained yogurt

Sleipnir: the eight-legged grey horse of Óðin

snekke: a small longship used in warfare comprising at least twenty rowing benches

svinfylkja: 'swine-array', a wedge-shaped battle formation

tafl: a strategy board game played on a chequered or latticed board

taufr: witchcraft

thegn: retainer; a member of a king or jarl's retinue

thrall: a serf or unfree servant

ting: assembly/meeting place where disputes are solved and political decisions made

utiseta: sitting out for wisdom. An ancient practice of divining knowledge

Valhöll: Óðin's hall of the slain
Valknuter: a symbol comprising three entwined triangles representative of the afterlife and Oðin
Valkyries: choosers of the slain
Varðlokur: the repetitive, rhythmic, soothing chant to induce a trance-like state
völva: a shamanic seeress; a practitioner of magic divination and prophecy
wergild: 'man-price', the amount of compensation paid by a person committing an offence to the injured party or, in case of death, to his family
wyrd: fate or personal destiny
Yggdrasil: the tree of life

THE NORSE GODS

Æsir, the gods; often those gods associated with war, death and power
Baldr, the beautiful; son of Óðin
Dísir, 'goddesses'; a group of supernatural female figures linked with fertility
Frey, god of fertility, marriage, and growing things
Freyja, goddess of sex, love and magic
Frigg, wife of Óðin
Heimdall, the watchman of the gods
Hel, both the goddess of the underworld and the place of the dead, specifically those who perish of sickness or old age
Loki, the mischief-monger, Father of Lies
Njörd, Lord of the Sea and god of wind and flame
Óðin, the Allfather; lord of the Æsir, god of warriors and war, wisdom and poetry
Rán, Mother of the Waves
Skadi, a goddess associated with skiing, archery and the hunting of game. Mother of Freyja.
Thór, son of Óðin; slayer of giants and god of thunder

Týr, Lord of Battle

Ull, lord of the hunt, associated with archery, skating and skiing

Váli, Óðin's son, birthed for the sole purpose of killing Höðr as revenge for Höðr's accidental murder of his half-brother Baldr

Vanir, fertility gods, including Njörd, Frey and Freyja, who live in Vanaheim

Vidar, god of vengeance who will survive Ragnarök and avenge his father Óðin by killing Fenrir

Völund, god of the forge and of experience

ACKNOWLEDGEMENTS

Before I got my first publishing deal for the 'Raven' saga I was living in New York with my then soulmate and best friend, Sally. This was 2006. I had written one novel, which nobody wanted, and to get over that disappointment I wrote *Raven: Blood Eye*. When it was finished I started working on a futuristic thriller to stay busy while I searched for a literary agent who would represent me and, I hoped, find a home for *Blood Eye* with a good publisher. It would be hard to overstate how much I wanted a publishing deal. I was, truth be told, desperate. I would wander round my local bookshop, McNally Robinson (now McNally Jackson) on Prince Street in the bustling, creatively charged neighbourhood of Nolita, lower Manhattan, imagining how I'd feel when (not if) my book was on the shelves there. Rather embarrassingly, I was even tempted to tell staff members that I was going to be a published writer, *so there*. You'll be pleased to know I resisted that terrible urge. And while I'm feeling confessional, another dubious pastime included coercing a designer friend to mock up book covers for my stories, which I'd then print out and wrap round Bernard Cornwell novels, just so I knew what it would feel like to hold my own book. Sad and creepy, or a powerful visualization exercise? I'll leave that to you to decide.

With every heartbreaking rejection letter received – and there were many – I sent off another submission and in doing so kept the hope alive, while Sally reassured and strengthened me. She never doubted (I married her of course) and, in all honesty, neither did I. Back in 1995 I had been interviewed as part of a BBC documentary and had said that my ambition was to be a writer. I was in a pop group at the time, so perhaps should have been concentrating on that, but even back then I knew what I really wanted.

Why am I reminiscing about this now, all these years later? Well, *Wings of the Storm* is my ninth published novel and my last Viking foray, for a while at least. And as I work on my tenth book, heading in a slightly new direction, it also seems a good time to look back to the beginning. I have a feeling it is important and healthy to try to recall, to 'feel' again that fierce need to be published. To remember the times I sat wide-eyed in McNally Robinson listening to guest authors – real, published authors – and hanging on their every word as though they had found the grail, the *elixir vitae*, and Harald Hardrada's battle banner, Land Waster. Theirs was an exclusive club and I wanted in. I was clawing at the door.

Eventually the offer of a contract came via my agent Bill Hamilton. By this time I would have signed it in my own blood. *Raven: Blood Eye* was published in 2009 and I've been working pretty hard, and loving it, ever since. But nothing is certain in publishing. If I write a book that doesn't sell, because there's no enthusiasm in the market for it, or else it's just terrible, it is reasonable to assume my publisher might not renew my contract. Publishing is a business and no business can afford to make bad investments. This industry doesn't owe me a living and I have no right to expect any new manuscript I come up with to be edited, copy edited, proofread, printed and bound, publicized and marketed, distributed, sold and bought. It is a privilege. An outrageous honour. It's a thrill every time I hold one of my books for the first time.

Here in this note then, it's my great pleasure to thank my publishers – Larry, Bill, indeed the whole of 'team' Transworld (there are too many names to mention here, but they know who they are!) – for introducing my stories to the world and for continuing to believe that I have tales that are worth the telling. It is because of Transworld that I get to spend my life writing stories and sharing them with you, kind and loyal reader. What a wonderful and extraordinary thing. I wonder what that desperate young man who wandered the aisles of McNally Robinson would think if he knew he'd be sitting here writing these lines ten years later. I suspect he had already seen it in his mind's eye. Even if he had no right to. But what's an imagination for if not to conjure that which should be impossible?

As for us, here and now, let's keep believing in new stories and wonderful adventures. Let's journey on together to see what we can find. We still have far to go, you and I.

ABOUT THE AUTHOR

Family history (he is half Norwegian) inspired **Giles Kristian** to write his first historical novels: the acclaimed and bestselling 'Raven' Viking trilogy. A long-held fascination with the English Civil War then led him to chart the fortunes of a family divided by that brutal conflict in the novels *The Bleeding Land* and *Brothers' Fury*, before co-writing Wilbur Smith's No.1 bestseller, *Golden Lion*.

In his recent novels – *God of Vengeance* (a *Times* 'Book of the Year'), *Winter's Fire* and now *Wings of the Storm* – he returned to the Viking world to tell the thrilling story of the rise of Sigurd Haraldarson and his celebrated fictional fellowship.

Giles Kristian lives in Leicestershire. To find out more, visit www.gileskristian.com